I0728676

TWO-FISTED JESUS TALES

BOOK 1: THE BOOK OF THE JOB

JAMES M. BEACH

MIND
FU

TWO-FISTED JESUS TALES, BOOK 1:

THE BOOK OF THE JOB

This is a work of fiction. All the characters and events portrayed, except for purposes of satire, are fictional and any resemblance to real people or incidents is purely coincidental.

Copyright 2017 by James Beach

All rights reserved, including the right to reproduce this book or portions thereof in any form.

A Mind Fu original book.

29 Grove St., #340

San Francisco, CA 94102

ISBN: 978-1-945451-00-3

LCCN: 2016908315

Cover art by Jason Heuser. Cover design by Kerry Hynds.

First printing. March 2017

4.9.4

<u>Two-Fisted Jesus Tales</u>

Book 1: The Book of the Job
Book 2: Doublecrossed

As revealed by prophecy to
Theo Hardwicke, D.D. (Doctor of Divinity)
Andover Mail-order Divinity School LLC

Transcribed by the Heathen
James M. Beach, Esq.

MORE

Sign up for my 100% spamless newsletter, and receive a free tale not published anywhere else.

To find out more, click here.

"Foxes have dens to live in, and birds have nests, but the Son of Man has no place even to lay his head."

Matthew 8:20

1

In a cheap motel off Route 66, Jesus cleaned his stepfather's .45.

It was just after midnight, December 25th. He didn't feel a year older. He didn't think he looked a year older either. He inspected the gun's barrel and then his reflection on its chrome exterior. Same long, flowing light brown hair and neatly trimmed beard. Same 6 feet of combat-hardened AmeriChristian manhood. He was clothed like a real American should be - cowboy boots, white T-shirt and jeans. He was eager and ready to go to work, at the job he was born to do. Still, another year had passed without the sign.

It should have at least been a little colder on his birthday. It was too hot to even close the motel room's door. The room's air conditioner had struggled mightily, with scant effect. Rendered ineffectual by secret weather machines? Created by the Devil's dupes to push the lie of global warming? Jesus had found no specific answer to these questions, nor had any of his true followers.

The gun was ready to go. He picked the pieces off the cheap motel room desk and reassembled it, occasionally glancing at the muted television. It showed earlier footage of President Thruppence leaving the White House. He was exiting well before the official re-inauguration of President Arack Bomraka, supposedly so that the returning First Family could enjoy Christmas back in the Oval Office.

Jesus did not begrudge Bomraka the opportunity to enjoy the holiday. It was just a mystery that the man really did appear to celebrate it. Hadn't Bomraka fought the War on Christmas directly from the White House, by saying "Happy Holidays"? Wasn't it obvious to all that once you swapped "Merry Christmas" for "Happy Holidays", "Hail Satan" could not be far behind? Surely people couldn't fool themselves that deeply into thinking they were doing the right thing.

All of God's true followers who still remained after the Rapture had experienced a brief spot of hope when Bomraka peacefully left office at the end of his second term. With the election of the moderately conservative Thruppence, it looked as if for the first time in many years they might reverse their homeland's leftward slide down the slippery slope of liberalism into the gaping chasm of tolerantly diversified Hell. They hadn't reckoned with the Demoncrat party's fiendish resourcefulness. Bomraka was back in for a third non-consecutive term, because the wayward Senate amended the holy Constitution as if they were in literal Congress with the Devil.

So, even on his birthday, Jesus continued preparing for the day he would be called to save America. Fortunately, it was not all unpleasant. Jesus finished reassembling his .45, set it down on the desk, glanced across the room and smiled.

On the room's sole bed lay a stripper Jesus had been showing the light, to save her from a life without true Christianity. She was face down, naked and exhausted. Soft moonlight drifted through the curtains, playing across her lovely dancer's back and glistening on her raven hair. Like many women before her, she had needed some explanation of how he could bring her to the light physically before marriage. Also like many, she'd had no idea what she was missing until he'd given it to her - the good, hard love of a real Christian man. After hours of joy and the inevitable female need for conversation, she'd slipped off into satisfied slumber. Not only satiated, but saved. Jesus had made sure she knew he could never stay with her. His mission left no room for any kind of stable life. The man she'd eventually marry and submit to in accordance with God's will would have a tough act to follow. If she ever felt lost with an inevitably lesser man, she could always pray.

Jesus lit a Marlboro, blew a smoke ring across the room, and considered the lighter in his hand. A good ol' Zippo, corners worn nearly round with wear. Like the .45, it had been carried by Joseph's grandfather in World War. From Pearl Harbor to the fields of Normandy on D-Day, they had kept him safe and warm. When Jesus' mother and stepfather Joseph had been taken to Heaven in the Rapture, they had left these keepsakes and not much else.

That had been the hardest day of his young life. Not only had his parents disappeared, but a car that had instantly lost its driver to the Rapture took the life of his young love, Alaine. It still broke his heart and stung his pride to know she must be in Hell. He'd failed her, listening with politeness and patience to her liberal ways, thinking they had all the time in the world for her to come around. If he had only pushed her hard enough toward salvation to make it stick. Then she might await him as she floated above, rather than burned for all eternity below.

The lesson had been hard, but clear. He had no time to waste with false kindness. His heavenly Father had given him a job to do. The last time Jesus had walked the earth, it was about peace, patience and understanding. That ship had sailed. This time, it was about kicking ass.

Which meant he had to stay on point. He should check his AOL, and see if his hidden followers had any news. He picked up his laptop.

The girl stirred. She turned over, opened her eyes, and smiled. He smiled back. She was a good woman with a good heart. It wasn't her fault she could never be Alaine.

"You're still here," she said.

"For now." He put the laptop aside and walked over, leaning in for a long kiss that left them both quite awake.

"I want more Bible study." She giggled and reached for him, pulling him closer.

Jesus sat on the bed and put his cigarette in the nightstand's ashtray, and put both his hands on her. "You know me." He smiled. "I like my teaching with active participation." He leaned in to kiss her again. She helped take his shirt off and pulled him to the bed. He lay down on his back, and she lay across him. Her fingers stroked from his mighty chest to his rock-hard abs, as his arm wrapped around her slender waist.

"I still don't understand why God doesn't just take out all the bad guys with miracles." she said.

"'Cause that ain't how my Father wants it to work, baby. He wants humanity saved the hard way, with muscle, grit and faith."

From her face, he could tell she didn't like this serious side so much. He tried to tailor his message for the audience, but that didn't mean they'd always be happy to hear it. Fortunately she was a firecracker. She grabbed him through his jeans and smiled as the serious expression left his own face.

"What have I got here?" she asked playfully. "Is this your rod and staff to comfort me?"

"Sounds like you remember your Bible just fine," he chuckled. He pulled her in for another kiss. "I'm still leading this lesson, though." She gazed at him with earnest eyes. He had seen this look before on many women's faces. It came from him being not just any man, but an actual savior to these daughters of Eve who'd lost their way. It was part of this job to show them that a real man could not only kick ass, he could also talk sincerely about their souls. Before he received the sign to go to war, he could use his God-given manliness to save women from Hell.

She reached around his probing hands to unbuckle his belt. She pulled his pants down and moved her hands across his thigh. "Why'd you get this?" she asked, stroking his thigh tattoo.

"It comes straight from the Bible, darlin'." The tattoo said *King of Kings and Lord of Lords,* "That's who I am, right in the Book of Revelation 19:16."

She scrunched her pretty face. "Ain't tattoos against the Bible?"

"Not all of 'em. Leviticus forbids tattoos with a father's name, but other tattoos are fine." He had toyed with getting other tattoos, like maybe a fish symbol or similar icons. Perhaps across his knuckles, to be the last thing seen by those who'd earned his fists. In the end he chose to not mark himself further. He was already unique in all the world.

She ran her fingers across his tattoo, and then upwards to his holy gun. It was his turn to drink in the sensation, for a moment not speaking further. When his eyes opened he saw her looking at him with a pleased smile. He grinned back. The minx. She liked distracting him. She came closer to him, allowing him to stroke inside her while his other hand drifted to her left nipple.

"Where'd we leave off?" he asked after a bit.

She had to concentrate too. "The Four Horsemen?"

"Right." He stretched and then caressed her as he gazed into her eyes. "The Bible describes the First Horseman as a white rider on a white horse, an archer with his bow. Obviously, this means the liberal lamestream media."

"Obviously?" she asked.

"Of course. Think about it. Launching messages over the heads of the faithful to the easily swayed. Thanks to this horseman, the first lamestream media of public radio helped elect the first American president to pollute our lifeblood with socialism, Franklin Delano Roosevelt."

"He was bad?"

"Yep. He fooled even some Christians at first, because he was a job creator. Only the true faithful saw his so-called Social Security for what it was: a plan straight from the depths of Hell designed to destroy America."

"And then what, my Lord?" she whispered, shivering with anticipation for the lesson she was about to receive.

"Then came the red Horseman of War. Not a real honest war where strong men clash and good men always win. No - this was the

War on Christmas. The war on depicting my first birth proudly in any public square, or worse, allowing that square to be shared with un-American religions." He caressed her hair, betting she would love it. He was right, she practically purred. "What's next?" he asked, testing her.

She kept her eyes closed, then opened them. "The third horse of the Apo - the Apocalypse?"

"Yes, third, the black horse of Famine." He pinched her nipple. She squealed - he liked that in a woman. She had fake breasts, which he generally did not prefer. They looked great onstage though. He focused. "The LIEberal agenda of dietary destruction. Where real, big American men from a big, American country are made to feel ashamed for their manly appetites. When the joy of sugar, white bread and real red meat was sacrificed for a long life free of heart attacks, and burdened with cowardice."

She moved her head down across his body. Neither of them spoke for a while, his lesson paused as he reeled in Earthly pleasure. "And then...?" she continued when her mouth was temporarily unoccupied. "What's the fourth?"

"The most fearsome horse of all," he declared. She hung on his every word, her lovely eyes wide open in the darkened room. "The pale horse of Death. The end of American manliness itself. The sickly end to the glorious warriors of America's roads - the muscle cars and their appetites for God's Good Gas... "His breath became heavier and more rhythmic. "The final liberal takeover of the White House, and with it BomrakaCare. Made manifest by the man known as Bomraka. The KenyAntichrist. And with him, hidden in the depths of liberalism, the Whore of Babylon."

She stopped for a moment, enthralled with his words. Enthralled with him. "What will happen?"

"At long last, Bomraka will come for the guns," he declared with fire in his eyes. "Just as, after the Rapture, the American dollar of the Founders was replaced with the sickly MexiCanadian Amero. Just as gay marriage became legal and parents lost the right to raise their children free of the lies of evolution. Last to fall, maybe by the end of next year, will be the right to eat bacon."

"Why won't God just stop him?" she asked.

"I told you before, darlin'. God doesn't work that way. He helps those who help themselves. That's why he sent me."

"Why can't you just stop Bomraka then?" she persisted.

"I can't start the war until I receive the sign," said Jesus. "Until then, I can only prepare." He sighed. Until he knew the time was right he could only watch as good Christian fathers were no longer able to shoot their God-given guns, unable to shield their children from science, forbidden from eating their fill of real red meat. He hoped some kind of sign would come before God's children had nothing left to live on but tofu and broken dreams.

"Once you see the sign, you're going to get all those horsemen, right?" she asked, breathless.

"They're just the start," he said, gripping her waist firmly. "I'm going after the Devil, baby." She cooed as he held her tight. He ran his hands down her lovely skin. "Not just his servants, like the Demoncrats and their President. I'm going for the Devil himself." He nodded toward the .45 he'd just been cleaning. "With that 1911 model Colt! For the Book of Revelations 19:11 declares that I am to come in righteousness to judge and make war!"

She moved her leg over his body, and slid on top.

"Yeah baby," he said with passionate intensity. "Yeah. Just like that!" His speech began to coincide with his movements.

"Uh-huh," she said. "Ohhhhhh...."

"Yeah! The lamestream liberal media won't even admit the Rapture happened to a single person. But we know the truth! We know they were many, baby!"

"Yes we do!" she said with passionate conviction, as Jesus entered her.

"We are left behind to finish my Father's holy plan!"

"Yes Jesus!"

He placed both his hands on her breasts. "With these hands, I will bring God's holy wrath to this spoiled, sickened Earth!"

"Yes! Oh yes!

"Do you see?"

"Yes!" she cried. "Yes, yes! Oh, do me Jesus! Do me, my Lord!"

The scripture lesson had just begun. This was not the only time that Jesus would come again.

2

—————

President Bomraka stared out from the Oval Office window and mused on the path that had led him back here. It was almost a mystery how it had all worked out. He had never even considered running for a third term, even a non-consecutive one. His wife had not wanted him back in this hard and thankless saddle. His daughters, both well placed in good jobs and dating fine people, certainly didn't need him to take another swing at the rather stressful job of running the country. He himself had been skeptical about returning to this job after a welcome four years of relative sanity, low stress and even relaxation.

But President Thruppence had just not done well for the country. When this opportunity had come along Bomraka's supporters and friends convinced him to take it. As he moved forward all obstacles had melted almost as soon as they appeared. It was strange, almost as if some unseen force was in action that helped some possibilities grow while others withered on the vine.

He shook his head. That was the realm of conspiracy theory, not politics. However he'd gotten back here, it was past time to get to work. Everything he'd accomplished in his first two administrations had been done while dragging half the country inch by inch, kicking and screaming towards something better. "Like herding cats" was a common saying; but cats at least wouldn't fight you if you tried to give them food. He had established a version of health care, to be called an authoritarian dictator. He had normalized relations with historically hostile countries, to be called a spineless appeaser. He had proposed job programs to both improve the country and put people to work, to have these efforts steadfastly ignored in favor of complaints about the healthcare system already in place. As if repealing the health program would even create the jobs people professed to want.

He considered himself a good judge of human nature. As a politician he had to be. You had to understand a crowd to speak before them. You had to understand a room and the people in it to make sure they understood you, and wouldn't turn on you before you even had a chance. But people's stubbornness still surprised him after all these years. It really seemed that if he offered them heaven on Earth they'd choose Hell just to spite him - and somehow think they had defeated him by burning their asses off.

Yet, and he smiled ruefully, he had once more taken the job. If he was honest with himself, it was great to have another chance to make things better – and also great to be back in the old game.

He leaned back in his chair and heard it give a familiar creak. He had missed it. The office was serene for now, and outside the world was quiet, with the stars shining down among the scant light of the city, and the Christmas tree with its many baubles reflecting in the moonlight.

It was always so pretty a view at night. And yet, he didn't feel as soothed as the last time he'd looked out this window, several years before. A feeling had emerged from the background of his mind into conscious awareness. There was something wrong. Maybe even very wrong. It was still so faint that he just could not put his fingers on. It reminded him of older feelings when he'd last sat in this same chair, four years ago. This time they were stronger, but they still were no closer to being clear.

He shook his head and picked up his pen and paper, almost old-fashioned now in the era of tablet technology. There was no better time than now to start outlining the broad strokes of his agenda. He already had a picture of it, but it always looked different when set down in ink. As soon as he had his general outline on paper, he would call in his Chief of Staff Rosio Dawnhell. She had come in early as well, he had seen her Prius back in her familiar charging spot. He wondered what she was up to.

The feeling still haunted him. He was just getting used to the new environment, he told himself. With any luck the feeling would soon pass.

Rosio Dawnhell watched the President from a hidden camera, as he gazed out on the White House lawn and its Christmas tree. It was bad enough such an obvious phallic symbol of the Christian patriarchy was still acknowledged, but she knew that playing lip service was unavoidable until the cause she served ruled the world. What was much more worrisome to her was the man watching it. In this moment that he thought was private, he didn't even seem to mind looking at the tree. This was supposed to be the Antichrist that she was born to serve?

Ever since they had come back to the White House, she was seeing less of what she needed to see. If he was supposed to bring about the end of America, where was his evil? Was he that brilliant and twisted that he could keep it hidden, even from her? Or was he so deep a cover agent, that he didn't even know himself?

She had hoped it would become clear, but after years of devotion to the Devil and the destruction of heterosexual man she still didn't know for sure.

She wondered for a fleeting moment, as she sometimes did: what if those who raised her were wrong? What if communism, Satanism and lesbianism didn't need to run together? What if America didn't need to be castrated and die?

Fortunately she had more to do than wonder about the President. On returning to the White House she had immediately taken advantage of the powers of the office. Her efforts had just paid off with a lead on a man she'd been tracking for years.

She resolved to stop questioning her faith. She wasn't here to doubt. She was here to make things happen.

It was time to get things rolling.

HOURS LATER, Jesus and his newest convert lay together. She borrowed his cigarette to take a drag. "Are all your lessons so intense?" She grinned.

"Only for those especially suited for this sort of saving." He smiled back.

She looked off into space for a moment. "How is it again we can do it unless we're married?"

"Like I said before baby. I'm duty bound to do whatever it takes to save you." He gave her a playful spank. "Also, you know, men are supposed to be good, but not tamed. So the rule's not as strict for men. More like a nice-to-have." He patted her on the head.

She smiled. "Am I nice to have?"

"Yes indeed." He kissed her again, and held her fondly in his arms. "Now give me a minute will you baby? I gotta check in on something." She kissed him and leaned back on the bed.

Jesus turned on his trusty old Compaq laptop. As it began its minutes-long task of loading Windows 95, he leaned back and took another puff. By the time the cigarette was nearly gone, the computer was fully awake. Jesus opened the AOL. Other laptops could run faster, "better" software with fancy names like "Chrome", "Firefox" or "Internet Explorer" and use the "Google". They also made it easier for the government to track him - something he definitely did not need.

He logged with his main username, AntiAntiC777. Just as he'd hoped, his leading follower Tex was online.

ANTIANTIC777: How's New America?

JCplace2b: Happy day here in many ways! Just contacted a perfect fit for our team. A master gunsmith.

JESUS CLOSED his eyes and pumped a fist in triumph.

AntiAntiC777: Your reward in the next world will be glorious!
JCplace2b: Helping you is all the reward I need.

JESUS LEANED BACK GRINNING. What a wonderful birthday this could be. Bomraka hadn't outlawed guns in his first two terms – he was bound to do it soon. With men like Tex on his side, they would be ready.

Jesus had recruited Tex after seeing the liberal media attack him. The man was a mighty dentist job creator from the holy state of Texas, and had flown straight to Africa to hunt the last remaining lion with his own two hands and a gun. When Jesus confirmed the man also knew the truth about EVILution, Ghenbazi and global cLIEmate change, he knew Tex was a true American destined to fight by his side.

He put the laptop aside and returned to the bed. She settled happily into his arms.

He nuzzled her ear and murmured, "Now that I've shown you the light, you're going to find a godly husband of your very own and make him very happy."

"Well, I'm so glad I met you, Jesus," she said. She kissed him, and put his cigarette back between his lips. "I know you'll have to go soon to save America. But I want to see you again."

"I'm so glad I met you too," he said, and paused. "So yeah, just, uh, give me your AOL address. I'll probably pass through some time again."

She nodded. Then her eyes opened wide.

"That's kinda how I talk when I forget someone's name," she said.

"Don't be silly, babe. We were about to leave things real nice here."

She sat up. "You do remember my name, right?"

"That's got nothing to do with your soul, honey. What's important is that you're saved."

"Come on. You didn't say my name. What is it?"

Jesus squirmed a bit. "Look, I see a lot of people and - babe, I'm just not good with names the first few times."

She jumped off the bed and stared back at him, stunned. "All this crap about Horsemen, and Seals and my soul, and we have sex three times in the same night, and then you can't even remember my fucking name?" Her face clouded with anger. "Just who the fuck do you think you are?"

"Baby! You know who I am. I told you. I'm the Messiah. I save a lot of people."

"What kind of excuse is that?"

"I know you're mad now. I'm gonna go for a walk before you say something to your Lord you might regret."

"You son of a bitch!"

Jesus threw up his hands. "I'll be back when you can have a conversation." He got off the bed, pulled up his pants, and threw on his shirt. His .45 went into a holster in the small of his back. Fortunately he hadn't taken his boots off.

"You stay right here! You-" Jesus stepped out of the motel room, and shut the door behind him. He could hear her voice rising in pitch and volume. Thankfully, she wasn't dressed enough to follow him out the door. Out of habit, he surveyed the stairway and the upper level of motel rooms - clear. He stepped out into the night.

That could have gone a little better, he supposed. If she still accepted him as the Messiah, she could still go to heaven. As long as she didn't try to kill him first.

That level of emotion meant passion, which also meant she'd make a good Christian. She just couldn't ever be...the girl he'd lost.

He ruthlessly struggled with himself to drag his thoughts away from Alaine and back to his mission. None of it was easy, but his path was never meant to be easy. Stretching a kink in his neck, he sighed. He might as well use the walk for practice. It was important to stay sharp. He began shadowboxing.

It had been a while since he'd tried to save a stripper. So much of his time had been spent working, preparing. Almost all of his plans were in place. The Christian militias had been dealt a terrible blow by gun control and a coincidental plunge in the number of domestic murders. That gunsmith Tex had found just might provide that last piece of the puzzle.

All across the country, righteous job creators just like Tex were weathering the assaults and insults of BomrakaCare and higher taxes. They were long past ready to drop their socialist fetters and be freed by the invisible hand of the market - the hand of God. AOL, still weathering the liberal takeover of the Internet, was there to keep the faithful together as America and the world waited. All that remained was for Jesus to know the time was right, and he could step forward to take back the White House for the coming Kingdom of God.

Then at long last he could end the pain of his followers – and he could find the woman he was meant to be with. For surely that was in God's plan for him as well. No one could ever take the place of the Alaine he loved in his youth, but someone close enough that he could really love not only as a savior but as a man. Not just another daughter of Eve who needed saving, fun as that could be – but a queen to share his throne, worthy of being the daughter-in-law of God himself.

For now, Jesus could only keep his own faith in his Father and a careful eye on his surroundings.

Back in the hotel room, the lamb he'd been trying to save stormed about looking for her other shoe. Unnoticed words appeared in Jesus' laptop chat:

JCplace2b: I think they're on to me! Cut this signal now before
The text disappeared from the screen.

3

———————

Jesus walked, falling deeper and deeper into a reverie. He let himself go and imagined how pure, beautiful and glorious their future world could be. As had only happened to him once before when he was but a teenager, his surroundings faded away. A vision fell upon him, and he Knew.

A bald eagle lay on the ground, covered in filth, awakening to the dawn shining on a city street. The sky turned red with blood, and the Eagle rose up. He saw a silver pistol and a golden sword beneath his talons.

The eagle shook off the filth that had been covering him; the accumulated garbage that decades of unbelievers had strewn atop it, hoping to hide and smother the creature's beauty. The Eagle grasped each weapon in a talon, and began to flap his wings. His wings, not 'hers' or 'its', for the Eagle was clearly a male – and a mighty one.

As the holy, masculine Eagle took flight above the city, the sword and the pistol began to glow. The Eagle expanded in size, his wings spreading across the land. Buildings, bridges and all the structures of man shook with the rhythm of his beating wings. Frightened citizens slowly emerged from their homes. Some to gaze in wonder at the Eagle, some to sing his praise, and others to cower in fear.

As the eagle flew higher, the sword and pistol burst into glorious fire.

The sword shot down a blast of flame. From either side of the sword's cross-piece came two more bursts of holy, magnificent fire. In the center of this flaming cross appeared a fist. Not a liberal fist, pointing upwards to defy the lord. A manly fist, with the knuckles coming straight at any doubter's eyes.

The eagle flew higher and farther, until he came to a mountain. To the top he flew. There, the eagle brandished his sword and readied to unleash the holy flame of judgment upon the world.

The eagle faded into the distance, taking with it the glory it inspired. The vision began to slip away. "Is it time?" he demanded.

Visions and memories mixed together. Scenes and images from his young life before he'd become the Savior mixed in a fog with jackals and eagles fighting on top of the corpses of demons, angels, Americans and Demoncrats.

The jumble cleared and fell away. He found himself staring across a black desert, with a night sky above him and a flaming red chasm beneath. An angel and a devil appeared on the chasm's edge. They turned to look at him, and then stood in silence.

"Tell me!" he screamed.

Still silent they pointed behind him. He turned, and saw that they were pointing at the twin golden arches of St. Louis.

The vision ended, and he returned to the world of the present. While under the vision's spell, he had walked back to the motel. From across the street, he faced the room he had just left and tried to understand what he'd been shown. That had been the first real vision he'd had since he was set on this path as little more than a child.

He recalled the symbol he'd seen, and wondered how to make a gesture from it that could go forth from man to man as a symbol of their faith. He made the sign of the cross, ending with a clenched fist over his heart.

That just felt right at least. It would henceforth be called the Crucifist.

But what about the rest of it? It still was not quite enough to at last break to the surface and strike.

Jesus stepped into the motel parking lot. His arms open wide, he implored the heavens.

"Now, Father!" Jesus declared. "I am ready! Let this be the day. The Day Thy Will Be Done. Let me see a sign!"

He closed his eyes, and stood in silence. Moments passed. He listened and heard nothing. He opened his eyes.

Nothing happened.

Jesus' heart sank. Why was his Father taking so long to manifest his destiny?

He stepped into the motel parking lot - and stopped.

He could hear the sound of helicopter rotors. He looked behind and up to see burgeoning silhouettes blocking out the stars. Black helicopters! At first nearly invisible against the sky if not for the heavenly light they eclipsed, as they drew closer they appeared to be thick as monstrous flies.

Two missiles shot from the nearest helicopter's torso. They arced toward the motel. He turned and ran for the room with desperate speed, knowing he would still be too late. The adrenalin shooting through him compressed time from seconds to what felt like hours, the cylinders of death seeming to pass above him almost leisurely.

The rockets fell screaming from the Heavens to the earth, and slammed into the motel room where he had lain just minutes before. A shockwave erupted that would have knocked a weaker man to his knees. It was followed by a wash of flame and smoke. Flaming debris rained down, lighting up the asphalt lot and surrounding woods nearby.

4

————

Time sped back up to normal. "Holy heaven," Jesus said softly. The upper floor had been demolished. The door to his motel room lay askew, flames licking around the entrance. The helicopter blades lowered to a hover. The ceiling was beginning to sink dangerously. There was no time to consider the risk. Jesus ran in through the smoke and still-settling debris to save his latest charge - and saw only her remains.

Even if he had the power to heal this time around, there might not have been enough left of her to heal. It was a miracle he had not been there too - a miracle that had only extended to himself. He shook with rage. She could have made America more Christians someday. Whatever her name was, she would be avenged.

Somehow, he must have been discovered. Who knew that he was here? Who could be his Judas this time around?

The sound of the black helicopters' blades brought him back to the present. Perhaps the things were waiting for the smoke to clear. He looked around the room. His laptop had been knocked to the floor. He stomped it until he was sure the hard drive was unrecoverable, and then kicked it into the flames growing in the room's far corner. He grabbed his denim jacket, miraculously untouched. From its weight his most important remaining possessions were in its pockets. He had no time to take inventory.

A helicopter approached closer.

He ran outside and up the stairwell to the second floor. From the railing he saw the helicopter lowering in, its rotor wash blowing the smoke away to get a clearer view of the motel room.

He put his back to wall at the edge of the landing, ran forward and sprang off the railing with a mighty leap. His outstretched hand caught the helicopter's lower landing skid. The monstrous insect dipped to the right and dropped a few feet from his unexpected weight. Hanging on with his left hand, with his right hand he drew his .45.

"Alright, you Demoncrat abomination!" he snarled. "Time to taste God's justice!"

He fired at the tail rotor. The slug bounced off with no effect. He aimed at the gas tank cover – and realized there was none. The monstrous helicopter must be electric, a full expression of the Devil's evil. He aimed his gun upward through the floor of the helicopter, and his bullets merely ricocheted off of heavy armor plate.

The helicopter rose in the air, dangling his feet higher above the motel roof. He looked back towards the parking lot, where another black helicopter was turning to face him. A rocket left its wings just as he let go. He hit the roof and began sliding towards the edge, as the helicopter he had been hanging onto was blown out of the sky. Flaming debris rained around him as he managed to holster his .45 and grab the edge of the roof. The flaming carriage of the helicopter hit the roof, its blades still swinging furiously. The roof collapsed and the edge Jesus was clinging to disappeared beneath his hands, leaving him to fall rolling to the parking lot below.

He rose to a crouch and glared through the smoke at the helicopters above. He was utterly outgunned, and this smoke couldn't hide him forever. He could be blessed by miracles, but he could not depend on them. As much as it galled him, he had to regroup to fight another day.

A door opened to his right. He whirled around to face groggy and shaken motel residents erupting from their rooms like frightened ants.

"Run, you fools!" Jesus yelled. "And read the Bible!"

The remaining black helicopters' blades grew louder, lowering towards him through the smoke. He ran through the burning half-collapsed motel to the back, pushing through crumbling sheet rock and cheap fallen ceiling tile to the bathroom. He wrapped his jacket around his head and shoulders and crashed straight through the bathroom window. He landed in the alleyway behind the motel and rolled to his feet. Just as he had his jacket back on a second set of rockets hit.

What remained of the motel collapsed in flames. He sprang to his feet and sprinted for the tree line - and almost ran right into ground troops sweeping toward the back of the motel. He dropped into the grass just as searchlights passed over his head, and crawled as fast as he could in a random crisscross pattern until he reached the relative safety of the trees.

Jesus crouched behind an oak, brushed some of the glass shards and ashes off of his clothes, and looked back at the motel that was now entirely engulfed in flame.

It certainly seemed he'd received his sign. The War on Christmas had at last become a shooting war.

5

———

From deep within the Environmental Protection Agency's secret black ops command center, Rachel Madcow sat in dismay.

She had come so close to destroying him. She had gone so far as to order a black helicopter to fire on its own kind to take him out. Yet somehow, once again, this mysterious man named Christ had slipped right through her fingers.

There was a knock on her office door. "Enter," she said morosely. Blabbera Wilters appeared. In addition to her public duties, she was the EPA's secret media liaison. Rachel had always disliked her. Wilters' older guard of Feminazi generally resented being outpaced by the younger and more fashionable "Third Wave" Feminazis – that new guard who concealed their bionic implants with eyeglasses and short hair instead of makeup. Rachel could feel professional jealousy surrounding her like a cloud of cheap perfume. "Tell me you found him," Rachel barked.

"He can't be far. Maybe we attacked prematurely-"

"Shut your mouth and find him," Rachel snarled. "Now!"

"Yes ma'am." Wilters closed the door, leaving Rachel alone with her fears.

There wasn't much time before she would have to report to Dawnhell. She'd better have some positive news by then. The last time someone disappointed the Chief of Staff, they were cleaning tofu out of the wood chipper for days. She shuddered and went back to her task with renewed intensity. There was a topographical relief map of the area to examine. Her eyes were drawn to some nearby woods.

JESUS RAN THROUGH THE WOODS, knowing that his respite would be brief. Somehow, the government had pierced his web of secrecy. Soon Bomraka's thugs would come in greater force, under the guise of some Federal agency. Perhaps it would be the FDA, or the EPA. Or OSHA, or NASA, or some other bureaucratic mask he hadn't bothered to remember. They would search for him among the people, using their government regulations to find any sign of Godliness they could extinguish.

The other end of the forest was in sight, where its edge would fade back into developed property. A small green island in a desert of occupied buildings.

He heard a rustling to his left. He crouched, drew his .45, and waited. A deer bolted past him. A less experienced warrior might think he'd already heard what he was listening for. Jesus knew to listen for what had disturbed the deer.

He waited in silence a few more moments. As expected, a jackbooted government thug appeared, looking for his trail. Jesus noted an acorn symbol on his sleeve. Of course – before patriotic Americans drove them into secrecy, ACORN was known for trying to register poor voters. They must have been seeking him with their voter registration drives, like Herod searching for the first baby Jesus.

The ACORN thug walked with a certain amount of confidence, not worried about covering his back. He could be the point man in a three-man formation. Jesus pulled back a little farther into the shadows.

"HE MIGHT BE in those woods, heading for the western edge," said Rachel. "Get some men there pronto. When we have the area surrounded, we'll burn it down."

"But ma'am," the commander protested, "how will we explain that to the civilian authorities? We've already blown up a motel. We're just supposed to be public health inspectors."

"We'll blame it on global warming! Just do it!"

Her hotline rang. She saw the caller ID and gulped. One of the few beings she truly feared was attempting to videoconference with her. "Call me when you have that patch of woods sealed off, and not one second before!" She disconnected, took a moment and a deep breath to steady her voice, and took the new call.

Rosio's face appeared on the screen. "Didja get him?" she asked without preamble.

"Not-" she began, and froze as she realized she'd just admitted failure. Backtracking would be even worse, so now she could only follow through. "Not yet. But it can't be Jesus, ma' am. He's a myth."

"I'm not asking for your opinion," Dawnhell declared. "Ya got the EPA ground forces out there, the county's OSHA team, ACORN, and half the black helicopters in Missouri. Ya had an advance line on his location. You not only blew up the motel he was in, you had one helicopter blow up another. And you still haven't caught him?"

"Ma'am, he - he's probably be in the ruins. We just have to find his body."

The resulting silence was much too long for Rachel's comfort. When Dawnhell resumed speaking, her voice was cold and calm. This served only to increase Rachel's terror.

"You know, you blew up an entire motel on Christmas. This will take a lot of effort to keep quiet."

"Our connections in the media can slant it sideways, ma' am," she stated. "We can-"

"Whatever you're about to say, don't bother," Rosio stated. "We're starting a new administration and are poised closer than ever to winning. Then this guy pops up on the map and you blow up a motel on Christmas to get him – and miss. Can you understand why that bugs me just a little bit?"

"Yes ma' am."

"Do you need to be reminded of how I deal with people that bug me?"

"No ma' am." No indeed, she did not need any such reminder now or ever.

Dawnhell looked at the watch strapped to her bulky arm, and sighed. "We've got a lot of things to do. I don't want this to even be a blip on the radar. You capture or kill whoever this dummy of a Christian is, and have a cover story in place in the mainstream media by no later than 5:30 AM EST."

"Yes ma' am."

"Good." Her voice softened a bit, shifting into the jolly tone that had beguiled and bewitched hapless millions. "You're one of my favorite besties. Let's make this work together, m'kay?"

Even though Rachel had been in the liberal mainstream media for many years, her heart still softened at Rosio's magic. "You've still got it, ma'am."

Rosio chuckled. "Have to be ready, always." Her expression hardened. "Now get to work! We'll be having a conference call with Strident's group at 9." Dawnhell ended the call with a stab of fat finger.

Rachel closed her eyes and spent a couple of moments sinking into deep relief. She still had her position. Her mistake would probably even be forgiven if she could produce some results. She shook her head to clear it, and got back on the line with her forces on the ground.

THE SECOND SOLDIER walked twenty feet from where Jesus lay in hiding, and then turned left. As soon as he was out of sight a third government thug appeared, passing on Jesus' right. Jesus was about to pounce but something told him to wait. This agent of ACORN also had a way of walking as if he wasn't worried about his back. Was a fourth hater of freedom behind him?

The third thug passed out of sight, and no fourth man appeared. Jesus began to wonder if he'd guessed wrong. Just as he was about to leave his cover and head for the edge of the woods, he heard the soft crunch of boots on fallen leaves. A fourth gunman was almost upon him.

It was best to handle this as quietly as possible. Jesus holstered his gun, searched the ground and picked up a fist-sized stone in each hand. The man drew nearer and stopped about twenty feet away. He scanned the space around him with practiced sharpness, seeking signs of his quarry every few paces.

Jesus waited until the man's head was faced away, and threw the first stone. It bounced directly off the soldier's skull. "Ow!" cried the soldier, turning and starting to bring up his gun - only to bring his face into contact with Jesus' flying right cross. He recovered and threw a flurry of desperate punches but he had already lost. Jesus slipped around his dazed strikes and wrapped his mighty arms around the soldier's neck, putting him in a sleeper hold. The government gunman fell into unconsciousness.

Jesus set him down softly, and scanned the nearby landscape. No one else seemed to have heard the struggle. He looked down at his defeated enemy and saw a young man barely out of his teens. Now that he was unconscious, the kid looked barely old enough to shave. Yet even after being hit with a rock, he had turned in time to nearly shoot his attacker. This sharpness and skill was worthy of respect, even in the hellbound. What trail of bad choices had led this valiant young man here?

Jesus looked down at the unconscious soldier's tag. It read "Elroy". The kid also had a walkie-talkie with an earpiece. He put the earpiece in and rifled through the kid's pockets, and came across a smart phone. He closed his eyes to mutter a quiet prayer of thanks. He might be able to warn his AOL brethren.

Jesus then found a wallet, opened it and frowned. The kid's driver's license was from Texas. That meant he had been raised strong and proud with discipline. For such a promising young man to be led this far astray by Bomraka's tricks…it filled Jesus' heart with sadness.

Jesus pulled the battery and SIM card from the smart phone, and put them in separate pockets. The captured walkie talkie's earpiece gave a sudden squawk

"Elroy!" came a man's voice clearly accustomed to command. "Report! Any sign of the search target?"

"Elroy reporting," Jesus responded, his voice muffled and low. "No sign."

"Fall back. Leave the blast range. The countdown starts on my mark." The Commander coughed. "T-minus twenty. Nineteen. Eighteen."

Jesus nearly cursed. He lifted the unconscious soldier's head and checked his temples and hairline. There was no sign of a Mark of the Beast implant. Perhaps he was too new?

"Sixteen. Fifteen-"

This kid wasn't saved. If killed he would go straight to Hell. The edge of the forest was nearly a hundred yards away.

Jesus hauled the unconscious soldier off the ground, and draped him over his shoulders in a fireman's carry. He ran for the nearest break in the tree line. Swelling sounds of incoming black helicopters convinced him to double-time it.

"Ten. Nine."

Ahead was a gap between the trees. He could make it if he dropped the soldier – but such a valiant fighting man deserved at least a chance at heaven.

"Three. Two… "

The clearing beckoned him like a far-away dream. Just a few more paces.

The explosion sent Jesus and his burden flying through the air.

Jesus came to moments later. His head was spinning and his ears rang, and he could feel something wet on the side of his face that he expected was blood. He closed his eyes and focused, then gathered himself up from the ground. The walkie talkie lay a few feet away, busted on rocks. He only had a minute or two before they found out this soldier was missing.

Jesus looked down at the young man, and reached into his jacket pocket. He pulled out a pamphlet with the real truth about the Bible and America. He stuffed it into the soldier's inner pocket. Then to make sure he'd stay out a little longer, Jesus punched him again.

If the kid had any luck, they'd think he had been knocked out by the blast and was incompetent. He would stay a grunt, never get promoted and never get a Mark. Then, if the kid really understood the pamphlet, and kept his mouth shut, his head down, and his Christian nature hidden until the time was right to strike, he might yet have a chance to find his way to salvation within the Army of the Lord.

Jesus ran to the next bunch of trees. No direction was better or worse than any other, as long as it took him out of the search radius as quickly as possible.

The next few hours were spent walking through the darkness of night with only heaven's thousand points of light to guide him. At long last he came to a highway. He approached the shoulder for a clear look. There was an overpass about a mile up. If God's fortune could smile upon him for the next mile, he might find just what he needed.

Jesus made his way along the shoulder, moving in a crouch so low he was nearly crawling. Swooshing hybrid cars occasionally interrupted the highway's quiet with their emasculated whines.

From the edge of the overpass, he saw what he had hoped for: an abandoned gas station. The liberal hybrid electric car armada was quickly rendering these symbols of American might obsolete. These once-beautiful Meccas of American motoring manhood still dotted highways and intersections, increasingly unused and unwanted – ghostly reminders of past glories murdered in the interest of "reducing pollution." What about the pollution that killed these gas stations – the liberal lies of lying liars?

This one would do him service. He walked up the overpass to what had once been the front office. A quick check revealed no motion detectors or silent alarms. The door lock gave way to a quick kick. He closed the door behind him, dragging a box of parts over to wedge it shut.

Everything inside the office was covered in dust – the couches, chairs and countertops and the magazines and clipboards laying on them. It looked as if the people who worked here had simply closed up one day and never returned.

He stepped into the main shop and from there into the mechanics' cramped locker room and washroom. This room had no windows, which was a relief. It was also less dusty and more filthy than the front office, which was somehow comforting. Good American work had been done here once, on real cars that used God's Good Gas. He found a sink and examined his face in the mirror. He looked quite a sight, with dried blood trailing down from a cut in his temple that hinted at his previous incarnation. He was very fortunate that it was a superficial cut. He washed his face and found an aged but unopened bandage kit in the garage's work bay. It would have been nice to have healing powers like before - but that Jesus was for a different time. Such was God's balance.

He poked his head into the front office to check the shop's windows, then opened the back door to listen while he examined the sky. He neither heard nor saw any sign of those monstrous black helicopters. The Demoncrat oppressors would hunt him until their end or his, but they appeared to have lost his trail for now.

He took some filthy couch cushions from the abandoned front office, laid them on the shop room floor and collapsed in exhaustion.

6

———

Rachel stared down at the hastily scrawled notes and frustrating reports covering her desk. With a savage swing swept them to the ground, to join the many empty cups of grande soylent green tea chai lattes. She sat back in her chair and buried her face in her hands. There was no sign of the Christian she'd been ordered to capture. What would happen to her career?

Her underlings were no help. The black helicopters just kept repeating that the target structure had been destroyed and all witnesses removed. The EPA agents and supposedly elite ACORN troops had no better answers – they couldn't find a trace of him. The room where his laptop was found held only female remains. No one else on the grounds matched his described age or gender. He was probably still alive and on the run – and they didn't even have a picture of his face.

There was a knock at her door. Rachel scowled "Go away! Come back when you have something on the search subject."

Wilters opened the door. "Jane, you need to-"

"What?" She launched out of her suit and stepped to Wilters with a fiery glare. "You don't tell me what I need to do! Do I need to remind you who's in charge here?"

Wilters didn't bother to hide her sudden pleased grin. Before Rachel could pursue this shocking new level of insolence, Wilters stepped aside.

There stood Rosio Dawnhell. In person. Just outside her office door. "Don't think there's a need for reminders, huh Miss Crabby-pants?" Dawnhell squeezed through the doorway, and motioned for Wilters to follow. Wilters closed the door behind them.

"So where's this Christ guy?" Dawnhell demanded.

"We don't know," Rachel said. "We-we think he's gone to ground-"

"You're darn tootin' he has," said Dawnhell. "Why'd'ya order an immediate aerial strike? Why didn't ya just contain the area?"

"We needed to take him out immediately. He was too dangerous-"

"Was that in any of your orders?" Dawnhell asked sweetly.

"No." She swallowed. "Not directly. But it seemed the most prudent way to..." Under Rosio's gaze, Rachel's sentence shriveled into nothing.

Dawnhell turned to Wilters. "Ya see how she failed, right?"

"Yes ma'am," she answered eagerly. "I believe I do."

"OK, tell me." Rosio folded her arms beneath her massive upper bulk and waited like an instructor testing a pupil. Rachel began to sweat.

"She strayed from her mission parameters by making a command decision for which she was not authorized. As a result, the target has escaped."

Dawnhell nodded. "Alrighty then!"

"Wait, that's not fair," said Jane. "I had good reason to attack!"

Rosio continued ignoring Jane, addressing her assistant. "Are we ready for the second part of today's lesson?"

"Yes ma'am," said Wilters.

"Good." Rosio faced Rachel. "When ya blow it as big-time as she did, then I do things like this." Her hand shot forward and grabbed Rachel by the neck.

She lost precious air to a gasp of surprise as Rosio choked her. She tried to pry Rosio's fingers, but even her bionic fingers were no match for Rosio's steely grip. Dawnhell increased the pressure.

Fueled by adrenalin, Rachel's efforts became increasingly frantic and had no more effect. Her vision began to darken at the edges, a shrinking tunnel focused on Dawnhell's blankly cheerful eyes with Wilters' shocked face behind her.

"Blabbera," asked Rosio cheerfully, "is that ol' lesson of mine gettin' through loud and clear?"

Wilters swallowed. "Yes'm."

"Anything more to say to your former boss?"

"No'm."

"Good," said Rosio. She eased up on the pressure.

Rachel gasped as she could reach air again. She coughed and spluttered. "I learned too!" she managed to say. "I'll never-"

Rosio reached over with her other hand and grabbed Rachel's head just under her chin. With a mighty yank she ripped Rachel's head right off her neck. Her headless body collapsed backwards, crashing over the desk and then flopping to the floor in death throws as it sprayed pulsing arterial blood all over Dawnhell, Wilters and the rest of the room.

Of the possible outcomes of this meeting, it was safe to say that Wilters had not envisioned this. She looked at the dead body as its twitching dwindled, and back to the now-separated head hanging by its hair from Rosio's meaty hand.

Rosio coughed politely. "Eyes up here."

Wilters brought her gaze to Rosio's face. She knew she should say something, anything, but no sound came out.

Rosio casually tossed the head away. It thudded to the floor and rolled into the far corner. "Focus, kiddo. Remember your training. Don't think with your human parts. Use your bionic implants."

Wilters forced her voice into steadiness. "Yes ma'am," she responded with clear effort.

"How're you gonna do better?" Dawnhell asked calmly.

"I - I won't be so obvious," she stammered. "I've already been planning since you've called. I'll make him come to us! I will use the media to set a trap he can't resist."

Rosio studied her for a second, and then smiled. "Congrats on your promotion, kiddo!" She extended the same hand she'd used to kill Blabbera Wilter's former boss.

"Thank you, ma'am." The coating of fresh blood and ripped throat tissues made Dawnhell's hand slick and slimy. Walters made sure to exert only the minimum polite amount of pressure.

Dawnhell nodded, and turned to leave. "Oh, one other thing. In private, I prefer 'Yes, mistress'."

"Yes, mistress." Wilters looked back to the office, and saw anew the headless body of her former boss sprawled across the floor. "Uh...what should I do with-"

"Get to work, and find this guy who calls himself Jesus Christ. Don't bug me with the details." Rosio smiled a friendly, soothing smile with just the right amount of teeth. "You don't want my management style to be more hands-on."

Dawnhell left. Wilters looked her former superior's headless body lying dead at her feet. She experienced an inconvenient bit of sympathy. Rachel had worked hard her whole life to break through that glass ceiling. She'd worked all the way up to it and cracked it. Then when her life was on the line, she hadn't been able to deliver - and the ceiling closed around her neck and took her head off.

She shuddered, and focused back on the present. There was the headless body of her former boss on one side of the office, the head in the other, and an entire office covered in sprayed blood. It was quite distracting. How would she get rid of that body and get the place cleaned up, so she could get to work?

At least Rachel's implants were probably metal and recyclable. Maybe the rest could be separated for composting. She called Facilities and arranged a pickup, then she wiped some stray blood off of the desk chair and took a seat. Wilters felt calm steal over her. The stakes were a little higher than usual, and circumstances of her unexpected promotion had rattled her. But she had experienced this kind of pressure before, the first time she'd had to cover up one of Ralph Nadir's blood sacrifices.

After years of toil and hard work, she had finally gotten her promotion. She rubbed her hands with glee, and pressed the intercom. One of her new inferiors scrambled to get her a grande chai latte, extra soylent green.

JESUS AWOKE. He kept his eyes closed and listened for the sounds of anyone nearby. All sounded clear.

He opened his eyes, stood up and took stock. He was in a fix, no doubt. He was also hungry. He was also free another day to fight for God's glory. It would all work out.

He stood, stretched his back, and began his own routine of movements and exercise. To some it might seem like yoga, but it was not. Yoga was a set of heathen practices that came from strange and un-American lands. This was something he himself had perfected over years of practice and prayer, a truly Christian exercise that he called YoGod.

As he tested bruises and stretched out tired muscles from his recent efforts, he reviewed his options.

The safest possible choice would be to retreat to the settlement of his secret followers in New Mexico - or as it would someday be known, New America. There a few of his most trusted faithful waited, secure in hiding. It would take a few days, but it wouldn't be too difficult. He'd have to keep his head down, maybe hop some freight trains. Once there he could regroup and plan how best to approach St. Louis.

He considered this safer path for the sake of thoroughness, but it was never really an option. He hadn't come back a second time just to be safe. God bless it, he was here to save America. He had to move forward right now and take vengeance for himself, his fighting AOL faithful, and that stripper whose name he was sure he would remember any day now.

So he would. Next question, as he stretched in his YoGod pose he called "Adam Missing His Rib" - how had Bomraka's forces come so very, very close to getting him, and sealing the fate of humanity forever?

The one way to find out was to go online. Which could put him right back in their crosshairs. He would have to be wily as a fox, and cunning as a serpent.

Jesus got up from his final YoGod stretch, "upward-facing God", and prayed. "Time to get to it!" he declared out loud. What did he have to work with? A captured smartphone and a shop full of tools. A plan emerged.

He rummaged through several tool chests until he found what he needed - a crowbar with a still-sharp edge, a roll of duct tape and a rubber radiator belt. Then he walked out to the where the road passed over the highway. It was near midday now, the sun staring directly down as the lunchtime traffic started picking up. He walked along the overpass' sidewalk until he stood over the highway, and kneeled out of sight from the traffic below. He reinserted the phone's card and battery and set it on the concrete. While the phone was booting up, he laid out the items he'd brought with him.

Several hybrid robot-driven drone trucks passed beneath him. How those un-American monsters had devastated the American spirit by removing personal responsibility from deadly accidents, for the paltry reward of saving several thousand American lives a year. This country was built with real, dangerous roads for American cars that were big and strong and just a bit dangerous like a man should be. He hung his head for a moment to lament the majestic diesel-belching 18-wheelers of old – driven to extinction by the Devil's EPA. A magnificence unseen since the dinosaurs of 6000 years before.

The phone's home screen lit. It was ready to use. He picked it up and held it sideways to reflect the sun, saw the smears on the screen from the last passcode entered and smiled. Maybe he'd been right about that kid he'd saved, because the passcode was actually in the shape of a cross. He unlocked the phone and proceeded directly to AOL. He spent further precious seconds opening a browser and logging in with a failsafe account known only to him and Tex, "JehovahJr".

He searched for the chat room he'd used last night. It was still there. Would any followers show up? He only had a few moments more before Bomraka's minions could get a fix on his location. He was about to log out when a message appeared.

FreeJC: It's a good time to fish, got good line.

This was Tex's failsafe username. "Got good line" was their predetermined signal that the line was secure. It meant they were safe to talk as long as they avoided trigger phrases the government would search for, like "gold standard", "free market" or "godless homosexuals." Jesus wanted to be relieved, but he still wasn't sure. Responding was risky. But Jesus also had to know. This man had been managing their entire network of chat rooms. Was AOL still safe at all, or had Tex been compromised too?

JehovahJr: What happened?

FreeJC: Can't tell you here.

His heart sank nearly as high as it had risen. That just didn't seem how Text would say it, or type it. Conversational subtleties could be tricky in chat rooms. He had to be sure.

JehovahJr: What's the best state for a real Christian to be in?

This was an inside joke that Jesus had shared with his lead online disciple for a couple of years.

FreeJC: The state of grace, of course.

That answer wasn't wrong. But it wasn't the one he was looking for. His good ol' Christian Tex would know the real answer: the State of Texas.

He started wrapping duck tape around the smart phone. Then it chimed. A new text message had arrived.

He lost the battle with his curiosity and unwrapped the phone.

The message said:

JESUS - YOU WILL FIND JUDAS IN EGYPT.

He stared for several seconds, his stunned gaze frozen to the screen. Then he nearly screamed in frustration. All he wanted to do was save mankind. He wasn't here to figure out riddles! He swallowed his anger. Whatever the reason behind sending that message, just receiving it meant someone had tracked him to this phone. He had to get rid of it.

He wrapped the duct tape around the phone until it was

completely sealed. Then he taped the phone to a radiator belt, and that mass to the crowbar. He then spent several tense moments waiting for the right vehicle to come along. He only had one shot at this.

At last, a long-distance hybrid drone truck appeared on the westbound side of the highway.

He climbed up on the railing that ran along the overpass. As the drone truck passed beneath him, he threw the crowbar downward point-first with all his might.

It penetrated the drone truck's flimsy plastic roof. He nearly whooped for joy. But the attached bundle bounced off with enough force to pull the crowbar free. He kept watching, hoping against hope, as it all slid towards the edge. Just before the truck disappeared around a bend, the crowbar was stopped by a riveted corner and the bundle came to a rest.

Jesus sat back down on the sidewalk, and breathed out. The phone was on a ride now. With any luck, they would track that thing for miles. That could give him just enough time to head in the opposite direction, toward St. Louis.

He walked back to the gas station, and didn't relax until he'd entered and closed the doors. Then he had a cigarette, relaxed his vigilance and allowed his mind to reel with his newest question.

JESUS - YOU WILL FIND JUDAS IN EGYPT.

What could it possibly mean?

If the government sent that text to trap him, why would they send something so cryptic? A message he didn't even understand?

It was addressed to him directly. It had to be the government. Didn't it? Who else could know he had that phone? Besides maybe God, and so far God had only talked with him through visions.

Further minutes of hard thought produced no answers. He pushed it all aside. He wasn't here to think. When something couldn't be figured out, it was time to fall back on faith and action. Jesus rummaged through the office drawers until he found an old oil-stained map. There was a bus stop not too far away, off a side road that looked small and less trafficked. If the line was still running and the government was still looking in the wrong direction, then God willing, he was on his way and his father would put his mission in his path.

Then he dropped the map to the floor in shock. He leaned down to make sure he'd seen it right.

Between the gas station and St. Louis lay what looked like a very small town named Egypt.

Rosio fidgeted for the entire flight back to DC. It was precious time away from the re-establishment of the White House office. Routines to be returned to, networks to reconnect, dark powers to reinvigorate. If there was anything she was even more mad about than the failure to catch this suspect, it was the time it was taking from her other projects.

There was reintroducing soy into school lunches, and expanding the amount of nonprofit radio spreading factual lies. There was scheduling flag burnings during football games, and charity drives for teachers so they could eventually buy their own military planes. There was resisting voucher education, and spreading subliminal messages of family-destroying hedonism through Planned Parenthood brochures.

It was funny, at the end of her last time in the White House it seemed that for the amount of effort they were putting in, things weren't nearly bad enough. Her underlings swore to her that the subliminal messages in Planned Parenthood were working, and yet straight couples continued to reproduce and have children. Even with all of the anti-gun messages being released into the media, the crime rate continued to drop. Even in places that were thankfully awful like Chicago, things seemed better than they had been. She knew that appearances had to be kept up enough to fool those who weren't real Christians into continuing to vote for the Democrats. They probably even believed it wasn't the "Demoncrat" party, and refused to see the silent "n" for "National Socialism".

But did appearances have to be kept up this well?

In addition, the way the stock market was actually doing better again, and the way some initial projections showed unemployment would probably go down again because of Bomraka's restored agenda, and how BomrakaCare had actually been saving thousands of lives every year...all these things made her wonder. Were she and the Christians both wrong? Was Bomraka actually a good man trying his best to help out the country, and actually succeeding?

She hoped not. Fortunately statistics could lie. This had to be a time that they were lying.

The plane landed and she departed, squeezing her bulk through the plane's aisles. She was able to leave quickly because she always flew first class. The physical comfort and convenience was nice, but the real comfort was that no matter what else was doing, she was also spending extra Christian Americans' taxes.

In the White House itself, President Bomraka looked around for his Chief of Staff. She was nowhere to be found, which was odd as she hadn't notified anyone of her whereabouts.

He had just seen the strangest report on the news, and wanted to confirm it with her. Some motel in Missouri had been blown up on Christmas Eve. Something about it was jarring to him. It seemed to link in with the uneasy feeling he'd had that same evening. It might have even been around the same time it happened.

He decided his mind must be playing tricks on him. Perhaps he was just going through a readjustment to the scope and the tension of the job. He returned to his desk, and resolved to keep an eye on this situation. Perhaps nothing would come of it, but if nothing else he could at least honor this feeling and see if it developed into a hunch that was worth pursuing.

7

After forty minutes of walking along side roads and wooded paths, Jesus waited for the bus in front of a convenience store. The store itself had too much allegedly healthy food for his liking, and officially only took Ameros. Ordinarily this would have incurred his wrath, but until he found out what this Judas' business was it was might be best to keep a low profile. Also, he was hungry. He postponed his righteous judgment and instead traded the teenage clerk some whiskey for some hot dogs. He ate them in white-bread rolls with the only condiment that ever mattered: American ketchup.

Sated and somewhat further rested, he stood outside and stayed watchful. At last the bus appeared. He checked his possessions – ammo, whiskey flask, coins of God's Good Gold sewn into the lining of his denim jacket. His .45 and Zippo lighter from his stepfather, his folding Reagan buck knife and his own two fists. He was ready.

The bus door opened. Jesus stepped inside, and saw there were almost no other passengers on board. The driver looked extremely bored. He also had a vein in one of his temples that looked like it could be hiding a Mark of the Beast chip.

"Ticket?" the driver said.

Jesus shook his head. "Don't have one. That machine only takes Ameros, which I won't let sully my hands. But on this day alone, and solely because of my great need, for this ride I will allow a devil's pawn such as you to have God's Good Gold." He opened his right hand, to show a golden eagle coin. "Maybe it can help bring you to righteousness. If not and you choose to contact the EPA instead," he held up his left hand in a fist, "then I'm'a have to smite you."

"The EPA?" the driver said, staring at him. "Smite?"

Jesus laughed. "We gonna play that game? I know the EPA wouldn't let you drive in their evil Public Transit system without a Mark of the Beast chip implanted in your head. But this here's real gold, and your bosses never need to know. Who knows, maybe it could lead one as lost as you to true salvation."

The driver stared at him for a moment. "Fine. Whatever. Get in."

Jesus gave him the coin, and found a seat in the back. As the bus headed to the highway, he pondered the road that stretched behind him.

8

Jesus had awakened to what he would call his second life at the end of a long and rainy morning. It was the day he turned ten. It was nearly ten years before the first election of President Bomraka, whom some true Christians even then were calling the KenyAntichrist. These concerns were still quite distant for an adventurous boy with Montana as his playground.

Everywhere one looked, one could see God's great glory made manifest. It was like any other fall Montana morning.

Even in the midst of heavy rain there were still meadows full of green grass, and unseen birds singing from the trees. The glorious mountains rose in the distance and yet seemed almost near enough to touch, thrusting up into the sky. There was time yet to enjoy God's bounty, as yet unoccupied by the struggle to save America.

His name was Joshua then. He ran through the fields at those mountains' feet, foothills and plains surrounded a wooded meadow with fertile fields.

As he walked back from this splendor to reluctantly complete his afternoon chores, an idea occurred to him. At first, he thought it might even be his. As the idea grew, it felt too big to have come just from himself. It blossomed into a vision, and pushed everything he'd once known into the background. It all began to make sense.

It was the future, and rain began to fall. Not the cool rain that cools and nurtures – the stinging, burning rain of hellfire coming upon the land. People screamed and fell before it to no avail - because they had not been saved. Their loving Father had given them every last chance to reach righteousness through faith, and they had failed. Now there was nothing else he could do. He would have to fulfill his promise and bring fiery retribution upon them all.

But wait! At the last second appeared a glowing stranger. Strong and mighty, handsome and bold, wise and brave, faithful and sure. He would fight the enemies of America, of God and of mankind. This stranger would right the wrongs done to not only Joshua's own family, but to all true Christians.

Joshua's family appeared, floating above this man in heaven. He saw that this mystery messiah's parents were his very own. A celestial light washed this view away, to reveal a gas station behind a cheap motel at the edge of the Montana border. It was his mother giving birth. The man he'd known as his father, Joe tried his best to help. Joshua knew this as the place they had to stop in the night, as they fled the un-American taxes forced upon them by the Demoncrats. He watched with wonder a new part of the tale they had never told him – how three wise job creators had come to visit, following a sign in the heavens. They brought with them three holy gifts: gold, whiskey, and tobacco for the newborn king.

A new light came again and washed the scene away. Now there was the lovely Montana mountains behind Joe and Mary, watching her son and his stepson as he grew into a mighty and glorious warrior for God. A Jesus who would take the battle to all their enemies. A throne appeared which he could see with ever-greater clarity, was set in the Oval Office of the White House itself. The glowing White House of Heaven, where God and Country meet.

This faded into an Angel and a devil, staring straight back at him. They stood at a road that forked, like a snake's tongue. Holding his gaze they pointed to one road which ended at the White House, and another road that led to a humble house with a family and children as an ordinary man.

The message was clear: this was his choice to make. He had been born to do it, but he still was a man who had to find salvation so he must choose.

He chose the path of mightiness

It was then the angel and demon both turned away so he could not see their faces, and looked ahead to the road now opening before him. An eagle rose beyond them, bearing a flaming sword. Jesus leapt to grab the sword and wield it. The eagle moved just out of his reach.

Before the vision completely faded he could see something else upon the road. It was an accident. It seemed odd and incongruous. An ordinary truck ran an intersection, slamming into a certain compact car. The smaller, hybrid vehicle didn't stand a chance.

No words had been said to him. No voice was heard. None was needed, it was all so clear. One moment, he was the same as most any child blessed to be American. In the next, he knew and chose his destiny.

He awoke from his vision a mere boy no longer. He found that he had walked in from the field almost all of the way back to the farmhouse. In that time he had seen blood shed by the valiant and the holy against the Demoncrat forces that plotted America's destruction. This battle would happen in his lifetime, in a place not far from here. He would be at the forefront, inspiring his fellow Christians to ultimate victory over those vicious, implacable and demonic entities - and then leading America into a glorious world of eternal splendor and peace.

The elders he still loved, whom he now knew with a very adult certainty could not be his parents. They were more like his caretakers. Especially Joe, the man who'd acted as his father. They would always have a special place in Jesus' heart. They'd raised him with goodness and love, and they no doubt still had much to teach him about the mortal side of life. They were proven the most blessed among all living by the simple fact of being selected as his parents. But from this point forward, Jesus would ultimately answer to a far greater authority.

By the time he got back to the house it had stopped raining. He found his stepfather Joe fixing the roof on their small but proud one-floor house. "Joshua," he called out in between hammer swings on shingles. "Did you bring the mail?"

"That's not my name any more," the boy said. "A vision came to me while I was raking leaves. You may now call me Jesus."

Joe dropped the hammer mid-swing, and sat down on the roof. Yet he was not as surprised as Jesus had expected.

"Your mother said this day would come." Joe shook his head. "But it's still hard to believe it's here at last."

"You may still call me son," Jesus said affectionately. "But you have to believe me. That's the way it is."

"I've known since the taxman chased us outta Bethlehem Texas, and we found our way here to Montana so Mary could birth you in a motel garage. Three wise job creators came by that night who'd driven for days, following a star. They said if you squinted real hard it shone red, white and blue." He nodded thoughtfully, and spat. "I believed 'em, and Mary too. So that's the way we raised you. But I wouldn't be a good father if I didn't test your vision, as well as your faith and purpose." He climbed down off the roof. "Take a ride with me to the fields, and we'll talk about it. Samson tore a hole in the fence again."

Jesus nodded. Samson was their prize bull. He was strong and willful, much like his namesake.

They went to the stable. Jesus was already large for his age but still a boy - he was just tall enough to mount his horse without help. Then they rode out to where their steers were grazing, in a thoughtful kind of silence.

As they rode, a thoughtful silence began. It continued for several minutes until they came around the corner of a dirt road. Sure enough, there stood Samson drinking water from a brook. The bad-tempered creature lifted his head up and regarded them as they approached.

"So," Joseph asked his stepson, "how would the Lord in heaven have this done?"

Jesus' heart leapt with eagerness. He sprang off the horse and marched towards the bull. When he was twenty feet away, Samson gave a warning snort.

Jesus spoke gently but firmly. "The place for you is inside a fence, my friend. You know this."

The bull did not move. He did, however, huff a louder warning.

"Are you sure you know how to speak to animals yet?" Joe asked nervously.

"He gets me," said Jesus.

"Don't look like he wants to listen even if he does," Joe pointed out.

Jesus looked up at the heavens and closed his eyes. He opened them again, and stared at Joe with force. "He don't have to listen." The manly tone he intended for his words was somewhat contradicted by a voice still squeaking with puberty. "This time I ain't no lamb, Pa – I mean Joe. I'm a lion and I'm takin' care of business."

The ten-year-old Jesus ran forward and took both of Samson's horns in his hands. The bull let out a roar. Fearful for his stepson's safety. Joe dismounted and brought his rifle to bear. Jesus shook his head.

"No, pa! I have to do this myself. Have faith."

Joe looked at the ton of animal that Jesus was riling up. He nodded and reluctantly lowered his rifle. "Okay. But if he harms a hair on your head I'm'a turn him into steak."

"Deal," said Jesus. "OK, Samson. Last chance to do this the easy way."

The bull roared again and swayed his huge head.

"Your choice," Jesus declared. "Now I will show you the dominion I have been given over all the creatures of the Earth. Let's do this!" He tried to twist Samson's horns.

The bull erupted forward with the speed of a freight train, and proceeded to drag him all around the meadow. Jesus ran along trying not to get tramped and attempting to bring Samson's head to the ground. His ten-year-old arms didn't even budge the beast.

A seed of doubt grew within his heart. Could he really do this? Had the vision just been some kind of walking waking dream?

The doubt grew exponentially when he saw Samson was dragging him toward a tree.

"You're not just a boy, son!" his stepfather yelled. "If you're the Son of God, you have to use your godly half too! You have to believe!"

Jesus felt for that glory he'd felt in his vision. His feet became faster, and he was able to run along with the bull. His hands gripped the bull's horns with white knuckles and felt red-blooded American strength flow into his arms.

Samson kept heading straight for that tree.

At the last moment, Jesus pulled himself over the horns to vault over the bull's head, and the bull ran into the tree with the force of a runaway train.

Jesus picked himself up from the ground and ran over to the bull. The tree trunk's bark was splintered, but it had not gotten the worst of the exchange. That would be the bull, which now wobbled on three legs out of four, still upright by drawing on some deep remaining well of sheer defiance.

"I'm the Lord, y'hear?" young Jesus bellowed. "You are under my dominion!"

The bull swayed for a few more seconds, then attempted to charge. It fell over unconscious.

"I've proven my dominion!" he turned to Joseph, relieved and proud.

"I had my doubts," said Joe. "For a moment, I was frightened. But that was a goddamn - oh, I'm sorry Joshua."

"My name is Jesus now," he asserted. "But don't worry 'bout the cussing. Talk how you talk."

"That was a goddamn miracle."

"Yep." said the boy happily. He got back on his horse and they began the ride back.

"Guess we can fix that fence hole now that Samson's concussed and cross-eyed," said Joe.

"Yep. And we didn't even have to make him into steaks yet. Show's God's mercy."

As Joe considered this wisdom, a new level of respect came into his eyes. "You're right. It truly does."

Jesus' heart filled with pride.

"So, I guess I'm your stepfather now," Joe said after a while.

"Yep. But you'll always be in my heart."

"Thanks, son. I mean, I guess my Lord...." He shook his head. "Gonna take a while to change how I've been talking."

"You can still call me son," said Jesus. "I'm proud to have grown up with you." He frowned. "But why didn't you tell me until now?"

"We had to be sure, son," said Joseph. "If we told you, you wouldn't be able to make the right choice. That's what the angel said to your ma."

Jesus nodded. He stretched his arms, and realized they hurt. "I wonder why my arms should hurt, if I'm the Son of God?"

They rode back for a full minute before Joe responded. "Well, if I were God and I wanted you to grow up right, then you'd have to work hard like any real American. Your heavenly father isn't just going to give you handouts 'cause he loves you. Ain't right. You've got to work hard to get strong and defeat people like any man worth his salt, because you're also the Son of Man."

"Thanks Joe," said young Jesus. "I feel like God put me in good hands."

"I'm as proud of you as any man could be of any son," Joe said.

"Let's go tell Mom I'm the Savior."

9

―――――――

The bus slowed to a halt, bringing Jesus back into the present. The driver announced "Egypt," with all the fanfare of a fart. That grand name of "Egypt" must have been given in better days, because today it didn't look like much of a town. Instead it looked like it was first in line for a good saving.

A quick look around showed no immediate authorities. The town probably didn't even have its own police, just relied on the Staties whenever they needed to hand off a drunk. Good – less chance of encountering any Demoncrat thugs. He could stretch his legs, and see if there was anything worth coming here for.

He was the only passenger to exit. As the bus drove off he saw the driver shaking his head in bemused relief. Most likely he was glad to be shut of such a potentially troublesome passenger.

Jesus forgave him and walked along what passed for the main street. There wasn't much to see. The town was, to put it politely, a dump. Jesus' heart went out to those who lived here. He wondered if, in his first time on Earth two thousand years before, he might have wept at such a sight. He couldn't do that sort of thing now of course. He had to be a living example of toughness and real manhood, both for followers and foes. How else would the sheep who needed saving learn the self-reliance and personal responsibility to help him help themselves?

If ever there was a town deserving tears, it was this sad remnant of former greatness that stretched before him. Less than a few blocks from the bus stop, the town petered out into nothing like the whine of a dying dog. There at the edge of town a lone bar made a last stand against oblivion. A swaying neon sign that had seen far better days announced it was "The Eagle". If this town had anything worth breathing in its sad air, that's where it would have to be. Whether it was a clue, a challenge, or just a glass of whiskey.

Jesus entered the alleyway right before it, checked his gun and put it back in the small of his back. Maybe he wouldn't need it. If he did he would be ready. As the son of God and a man of action, he wasn't much on planning but he liked to be prepared.

The front door was worn, but rugged at least. Inside the place looked better, barely. It was all wood, some of it splintered but most of it polished, with scattered townsfolk inside. Not one head or scalp bore the outward indications of a Mark of the Beast implanted. There was at least the sound and smell of a jerry-rigged generator inside - a welcome sign that people were still independent enough to make things work with good ol' God's gas, and refuse the Satanic temptation of solar power.

Real, manly rock music was playing too. Not this modern fiddle-faddle with bleeps and blaps made by pale bony boy-men on Mac computers. Jesus nodded with satisfaction.

He walked over to the bar and took a seat. "Budweiser, Maker's Mark, and a pack of Marlboros."

The bartender sized him up. "Reds?"

"Is any other kind really a cigarette?" The bartender flashed a quick smile, put a pack on the bar and began to pour. Jesus picked up the pack and struck it against his palm to make sure the cigarettes were tight. He examined the wall behind the bartender. American flags, banners and posters of patriotic football teams, and pictures of the bartender and what must be his family.

The bartender placed the drinks before Jesus. "13 Ameros," he said.

"Ain't got none of that."

"Credit card?" asked the bartender. Jesus shook his head. The bartender's expression became less welcoming. He casually reached a hand under the bar. "We don't give nothin' out for free here, mister."

Whether the bartender was preparing to grab an axe handle or gun, Jesus couldn't help but like this man's strong attitude. "That's what I like to hear." He put a gold eagle dollar on the counter, and watched the bartender's face.

The bartender looked back at him with a shrewd expression. "If I took some sort of non-credit payment, some sort of solid gold as payment instead of an Amero, why that would be illegal."

"Heavens," said Jesus with a grin.

"But, seeing as you just rolled into town without Ameros or credit, why don't you just have these on the house." The bartender set the drinks before him, and when he'd lifted his hands the gold coin had disappeared.

Jesus took a sip and closed his eyes. Good whiskey.

Right at that moment, the music changed to a song he hadn't heard in years, by a '70s hard rock band named "Nazareth". Few people even remembered the band any more. The song was one of his favorites - "Don't Judas Me".

It couldn't be a coincidence. Jesus whirled around to see who'd played it. He saw an old man standing next to the jukebox, holding a wooden box the size of a small briefcase. The geezer was stooped with the weight of years but standing proud as he was able, and staring straight back at him.

"Do you know who I am?" Jesus asked.

"I might," the old man allowed.

"Did you send me a certain message?" Jesus asked him softly.

"I just might have." The old man stated with smug lightness. "Why do you ask?"

Jesus put down his beer and clenched his fist. "Because you need to either give me answers or say your prayers!"

The old man moved the box to the crook of his arm, and raised this hands in a calming motion. "Slow down, daddy's boy. Whyn't you take a seat while I explain things."

Jesus' face went pale with wrath. "You sold me out, me and my Christian AOL brothers, and caused the death of...of that girl ... And you want me to take a seat?"

"A-yep."

Jesus was a bit taken aback by his calmness. "Vengeance is mine. And I aim to collect it!" He reared back to let fly with a good ol' John Wayne haymaker, straight for the son of a harlot's chin.

"Why only claim vengeance when you can claim this instead?" The old man held up box. "Go on, open it."

Jesus stood there for a moment, torn between wrath and curiosity. Curiosity won. He grasped the lid and yanked it open.

He let out a long, low whistle.

There, perfectly fitted in red velvet, lay a beautiful, gold-and-silver-plated Army issue Colt .45 revolver. He'd fired many guns in his life, but this type had always been his favorite. He'd never seen one this...exquisite. He usually didn't like that word, because it was kind of gay. But just this once it fit just right.

Jesus checked the chamber and the action. Perfection. On the grip, an eagle's golden wings soared above his Crucifist. An engraving on the barrel declared *E Pluribus INRI*. All this was traced in gold inlay. The overall effect was not just beautiful - it was unequaled.

In the velvet case, above where the gun had been lay seven cartridges. Each had its own slot, and each was of similarly singular workmanship. Light filigree traced every one. Jesus hesitantly reached forward to run his fingers across a shell. The casing was somehow cool to the touch, even cold. The bullet in the tip was somehow warm.

Inside the case's lid was a shoulder holster. It was of the finest leather, worked in a simple and understated eye. A sharp eye would detect a master's touch there as well, but its quiet elegance served more to offset the gorgeous beauty of the weapon – like a perfect mate.

It was also the gun he'd seen in dreams. It was the heavenly counterpart to the .45 of his earthly heritage.

"Word," Jesus said softly.

"You wouldn't believe what it can do as well," the old man added with pride. "Amazing things."

Jesus returned his gaze to the gun's maker. "You know who I am. Just who the Heaven are you?"

"My name is Hieronymus Godwin. This is only the first of many holy weapons I have made for you."

"Then why the Heaven did you betray me and my entire team?" said Jesus. "Matter of fact, gun or no - why shouldn't I break your neck on general principle and let the Devil sort you out?"

"All good questions. If you'll take a seat, I'll answer 'em one by one." He pointed to a table where his drink already sat.

Jesus looked around. They were attracting some attention, from the bartender as well as the bar. His options were quickly narrowing to either swing or sit. The man was probably too old to outrun him if it came to that. Jesus picked up his beer from where he'd placed it and reluctantly walked over to the table. The old man sat across from him.

"I betrayed you," he said in a lower voice, "because I need your help."

Jesus blinked. "Either you need to drink less," he said slowly, "or I'm gonna need to drink a little more."

10

———

Rosio Dawnhell looked over the inside of her lair. Everything was dusted and in order, and the soylent green tea chai lattes and scones were laid out for her coming guests. She opened the doors to her guests. "Welcome, comrades! The Death Panel is convened!"

"Mistress," mumbled the documentary filmmaker Michael Max around a muffin he'd stuffed in his mouth. Scattered crumbs fell over his shirt as he barely managed to fit through the double doors.

Blabbera Strident came in next, with a cheery "Hi, Rosio."

"Great to see you again, boss!" bellowed their mutual backer George Sauron, letting his reptilian tongue slither loose from beneath his human one, as he liked to do in private.

Jane Fondue walked in last. "Hi, Mistress." The doors slid closed behind her. They went over to a circle made of couches with one chair at the head. They all sat at the couches, Sauron and Max each taking up most of theirs.

Dawnhell sat at the head of the circle of chairs, arranged as a pentagram. "I welcome you all to our reconvened new Death Panel! It's been a busy four years, but before we get into it are there any questions from our newest members?"

"How many people know about us?" asked Fondue.

"Only the most conservative of Christians suspect. The rest think we're a crazy misinterpretation of BomrakaCare. Let's keep it that way! Next?"

"What does Bomraka know about us?" asked Sauron.

"We are not to ever discuss this with him," said Dawnhell. "Your orders on this are quite clear."

"...but Bomraka has to be in on it! Why else would the government pretend to help people, like those socialists overseas?" asked Fondue.

Max nodded. "He did call it the American Affordable Care Act, or AACA. That's obviously the American AntiChristian Act!"

"Never mind your speculation." Dawnhell declared. "Any other new questions?" There was a respectful silence. "Good. Reports?"

Max hurried to speak, his latest pastry unchewed and falling back into his throat. He started gasping. Fondue sighed, annoyed, and punched him directly in the stomach. He sprayed all seated with a stream of half-eaten crumbs and stomach acid.

"Satan bless it!" cursed Sauron. "I just had this suit dry-cleaned."

"I know, ew," said Fondue.

"We'll clean it up later," Rosio declared. "Report!"

Strident spoke instead as Max struggled to get his breath back. "After our initial survey, Hopewell's administration has worked even better than expected. Gay marriage continues to rise." She frowned. "It still doesn't seem to be destroying straight marriage as we hoped. It seems to be reducing levels of hate and unhappiness, in fact."

"Thank you. Jane? How goes diet and exercise?"

Fondue beamed. "Americans are eating more yogurt and tofu than ever. Our plan is working! Meat-eating increased slightly as well, but nothing we can't deal with."

Rosio turned to Sauron. "And the United Nations initiative?"

"We've increased stockpiles of blue helmets and uniforms in every major city, mistress," he said. "We've been able to camouflage them in plain sight as supplies for Planned Parenthood."

"My movies are decreasing the desire for guns among the young," Max added, now that he could speak.

"Good, good," Dawnhell said approvingly. She turned to George Sauron. "And BomrakaCare?"

"It appears to be increasing state power as desired. But I....can't help but wonder...."

"Wonder what?" Rosio asked sweetly.

Sauron twisted in his seat and looked uncomfortable. "What if the United Nations really doesn't want to conquer America?" The sentence hung in the room like an unpleasant smell. Sauron grimaced and wiped some sweat from his face. "The Thruppence administration watered down BomrakaCare a bit – and that did seem to hurt America slightly. So it would – it seems that BomrakaCare is actually helping America somewhat?"

"That's strange," Strident admitted. "I thought it wasn't supposed to do that."

"We must trust in our secret overlords' plan," said Dawnhell. "All that matters is that their wish is fulfilled, and BomrakaCare is continuing to expand."

"Yes it is, Mistress," Strident answered with appropriate deference.

"Good. Back to you, Ms. Fondue. The switch to hybrid transportation?"

"It continues," said Fondue. "Although I'd prefer if people walked or jogged. That way their lives are less pleasant and more painful. And..."

Dawnhell stroked the flesh on her chin thoughtfully. "Something else concerning you?"

"Now that we're talking about it...Some of the things this Death Panel is planning might...that is they appear..."

Rosio said nothing, and let her flounder for words.

After several moments, Strident voiced what Fondue was afraid to say. "Sir, the hybrids lower pollution, and reduce dependence on oil. So, some may wonder if....if Bomraka's liberal policies are actually of net benefit to America?"

"Our overlords have been very clear," Rosio stated. "They are only to be implanted in key circumstances. This is all dependent on plans we do not need to know."

Sauron looked disturbed for a second – so disturbed that it showed through his human mask. "Does that mean you don't know either?"

"You let me worry about that," said Dawnhell. "For now, do as I say."

Max and Sauron looked at each other, and almost spoke. Strident wisely kept her face very blank.

"There is a new matter that I regret to speak of," said Rosio. "It pains me that we must deal with distractions. But a man has emerged who calls himself Jesus Christ. We've managed to capture one of his followers, but so far, he has eluded capture. Madcow failed me, and was dealt with. Blabbera Wilters is on it, but I don't know if she's up for the task. So this is your new top priority. Use all your dark skills, your cunning, and all your media contacts. We must find him."

"All of our efforts on hold, just to catch one man?" asked Jane Fondue. "Why?"

"That's above your pay grade. Just do it."

"Yes mistress," they said as one.

Dawnhell stood. "Good. Now if you'll excuse me, I have work to do. We'll reconvene next week."

They stood and left, Michael Max not even making it to the door before he'd pulled another muffin from his voluminous jacket pocket.

Rosio shut the doors behind them, and massaged her temples. Good Satan, what she had to work with to get things done.

11

———

Jesus stared across the barroom table at the man who called himself Hieronymus Godwin. The old man returned his stare without an ounce of concern.

"And just what is it you need help with?" Jesus asked at last.

"A job."

Jesus laughed. He found himself almost admiring this coot's audacity. He folded his arms. "Oh really? What job is that?"

"To bring me a woman."

Jesus laughed again. "Get her yourself!"

"I can't," the old man said. "I've grown old and weak, like this dying town, waiting for you to arrive. Making weapons for you to someday come and save us." Tears grew at the corners of his eyes. "I paid so much attention to that goal, I lost my only granddaughter. Gone to secular humanism!" He grabbed a bar napkin and swiped away his tears. "I'll be damned if I'll let her go to Hell because I failed to teach her right!"

Jesus stared back in open-mouthed shock. "Why, damned is exactly what you'll be! Your visions are a clear sign from God! You're supposed to give those weapons to me, not hold out on them and string me along like - like you're going on strike against a job creator! The creator of all jobs - God! There ain't no unemployment line in heaven!"

Hieronymus leaned back and folded his arms. "Don't care."

Jesus sighed and a bit of sadness came into his eyes. "You know my mission is to save mankind. If you get right with me and my Father and hand over more of those weapons, I can see about forgiving you. If I have to get mean and beat you up to save America, you know that's what I'm going to have to do."

The old man tapped his jaw. "Suicide tooth. Right here. All I have to do is bite wrong. You already know I don't mind Hell. Next?"

Jesus searched the old man's face. The buzzard was serious. "You blasted old Judas. Everyone has a hard-luck story in these troubled times. I can't just set aside my sacred job to save all mankind to bring you back your granddaughter." He was too exasperated for a second to find words. "It ain't even efficient!"

"Devil take your job!" Hieronymus spat.

"That's it. Listen here, you blaspheming buzzard-"

"No, you listen to me. You need me. I've got the weapons you need to win! Tools you need to do your job!" He leaned in. "You won't get a lick of it unless you go and bring her back to me."

"Whoever is this woman?"

"What's that matter?"

Jesus leaned back impatiently. "I've got a lot to do, and a powerful need to do it. There's a lot of different folks need savin'. Weapons of my divine dreams or no, you want me to go and kidnap some woman to save her, you got to make the case for why."

"She's my granddaughter." His voice broke. "Lily Jane Godwin." He waited for a response.

"Should I know who that is?"

"You might have seen her on TV. She's a..." the old man paused before he found the strength to continue. "She's a reporter." The words were so heavy with disgust they barely escaped his mouth.

The man's tragedy became all too clear. Jesus tried to put a good face on it. "Well, she still could make it into Heaven. Just look at Fox."

"She works for ABC Atlanta."

"Oh...." Jesus' sentence trailed off into nothing. For a man of faith like this codger to have his only living relative, his dear granddaughter, working for the network that had enabled such a demon liberal as Blabbera Wilters and her hideous harpies on that show *A View*... this explained so much of this poor old man's pain. "How'd it go that way, old man?" he asked softly.

Hieronymus told a sad, oh-too-typical tale of liberal feminist waywardness. The old man's son and daughter-in-law had vanished in the Rapture, just like Jesus' mother and stepfather. His wife had died many years before. Hieronymus realized he must have been spared for his work, and his beloved granddaughter Lily must have been too young to go with her parents too. Or so in his loneliness the old man had prayed.

He then began receiving visions on a constant basis, of divine weapons to be made for the coming Savior of Mankind. Afraid of what a talkative student might say in a government public school, and without the wherewithal to home school her properly, Hieronymus had hidden his mission from her instead. To forget his own pain of separation from his wife and children, he dove into long hours at work designing, building and crafting with divinely driven ingenuity.

"She grew up strong and beautiful, like her mother and my own dear wife Lucille. In my passion to execute the visions, I didn't notice Lily was growing away from me. I let her go to college, thinking that when she returned, she would be ready for me to share my Godly mission." He blinked back tears. "I waited too long. They filled her pretty head with all sorts of impractical and anti-Christian nonsense about the media, her rights, and evolution and global warming." He nearly sobbed. Moved in spite of himself, Jesus put a hand on his shoulder to comfort him.

"Didn't you try to talk with her? Share the importance of your work?" asked Jesus softly.

"The first time she came back home to visit, I tried to share with her my visions. But I was too late. She had become - a Democrat."

"No!" said Jesus.

"Then she got a degree in the Liberal Arts. In communications! I told her how close that was to 'communism', but she refused to see it. After a few scant years, her cursed college degree and God-given beauty had helped her move up the ranks of the liberal media. Now that Bomraka has usurped the White House a third time, their spell will take her completely. She'll be promoted to a talk show, I know she will!"

Jesus placed a hand on the old man's shoulder. "In spite of all you've done to me, I feel for you. Your own granddaughter, a part of the liberal elite and all that goes with it - helping Bomraka, the Demoncrats, and all their ilk keep the greatest country that ever could be away from the one true God who made it." He removed his hand and scowled. "Unfortunately she's the sort of person I'm here to fight against. I'm on the clock against the Devil. I can't put the salvation of all mankind on hold just so you can try and talk her out of being liberal."

"Yes you can. You do that and I'll give you the tools you need."

"How would you even change her mind, if I did bring her back?" asked Jesus. "Hard enough to get a liberal to watch Fox."

"That's your problem," the old man retorted. "And I sure ain't getting any younger. So you better hop to it, lickety-split!" He pulled a picture from his pocket, and handed it to Jesus. "Here's what she looks like."

Jesus took one look at the picture and the blood left his face. He threw it down on the table, and stood up ready to fight. "How did you get this?"

Now it was the old man's turn to be surprised. "What do you mean? That's her. That's my granddaughter."

"I can't tell from this photo. What color are her eyes?"

Hieronymus' own eyes narrowed. "You've seen her?"

"When was this picture taken?"

"Just a few months ago. Why?"

Jesus examined the picture, closed his eyes, and examined it again.

She looked just like Jesus' first and so far his only love - Alaine. Enough to be her twin sister.

"You just saw some kind of sign from God, didn't you?" the old man said, with disconcerting insight.

Jesus held his breath for a long moment. Finally he let it out. "She looks just like someone I used to know." He looked troubled, and then shook his head. "I can't pretend to understand all of my Father's grand designs. He doesn't speak to me directly. I can only guess from what I see, like any other man." He handed the picture back, and pointed at the case on the table between them. "That gun must be unique. In all the world, I've never seen its like. It clearly plays a part in how I'll save America." Jesus nodded to himself. "Which means you must be a part of my father's plans as well. When you betrayed my AOL chatroom, that must have been pre-ordained. It could even be that the Feds were already on my trail, and you just saved my ass by springing their trap before they had me." Jesus leaned in close. "For those reasons, I won't take vengeance on you today. But those reasons aren't nearly good enough for me to put my life's work aside to trust your flimsy word and take on a job to kidnap your wayward granddaughter."

Hieronymus leapt to his feet. "But you have to help me!" the old man cried "You're her only hope!"

Jesus kept his face stony smooth, and spat. "I don't got to do nothing but be the son of God and save mankind." Inside his heart, he was having a hard time with this decision. He reached into the gun case, took the gun and scooped out the bullets. "This at least can help me in my mission, so I'm keeping it. As for the rest of what God told you to make for me, you better deliver it before your time is due." Jesus took out the shoulder holster, and pushed the case to the side like a leftover plate of food. He stood up from his chair.

"You can't just leave!"

"Watch me." He put the new pistol and holster in his inside jacket pocket. "I pray you see the light before it's too late."

Hieronymus watched in silence as Jesus turned his back and walked out the door. He finished his drink and choked back bitterness. "I already saw the light," he said to no one. "It blinded me. I hope for all our sakes it hasn't blinded you."

12

J esus let a quick pace take him out of Egypt, with his hands
clenching and unclenching. He knew his mission lay before
him. For the sudden reappearance of the very likeness of
Alaine, he could make no sense of it.

He had lost Alaine years ago, through a chain of events that had
begun the first day he'd been confirmed as mankind's savior. It all
still felt like it could have been just yesterday.

His mother had taken the confirmation of his being the new
messiah about as well as could be expected.

"MY BOY!!" she cried. "God can't take my boy! Oh, I knew the
night that goddamn angel came, the Lord would break my heart."

"Marian! Don't talk like that!" Joe said.

"Oh, you're all fancy and formal now, ain't you? Now that you
know for sure we've got God's son here. Couldn't just believe me
when I told you! I remember how you weren't so keen to raise him!
You wanted to put him up for adoption!"

"What do you expect?" Joe said. "I'm outta town one weekend and
you tell me some angel visited you, then eight months later out pops
a boy who doesn't look a lick like me! That took a lot of work, and we

didn't even go to one of them high-falutin' marriage counselors that say we need to talk as equals!"

"Never mind that! Oh Lord why??" she screamed. "Why can't you just let me have my boy?"

Joe looked at her a bit longer, and went to embrace her. She struggled a bit, then gave in and hugged him back. Jesus put his arms around them both. They stayed like that a long time, until finally his mother pulled away and went upstairs to bed.

Joe walked to the china closet, opened the lower drawer and pulled out a bottle of whiskey and two glasses. He led Jesus out onto the porch and sat on the steps. Jesus sat next to him. They looked out on the rain-swept view as Joe poured a glass for himself, and then for his stepson.

"Thanks Pa-," said Jesus. He caught himself, and decided it was still alright to call Joe his father. "Thanks Dad." He took a sip. Joe hid a smile as Jesus tried not to cough. Half-God or no, that first sip of whiskey is always stronger than one might think.

He took another sip. "I don't understand," he said eventually. "Why was Ma carrying on like that? Doesn't she get this is a good thing? Maybe she didn't hear it right. I'll just explain to her about what an honor it is." He stood up to go upstairs.

"No!" said Joe. "I know you're the son of God, but you've got a lot to learn about women. You just better leave her alone for a bit." His adoptive father lowered his voice. "Anyways, you can't go paying attention to everything women say. Sometimes you have to pretend to listen, and let it just wash over you."

Jesus sat down again, and looked back at Joe's face. Joe had taken a firm and sad expression. "What's going on, Pa?"

"Something else we got to talk about. You know what this means now, about that girl you like so much."

"What about Alaine?" Inwardly he cringed. He could guess what was coming, and he had no defense.

"I think you know what I mean. You're gonna have to take her salvation more seriously."

"I'm tired." He started to stand up.

Joe put a hand on his arm and sat him back down. "You're gonna think about this 'cause you have to. You know Alaine's daddy. He's a good man in many ways, but he don't believe in God. That means she don't either."

"So what?"

"Now don't you sass me just because you found out you're the Messiah. You're still big enough to go over my knee. It ain't just me, but your father up above you got to answer to."

"I'm sorry pop, but I just don't see what she's got to do with this."

"You're close to lying to me as well as yourself. I'll spell it out. If she don't believe in God and you don't convince her, she becomes your enemy. You'll have to fight against her and if you win, she goes to hell. And you will have put her there."

Jesus jumped to his feet. He tried to talk a couple of times but couldn't find the words. At last he found something.

"I can't believe that my father in heaven would create someone as good and kind as her, just to send her to hell for all eternity." He set his jaw. "This has to be a test. I'll find a way."

Joe put the top on the whiskey bottle and stood up from the porch. He looked into his stepson's eyes and nodded. "Just let an older man tell you something your visions might not. There's always less time than you think."

JESUS COULDN'T HELP but turn the memory over and over in his head. As with so many times before, it brought him no new resolution.

His job remained. It was time to head onward to the city of his visions, St. Louis, on foot if he must, to find out his next step. He found himself momentarily gripped with a flash of righteous anger. The nerve of that old coot to deny him the tools he needed for his holy job! He told himself that at least he'd gotten a kickass new gun out of the deal. He patted his jacket pocket with some satisfaction. He sought some comfort in that, his new shoulder holster, and as his backup piece the good ol' .45.

He squared his back and got to it, trying to clear his mind. The more he walked, the more his thoughts drifted back to that old man's photograph, and his granddaughter's likeness to Alaine. Was it a sign? Or just a test? Could it even be both?

Several hours of walking later, he didn't feel any nearer to a resolution. He needed rest and food; it would do no good to face the enemy exhausted. A vehicle recharging station became visible in the distance. As he drew closer he saw that this den of sun-derived electricity for energy efficient electric vehicles was open. His wrath smoldered. They were indeed efficient – for evil.

Their day would come. In the meantime, this store might fill his needs. Just to be safe, he stepped back into the meadow, and approached the station from the back. There were no signs of surveillance. He walked around and in the front door. The sleepy teenage clerk barely registered his existence. Jesus suspected that the kid probably paid the same attention to the Bible.

Jesus grabbed some beef jerky, a couple of energy drinks and a bag of pork cracklin's with real preservatives. Real man food as God intended. For the next time he might break bread with the true faithful, he picked up a pack of Twinkies. An "Angels" baseball cap completed his selections – one never knew when he might have to hide his face from cameras. Approaching the counter, he prepared himself for the necessary effort to save this teen clerk. Perhaps he could be talked out of listening to rap music, or at least be convinced to not accept his paycheck in Ameros.

Behind the clerk, a television babbled the morning's so-called news. "...commute this afternoon. Traffic is backed up for hours into St. Louis due to surprise mass inspections by the EPA."

"Nine fifty-two," said the teen.

"Can you turn that up a bit?" He needed to find out more about these latest boulders in his path.

The kid complied. "Driving in?"

Jesus nodded. "Thinking about it."

"Yeah, they're doing a surprise vehicle inspection. Sure looks like a mess."

"That it does." A heck of one. Either Bomraka's minions had seen through Jesus' subterfuge with the phone, or they were covering all the bases. So the bastards were flexing their muscle, forcing real American gas-burning cars, trucks, and vans to wait as pussified hybrids and electric buses passed through with ease.

He watched the screen as two EPA thugs singled out a small older vehicle of American make. A Ford - the only American company with the God-given guts to not take a government bailout. The injustice of it made him grind his teeth. That driver would almost certainly end up with some sort of ticket. More money paid to the government, so it could then tax and ticket good Christians even more. It was truly worse than Nazi Germany.

"Uh, so, nine fifty two, mister," the kid said again.

Jesus grinned. "What? You in a hurry?" His face went serious again. "Let me tell you something about the Amero - "

"In other news," the head news babbler continued, "the Justice Department announced an important arrest. The second-in-command of an underground right-wing terror cell."

Jesus halted midsentence. "What did he just say?"

"Been on the news all day," the kid said. "They caught some whacko on AOL. Said he was working for Jesus Christ. Who knew AOL was even still around?"

"- Texas businessman Kevin Adamapoulos, who had the AOL 'handle' of 'JCplace2b'. He will be taken to the St. Louis City Courthouse for arraignment this evening. His suspected terror cell leader is still at large. Back to you, Ted."

The screen switched to another news babbler. "Thanks Bill. Well, sounds like he's got more heat on him than Global Warming!" The liberals all had a nice chuckle together. "Up next, the weather, with our brand new announcer!"

Jesus leaned his head back and sighed. It had to be a trap. There was no other reason why they'd announce Tex's arraignment on the lamestream media.

He also had no choice. First his visions pointed that way, and then the honor of God-given American manhood required action. He had to go to St. Louis and save his faithful disciple, come what may.

"What were you saying about the Amero, mister?" the kid asked.

"I ran out of time to say it. Here," he flipped the kid a gold dollar. "And here's an extra tip: read the Bible."

The kid looked at it in awe. Jesus turned to leave. "Don't you want the change?" he asked.

Jesus shook his head, and set his jaw. "I don't need the change or the hope. I got the truth."

He hit the pavement and steeled himself. The Revelation of St. John seemed to indicate that he would live to defeat the Antichrist, but gave no guarantees. If he ended up dead anyway despite his best efforts, then so be it.

He turned his mind to practical matters. It was good he'd gotten off that bus when he did, back at Egypt. EPA thugs would almost certainly be checking any of the public transit liberals loved so much, as well as checking cars at random. He would have to find a way in past their search. But how?

Jesus put his Angels hat on, leaned against the corner traffic light and ate his man food. He washed down the beef and pork products with a refreshing energy drink, as he checked the cars stopping at the light. Many of them were headed towards the on ramp to St. Louis. Maybe, just maybe, one of them could help him slip through the blockade.

A Prius stopped. The EPA would probably let it through. But even if he could convince a Prius driver to do right and serve God, or choke him out at a stop light and not be noticed, could he subject himself to sitting inside one of those anti-gasoline electric-powered sin boxes and still call himself a Christian?

He let it pass. Several other cars came and went. He examined each of them for strippers who might need saving, finding none. His meal of manly drinks and pork products completed, he let the empty wrappers drop to the ground in accordance with man's God-given supremacy over the environment. After several minutes he saw a matronly woman pull up in a station wagon. He had just stepped forward to knock on her window and see if she might accept his gospel or be quietly subdued, when what looked like a better shot came up behind her. He left her car continue as a white minibus approached with "St. Louis Christian Ministries" emblazoned on the side. When it stopped at the light he saw to his dismay that it was also a hybrid. Dealing with any post-Rapture Christians was always risky. What sort of self-called Christians would drive such a mockery of a vehicle, that didn't always run on God's Good Gas? He could excuse himself if he had to – others who did the same, he wasn't quite so sure. He let it pass without attempting to wave it down.

He prayed. As had been the case for his whole life, he received no audible response. He understood his Father was silent to all of mankind – and as his son, it was his mission to win back Earth the hard way, as a man. Still, he sure would have appreciated a bit more direct guidance from time to time.

Then around the corner came the most unlikely blessing he ever expected to see.

"St. Louis Scrap."

A recycling truck. A repurposed dump truck, with a loosely-tied tarp on top. It must have come out into the suburbs, to find more abandoned metal to feed liberal America's diseased appetite for reusable resources. Its very existence was sinful. But if he could use the enemy's tool against him then it was perhaps poetic justice.

Jesus looked away until the light turned green, to make sure the driver wouldn't notice his interest. Then as the end of the truck passed by him, Jesus grabbed hold and swung onto the back with one smooth motion. He quickly scrambled up, and found his way beneath the tarp -

And into a pile of recyclable debris. The top layer was mostly cardboard, plastic and something that looked like curtain rods. The junk shifted as the truck headed up the highway onramp. Jesus appeared to have chosen well. The smell could be better, but he settled in to make the best of it.

His father must really be testing him. He moved some of the rods aside. Then he realized what he was surrounded by, and could barely contain his rage. They weren't just rods - they were guns! The Bomrakaites must have reached a new stage of their plan - America's guns were being melted down! What would they do - turn them into plowshares? More like pitchforks for the Devil.

He consoled himself that the stripped bones of these once-great American protectors would be his own personal salvation, and help to save America again. He didn't have to like it. He dug deeper until he was completely covered in scrap.

Now he would wait. The next miles would tell if his ruse worked, or if instead humanity would succumb to a thousand years of eco-friendly healthcare-covered darkness.

After about 40 minutes, the truck slowed and came to a stop. Jesus heard idling cars around them, which meant they were still on the highway. They must be coming towards a checkpoint. The truck moved about a car length forward and then stopped again. He cocked both his guns and ears, tuning out the many squeaks of sliding, sometimes rusty gear beneath and around him. The truck continued its start and stop motions for a bit longer, and then pulled over to the side. The driver turned the engine off.

A man's slow footsteps approached. Jesus heard a voice say "EPA check" - the rest of the dialogue was too low to make out. The driver's side door opened, and the truck's springs shifted minimally as a man stepped onto the road. Jesus presumed the driver's papers were being checked. A pair of voices increased in volume as they approached the back of the truck. The truck's springs shifted again as someone stepped on the back bumper and lifted the tarp. Small bits of light shone through the debris above Jesus. Lying beneath the cardboard and plastic, Jesus touched a hand to his divinely inspired shoulder-holstered revolver. Would it soon be time to find out what it could do?

"You really think some Christian would hide in the recycling?" he heard the driver laugh.

"Probably not," the EPA thug responded. "But you never know how much of a pussy people can be."

The man's voice practically dripped with oily elitism. Jesus' eyes flashed fury and his right hand drifted a little nearer to the trigger of his .45. The tarp continued movement. The oil jack-booted EPA thug stepped back for a few seconds, and asked some more questions.

Then the tarp slid back in place. When the truck resumed a normal speed, Jesus relaxed and closed his eyes in silent prayers. He thanked his Father for helping him manage his anger, and begged forgiveness for not immediately answering the ultimate insult, pussyhood, with a rebuttal of manly American violence. His path was difficult and beset with challenges. Sometimes he just had to let some things wait for a full reckoning.

The truck drove for several more minutes. Finally it came to what had to be a stoplight. He carefully pushed his way to the top of the filth and debris as quietly as possible, and peeked out from beneath the tarp. It looked like they were driving through a residential area, with no vehicles behind them.

He slipped out of the back, dropped to the street and made it to the corner just as the light turned green. He had a couple of bruises from the metal and some oil stains on his denim jacket, but otherwise he was none the worse for wear. The truck pulled away, and Jesus gave a sad wave of goodbye to the lost guns, never again to know a human touch. It was up to him to save the Americans who could avenge them.

13

———

Jesus took stock of his environment. He'd made it into St. Louis! He was on track with the job he'd received from his vision, and saving Tex was the first part of it. Once that was done God would guide him more. A few miles past this ordinary suburban area with row houses, he saw the famous and glorious golden double arches of St. Louis. Once there had been only a single arch, but the holy job creators of McDonald's had made them into two and painted them freedom fry gold.

What did he see then, but the same Christian minivan he'd seen before. The dump truck must have gotten ahead of them, which meant Bomraka's minions must have searched the Minivan thoroughly even though it was a hybrid. He'd made the right choice, and felt comforted in his Father's silent guidance.

He selected the golden arches as a goal and began walking towards them. There was much he had to do before nightfall. Figure out an assault plan, clean his clothes, eat...

"Pardon, friend," said a voice behind him. Looking behind him, He saw that the same minivan had just pulled over. The driver had rolled down his window. He was in his early 30's, lightly balding with brown hair and a face that was pale, kind and kind of soft. "Need a ride?" the driver asked with an open friendly smile. Next to him on the passenger seat was a black man in his early 50s. Jesus didn't really see race, it just meant the man was much more likely to vote Democrat. On the plus side the guy did have a certain watchful, alert posture that seemed ex-military. So he could really be a conservative Christian and true American. It was important not to rush to judgment. Other people were seated in rows behind them.

"That's a kind offer." Jesus said. "Why me?'

"Well, here we are, just coming back from a mission for the Lord," the man said. "Looking like a hardworking man as you do, and also looking so much like the Lord, it just seemed right."

"Looks like you've had a hard day, too," the passenger added.

Jesus smiled. "God's work gets a bit dirty sometimes."

"Don't we know it." The driver's smile was both soft and sincere. He thought he knew, at least. "So how 'bout a ride?"

"Well," Jesus answered slowly, "I sure wouldn't mind to sit for a while." And that was the God's honest truth.

"Then step on in, and give your feet a break," the driver said. "Where you headed?"

"Downtown."

"We'll get you halfway there at least."

"Glad to, friend!" Jesus said, with real gratitude. He liked the look of these Christians after all. The minivan's sliding side door opened, and other passengers including a minister, greeted him. He made his way into an empty seat in the second row.

Just as the door closed he saw a Prius come around the bend. It was a camo squad car version full of Bomraka's Environmental Police Assassins. They must really, truly want him badly. They were instituting a second-level of search. Now he was stuck with a bunch of civilians.

His stepfather's .45 dug painfully into his lower back. Jesus resolved to ignore it, as well as the new magnificent revolver in his side holster. He shouldn't pull yet. Their hearts might be in the right places, but they might not be experienced enough as Christian warriors to calmly accept a gun's holy righteousness in truly Christian hands. He especially needed the next few minutes to go smoothly. Once he had Tex out of the EPA's clutches he could take more risks, but he had to save his partner first.

Unaware of the EPA danger ahead, the driver found Jesus' eyes in the rear view mirror and waved hello. "My name's Aaron Morehouse. That's Barclay Andrews," the man indicated the black man sitting next to him." Jesus greeted them both with a nod. "And that's Minister Simone, and the rest of our flock." The other passengers introduced themselves.

"Pleased to meet you all." If he told them his first name was Jesus they might reasonably assume he was an illegal, and he didn't want that. He'd love to tell them the full truth of who he was, but even though they were Christians they might not be able to handle it. "You can call me J.C., but my last name isn't Penney." The others in the car seemed a nice and somewhat standard group of American churchgoers. One or two of them smiled politely at his joke. Jesus forgave them all for not laughing. "Where you all coming from?" he asked, partly to evade any questions they might have for him and partly from real curiosity.

"Helping some poor folks rebuild their homes from last week's storm," said Barclay.

"You mean that storm that's supposed to be due to global cLIEmate change?" asked Jesus, leaning heavily on the "lie" part to make sure they got the point.

Aaron and Barclay both chuckled. "That would be the one," Barclay returned.

Over Aaron's shoulder, Jesus saw the EPA thugs drive past them. He thought they were in the clear. Then one of the thugs looked back at the church minivan. Jesus raised his hand over his face as if to deflect the setting sun.

The EPA man held on for a second, and then pointed at another car ahead. The Prius passed them by, on towards more polluting vehicles.

Barclay noticed Jesus' movement and followed his eyes to the EPA car ahead in the distance. Barclay eyed him a little closer than he liked.

"The Lord sure does work in mysterious ways," Jesus said to himself.

"How so?" asked Aaron.

"Hm?" He realized all the other passengers were waiting for him to respond. He struggled to recall the thread of recent conversation. "Well, surely God caused that storm so you could go and help those folks, and they could see the might of your Christian faith. He hurt them to help them, like any good father."

The other passengers nodded and smiled, including Minister Simone.

"What's your profession, son?" asked Minister Simone.

"Oh, bit of everything," said Jesus.

"Carpentry?" asked Aaron, chuckling. "You bear a passing resemblance to our Lord."

The other passengers laughed. "Certainly a good role model for any man." Jesus smiled. "But that's not my kind of job right now."

"You look like you been workin' at least, no shame in that." Barclay said. Jesus agreed. These church folks mostly didn't look up to taking Bomraka and his Demoncrats head on just yet. Their hearts did seem to be in the right place - maybe they just needed a little nudging to get with it.

"Would you folks like to hear a story?" asked Jesus.

"Sure!" said Aaron.

"Nothing like a good tale to pass the time," said Barclay. The other passengers nodded.

"Y'all know the parable of the mustard seed?"

"Surely," said the minister. "It's about how a tiny seed of faith when nurtured can grow into a mighty tree that offers not only fruits, but shelter and a place for birds to sweetly sing." Several other passengers nodded agreement.

"That is a pretty way to put it," said Jesus diplomatically. "Well the other day, I saw some mustard left alone. It was in the ruins of a former Burger King." He waited.

"Not quite clear on the meaning of that," the minister said.

"It's like this. Nowadays in our fallen country, many seeds of faith should also be sown in the free market."

"The free market? But why?"

"Because the free market is God's market. His is the invisible hand that makes it just."

"Now hold on, son," Minister Simone said. "The Bible itself says love of money is the root of all evil."

"That's just 'cause way back then, it was. Money wasn't American yet. When the good ol' American dollar was backed by God's Good Gold, it was the best money there ever was. If you don't love the dollar and all it still stands for, you don't really love America or God."

The minister's face became troubled. "I don't know if I agree with that interpretation. If we're helping folks, I don't see how it matters if it's done in dollars, Ameros or anything else."

"I'm sure you folks think you're helping," Jesus allowed. "But the only real way to help people is through the free market. That's why God gave it to America."

"But that's just-" Minister Simone began.

"Why don't we let him finish the story at least," Aaron cut in.

"Ain't much more to tell," said Jesus. "Just something to think about. In our country, these seeds of capitalism, these abandoned mustard packets in the fast-food chains that once shook the world in their majesty and might, these places that were supposed to be so unhealthy –what has replaced them? Smaller and supposedly healthier things that have made people lose their faith in the free market, just as many have lost their faith in Heaven. And all those seeds will lay fallow like little empty mustard packets, until people nurture the faith in the free markets and in the churches by deregulating 'em both and bring America back to the Lord's fold again."

From their faces, some in the van were moved and others were resistant.

Jesus caught some red and blue lights in the rear view mirror.

The EPA thugs were flagging them down.

"What is it this time?" Aaron grumbled as he pulled over to the curb. The EPA car stopped behind them, and a thug stepped out. He walked over to the driver's side. "Emission papers?" the Bomrakaite asked. This thug's voice wasn't oily with elitism like the last one. His was a more perky evil, like Satanic solar power.

"Sure thing," said Aaron. Barclay dug some paperwork out of the glove box and passed it along. Jesus sat low in his seat as if he was tired from a long day. His hand just happened to reach under his denim jacket, to rest on the gun Hieronymus had made.

The EPA man checked the paperwork, and handed it back to Aaron. Then he noticed Jesus. "Why's he so dirty?"

"Just working hard like the rest of us," said Barclay.

The EPA thug looked at Jesus again. "Seems he kinda got the worst of it. Been riding with you the whole time?"

"Yep," said Barclay. He gave a quick warning glance at Minister Simone who held his tongue. The big government Gestapo EPA thug turned back to Aaron. "Make sure you don't rev the engine too high," he threatened. "We're trying to save the environment here."

"Yes sir," said Aaron. The EPA man waved them back onto the road.

Jesus relaxed. Apparently, they didn't have a reliable description of him yet.

The minister sighed. "I wish you hadn't put us on the spot like that, Barclay. I don't like lying."

"Lying to the EPA ain't a sin, it's a duty," said Barclay. Aaron nodded, and Jesus smiled. He liked these guys more and more.

14

───────

President Bomraka needed to speak with his Chief of Staff, and no one seemed able to find her. He took it upon himself to search the White House. Finally he tracked her down to a basement room, and to his surprise found her in a video call with Blabbera Wilters.

"Babs!" he said over Rosio's shoulder. "What a pleasant surprise. Are we setting up for an interview sometime soon?"

"I was hoping so," Wilters said. She appeared to be recovering from a bit of shock at seeing him. That was strange, he thought. This was the White House – was she expecting he would only be at his desk? "Rosio was just telling me that you don't have much time available."

"Always happy to make time for my supporters," the president said. He smiled his famous smile. "Your check was quite generous, as has been your attention to so many of our causes. You seem to have quite a lot invested in them."

Blabbera allowed herself a smile. "More than you may know," she chirped. "How are you liking the Oval Office again?"

"I'm glad to be back."

"We are to glad to be back too – that is, glad you are back too.

Perhaps you'd be free sometime in early April to come onto The View?"

"Yes, I think so," said the president. "Arrange the details with Rosio. Good to see you."

Blabbera hung on a bit awkwardly. Bomraka coughed politely, and she apparently got the message that he wanted to talk with Rosio and hung up. He had thought Wilters was more perceptive than this, but apparently not today.

"For a celebrity donor, she really does like to talk with you a lot," the president said.

"She's got her finger on the pulse of a lot of things," said Rosio.

"I remember how often she used to visit in my last administration," the president mused. He started to speak again, but since Rosio and Wilters seemed to be close friends he chose not to state his next thought about Wilters. It wasn't quite fair of him, but it often seemed that when Wilters, Madcow or other of his supporters started calling around, good plans went bad and bad situations got worse.

"Now," the President said, "what's going on with this Christian terrorist group?"

"Well, I passed on your request to circulate an all agency bulletin to the FBI, CIA, NSA. and all local law enforcement agencies. There hasn't been any sign of the group just yet."

"Yes, yes, of course...but what is this report that the EPA is involved?"

Bomraka could swear his assistant suppressed an expression of alarm. "Where did you hear that?" she asked.

"Never mind where. What are they doing being involved in this? We're trying to get gas usage down, not replace law enforcement."

"I don't know. Perhaps the group has some link to Eco terrorists," she improvised.

Bomraka raised his eyebrows. "That would certainly be a surprise, conservative Christians working with Eco terrorists. But I guess not much is surprising anymore." He shook his head. "Just keep me posted, will you? I don't want any of this nonsense getting out of hand. Got another four years to make progress for the American people I don't need stuff like this mucking it up."

"I'm sure you don't," said Rosio with a smile. He nodded and walked away, feeling less settled than before. There was something unsettling about the particular way her smile had bared her teeth.

15

______

After another 20 blessed uneventful minutes, Aaron pulled the minivan into a church parking lot. All the passengers exited, and at long last Jesus was able to adjust the .45 in the small of his back. It had felt like it had pressed a tattoo of its outline into his spine.

He took a gander at their church. The building itself was small, but well-kept and proud with a big cross in front for all to see.

The congregation bade polite farewells to Jesus and each other. "You should come to a service some time," said Minister Simone.

"I just might take you up on that," said Jesus. "I'd have a lot to share. Go with God, y'all."

All except for Aaron and Barclay headed for their separate cars. With the minister gone, Jesus felt he could speak more freely. "Thanks for picking me up, and then for talking to the EPA thug there. You guys definitely did me a solid." Barclay had earned his trust. From the way he'd dealt with the EPA, he was certainly no liberal.

Barclay smiled. "Ain't no thing. Where you headed?"

"A hotel room or something. I'll just walk downtown from here."

"Alright then, it was a joy having met you." Barclay waved goodbye, and walked toward his car. Jesus waved back, glad to have met him and have his faith in real Christian black Americans reaffirmed. They needn't all be Demoncrats.

"You don't have a place to stay yet?" asked Aaron. "Why don't you stay with me and my family?"

"Thanks friend, you're kind. God will provide for me."

"You really should stay over," said Aaron. He was a good Christian man who wouldn't take no for answer. "We've got a fine pull out couch, and like any city, St. Louis can be rough at night." He pointed to his vehicle, and Jesus gave it a gander. It was a fine work van, entirely powered by gasoline. The magnetic vinyl sign on the side announced "Morehouse Plumbing Equipment - Sales and Rental." Selling plumbing gear was not the most glorious of jobs, but a solid American tradition that was untouched by modern liberal ways.

Jesus considered it. He liked this man's persistence in helping a fellow Christian. And it would greatly reduce his risks. He had no fear of any civilian he might meet, but the government was looking for him hard. Sometimes Jesus' Father offered help in ways that weren't so mysterious.

"You know what, Aaron my friend," he said at last, "I'll be glad to take you up on that."

16

___

Aaron's house was a small but proud one-story structure, on the edge of a suburb that seemed to have somehow escaped most of the scars of liberalism. "No solar power," Jesus noted approvingly.

Aaron nodded. "Just doesn't feel right. I know we could save money even without what the government could refund us. But coal is..."

"Real. From God's Earth."

"That's just the word. Real."

They walked inside. A woman came toward them, with a young boy and a girl close behind. "Daddy!" the kids exclaimed as they all embraced Aaron. Then they noticed Jesus, and stared with curiosity.

"And who are these adorable rascals?" asked Jesus.

"This is my wife Hannah, and my son Christopher, and daughter Jenny. All of you, meet J.C."

"To my friends, my name is Jesus." He shook their hands.

"Is that really your name, mister?" said the boy named Christopher. "And not Hay-sus?"

"I am so blessed."

"You sure do look like him," Jenny said.

"That he does," said Hannah.

"Who is he?" the boy asked.

"A new friend I just met," Aaron said. He tousled the boy's hair, and smiled to his wife. "A good Christian man just come into town, who could use a place to stay for the night."

"That's all I need to hear. Come on in!" She kissed her husband on the cheek, and pointed to the couch. "Take a seat. Dinner's in half an hour. Jenny, set an extra place." Jenny nodded and ran to the kitchen.

Aaron's son Christopher piped up, "What you in town for, mister?"

"A job for my Father and for a good friend too." Jesus smiled and gave the kid's shoulder a friendly punch. "I sure am grateful for the place to rest. You guys like Friday Night Football?"

The answer was an enthusiastic and multiple "Yes!" Aaron put the game on, and the males settled in to watch as the ladies prepared dinner just as God intended. A fine time was had enjoying the commercials, with their many tales of fine products that job creators still had to offer. Then right before they were called to dinner, the broadcast took a dark turn.

"Breaking News. The captured Christian terrorist has announced he will accept no legal representation, and says he expects to be released soon on the authority of, quote, "The only real judge, God." Authorities are considering this a reference to his terror cell and cult leader, who is still at large and is considered armed and extremely dangerous. There is a reward of 200,000 Ameros for any information leading to his capture. You can call the police immediately and anonymously at-"

Aaron turned the TV off. "Time for dinner anyway. Come on, kids."

"Didn't like that news?" said Jesus.

"Not right for them to call a terrorist a Christian," said Aaron. "No good Christian would do the things he's accused of."

Jesus weighed his words. "Maybe he is a Christian. He's just not a terrorist."

"What do you mean?"

"It's a good Christian's job to fight for what's right, no matter what. That's the difference between the terrorists and us, don't you think?"

"I surely do," said Aaron.

"Well there you have it. If he was a true Christian, he must have been something that needed to be done. A true Christian can't do wrong."

Aaron considered that. "I like that. But something doesn't seem quite right about the logic."

"Don't worry about the logic. Just concentrate on the feeling. That will lead us to the truth."

They sat down at the table. "Who wants to say grace?" asked Aaron.

"I want Jesus to say grace," said Christopher.

Hannah looked at him skeptically. "Now Christopher, that's close to cracking wise."

"Happy to have that honor," said Jesus.

"Well then, be our guest," Aaron said.

Jesus folded his hands and bowed. "Lord, Father, bless this food, and this loving family. May they escape the coming tide of blood that will wash over this nation in, cleansing it of all the filth who stand in the way of your forgiving love. May this family wade through the guts of heathens and ascend to the heavens in your embrace. In your name, Amen."

"COOL!" Christopher and Jenny both exclaimed.

"A bit strong, don't you think?" Hannah said to Aaron softly.

"The kids love it," Aaron pointed out. "I've never heard them take to a prayer like that."

"You're right, I guess, " Hannah admitted.

LATER THAT NIGHT as she put their children to bed, Aaron brought Jesus a pillow and a sleeping bag.

"You sure do have a fine family here," Jesus said as he settled in. "Heartwarming just to be around you all."

"Why, thank you!" said Aaron. "We do the best we can. I'm blessed enough to have a job where we can afford to school them at home." He took a seat in the oversized chair next to the couch. "My and Hannah's parents all went in the Rapture, years ago. We wondered why we'd been left behind. The only way we could think that we'd failed, was that we'd considered putting our kids in public schools. Even looked at a few. Since then it's been home schooling all the way. It's so worth it." He sighed. "Not always easy, of course. We tried to work together with some other home schooling parents. You know, some of 'em aren't even Christian?" They shook their heads in shared commiseration.

"I wonder what they'd think about that man the government's going to put on trial tomorrow." Jesus ventured, testing the waters. "The so-called Christian terrorist."

"I don't know what to think myself," Aaron admitted. "Hannah and I sure don't like the direction this country's gone for the past few years. All this stuff about healthcare and the environment and helping people who aren't Christian, and not near enough from our government about God. We thought we had a ray of light there with Thruppence for about a minute. But they must have gotten to him or something because he didn't get much of anything fixed, and now we're worse off than when we began." Aaron blew out a breath and put hand to his forehead. "I love this country, and I love God. I also love my wife and children. I just don't know if taking up arms against the government is the Christian thing to do."

"What might it take for you to change your mind?" Jesus felt sure he already knew the answer.

Aaron thought about it. "Someone worth fighting for."

"You're a good man. I'm sure that someone will appear - and closer and sooner than you think."

"I hope so." Aaron stood. "Sleep well."

"Sleep well."

17

The next morning, Aaron was kind enough to drop Jesus off downtown on his way to work. Jesus bid him farewell, and then set to the job his Father had put before him. He found the corner of a closed doorway and checked both his guns. Judging from the height of the sun in the sky, he had some time to kill before it might be time to kill.

Jesus wandered around the area a bit, eventually finding himself beneath the famous Golden Arches and drinking in their golden beauty. That inspired him to look inside the McDonald's at their base, to remember what he was fighting for: Gold, Guns, Gas, and God – which together had formed Good ol' American business values. If they kept those in their hearts, America could be saved. If they let those values slip away, then the country God made to save the world would slip into sin and be damned for all eternity.

There was a touch of sadness to the Arches. They represented both a height and a fall. He almost bought an Egg McMuffin in recognition of McDonald's past devotion to God's Freedom Market. But Bomraka and his vipers had not only spread the Amero to McDonald's - the great restaurant had also been forced to offer tofu burgers and some substance called seitan as a breakfast sausage substitute.

Seitan – which was literally pronounced just like Satan. How obvious could the liberals be?

It was time to scout the jail they held Tex in. As he walked, he stuffed his glorious mane of hair beneath his "Angels" baseball cap. It galled him to hide his purpose, but this was still a silent war. At the plaza, some no doubt union crews were setting up stands and lights for the press conference. Jesus walked around the block, measuring the footsteps around the expected entrance points. He had just about lined up a plan of attack he thought might work, when shadows near the rooftops caught his eye. They didn't quite fit the details of the roof. From the corner of his eye he kept a watch on one shadow until it shifted.

Snipers. He left quickly.

There was no way this was just the EPA's handiwork. It was just crazy to think they had snipers. They must now have been joined by the FDA.

In any case, they were clearly dug in. The inescapable conclusion was that there was no way Jesus could pull Tex from that building and escape without a miracle. And without a miracle, it would be suicide –a sin he was not allowed to commit.

After the arraignment was concluded, the St. Louis police brought the cuffed Kevin "Tex" Adamapoulos into the parking lot beneath the courthouse. There he was handed off to the waiting Federal guards, who were all dressed in head-to-toe black tactical gear and gas masks, with "FDA" labels over their vest pockets. The local police were a little bewildered that this fell under the authority of the Food and Drug Administration but signed the forms in silence and walked away.

As soon as the police were gone, the FDA guards relaxed. "Some press conference," one guard snorted. "Christian punk didn't even have the guts to say he was guilty."

"I ain't got nothin' to say to any o' your sort," said Tex.

"Just said something though, didn't you?"

Tex turned red. "Curse you and your liberal tricks! Jesus will save me!"

"Your boy never did show up, did he?" the same guard taunted.

"You'll see him! If not today, then the day you go to see your Maker."

"Evolution made me."

Tex looked at him a little closely. "In your case, maybe you did come from a monkey."

"Oooooh," said another FDA attack specialist. They laughed.

"I told you that so-called Jesus clown would pussy out," said one guard to another. "Looks like you owe me five Ameros."

The EPA brought around their custom Kevlar-armored stretch Prius, and loaded Tex into the back. He was followed by an FDA man on either side. Two more got in the front of the Prius, as the other two EPA men boarded waiting Segways with mounted gun tripods

The Segway-riding gunmen emerged from the parking garage and led the way, followed by the strangely ominous Prius

The driver adjusted his visor to block the sunlight, as the sun was just beginning to fall behind the city skyline. "Sure is kinda nice here," he said. "Everywhere smells like French fries though."

"Sure does," the passenger agreed. He saw a patch of cable lying on the road ahead. "Hey, what's that?" His eyes widened. "Hit the brakes!"

The cable jumped to engine height and locked in place. The Segways flew over it and launched their mounted EPA soldiers with great force, the vehicle's gyroscopes unable to handle American steel. The Prius reached the cable a split second later. A lightweight car even with its plastic Kevlar armor, Prius flipped end over end. It lay on its roof, its impact-absorbing front end crushed and the entire car immobilized.

The driver opened the door and fell out, still dazed from the crash. Jesus ran over from the pole the cable was tied to, and rewarded the EPA man's resilience with a right cross to the face. The thug went down hard. Jesus ran around to the passenger side to find EPA thug still belted in, upside down and struggling with his seat belt. Jesus cursed Ralph Nadir for forcing the seatbelt on America. The man should have hit his head and at least fallen unconscious. If Jesus took a shot then a stray bullet could hit Tex. This last remaining result of liberal pussification, the seat belt, might have been part of the Devil's plan for just this moment.

"Freeze!" Jesus said as he advanced, his stepfather's .45 drawn and ready. "Don't make me send you to Hell without a chance!"

The man stopped his struggle for a moment. "What kind of - no! Are you that terrorist we're supposed to capture?"

"The Christian," Jesus corrected. His eyes hardened. "What's your choice?"

The man said nothing.

"Last chance," said Jesus. "Do you stand with us, or do you stand against my Father?"

The man answered by going for his gun – and Tex reached forward, also upside down and strapped in, to choke the EPA thug with his own his government-mandated seatbelt. If that wasn't justice, Jesus didn't know what was.

Jesus went to the back passenger window of the flipped Prius and smashed it open with the butt of his father's .45. Tex slid out the window.

"Good Lord, it's good to see you," said Tex.

"Likewise! How are the other Demoncrats in there?"

"Taken care of." Tex took a step and winced. "Did hurt my leg a bit though."

"You uncuffed yourself too, that's fine work."

"I follow a great savior."

Jesus saw civilians emerging from cover. Some deluded dupes would no doubt be calling 911. "Then follow me out of here! It's about to get pretty hot." Jesus helped Tex along as best he could, his follower grimacing as they achieved a limping run. They turned the corner just as sirens began to sound. Five blocks later they found a suitable alleyway away from prying eyes.

Jesus checked out the other end of the alley as Tex leaned against a wall to catch his breath. "How much time we have to disappear?" Tex gasped.

"Gotta be ASAP. If we can break into a basement we might be able to pop out on the next corner..." He spotted a basement entrance. "There!"

Tex groaned and fell to the ground, holding his sides. Jesus ran back. "Your leg that bad?"

"Ugh! My stomach," said Tex. "Must've been something I ate..."

"Well we don't have time for indigestion! Help me with this door-"

Tex groaned louder. "It's...vibrating..."

Jesus squatted next to him, as a distressing idea took form. "Tex, what did they feed you?"

"They said it was real meat...but it didn't taste like it...I hope it wasn't...." He was starting to sweat. "...Tofu."

Jesus' face went pale. "Tex! You know that stuff is poison. It's made to gradually weaken you to God's good meat. It probably even has fluoride."

"I'm sorry...I know I shouldn't have eaten it...but I was hungry, I was weak..."

Tex vomited a small amount onto the pavement. Jesus looked at his disciple with increasing worry. "That's a bit quick to sicken a man, even for tofu." He leaned forward to sniff it. His nose wrinkled.

"That's not just any tofu, blast it! They've slipped a Mark inside you!"

"A Mark?" said Tex, barely comprehending. Then it hit him. "You're saying I swallowed a Mark of the Beast?"

"They're using it to track you and find me! They can trigger it at any time. If only you'd stayed strong, and not been fooled by their false food!" Jesus frantically scanned the alley.

"I'm sorry Jesus! Oh God, how it hurts!"

"There - there has to be some way to block the signal-" His eyes landed on a dumpster halfway towards the alley's other end. "Quick, let's get you up and in there! Maybe the metal will disperse it, like a good tinfoil hat!"

"I feel - it's like it's shaking -"

Jesus got him to his feet, a task complicated by Tex's pained writhing. "Help me get you in the dumpster! Get-"

A final beeping sound was heard from within Tex's stomach. He locked eyes with Jesus in stark fear. Jesus hit the deck.

Tex exploded.

Jesus stood, his ears ringing. There was nothing left of Tex except his smoking cowboy boots.

"Farewell, my friend." He bowed his head. "You'll be creating jobs in Heaven now."

18

———

After several hours of walking at a fast clip, keeping his long hair back under his cap, ducking in and out of doorways and doubling back on his tracks to check for pursuit, he finally felt he could rest. He sat behind a diner that had just shut its doors and started its evening cleanup.

His whole mission had gone straight to perdition. Why would God bring him all the way to St. Louis, just to make him fail?

Behind him, he heard the kitchen crew turn to tonight's football game, as accompaniment to their clanking dishware. He wondered morosely if the sign he was receiving was God just wanted him to quit and become a dishwasher.

Then he heard a voice he hadn't heard in over fifteen years, that he thought was lost to this Earth forever. He stuck his head up to see into the restaurant's back window.

On the television Hieronymus' granddaughter. She not only looked just like his lost Alaine, she sounded like her too.

"This is Lily Godwin, with breaking news. Tragedy struck St. Louis earlier this evening. A caravan transporting the only known lead to a Christian terrorist cell was attacked. The suspected terrorist and his cohort or cohorts fled on foot, before the escaped prisoner inexplicably exploded in a nearby alley."

He barely registered her words. So there she was - Lily Jane Godwin. She only looked even more like his Alaine than Hieronymus' picture let on – she sounded like Alaine. She even moved like her. Probably laughed and kissed like her as well. He still couldn't confirm the colors of her eyes, the damnable camera never came close enough.

He watched until her segment was done, and the subject turned to entertainment. He spun away from the window and sat down hard.

After long thought, which he never enjoyed, the only way he could make sense of it all was that Tex's life had been sacrificed so Jesus would be put on this new path. A path that led towards Lily and towards the job that her grandfather had requested. It was sad that Tex had to die, but his reward would be great in heaven. For Jesus on Earth, the new path would bring the weapons God had inspired, placed right in his hands.

The trouble - the challenge, he corrected himself – was how to accomplish this new job set before him by his Holy Father. He would need to put a new team together right quick. Bomraka's thugs were after him like a feminist after a man's spirit.

His AOL cell of active agents was gone. His followers in New America appeared to still be safe - but if he pulled any of them out of hiding, he could compromise their haven too. He had to find new allies in the real world. Hearts in the heavens, boots on the ground.

Where could he find them? There was only one answer. That also, he took heart in realizing, was why his Father had sent him to St. Louis.

It all made sense now. He relaxed and said a prayer of thanks. There was no more need to think, his plans were set and Tex was in heaven.

He moved further from the restaurant's back window, and found a place to sleep. He rested better than he had for days, although still experiencing some disturbing dreams. In some he danced like a clown, in others he was a mighty warrior alone in a graveyard. Again, just before he awoke, an angel and a devil pointed behind him.

This time, right before he woke up, they both pointed to a city past the horizon - Atlanta.

The dream faded, and he opened his eyes. This dream hadn't had the full overwhelming power of a vision, but it probably did merit some attention. "One thing at a blessed time," he said, as he rose. The first glints of the morning sun shone into the alley, as he field stripped his guns.

AFTER SEVERAL MORE HOURS OF walking through the city in the early morning hours, ducking in the shadows to avoid cars and shielding his face from traffic cameras he was near his objective. The Twinkies he'd purchased before St. Louis were a little worse for wear, but still sealed in his inner jacket pocket. He stood behind a nearby tree and checked his guns. From the position of the sun, it looked to be about 9:00 AM.

Jesus tossed his baseball cap aside, and freed his glorious golden mane of hair. He drew his .45 with his right hand, and took off the safety. The gun from Hieronymus in his left hand had no safety.

At that exact moment, the church bells rang.

It was time to go to service.

He drew a deep breath, and ran forward, gathering speed as he neared the entrance. He used the handicapped ramp, putting it for once to a truly American use and not just coddling special interests. At the last second just before he hit, he spun around so that his back and mighty shoulders smashed straight through the front doors.

Just as he'd expected, he flew past two armed members of President Bomraka's forces were waiting inside.

19

Jesus stood with his back to the church's surprised congregation, with a different gun pointed at each of the two government minions. They stood frozen, both their weapons still holstered. He had the drop on them.

He'd guessed that they would try to ambush him by staking out the churches he might visit – the real Christian ones. He'd prayed that between this and covering all the public transit methods out of town, their forces would be spread thin.

"I'm Jesus!" He declared. "Don't make me judge you. This is your last chance. Repent the EPA's guidelines and all their ways, or doom your soul to Hell!"

The EPA thug to Jesus' right was slightly closer. He started to move but stopped when he felt Jesus' steely gaze.

The thug to Jesus' left went for his gun.

Jesus kicked him in the gut, and took aim at the EPA minion on his right with the glorious revolver Hieronymus gave him. The thug was bringing up his gun as well. Jesus pulled first.

A deafening thunder sounded as seven gouts of flame shot out from the sides of the barrel. The minion's head just disappeared.

Ears ringing from the blast, Jesus whirled back to the remaining

EPA thug and aimed his stepfather's .45. "Don't do it, man!" Jesus warned. "At least get saved first!"

The thug reached for his gun anyway. Jesus fired a single shot from the pistol he'd been given by his stepfather.

The EPA man's lifeless body slumped against the wall and slid down, the blood mingling with the pool coming from the other soldier's headless corpse. Jesus scanned the church interior and saw no other gun-wielding Demoncratic dupes - just a room full of parishioners, staring at him in open-mouthed shock.

He looked at the gun Hieronymus had given him, and then at the headless remains of the soldier he'd first shot. In the wall behind where that minion's head had been, a circular hole was now wreathed in ash and small blue flames. Beyond that, outside, he could see a hole in the side of a building fifty feet away.

By his Father, what a weapon. He had never seen the like. And the recoil had been less than the kick of a baby through a mother's stomach. He shook out the cylinder, to stare at the backs of the remaining six bullets in wonder. What kind of weapon was this?

He would definitely be conserving that ammo. That was for sure.

He turned towards the bodies of the EPA thugs. "Tell the Devil I'm coming for him." He holstered Hieronymus' gun, and held the .45 in his right hand level as he faced the assembled congregation.

"You just - you just killed them!" babbled an old man in the pew to his left.

"They were warned," said Jesus. In his peripheral vision to his right, Jesus saw a woman pick up a cell phone. "No outside contact!" he ordered. "This is between you all, me, and Heaven until I'm out of here." She put the phone back in her purse and closed it.

"How'd you know those soldiers were standing there?" asked Aaron. His wife Hannah stood next to them, and their two children with eyes big as Bibles.

"Those weren't soldiers – they were government thugs. I knew they would be waiting for me, like a taxman waiting for a job creator."

"Who are you?" asked another parishioner.

"It's the hitcher we picked up in the minivan the other day!" Minister Simone screeched from behind the pulpit. "He must be the Christian terrorist they were looking for!"

"That's Mr. Jesus the Christ to you," said Jesus. "Your Lord and Savior returned. This is my Father's House - so either stand with me or get evicted."

"Now, son," Minister Simone said, "I don't know what you're thinking but-"

"Yeah, I think you do know what I'm thinking." Jesus walked up the aisle towards him. "I'm thinking that you hide behind those robes every Sunday and pretend to follow my law - while you let them teach evolution in the school? What sin will you let them teach next, global warming?"

The minister's face flashed with fear as he struggled to find words. Jesus' eyes narrowed. "You teach them global warming is real in Sunday school here? You sick son of a bitch!"

"Yes, but...the science is pretty accepted and it doesn't mean God can't have made the Earth that way...look, why don't you just calm down a second and-"

Jesus fired his stepfather's pistol once. While it was no match for the gun Hieronymus had made, the results were still quite impressive. The shot burst through the podium into the preacher's leg. Simone fell down shrieking.

"You deserve much worse," he told Simone, "for all the people your teachings sent to Hell. But I'm gonna give you one more chance. Start praying silent - and don't say another word." The Preacher wisely held his tongue and kept his moaning low.

He holstered the .45 and faced the flock. "Now people, listen up. I'm back and I'm strong!" He threw his head back, proud and beautiful like an avenging Eagle of the Lord. "But I ain't here to do it all myself. Even if I could, that's not how my Father wants it. He wants Real Americans to prove their faith, by joining me to save mankind. So I need some new disciples."

"You've got my attention," said a choir leader. Jesus recognized him as Barclay.

"Glad to hear it!" He turned back to the rest of the crowd. "You should all know, we might not all make it back alive. But if we're able, and God willing, we're going to strike blows for truth, justice, and the God-given American Way until the Demoncrats fall down!"

"How do we know you're Jesus Christ?" another man asked from the crowd.

"Look into my eyes. You either have faith or you don't."

The church was silent for a long while. Doubt and uncertainty filled the air, thick as the darkness before the dawn.

Aaron spoke into the silence. "I'm the first person here to have met you. From the beginning I knew there was something different about you. Something that just felt right." He took a deep breath. "I want my kids to live in a country ruled by God." He swallowed nervously, but kept his resolve. "You look right, you sound right, and it feels right. I'm with you."

In most military situations, Aaron was nothing much to look at - pasty white, a little fat, a little bald. Jesus face shone with pride. The man was showing more guts so far than anyone else besides Jesus himself.

"Aaron, no!" said his wife Hannah. "You can't leave us! If you - if you didn't come back- I don't know what we'd do-"

Aaron took Hannah's face in his hands. "Dear heart, you'd raise a son and daughter who knew their father was a Christian man. We've been worn down by secular humanism and Hollywood, year after year. It's time to take a stand."

"But why does it have to be you?" Hannah asked, tears beginning trails down her cheeks.

"This must be why we were left behind when so many more were Raptured," Aaron said. "To do God's work."

He hugged and kissed his wife, and shook his young son's hand.

"Dad, do you really have to go?" Christopher asked softly.

"It does look that way, son," he said.

"Don't!" his darling daughter Jenny cried, as she wrapped her arms around him and tears filled her eyes.

"I guess I have to," said Aaron. "So you all can grow up in a right

America." His face twisted with the pain of holding back tears of his own. "Don't make me cry now. Hug me."

The family embraced. "We'll met again," said Aaron. "As sure as God saved Abraham."

Aaron walked over to Jesus. "I don't know-" Aaron started. "I mean, should I bow, or..."

"A good ol' American handshake will do," said Jesus. They clasped hands like men.

Jesus pulled a pamphlet from his pocket. He handed it to Hannah. "You and your kids go, right now. Don't stop by your home first, it will be watched by the time you'd get there. Follow these instructions. They include an AOL account and password. We'll be in touch with you as time and our mission permits. Go with God."

Hannah looked at him, and wiped her eyes. "We will, my Lord." She grabbed her children. "Come along now," she said. "Your father has a job to do. So do we."

Aaron's family left quickly. Jesus and Aaron looked around the church room.

"Any other real Christians in here?" Jesus dared.

Barclay stepped forward. "I wondered if you might be the righteous Son returned from the second I saw you by the roadside. Now I know it."

"You can't be serious!" said a singer, still standing back behind him.

"You better believe I'm serious. How about you? You gonna try and stop me?" The rest of the choir couldn't meet his eyes. Barclay stepped over the minister, and down from the stage. He took off his robes and tossed them to the side. "I ain't a choirboy no more."

Jesus shook his hand proudly. "Then do you both swear to join my crusade?"

"We do," said Aaron and Barclay, in perfect unison.

Jesus whooped for joy. "Then by the power invested in me by my Father, I christen you the first of my New Disciples! Like saplings that grow into a mighty forest, you, Aaron and you, Barclay will help us swarm the land and crush the evildoers of evil! Barclay, you will be our black oak, strong and mighty. And you, Aaron, will be like pine, that's kind of white and soft but ready to shaped and stained and hardened by fire."

"I'm not sure that's how it works," someone said from the congregation.

"Look, I'm not a carpenter this time around, alright?" Jesus responded, exasperated. He looked around at the rest of the chastened churchgoers. "Anyone else in here got the faith and guts to join us?"

The rest of the congregation shuffled their feet and looked aside.

"All right. Just remember when you meet your Maker, you had this chance. You won't have many more. Don't be lost when the time comes - because my day will come like a thief in the night."

They left the congregation and shut the inner doors behind them, leaving more than a few who were ashamed for not joining this man called Jesus.

20

———————

In the church's lobby, Jesus directed his new disciples to the remains of the downed Bomrakaites. "Get their guns. We'll need 'em. Then we better get a move on," said Jesus. Barclay and Aaron kneeled down and pulled the weapons and ammunition from the government thugs' bodies. "Alright. I got a lot to teach you. But first, we gotta get out lickety-split. The government will be here in minutes. Follow me." Jesus led them down streets and through alleyways at a quick pace, putting as much distance as possible between them and the life they'd left behind.

"How will the government know so fast?" Aaron panted.

"I'll bet one o' your former so-called Christian church members is callin' the EPA right now," said Jesus. "Global warming my foot."

Barclay nodded, less out of breath than Aaron. "Ever notice how someone in that church was always bringing up climate change when you're just talking about how strange the weather is?"

"I guess I didn't want to believe my own fellow Christians could be so wrong," said Aaron.

They came to a corner. Jesus motioned for them to drop back, and stuck his head around to check the street. The coast was clear. He beckoned Aaron to come closer and leaned in, thoroughly examined his new disciple's temple and scalp. Barclay was examined next, and raised an eyebrow but said nothing.

Jesus leaned back, somewhat satisfied. "Either of you ever had one of those official government vaccinations?"

"My parents didn't believe in vaccinations, and most of my family survived," said Aaron.

"I only got vaccinations from the military," said Barclay.

"That's different then," said Jesus. "We can trust the military, they really aren't part of the government." He nodded. "Good. It looks like neither of you have the Mark of the Beast implant." He checked the street again. Still clear. He led them out of the alley and resumed the previous double-time pace. They followed him up the street.

"What do you mean, a mark? Like a scar?" asked Aaron, unaccustomed to the exertion and beginning to huff a bit.

"You're a mark," joked Barclay.

"Not that kind of a mark - the Mark of the Beast. Sometimes when they're giving you those supposed vaccinations, if they think you might be a danger they put a chip in you." Jesus pointed to his left temple. "It floats in the bloodstream until it ends up here. The Mark of the Beast. A cyber tracking chip that can also explode your head."

"I thought that was just a rumor," Aaron said.

Jesus chuckled. "You got a good heart, Aaron, but you trust a bit too much." He turned to Barclay. "Army?" Jesus asked.

"Me? Navy. Seals." Barclay scowled. "Don't you know everything?"

"That's my Father's job. I'm just here to show a good man can make things right."

"Maybe we should stop by my house, get some supplies," Aaron suggested. "I got some food stocked up, and some guns."

"Nothing doing," said Jesus. "Your former homes are the first places they'll look for us." He saw Aaron's face sink. "Sorry, brother. You can't go back. This is the journey. You've got a lot you'll have to get used to pretty quick."

They approached a parking lot, and stopped at the bottom of a chain-link fence. Jesus lifted up the bottom, and motioned for them to step through. Once they were in, he vaulted over it.

"So, if we get hurt you can heal us right?' Aaron asked.

"Nope, sorry cowboy," said Jesus. "This time around I ain't got no healin' powers. I'm here to fight and win just like an ordinary man." He grinned as his eyes surveyed the parking lot.

"I see," said Aaron, his face falling a bit.

"You got faith?"

"Of course," said Aaron, sounding almost offended.

"Then that's all we need. That, and to get the Heaven out of here." Jesus found his target. "This should do just the trick."

He approached a king-cab pickup truck, checked quickly for witnesses, and then broke the driver's-side window with his jacketed elbow. As the car alarm rang out, he reached through the broken window, jerked open the door, pulled a buck-knife from his boot and dove beneath the dashboard. A few yanked-out wires and some quick splicing, and the car alarm was silenced. A few seconds more, and Jesus had brought the engine to life.

"Isn't this stealing?" Aaron asked.

Jesus pointed at the Teacher's Union sticker in the back window. "Not if it's from the enemy. Then it's just smart. Like not paying taxes."

They hopped in the truck, and Jesus took the wheel. Aaron was still closing the passenger door as they sped off. They had just exited the lot when police cars erupted onto their street and rushed toward them.

"Fellas, hold your shoulder seatbelts across your chest," said Jesus. "Don't buckle 'em in of course. But for now we have to play along." Barclay and Aaron grabbed the unmanly safety belts and held them across their chests, in feigned submission to the tyranny of government safety regulations. Jesus flexed his knuckles on the steering wheel, but otherwise kept driving straight and calm.

The police cars went straight past them. Barclay and Aaron exhaled in relief, and released their safety belts to resume riding like free men.

"What's next on the plan, Son of Man?" said Barclay.

"I've got a job to do, which I'll let you two in on. But for now, let's find a place that we can be left alone a bit."

JESUS and his new disciples rode in a contemplative kind of silence all the way out of St. Louis. Jesus turned off main roads as quickly as possible. Soon he found a farm with cows grazing peacefully in a meadow, and took a dirt road that ran parallel to its fencing. Minutes later, with thanks to Providence, there was a grove of trees to hide the truck.

They exited the truck. "Welcome my brothers!" said Jesus. "The first thing you gotta learn is the sign of the Crucifist."

Barclay frowned. "Ain't that a papist thing?"

"No, no," said Jesus. "This is a new thing. A right thing." Jesus showed them the sign that ended with the first over his heart. After some difficulty in coordination on Aaron's part, they mastered it. "Wonderful," said Jesus. By his Father, it was good to have some comrades in Christianity.

"Now let's break some bread." He walked them over to a nearby tree and sat in its shade. He reached into his jacket and pulled out his Marlboros, his whiskey flask, and finally a rather mashed Twinkie still in its wrapper.

"This is flesh of my flesh, and blood of my blood, and soul of my soul. The red," Jesus held up the Marlboros, "the white," he held up the Twinkie, "and the blue." The steel blue flask completed the picture.

He gave each of them a cigarette and passed the flask of American whiskey. Aaron declined both at first, to receive a warning frown. Barclay took a shot, and then Jesus lit his cigarette for a deeply satisfying puff. Aaron changed his mind and accepted the cigarette, had it lit, and proceeded to cough harshly.

Jesus clapped him on the shoulder. "Don't worry, we'll toughen you up."

"I look forward to it," said Aaron between hacks. Barclay handed him the flask next, and Aaron proceeded to cough some more.

"It's been a long, hard day, but a good one," Jesus continued, over Aaron's hacking. "Spreading the word, and slaying the evil. Everything else is just details." He took a puff from a cigarette himself, and began opening the Twinkie. After a brief struggle the divine treat was freed from its surprisingly durable cellophane shell. He passed around the mashed but still whole Twinkie to complete the communion. As Aaron gratefully took a bite of something that didn't hurt, Jesus leaned back onto his hands. "So now I'll tell you a bit more about the job. You can tell me if you got what it takes to do it."

"Don't you already know?" said Barclay, a bit hurt.

Jesus grinned widely. "I do now."

Aaron passed his portion of the Twinkie to Barclay. "Before we get all the way into that...can I get some assurances?" Aaron paused, as both Barclay and Jesus looked at him in surprise. He took a deep breath and continued. "I know I should have faith, and I do. But I also have a wife and children. They're on the run now, leaving behind our friends, our home, everything we know - and at a terrible risk. I need your personal word, as not just the Son of God but as a man, that my wife and children will be safe. If something happened to them, I - I just don't know what I'd do."

Jesus stared at him for a second. "Well, you are manning up right away. Demanding my Word!" He laughed heartily. "You got a brave good heart in there. Aaron, I swear that your family will be as safe as anyone can be. The Lord will provide to his good servants."

"That is such a relief to hear, my Lord," said Aaron, his shoulders relaxing as he unburdened himself from some of his fears.

Jesus patted him on the shoulder. "Yep, they'll be completely taken care of. If not here, then in Heaven."

"Sure - wait, what?" Aaron felt less settled. "That was kind of the point, Jesus. I kind of want to know that they'll be-"

Jesus put his hand over Aaron's mouth. "Shush!" Jesus whispered. Jesus pointed at his ear and then the sky. A moment later, Aaron heard a sound: the faint buzz of helicopter blades in the distance.

The noise became slightly louder, and then stayed the same

volume as they hovered. Finally the helicopters faded off into the distance - seeming to go back the direction they came.

"We better get set to run, guys." Jesus put away the whiskey and cigarettes, and had a final mouthful of the Twinkie. "They'll identify the truck, and then they'll scan the woods this time."

"What are the odds we can run out of range before they get here?" asked Aaron.

"Zero," answered Jesus.

"Second pass, they prob'ly gonna run those infra-red cameras," said Barclay.

Jesus nodded grimly. "That's why we got only one option." He pointed at the nearby field. As if understanding his words, a cow responded with a moo.

21

———

Back in her office, Blabbera Wilters found herself shouting at the commander's face on the screen. "What do you mean there's no sign of them? They found the truck! Infrared revealed that the engine was still warm!"

"They scanned all the nearby fields."

She slammed her bionically enhanced fist into her desk. "Then they must have gone back to the highway on foot! They might hitch a ride!" Blabbera said, on the edge of panic. "Scan all vehicles in an expanding search radius."

Another connection appeared on the screen. Her heart plummeted – it was Rosio. She quickly switched connections and opened her mouth to speak.

"Don'tcha waste my time with excuses," Dawnhell said through gritted teeth, before she could say a word. "I already know ya failed. You don't think you're my only source of info, do ya?" Her scowl deepened. "You need to get on the ball and get this done."

"We - we have this Christ man's picture now, from a cellphone in the church he attacked," Blabbera stammered.

"Then start broadcasting it. I don't have the time to fly out there and handle this in person. Take care of this before I make time."

"Yes sir! And I just want to say, I apologize for-" The connection cut off before Blabbera had a chance to finish. She sat down hard.

Her predecessor Madcow, that little viper, had been in this same situation. Now it was Blabbera's turn to sweat, and she did not like it. Not one bit. She shivered. Was she beginning to see something in Rosio's eyes? Something that looked very much like hate?

She had to make sure the releasing of this man's description to the media went exactly right. There was a promising young anchor-woman in Atlanta who would do a fine job as the face of the manhunt. She would fly there with her best agents right away. She decided to bring her favorite Emmy too. One never knew when it might come in handy.

22

———————

Jesus and the disciples lay in the fields on their backs, directly underneath compliant cows. Soon, the last slashing sounds of helicopter blades faded into the distance

"This better have worked," whispered Barclay. "'cause this sucks."

"I'm not exactly a fan of this position either," complained Aaron. He started to poke his head up, and got an udder in his eye.

"Stay still!" hissed Jesus. "Stop talking!"

They kept still for a few more minutes. Then Jesus gave the okay, and they emerged from under the cattle.

"Praise the Lord, we're saved!" said Aaron.

"You're welcome, think nothing of it." Jesus stretched, smelled his shirt and grimaced. "We got a lot to be grateful for, but cleanliness ain't on that list."

"So much for using that truck," said Barclay.

"Yep. They'll be expanding their search radius from here at least, so we should be good for a while."

"Great!" said Aaron. "Can we, uh...think we can get back to my family's safety?"

"Thought we already finished that," said Jesus.

"Well," said Aaron hesitantly. "I guess maybe I wanted a bit more clarity on their safety before the afterlife?"

"You got faith?" asked Jesus pointedly.

"Of course I do! Wouldn't be here if I didn't."

"Then use it. Now focus. This is a mission from God here." He stood up. "I'm here to do a lot of things. The foremost point of all of them is to save America and therefore save mankind."

"Of course," said Aaron.

"That's why we joined you," said Barclay.

"Right. So that's a big job, and there's a lot of smaller parts to it. God won't just come out and tell me what they are, you know? I have to earn everything I get, and prove my faith like every other man. Find the signs. Interpret them according to the only truly holy documents, the Constitution and the Bible."

"Amen," said Aaron.

"Hallelujah," Barclay agreed.

Rare for Jesus, his face became unsettled and he began to pace. "A few days ago, things went absolutely wrong. The Demoncrats hacked my AOL, blew up my motel room and a stripper I was trying to save, and caught my number one disciple. I was Judased by a man God told to help me. In fact, he's the very same genius who made this." Jesus pulled out his divine .45 and handed the gun to Aaron.

Aaron looked it over and was impressed. He didn't know much about guns besides that every good Christian should have at least one, but even he could see this gun was amazing. It fairly glowed with beauty, elegance and power. "If I hadn't seen that soldier's body, I wouldn't believe something this beautiful could have that much power." He passed it to Barclay.

Barclay whistled as he turned the gun over in his hands. "This is amazin'."

"Yep. I've only got 6 of those bullets left. Also, Aaron, you have to remember: that wasn't a soldier. That was a government thug."

"How do we know if they're soldiers or thugs?"

"Why, how Christian they are o'course." Barclay gave the gun one more admiring look before handing it back. Jesus held the pistol up so it gleamed in the sun's light. "This is only the first of many weapons this man has made for me. He is the key God has been waiting for me to find so we can take America back. But the blasted coot just refuses to help me unless I do one thing for him: bring back his granddaughter Lily Godwin."

"Why, that's that new anchorgirl on ABC!" said Aaron. "I saw her give some news about that so-called Christian terrorist. The one you tried to save."

"Why does he want to bring her back?" Barclay asked.

"To save her from liberal doom. The message I've been getting from my holy Father through dreams and bits of television is that all my other plans on hold 'til this is done."

"Well, all right then," Barclay said. "But I gotta say, so far she sounds like a side job. You could just put her to the wayside, and get to her in due time. Unless maybe there's more to it?"

"You are wise. That's just the half of it." Jesus breathed out. "The rest of the problem is, she looks exactly like a girl I knew who died over 10 years ago. Her voice too. A girl who...well, there ain't no other way to say it. A girl I failed." He stroked his lightly bearded chin. "So this could be a chance to make that right, somehow. It's almost as if - I'm supposed to make some kind of choice." He smiled. "So what I find works in these kinds of situations, is just to go ahead with what feels right! With faith in our hearts, the answers will be revealed!" He clapped his hands together. "We're gonna go save her. You guys with me?"

"Of course!" said Aaron. "Saving the helpless? Fighting the Godly fight to save America? We know that's what we must do. What's the plan?"

"Not so much on planning, boys. I'm more of a doer."

"I am so glad to hear it," said Barclay. "Some of us are real Christians and have been waiting for this moment. You can lead our people back from Demoncratric temptation, and deliver us from secular evil."

"Yeah!" said Aaron with great enthusiasm. "Especially since Bomraka's election proves there isn't even racism anymore!"

Barclay looked a bit uncomfortable. "Well, I wouldn't go that-"

"Alright!" said Jesus. "We're all on the same page. Let's hit the road!" He clapped his hands together. "We got all we need to make this happen."

"The two machine guns we grabbed off of those soldiers back there, two hundred rounds of ammo, and our swinging'..." Barclay paused.

"You can say it," laughed Jesus. "I'm not one to fret strong language."

"Our necks," said Barclay.

"We also have the greatest weapon of all – our faith!" Jesus raised a mighty fist upwards to the heavens. "As long as we're on the right path, and unless he feels like getting mysterious, my Father will provide. New Disciples, it's time to hit the road!"

23

____

Bomraka stuck his head around the door of Rosio Dawnhell's office. "Rosio, can we talk for a second?"

She preferred that they didn't right now, but she really couldn't say no. "Sure, Mr. President. What's up?"

"What's all this FDA and EPA activity? It looks like they're being used to go after that Christian terrorist. Since when do they work together on anything, let alone counter terrorism? It doesn't even make sense."

She decided to test him. "Because of how the economy is going to be affected by the jobs stimulus, the FDA and EPA will have to work together. When the stimulus economy doesn't create jobs, the people will turn to the FDA to keep their food safe. And since regulation is always bad for the market, the food will get worse. Then people will start burning more oil to drive to different supermarkets, so we'll have to keep people from driving more by limiting the amount of gas they use."

During this entire statement his face had grown continually more quizzical. Rosio's heart fell.

He held his chin as he was silent for a long moment further. "Rosio, not a single one of those things are true."

"That's not your plan?"

"It's not even close." Rare for him, he briefly struggled for words. "Where did you get the idea that I want any of those things?"

"I just – I thought that was the clear implications of your policy."

He frowned. "But that makes even less sense. When has a jobs program ever hurt jobs? Why would less regulation result in better food? And who ever said we want Americans to drive less?" He shook his head. "These are all things to improve our country. Just look at the statistics."

She gave a shocked laugh. "But those are just numbers sir. Even Christians know they don't tell the real story."

"Even Christians?" His face became even more confused. "I'm a Christian."

She couldn't even process that. He must be sleeper agent, she told herself. His programming just had to be that deep.

"Rosio, how long have you known me and worked with me?"

She knew the answer to that. As far as he knew, "Ten years."

"You're supposed to help me be effective, and be my informal liaison to get around the red tape. Not make it more confusing. Talk to the FDA and EPA, and tell them to keep to their own tasks and leave the manhunt up to the professionals. We don't need them confusing the general public. Okay?"

She swallowed her growing disappointment. "Yes sir."

"You're not even supposed to be making calls like this. Let alone without consulting me." He paused. "Are you...up to this?"

Fire flashed in her eyes at the thought of a man even questioning her capability. "Yes sir," she managed. "I won't let it happen again."

She watched his back recede up the stairs to the Oval Office. Her heart sank. He had to be a secret Muslim. At least let him be that.

24

———————

Jesus and the New Disciples set on down the highway. After a few minutes of walking, Aaron began cautiously, "So, about the whole thing with my family again-"

"A Wal-Mart!" said Jesus. "See the sign? It has to be a sign!" He pointed down the road and nearly jumped for joy. "Holiest of stores, it must be part of our path to the salvation of America." He rubbed his hands together. "That's it fellas. That's the next step of our mission."

Aaron and Barclay looked at each other, the Wal-Mart sign, and then back at Jesus.

"Guys, have some faith," said Jesus, annoyed. "That's got to be it. Now we just have to figure out how to get in it."

"We can't just walk in?" said Aaron.

"No! Come on, man. The enemy has to know Wal-Mart is a remaining bastion of godliness. They will be examining any real Christians very closely. Probably posing as food inspectors or OSHA or some such. This will take some figuring out."

As cars and trucks sailed by them on the seemingly endless flatness of the Midwestern landscape, they discussed the problem from every angle they could conceive. After a long day of walking that had brought them within a few miles of the Wal-Mart, they still could not settle on a plan. Jesus led them off the road and found a spot to sleep in some tall grass. They folded their jackets for pillows, and shared the rest of Jesus' stock of beef jerky before settling in for needed rest.

As Aaron was starting to drift off, something about the beef jerky wrapper caught his eye. An idea came to him. He sat up as if something had bitten him. "I've got it!"

"What, did you find something in the grass?" asked Jesus.

"Inspiration! This must have come from God above!"

Barclay and Jesus leaned up on their elbows. "Well?" asked Jesus.

"We'll be fine just as long as," Aaron paused dramatically, "we dress like Mexicans."

"You drunk?" growled Barclay.

Aaron shook his head. "I never drink to excess."

"You must be."

"I think I see where Aaron is going with this," said Jesus. "Since Bomraka and his Demoncrats kept reading the Constitution like we couldn't just throw out illegals, and kept telling lies that the Free Market was responsible for bringing 'em in, they're everywhere. We have to make their trick work for us." He grinned. "That's what works so best about this idea! We can just pretend to be them! Liberals can't look at us. The question is, how do we pull off the disguise?"

"That's what really made it come together for me," said Aaron. "The next convenience store should have everything we need!"

They immediately got back on the road, and found a convenience store within a mile. Just like the one right outside St. Louis, a pimply teenaged boy sat behind the register. This was definitely a worse case. This kid's pimpled face was curled in what might be a permanent surly sneer. As the lost child of liberalism gazed at them with a dull-eyed stare that would better befit a goat, Jesus saw his Penn & Teller t-shirt and the copy of Mad magazine he was reading. Sorrow struck him to the depths of his heart - so many lost sheep to save. His eyes left the teen and took in the store. "I don't see anything that can help us," he said to Aaron.

"There's what I'm talking about, right there." Aaron pointed at some cheap straw sun hats. "We can make them into sombreros."

Jesus looked at him, but for once said nothing.

"So we can look like mental patients?" asked Barclay.

"If we only wore the hats, maybe," said Aaron. "But we also have this." He pulled some shoelaces and some brown shoe polish off the rack. "And – yes, here!" He laid his hand on several patterned woolen blankets. "We can cut holes in them and make them ponchos!"

"What would you use the shoelaces and polish for?" asked Jesus. Aaron showed him.

Barclay turned to Jesus. " Do you really think this will work?"

Jesus said nothing for a while longer. Then he sighed. "Through faith all things are possible. We need ammo, man food, and probably light camping gear as well. Wal-Mart's the only place that will have everything we need."

"Wal-Mart really does have everything," Barclay agreed.

"Yes. When the family of blessed job-creators who ran it were summoned up to Heaven in the Rapture, it fell into enemy hands. They watered down its holy free-market righteousness with the devil-scourge of unions. But even the Demoncrats had to leave some of it intact. It just has such great stuff and low, low prices."

"How we gonna pay once we get in? I don't think we have enough to trade."

"It's war now," said Jesus. "We can't wait to see if we're dealing with Christians. We gotta take what we need to win. Starting in this store here." They snuck out without paying, and began the long walk to the Wal-Mart.

They had gotten twenty feet along to find the kid running after them. "Hey! Hey you guys have to pay for that stuff."

Jesus looked the kid over. "You've got more guts than I expected. We're not gonna pay, but there's good news in that for you."

"Huh? What's that, mister?"

"If you become a real Christian, you don't have to pay for anything either."

The kid's face lost its sneer. "Huh?"

"Is your boss a Christian?" Jesus asked.

"I don't think so. You know, he's got a funny last name."

"Then there you go! Christians are saved and forgiven no matter what – and anyone who isn't a Christian, they're going to Hell anyway. You can do anything to them that you have to. For America."

"Really?" the kid said. He laughed with sudden delight. "That's awesome!"

"Isn't it?" said Jesus. He saw with some surprise that Aaron and Barclay seemed to be having a bit of trouble with this concept. "Look, fellas. It's not that hard. We're right, they're wrong. We're saving America, so if they're not with us they're against us. Every bad thing we do to them is a good thing we do for God."

"I guess you're right," said Aaron.

"It just feels kinda wrong though," said Barclay.

"You guys have faith, right?"

"Of course we do!" they both said.

"Then just let that faith tell your feelings how to feel."

Aaron scratched his head. "But wait. I thought you said we were supposed to go with how we feel?"

"Except if it contradicts faith of course," Jesus explained with godly patience.

They all took this new wisdom in, and eventually they nodded. Jesus smiled. He had gotten through. "Now kid, go back and take what you want, and make up any story you want. As long as your boss is not a Christian, God will forgive you."

"Yes sir! Oh boy, this is great! What's your name?"

"Jesus, son."

"You're the best!" The kid ran back inside the convenience store and began poking around in the cash drawer.

"Yes I am," said Jesus with satisfaction. "You see, guys? You never know who can be saved." It felt so good to be in public now, making a real difference for America. "Let's get some rest, and in the morning start walking the walk."

25

They journeyed along the side of the highway for several hours. Cars whooshed by, heard and largely unseen. At long last, the welcome sign for Wal-Mart appeared around the bend.

"Whew," said Aaron.

Barclay nodded. "After that walk, I think I might need to get some new shoes in there too."

"It's been too long," said Jesus as a tear ran down his cheek. "All those aisles of quality goods at prices easy to afford...It may be the closest thing on Earth to the promise of Heaven."

They cut holes in the blankets, and draped them over their shoulders. Then they took the shoelaces and shoe polish, and fashioned slick curling mustachios. Once these were attached with duck tape to their upper lips, the sombreros were added to the mix. Their transformation was complete.

They walked in. "Welcome to Wal-Mart," the greeter said, looking at them a bit oddly.

"Hola," said Jesus.

"Si, gracias," said Barclay.

"Empanada," said Aaron.

The greeter looked away, and let them pass unchallenged.

"Let's move," whispered Jesus.

"I'll get the camping gear," said Barclay.

"I'll get the man food," said Aaron.

Jesus nodded. "Also swing by Housewares and get a couple of flags. Big ones, at least six foot. And a couple of police scanners. I'll get the guns and ammo."

"Once we have it all, then what?" asked Aaron.

"We'll meet up in the grocery section," " said Jesus in a low voice. "If all's still clear, we'll head on to the registers Any trouble, follow my lead."

They claimed shopping carts and started in. Aaron grabbed fistfuls of camping gear, and went to Housewares. On his way he passed the electronics section, and detoured to pick up a police scanner. He passed a row of televisions tuned to the same channel, and stopped. The televisions were tuned to One World Channel (known to most of the non-Christian dupes as MSNBC).

Who should Aaron see on television but the very woman Jesus wanted to rescue from enslavement by the liberal media. She was very beautiful, with a face that was hard to forget. Over a series of pictures showing her interviewing famous people, reporting from the street and relaxing in some sort of fine apartment a voice announced "Coming up next week on The View – rising media star Lily Godwin on balancing career and sexiness!" Aaron stepped in closer to see more. The commercial ended, and a news report resumed.

An anchorman named Bret Stormbreaker began discussing a shooting that had happened in a church the day before. Aaron realized they were talking about his own church. He was seeing his own life's events through the lens of the liberal media.

"Aaron Morehouse was an ordinary plumbing salesman with a good job and a happy family. Barclay Andrews was a decorated veteran. They were part of a Christian community known for charitable works. That all ended yesterday with a tragic shooting that left two soldiers dead, a preacher injured, and a community in turmoil. If you see any of these men," the camera cut to a picture of Aaron from a church picnic in happier times, then to Barclay from the same event, and then to a blurry cell phone image of Jesus that had been taken in their former church, "turn them in immediately for a 300,000 Amero reward!" Stormbreaker unleashed a dazzling smile at the viewing audience. "You will also receive a personal dinner and televised interview with celebrity Blabbera Wilters!"

Aaron pulled his sombrero a bit further down over his face. He hurriedly found a shelf with police scanners and put them in his cart. One of them dropped to the floor with a clatter. A child in a shopping cart heard the noise, saw Aaron and then looked at the televisions which had just been showing his picture.

"Mommy," the little girl said. "Look, look at-"

"Hush, honey," the mother said, embarrassed. "We're not supposed to notice illegals."

"But mommy, that's-"

"Hush!"

Jesus and Barclay rolled their carts up next to Aaron. Barclay's cart was piled high with manfood, and Jesus' cart filled to the brim with ammo, shotguns, and Kevlar vests marked "special clearance".

"Taco!" Aaron said at a volume he hoped any civilians in earshot could hear.

"Quesadilla!" Barclay responded.

"Ready to go?" Jesus said under his breath.

"Got my stuff," said Barclay.

"Got mine too," said Aaron. "We should get out of here right away. Our pictures are all over the news," said Aaron. "I'm a little worried-"

Jesus' expression hardened. "This is the path. If we must bathe in blood to save America, that's what we must do." He pushed his shopping cart down the aisle towards the registers. Barclay and Aaron followed.

Barclay noticed Aaron's worried expression. "How you doing with all this?"

"It's so strange to see the world with new eyes. If you hadn't told us she needed saving, I'd have thought she was just another pretty liberal moving up in the world and appearing on The View."

Jesus whirled around and grabbed Aaron's shoulders. "What did you say? The View?"

Startled, Aaron nodded.

"Then they're sure to give her a Mark soon. We need to get going." Jesus pushed the cart at a pace that was close to a run. Aaron and Barclay struggled to catch up. Their speed resulted in increased scrutiny from other customers, which did Aaron's nerves no good. Jesus and the New Disciples turned onto the main aisle that went past the registers.

Jesus stopped, and they halted behind him. "Okay, men. Spread out and take separate cashiers."

Aaron went to a register almost all the way to the left entrance of the store, Barclay somewhere around the middle, and Jesus got into the aisle furthest to the right.

"Security in aisle two," said a voice over the intercom. "Security in aisle two." A door opened in the far wall behind the cash registers, and a team of men in black uniforms ran out. They headed straight for Aaron.

"That's it!" Jesus shouted. "Let's do this! FOR HEAVEN!! DUCK, SINNERS!"

Jesus leapt onto his shopping cart and pushed it along the back aisle towards Aaron. As the cart rolled past one shocked cashier after another he lifted a machine gun in each hand and fired at the security guards. Unprepared for the sudden action, they ducked behind the electric razor display that separated the check-out lanes from the rest of the store.

All the cashiers and customers ducked for cover. Aaron and Barclay took their shopping carts and ran to Jesus. Jesus tossed a shotgun to Aaron and then a hunting rifle to Barclay. Aaron somehow caught his weapon without shooting anyone, and proceeded to aim in the general direction of the security guard near him. Barclay ran to the wall and put his back to it, keeping his head low.

"You two keep an eye on all of 'em!" Jesus said. Barclay and Aaron nodded.

Jesus leapt off his shopping cart, pointed it towards the electric razor display and pushed it forward with all his might. Then he ran and jumped onto it. Just as it collided with the display, he leaped off and executed a perfect back flip with a twist, going over the highest shelf of products and landing on the other side like an avenging angel – with his guns pointed at the backs of all four security guards.

Aaron and Barclay emerged on either side of the display.

"Y'all Demoncrat dupes are covered," Barclay growled. "Don't do anything stupid."

"Good work, Barclay!" said Jesus. He gestured towards the rest of the store. "Aaron, keep covering everyone else."

"Right! Sorry." Aaron aimed his gun back towards the store's customers.

"Now listen up, you thugs in uniform," said Jesus. "This is your last chance. You're probably all in a union, but I can forgive even that with my unconditional love – if you do one thing."

"Isn't that a condition?" asked one guard.

Another squinted, and his brow furrowed. "Is that a...a shoelace ducktaped to your upper lip?"

"Never mind that. Do you accept me as your Lord and Savior?"

"Who are you?" asked another.

Jesus laughed. "Don't you know? Look at me. I am your Lord and Savior Jesus Christ! And I'm here to take God's country back from your evil master!"

"Look man," said one guard, "We don't even have guns, just Tasers."

"Why do you think you're getting this chance?" said Jesus.

"The real Jesus wouldn't shoot people!"

"Try me and see." The man stared for a second, and went for his Taser. Jesus squeezed the trigger and shot him in the leg. The guard went down. "Take that in remembrance of me." He turned to the other security guards. "Anyone else want a bullet? Are you with me or against me?"

"Um, with you," the man in closest range said. The others nodded quickly.

"Good choice!" He smiled. "There's hope for you all yet. Whyn't you all take off your gun belts and put all your cellphones on the floor here. Then take a seat." The guards did so. "Barclay, grab 'em and put 'em in your cart. Once we're outta here, y'all go and get some real American Bibles out of the book section. Send the bill to President Bomraka." Jesus beamed at his disciples. "Great flanking! First time in a long time that someone's had my back."

"They're gonna bring reinforcements," Barclay said.

"Of course. Aaron, we got everything?"

"Yes, Lord."

"Proud o' y'all." Jesus turned and addressed the customers and cashiers, still lying down or crouching behind registers and counters. "The rest of you, remember this is all for America! Get some God and get some freedom!"

Jesus and his new disciples grasped the handles of their brimming shopping carts, and double-timed them out the exit. The doors slid shut behind them.

"I don't understand," said one customer to another. "They speak English? I thought they were Mexican."

Once outside, Jesus saw a pickup truck at the edge of the parking lot. "There! Quickly!" The trio began to run. They were almost all the way when a magnificent station wagon pulled in front of them.

It was a beast straight from the 1970s, with a huge 420 cubic inch overhead camshaft-injected blower sticking from the hood.

A Latino man stepped out. "I'm sorry," he said. "I don't mean to intrude, but I know who you are."

26

————

Barclay's hand strayed near his pistol, beneath his woolen blanket.

"And who might that be?" said Jesus.

"El Señor. Our Savior. The Jesus," the man said. He made the sign of the cross, and looked at Jesus expectantly.

"That's me," Jesus said. He removed his sombrero and false mustache. "But that's not my sign. That's the sign the papists make."

"How is it different for you?"

"I add the missing ingredient." Jesus held up his fist. "This in the middle. That makes it the Crucifist." He clenched it over his heart.

The man's eyes became wet. "At last I know it is you! After so many false prophets, you make the sign of the cross with the true fist of freedom!" He embraced Jesus.

Barclay and Aaron looked alarmed, and stepped in. Jesus waved them off. "It's alright, I can tell he's not gay." After a few short moments he gave the man a quick pat on the back, the warning signal straight men give each other that it's time to stop hugging.

The man stepped back, embarrassed. "I don't mean to be so excited," he said. "It's just been so long, my family and I have been so alone among my people...I feared you may never come. Here at last you are!"

"Yep, I'm back – and better than ever! We have to get going. I've got a lot to do." Jesus looked him over. "We could use another man."

"I'm with you," he said. "I and my car is at your, how you say, disposal."

Jesus examined the vehicle. It gave him great pleasure to see this was no shamefully neutered fuel-efficient insult to god and man. A large and glorious beast that hailed from the grand gas-loving days of the 1970's, it had three rows of luxurious seats with room for cargo and was capped off with a muscle-car blower declaring its virility for all to see.

"I don't need to look gift horsepower in the mouth," said Jesus. "Gimme the keys. Everybody in!"

They threw the goods they had earned with their own might of arms into the back, letting the carts loose into the parking lot. Adam and Barclay dove into the second row of seats as their new friend jumped in the passenger seat in front. Jesus jammed the gas pedal all the way down to the floor before the passenger door was fully closed. They sped down the ramp and back onto the highway.

A group of Black helicopters swooped over them towards the Wal-Mart without giving them a second look.

"Our disguises worked like magic!" said Barclay.

"Not just like magic," said Jesus. "Like a miracle." He took out his cigarettes, and offered them around. "What's your name?"

"I am Hector."

Jesus extended his hand, and the man shook it gratefully. "Please to meet you. This is Aaron, and this is Barclay."

"How did you see through our camouflage?" Aaron asked.

"It would have fooled most white people," Hector said. "But we Latinos know that most illegals don't wear long black mustaches made from shoelaces, or sombreros."

"Huh," said Aaron. "That's so weird."

Hector coughed. "What is that we will do, El Señor?"

"We're going to rescue a woman from the clutches of the LIEberal media. She is the key to the tools that will help us overthrow the Demoncrat party, and their leader, the KenyAntichrist Bomraka." As they spoke, Barclay began checking their new weapons in the back seat.

"I see," said Hector. "Where is this most important señora?"

"In Atlanta. She's a reporter for ABC, which is bad enough. Unless we can save her, she will soon be pulled into the dark web of Feminazism that is The View. "

Barclay racked a shell into the chamber of his shotgun. "Not on our watch."

Hector whistled. "If I were not sitting I might jump for joy! Yes! You strike straight at the heart of the beast!" His smile wavered. "But there are likely to be many sinners in your way."

"Then they'll either get out of our way, or my Dad will sort 'em out." Jesus' expression sharpened as he looked deeper into Hector's words. "For all those sinners who fight for me, I can forgive a lot of sin."

Hector closed his eyes and raised his fists in joy. "My heart is lightened to hear of this. Because that is what I would ask of you." He lowered his fists and hung his head. "I have some in my family, they would vote against the liberals but they are illegal. Also, perhaps even worse, some of them are..." He bowed his head in shame. "Catholics. They could become good people, if it were not for their sin in worshipping the false Catholic god, working without papers and taking jobs from real Americans." He raised his eyes to Jesus with scant hope. "If I help you on their behalf, can they be saved? For that is what I would ask from you - that you can grant my people the guidance to become true Americans."

"I want similar things for my people," said Barclay. They read each other's expressions, and then shook hands in one of those ways unknown to white people.

"All who can help me with what I need, can be forgiven," said Jesus. "All they must do is follow my every single order without question."

"Wonderful!" said Hector. "Because I think we can get you inside the TV station that has the señorita!"

"How?" asked Aaron.

"The station must be cleaned, right?"

"Yes," said Aaron. "But...? OH...!"

"Yes, that's right! There's no way liberals could do honest work themselves. So they must hire cleaners! We have a cleaning company, so with luck you can all slip right in!"

"My God, you're right!" said Jesus. "There's no way feminist women will clean and cook as God commands!"

"Are you sure you get the right security access for the cleaners?" Aaron asked. "When I was a plumber and we had a big contract, we still had to sign in at the front desk."

"I'm sure someone in my family has access. As you know, all of us Latinos really do know each other."

"All right!" said Barclay. "It's all coming together."

"We really are on God's road after all," said Aaron.

Jesus stroked his chin in thought. He snapped his fingers. "This is just perfect! Aaron, you know those flags we got? Here's what I need."

ROSIO HUNG up her encrypted desk phone so hard it cracked the plastic. She could not believe how incompetent her servants were being. This Christ had been able to get out of a Wal-Mart of all places, in some sort of disguise that seemed to make him, and even his possible servants, literally invisible.

It was starting to feel like a plot. More heads might roll after Madcow's if people didn't get it together pretty damn quick. She made a few more notes, and steeled herself for what would have to happen next – a visit upstairs to the Oval Office.

As angry and vengeful as she was when her plots were foiled, she could only imagine the incandescent rage Bomraka was experiencing. Even sleeper agent programming wouldn't be enough to hold back his true inner nature after this public humiliation and setback.

This would have to crack his cool. It would be a threat to her life, but at least she would finally see the true face that she was fighting for.

She took the stairs, not immediately hearing any struggles or screams of the dying. Had he already liquidated them all, in a rage all the more terrifying in its silence like the deadliest assassin possible? When she reached the top of the stairs, she looked around the hallway on the way to his office. She rubbed her eyes to make sure she was seeing things correctly.

People were still seated at their desks – all of them! None of them appeared to be dead. The ones who were moving around didn't even have wounds. Not so much as a broken leg, or even a bruise. One even smiled at her! She returned the smile frostily, and hurried past the troublingly undamaged staff to knock on the Oval Office door.

"Is that you Rosio?" His voice came through the door, a bit annoyed but otherwise calm and cool.

She opened the door, and to her dismay saw not a single sign of unholy wrath. No destroyed furniture, not so much as an overturned chair. His eyes were most definitely not glowing red, and there wasn't so much as a scent of brimstone.

She stepped inside the room and closed the door. How could he have this much control over himself?

"What the Hell just happened, Rosio?" he asked. "I understand this terrorist just shot up a Wal-Mart and just walked away without a trace? Possibly with supporters, and without a single lead?"

"We're thinking..." she decided to test him. "We might have to start banning guns for all Christians in the Midwest."

Bomraka raised a quizzical eyebrow. "How does that connect? Let alone help us catch him?"

In that moment she knew that there was no way he could actually be the Antichrist. Her childhood dreams fell crushed around her feet.

She kept her face frozen in a cheerful smile. "You know we have to stop him right?"

"Of course we do," said Bomraka. "What kind of a question is that? But we need to stop screwing around with the EPA and FDA and whatnot. We need the FBI on this."

She couldn't refrain but one last attempt to see if he was the man she needed him to be. "How about Seal Team 666?"

The president looked at her a little oddly. "I think you added a couple of sixes there. We're not at extrajudicial assassination yet. What do you have on him?"

"Just that he's a Christian."

"He's a terrorist really."

"Even though he's not a Muslim?

The president didn't even know what to do with this sentence. "Okay. Rosio, this pains me, but your duties are now confined to handling my social calendar and dealing with party donors."

"Are you sure you don't want any more help?" she asked. Now that he clearly was not even a sleeper agent, she liked the idea of his being in control of the search for Jesus even less. He might not even kill this Christ.

She found herself wanting to kill Bomraka even more than Jesus. All these many years working for him, thinking she was helping to smash the patriarchy and create a new human species without men by female stem cell cloning – and it turned out the President was just another ordinary man.

Her masters must have a reason for all of this, she told herself. She must not strike against him until she was sure.

His words came in as if from a distance, as he said "Yes, don't worry about it. Maybe get yourself checked out. You seem to be - a little stressed perhaps."

"You got it sir," she chirped, and left.

He might have a point in spite of himself, she thought. She could definitely use some relaxation while she figured this all out. She'd always found food comforting.

She wondered who she might be able to eat on such short notice.

27

———

Jesus and the New Disciples passed the miles to Hector's home in a happy blur of companionship and Christian problem-solving. Soon they reached the outskirts of Atlanta, and a short while later arrived at the poor but proud home of Hector's cousins. Barclay was relieved that they had a garage to pull their borrowed vehicle into. Faith was fine, but it sure didn't hurt to also be off the street.

"Before we go in to see my family, maybe you guys want to...take off your disguises now?" asked Hector.

"Of course," said Jesus. "We don't want to confuse anyone we can convert."

Hector scratched his head. "Yes...confuse...sure. Thank you."

Hector went ahead into the house to gather his relatives for their shot at salvation. An hour or so passed, as they heard cars pulling up and people entering through the front door. Under Jesus' direction, Aaron made some modifications to the American flag they'd liberated from the Wal-Mart. Just as the flag was finished, Hector asked them to enter the living room. They found a room full Hispanic folks, about 15 people in total, ranging from a little girl of nine to men and women in their 70's or higher. Jesus stood proud, and removed his denim jacket to reveal his hard-muscled body, with his silver .45 thrust into his waistband.

"You look just like him, but with a gun this time!" said an old woman with her hair in a bun, who then made the sign of the cross.

"That's right ma'am," said Jesus. "But it's not just about me. Aaron?"

Aaron pulled out his modified flag. "It's about the flag!" he said. "That goes with the new sign of the cross!" Holding the flag proudly in one hand, he made the sign of the Crucifist with the other, ending on his chest.

"Both look a little different?" said a younger man in his 30s.

"Sharp eyes," said Jesus. "They are different. The sign is how it should be – strong like America. This flag is how it should be - with 49 states." Jesus raised his voice in passion. "The only real states of America. Who can guess what false, unholy, LIEberal state have we removed from the holy flag?"

No one really answered. "Come on, someone try," Jesus cajoled.

From the corner of a room, a middle-aged mother took a guess. "California?"

"Good guess! But Ronald Reagan himself came from California, which saves it from God's wrath."

The gathered folk considered. At last a father raised his hand. "Alaska?"

"Oh no. Alaska was saved by St. Palin." A couple of his listeners looked at each other, and a little girl behind them raised her hand. "Little girl, you have a question?"

"I didn't know she was a saint," she said softly.

"I don't blame you, you're too young to know. You just tell your parents to get with it. Sarah Palin is a saint to any real Americans." Jesus smiled and spread his hands to the group. "Anyone else want to guess the state?"

"We don't know, tell us!" was the eager answer.

"The answer is - Hawaii! Because when that RINO Eisenhower made that foreign stain of sin a full US State, Bomraka gained his foothold! Once that false island of un-Americans is made back into a colonially occupied US territory, the rest of the real states can once again be by God's grace the greatest country on Earth."

The crowd murmured to each other as they considered this.

"But America is still the greatest right now, right?" a middle-aged woman asked.

"Of course," he said, a bit surprised at the question. "It's just that if we can win, it'll once again be even more the greatest."

The room full of Hispanic wisdom-seekers thought on this a bit longer. Finally, an older man spoke. "Hector says that, with your help, we can be saved and forgiven for being illegal, and even for being Catholic. What would you have us do?"

"Accept me as your lord and savior, kiss this flag, and help me on this mission, and all your sins of working in America without papers or the right God will be forgiven."

"What about the people who hired us?" asked a teenaged boy.

"Huh? What about 'em?" said Jesus.

"Hush!" Hector ordered the boy. "There have been enough questions - I'm sorry, El Señor. My sister's cousin's child. He knows no better."

"No, let's hear him. What do you mean, the people who hired you?"

"I guess I mean, if it's a sin for us to work without papers, what about the white American citizens who hired us? We wouldn't come if they didn't hire us. Shouldn't they be punished too?"

Jesus was greatly saddened. He walked over to the boy and placed his hand on the boy's head. "It's not your fault, son. The liberal media won't explain these things truthfully. All of you listen close, now." He beckoned them closer with his hands, and smiled as they all moved in closer.

"Now when someone who's running a company does something for profit," said Jesus, "it's not a sin. It can't be, if he's doing it for a proper company."

"Why not?"

"Because, my boy, every American company is born a holy creation of God."

"Every single one?" the boy said.

"Every one," said Jesus. "And they stay holy by following God's laws. Chief among those laws, the law of the free market. Where my father's invisible hand is always at work."

The crowd murmured some more among themselves. Jesus waited for them to subside before he resumed.

"The free market means companies have to operate on profit," Jesus said. He held his hands up to the heavens. "So if a company that obeys God makes a profit, it just can't be a sin."

"Why's that?" the same teenager asked.

"Boy, you just keep askin' those questions, don't you?" Jesus chuckled ruefully. "Because, unlike people, companies never rebelled against God and left the Garden of Eden. So they are born without sin. And so as long as the companies make money, the people who run them are proving themselves to be beloved of God. That's why they should never go to jail or even be personally fined."

"Even if it's a liberal company?" the teenage kid persisted.

"Of course not, that's different," said Jesus. "If the company is doing something liberal, then it's entered a state of sin. If they are being liberal they are acting against God, and so they go into a state of sin and can no longer operate in the Free Market."

"Ah, I think I see," said the boy. "So the Free Market is like Eden."

Jesus beamed with pride. "Exactly!"

"Ah, I see!" Hector exclaimed. "That's why liberals hate corporations. Because most corporations do God's work!"

A little girl spoke up. "Can I still have toys like dolls that are made by corporations even if my parents are illegal?"

Jesus looked stern. They all held their breath. "Ah, just messin' with you," Jesus said. "Of course you can have toys!" Everybody laughed. "Toys come from corporations, so they bring you closer to God. Just don't go to a Catholic church anymore and make sure you don't vote Democrat, and God will provide for all of you."

"Thank you Jesus!" the girl's mother proclaimed and clasped her hands in joy. "I had feared we were lost in sin - but you show us the way! We can work our way to salvation!"

"Yes, you get it!" said Jesus. "Just like the Cubans - they came here illegally, but they voted conservative in a swing state - so they're saved! God loves those who help themselves, by helping the right people! Help me, and be blessed not just by me - but by God's will as shown by the greatest country in the world!"

"We can save ourselves as long as we are of use to El Señor!" Hector cheered. His family of righteous hispanic Christians joined him, and even the surly teenagers were moved.

Jesus closed his eyes and felt the joyful noise wash over him like a wave. It took a glorious while to fade. "It's been a long time since I spoke to a crowd," he said at last. "Damn if it doesn't feel good. I can see why I liked it so much in my past life. But this time, I'm not just about teaching." He pulled out both his guns and pointed them at the ceiling. "This time, I'm about TAKIN' CARE OF BUSINESS! Are you ready?"

Hector's family cheered again, now fully restored to the blessings of Christ.

"Then, let's give ABC Atlanta a housecleaning they'll never forget!"

28

Jesus and the New Disciples prepared well into the night. At Hector's recommendation they didn't reuse their disguises from Wal-Mart. Instead they went a more subtle direction, using the uniforms of cleaners. Their getaway vehicle would be Hector's station wagon, with his relatives' cleaning equipment hiding their weapons. They would go in right before Lily Jane's evening broadcast. Phase 1 would be to rescue Lily herself. Once that was accomplished they could go into Phase 2.

Jesus broke bread with a fresh Twinkie, and inducted Hector into the ranks of the New Disciples. Then he led them in a prayer for holy victory. After that he set them to stripping and checking all of their guns. They filled backpacks with ammunition, breaking and entry tools, and medical supplies they hoped they would not need. Just in case, they also added protein bars, cigarettes and whiskey. At Aaron's suggestion, they even included a small amount of bottled water - making sure first that it wasn't some pussified version that was "natural" or "filtered".

Jesus noticed Aaron checking his pack again, a bit intensely. He sent Barclay and Hector to start packing the car, and went over to Aaron. "Something troubling you, brother?"

"The bandages, Lord," Aaron sighed. "It really brought it home to me. This is a dangerous venture. It's for you and God, and I have no regrets," he added quickly. "It's just...it does make me wonder if I'll ever see my family again."

Jesus clapped him on the shoulder. "I believe I'm just in time. Why don't you come in here for a minute."

"What's going on?"

"Got a surprise for you, buddy! Follow me. As always, I suppose," said Jesus with a friendly grin. He led Aaron to a private room with a computer. Aaron saw his Hannah smiling at him on the screen.

"Oh, thank you Lord!" said Aaron. "Honey, how are you?"

"Good! We're wonderful! Oh, it's so good to see you!" Hannah said.

Jesus flashed a grin. "Gonna see how they're doin' down there. We'll honk the horn when we're ready to go." He closed the door behind him.

"Where are you, honey? How have you been?" Aaron asked. "I've been so worried about you."

"We've been fine! The instructions in Jesus' pamphlet were perfect. We're in New Mexico now – they call it New America. We're safe! And free! The schools don't teach evolution, and there are no free lunches for anyone, and they don't even have tofu. It's like Heaven on Earth!"

"It's good just to hear you so happy," he said, wiping away a tear.

"We've got someone else who wants to say hello," said Hannah. She pulled their son into view.

"Christopher!" Aaron exclaimed. "Have you grown bigger since last I saw you?"

"Not yet! But I'm gonna fight for God like you some day, Dad, you watch!"

"I surely will."

"And where's Jennifer?"

"Right here Daddy!" she stuck her head into range of the camera. "I've been learning all about how to cook real manfood!"

"That's my little girl!" He sighed. "It's so good to see you all again, and see that you're doing fine."

Hannah beamed back at him. "And how are you, my warrior for Christ?"

"I'm good. I'm learning so much. He is every bit the man we need him to be. He's strong, and fearless, and I've got faith that's he's the one God sent to make things right." Aaron faltered for a second. "Can you – can you all put your hands up to the camera?"

Hannah did so wordlessly. His son and daughter followed. Aaron put his hand to the screen on to where it looked like it touched theirs.

"You'll have other people joining you soon," said Aaron. "Good people. I met them last night. The family of our newest fellow disciple, Hector."

"I look forward to meeting them, honey," said Hannah. "Even more, I look forward to being with you in person, my warrior for Christ. And...doing all sorts of things," she blushed.

Aaron smiled in joy. "Me too, honey." A horn honked from outside. "I have to go," he said. "Stay safe, all of you. You mean more to me than all of the heavens and the Earth."

She nodded tearfully. Neither of them cut the connection. At last Aaron decided it would have to be him.

He stared at the black screen for a second, wondering if he would ever see them in person again. He shook his head and grabbed his backpack and walked downstairs into the waiting car.

Jesus noticed that Aaron was wiping at his eyes. Any other time Jesus might have reproved a disciple for such unmanliness, but he knew that becoming a divine warrior was a long process. Aaron's heart was in the right place, he just needed to toughen up a bit.

As Barclay drove to Hector's wagon to their mission objective, they turned on the police scanner Aaron had taken from the Wal-Mart. Their attention was soon rewarded with an APB for "Illegal aliens involved in a Wal-Mart incident."

Aaron grinned. "We're getting more and more famous."

"Outlaw life starting to appeal to you, Aaron?" said Barclay.

"I have to say, now that I know my family's safe...it just feels right."

Jesus nodded. "When an outlaw can follow God's law, it sure is the best of both worlds." He pulled out his pistol and checked the ammo.

"Let's go be outlaws for God."

29

They pulled off of the highway and took side roads to the front of ABC Atlanta's main headquarters. It was a low building of only 3 stories in a modern style. The sinful building's height and partial seclusion suited the low character of the media elitists Jesus expected to encounter. Turning right immediately after the building, they went down a short road to the back gate, just off of a cul-de-sac. A steel broadcasting tower reared several stories above the parking lot, topped with a satellite dish. Several other, lower dishes were scattered about the parking lot, also broadcasting their largely liberal poison into the country.

They rolled up to the gate and pressed an intercom button.

"Ensenada cleaning," said Hector.

"Oh?" a distorted voice responded through the speaker. There was some barely audible shuffling of paper. "We don't have any cleanings scheduled for today."

"This is for Lily Godwin's office," said Jesus, leaning past Hector to reach the intercom. "Everything is to look good for her special event tonight."

"Oh," said the guard. "Hold on while I check with her office."

They waited. "If this doesn't work, will we have to blast our way in?" asked Aaron. Jesus shushed him.

The intercom voice returned. "Alright, she didn't have you scheduled but come on in."

The gate buzzed and slid open. They drove to the rear entrance of the building. Hector turned the car around so that they would be able to leave quickly. They exited the car holding mops and brooms bundled together, and several mop buckets.

A security guard opened the back door atop a loading dock. "Sure is a lot of stuff you got there," the guard said cheerfully as they walked past him. "That much to clean up in one star's dressing room?"

"There's a lot to clean here, believe me," said Jesus, the last to enter the building.

"Alright, well, the freight elevator is that way." The guard pointed down a hallway. "Her dressing room is on the second floor. Third is the broadcast studio, you probably want to avoid it."

"Thanks," said Jesus. He produced a gun from his mop bucket. "Now think fast!" he said.

The guard went for his gun, and stopped.

"That's right," Jesus nodded. "Think about your soul and salvation."

"Alright?" sad the guard. "What are you guys doing, anyway? Don't you know this is a TV station, you're going to get in a lot of trouble for not a lot you can even steal."

"Guys, tie him down so he can think about the Bible for a bit." The New Disciples pulled rolls of duck tape from the buckets and set to work. When that was done, they untied the bundles of mops and brooms to reveal machine guns, shotguns and rifles.

"Now let's get to it," said Jesus. They entered the freight elevator and took it to the second floor.

The elevator door opened into a carpeted hallway. The decor was decadent and foreign-inspired, with the subtle arrogance of latte-sipping liberal elitism oozing from every inch. There were way too many books, and instead of paintings of American glory or even a pretty countryside the paintings were strange agglomerations of lines, colors and shapes that made no sense. Jesus hoped they were from foreign lands. He didn't want to believe they accurately represented the debauched state of current American art. And of course, there was not one single American flag.

"*Muy sucio*," Hector muttered.

"Come on, man, speak American," said Barclay.

"Sorry. It is very dirty in here...and not just the floors."

They finally reached a bored secretary who buzzed them in. Passing her they found themselves in another hallway. This had less decorations and more blank hallways with closed doors at each end, almost like a regular corporation that wasn't in league with the Devil.

"This is it," said Jesus. "This is as far as we get with disguises." They took off their cleaning uniforms.

"Shall we all go in?" asked Hector.

"I think I'll have an easier time finding and talking some sense into the girl by myself. Wait here and get ready for phase two."

His disciples all nodded. They took flanking positions and checked their ammunition. Jesus went to the end of the hallway and stuck his head through the door. No one appeared. He tucked both his guns away, and walked nonchalantly into the hall.

A couple of apparent media workers in headsets glanced at him but paid him no mind. When the hallway came to another corner he saw a room labeled "Lily Godwin."

This was it. In spite of himself, he swallowed nervously. He tried the door, and found it was unlocked. He entered the room.

There she was, the lovely, even bewitching girl from the photograph. She was facing him, paused in the act of brushing her hair before a mirror. She was dressed in fancy newscast clothes. No amount of liberal fashion could hide the beauty of the raven hair falling down her back. She was even more beautiful than the picture. Up close he could see her left eye was blue, and her right one green. His heart leaped. One pure and one witchy, just like Alaine.

"Are you the cleaner I was told about?" she asked.

He couldn't help but chuckle. "In a way, girl. In a way." He had to ask. "Alaine? Is it really you?"

"What?" She stared at him. "Are you feeling alright?"

There was no sign of recognition in her eyes. Looking closer, he could see she was.... *almost* the same. There were some differences. Her cheekbones were slimmer. Her eyes were a little wider, her voice a little brassier. They stood in contrast to his memories. Lily was like enough Alaine to be her sister, but was not her.

"My name is Lily Godwin. I think you've got the wrong girl." She waited for him to say something, time which he spent staring at her further. "So, uh, no offense but I'm getting ready for an important meeting – if you're supposed to clean, can you get to it?"

"Then we are just in time to save you from the Mark as well," said Jesus. "God's mysterious ways. You yourself, you're like a flower with thorns. One part lovely femininity, and one part witch...."

"Okay, now you're creeping me out." Her eyes opened wide with sudden recognition – and it saddened Jesus to see eyes her eyes fill with fear. "You're that – the leader of that Christian terror cell!"

Jesus shook his head. "Don't believe everything you hear on the news." It must be some kind of sign that she looked so much like his Alaine and still wasn't.... but why would God make a sign like that?

Maybe it was just to let him know he was on the right path. He nodded to himself. That worked. He could leave all the details to God. "Alright, Lily then - I don't have a lot of time to explain, so listen close. I'm Jesus. I'm the second coming of salvation - only this time, I'm here to kick ass." He saw the fear in her eyes increase, and for once his tone softened. "Don't you worry, okay? Nothing improper is gonna happen here. We're just gonna get you free of this place."

"Well, um, thanks, but I'm really fine here, really."

"No, you're really not. You're in a straight unholy situation here, dealing with bad people. You just have no idea what kind of danger you're really in..." She stepped all the way against the wall, as far away from him as she could.

"Please listen, ma'am," he tried again. "I'm sorry to rush you like this, I know you got a lot of questions and I wish this wasn't how we had to meet. Look in my eyes. Can you trust me?"

She looked into his eyes. "I just met you. Why in God's name would I trust you?"

"God's name is exactly why you should, ma'am."

"I need a lot more than that."

Jesus noticed the clock on the wall. Not much time left before Phase 2 of their plan would have to start. He had to wrap things up here. Ordinarily, if a woman stood in the way of an important plan, it was time to assert the Godly position of man leads, woman follows.

Somehow, he couldn't do that.

"I can tell you this, ma'am. It's about your grandfather."

"My grandfather?" she exclaimed. "Have you – have you done something to him?"

"Not a thing, despite extreme provocation. But he's in mortal danger, and you're the only way he can be saved. I can't explain anything else. You have to come with us, Lily Jane." That was all close enough to the truth. If anything, it understated the risk the old man was taking by withholding the tools Jesus needed to defeat Bomraka and his Demoncrats. The old man's immortal soul was on the line.

She stared at him, as seconds ticked by. "How do you know my middle name?" she said at last.

"He told me. Now I know you have a lot of questions. But time is of the essence. We have to get going."

"I'm not sure yet," she said. "Why should I trust you for a second?"

"Because I'm asking you to."

"I need a little more than that."

"Then how's this?" he smiled. "I can promise you it will be one Heaven of a story."

She came to a decision. "Alright then." She picked up her smart phone from a nearby chair. "Let's go take me to my grandfather."

He shook his head. "You can't bring that. They can track you with it. You're gonna need to leave that here."

She rolled her eyes. "Seriously?"

"That's the only way this can work."

"Fine." She said something below her breath as she dropped the phone back on the chair.

"What was that?" he asked.

"You don't want to know," Lily responded. "It wasn't flattering. How are we getting there?"

"This way," said Jesus. "And keep quiet, our success depends on it." He held open the door, and she walked into the hallway. As soon as he let go of the door, he pulled out his stepfather's pistol. Startled, she opened her mouth to speak. He held his finger to his lips; she subsided, still unsettled. He took her gently but firmly by the upper arm, and led her back to where he'd left the New Disciples. They stood waiting, guns at the ready.

"Howdy ma'am," said Barclay. "Glad you could join us."

Lily eyed the guns. "What does my grandfather have to do with this?" Lily asked. They looked to Jesus, asking with their eyes if they should tell her. Jesus shook his head.

"Are we about ready to go?" asked Aaron, changing the subject.

"He started to get a little worried," said Barclay.

"So did he!" said Aaron.

Jesus chuckled. "Alright, men! Now for Phase 2."

Before Lily could object, Jesus pressed his finger to his lips again. They walked back into the freight elevator, and Jesus pressed button #3.

At the end of the hallway they took a left turn, to see a locked door with a lit sign above it saying "On Air".

30

"Alright," said Jesus. "It's blinking! I think that means they're about to go to commercial. Are you ready, men?"

"More than ever, Lord!" said Aaron. Barclay and Hector cocked their guns.

"What?" asked Lily. Surprised, they turned to face her. "You're going into the TV studio? You said you were taking me to my grandfather!"

The "On Air" sign changed to "Off Air". "Let's roll!" said Jesus. He fired at the lock with his stepfather's 45, and hit it clean. He kicked the door and they stormed in. Hector, Barclay and Aaron spread out immediately. Jesus pushed Lily behind a cabinet. "Stay there, you'll be safer! Barclay, stay with her. Hector, go into that booth up there and bring 'em out." He pointed to a studio booth that had three crew members in it, with headsets on. They hadn't noticed Jesus or his men yet. "Aaron, follow me!"

Jesus marched straight in to the center of the show.

There sat the lead anchorman Bret Stormbreaker behind the news desk, having his makeup touched up by a small and rather pretty girl with short black hair.

"Look out Bret, he's got a gun!" yelled Lily.

Bret saw Jesus with a pistol in each hand, and turned pale beneath his makeup. "Security!" cried the anchorman as he reached for something beneath the desk. The makeup artist turned, gasped and dropped beneath the desk as well.

"Everybody, I advise you all to hold still and say your prayers," said Jesus. "This will all be over soon, no harm done save to the Devil."

"Someone call security!" Stormbreaker insisted.

"No more security for Bomraka's minions," Jesus declared. "You better take your hands from underneath that desk or you start explaining yourself to St. Peter at the gates." Jesus heard a sound to his left. He whirled back with Hieronymus' revolver in his other hand, just in time to see three security guards about to grab their guns from their holsters.

"I got the drop on you," Jesus pointed out. "Don't make me send you to Hell. Hands up now." They slowly raised their hands. One of the guards' eyes flicked to a point just over Jesus' shoulder. He whirled around to see Stormbreaker had a gun! Jesus raised his arm to fire - but Stormbreaker's gun was already almost aimed. Adrenalin expanded the moment into an eternity as he tried to force his arm to move faster, but it was still a moment behind Brett's. Without a miracle he wouldn't make it in time...

Stormbreaker grew a red hole in his shoulder, and blood splattered across the green screen behind him. He went down. Jesus ran over to him and finished knocking him unconscious.

The gunshot hadn't been his. Behind him, Aaron lowered his rifle.

"I used to tithe gold to the cause of Christ," said Aaron. "Looks like lead works too."

"Good one!" said Jesus. Blessed if he wasn't proud of how that man was coming along. "Over there, get their guns!" Jesus pointed to the security guards. Aaron ran over and quickly stripped them of their weapons. While he was doing that, Jesus caught a glimpse of several crewmembers try to make a break for a different door. Jesus ran over and to find that Barclay and Hector were already corralling them. As if they had been working together for years, Jesus and his men brought all the crewmembers and guards against the wall next to the news desk next to Stormbreaker's bleeding, unconscious body.

"Alright all of you, take a seat. You! Makeup girl!" Jesus bellowed. "Come on out now and join the others."

The makeup girl tentatively stuck her head above the news desk, and then emerged. She walked over to the others. There were ten people total - seven civilians, and the three guards who'd been caught flatfooted.

"Good! Now, those security boys, I don't like 'em being awake." The New Disciples jumped to it. Three thuds resounded, and the guards fell to the ground, unconscious. "Fine job, men! You're all learning mighty quick." He turned to the still-conscious crew. "Now, here's the deal. This is a one-time offer. If you do exactly what I say for the next several minutes, and promise to follow the Bible for the rest of your natural life, I'll not only let you into Heaven - I'll reward you with freedom here on Earth. Got that? Nod your heads."

The crew nodded numbly.

"Which one o' you was the cameraman again?" One crewman raised his hand. "You come here. Who else we need to do a broadcast." The cameraman didn't answer. "Now, boy!" said Jesus.

"Uh, someone to switch the camera feed I guess."

"Which one of you does that?" Jesus demanded.

A moment of silence followed, and then a geeky man in a slightly nicer shirt raised his hand. "I'm the show producer. I can could do that."

"Alright. You two stand to side. Disciples, bind the rest of them from acting against my will."

"Uh...." Said Aaron.

"Duck tape," said Jesus. He tried not to roll his eyes. Aaron still wasn't that quick on the uptake.

"Got it."

The New Disciples pulled out rolls of duck tape, and set to work. As they did, Jesus split his attention between the two unbound crew members and the rest of the studio.

"Done, Jesus!" said Aaron.

"Good. Now, camera guy! When that next commercial's done, you're gonna focus right in on me and don't cut it till I say so. Right?"

"Yes sir," the cameraman mumbled.

"How much time 'til we're back on the air?"

"We just started a two-minute quick commercial block," another man spoke.

"And who are you?" asked Jesus.

"I'm the assistant show producer," he said, his voice quaking. "You've got about a minute. Unless you have the camera cut in right now-"

"Heavens no!" said Jesus, offended. "Some business paid for that time. You want me to steal? From a job creator?"

"No sir," the man mumbled.

"That's what I thought," said Jesus. "You just go in the booth and get ready. Hector, follow him." Jesus called out. "Barclay, how you doing back there?"

"All clear," said Barclay. "Your girl ain't too happy though."

I bet, Jesus said to himself. "Lily, in about a minute or so it should be a lot more clear for you.

"Fifty seconds," said the show producer.

Jesus scanned the room again. "Hector, make sure we've got everyone in here and the doors are locked. Something don't feel right."

"Forty seconds," the show producer announced.

Jesus looked around the studio again. "You sit over there." He indicated a chair with a wave of his pistol.

The producer got up and went to his new seat, eyes wide. "Thirty seconds," he said.

Jesus pointed at a camera. "This one the main one?" The cameraman nodded.

Hector came back in. "No else is here."

"Twenty Seconds."

"Disciples, watch the entrances! " Jesus ordered. "No one must interrupt us! This may be the only chance we have to get past the liberal media filter."

"Twelve. Eleven. Ten…"

The cameraman was still counting down. Jesus faced the camera as the man started using hand signals for three, two…

"Hey there, America." Jesus smiled. "Bret Stormbreaker ain't in tonight. He's been judged, and there's the verdict." Jesus jerked a thumb over his shoulder, to indicate the red wash of Stormbreaker's blood across the green screen. "The so-called news was scheduled to sing you all to sleep, with some soothing liberal lullabies some of you actually believe."

Across the continent, Rosio Dawnhell spit out her tea. She spluttered. "Tell Blabbera Wilters! NOW!" Her frightened servant scrambled to obey.

Back in the television studio, Jesus continued. "World news this, economy that, and then Bret here was gonna fill your head with lies about the alleged science of predicting God's weather. Got something a little different tonight!" He raised his hands in joy. "A wake-up call from your Creator, and for the Demoncrats, and for the KenyAntichrist President Bomraka!" He placed his arms on his hips. Bless it, this was all going so well.

"You're probably wondering who I am." Jesus made the sign of the Crucifist. "None other than-"

He heard a sound far back in the studio, and saw Lily slump unconscious to the floor.

"Look out Lord!" Barclay yelled. Jesus looked away from Lily just in time to whirl where Barclay pointed, and duck something slicing through the air just above his head. He jumped back to barely avoid the return strike of a golden-colored object the size of a bowling pin as it flashed past him, thudded into a nearby lighting stand and knocked it down in a sparking crash. The miss threw his opponent off balance, causing her to regroup and giving him a second to see who he was facing.

When he saw the face of his attacker he couldn't help but laugh. It was so perfect. Just as he'd always suspected.

"Blabbera Wilters?" the makeup girl gasped.

31

"Y ou were waiting until our backs were turned, weren't you?" said Jesus.

Barclay cocked his shotgun. "Say your prayers, media demon bitch!"

"Do you dare to take me on yourself, so-called Messiah?" Blabbera challenged. "Or will you hide behind your guns?"

"No one shoot her!" Jesus ordered. He holstered both of his guns. "Stay near Lily and keep her safe! Leave this one to me."

"You won't even have time to say your prayers, you fool." Broadcasting live now, the cameraman zoomed in on her. In her left hand, she brandished the shining implement that had nearly bashed in his glorious head - and Jesus realized it was an Emmy.

Jesus barked with laughter again. "Why not just a hammer and sickle?"

"Because that would be only one blade," she sneered. She grabbed the Emmy in both her hands and gave it a sharp twist. Twin gleaming blades thrust out with a clang, each two feet in length, from either side of the golden idol she'd been given for her work. She moved her trophy-turned-death weapon in an expert figure eight, the blades making a whooshing sound as they sliced through the air.

Then Wilters noticed the cameraman. She turned pale. "By tofu! Are you still broadcasting? Why haven't you cut the signal?"

Jesus stabbed a finger at the cameraman. "You keep filming if you know what's good for you! Boys, if she gets near him you can shoot her!"

"Big talk," she snarled. She whirled her blade around her.

"How can that withered crone even move that fast, let alone swing that weapon with such skill?" mused Aaron.

Hector scowled. "It must be the evil of heathen yoga."

She sneered. "And that's not the half of it, you sad little boys!"

"What else you got?" said Jesus. "You won't even last us to commercial!"

"Think so, do you?" She whistled. "Alright ladies, show yourselves!"

The ceiling behind Wilters shattered, and down jumped nine more brassy broads in functional pantsuits. Some held laptops, others held notebooks, still others coffee cups. Like a trained cadre of feminist liberal death, they twisted these implements of the office workspace as one. Blades, spikes and metal balls on chains shot out, for her feminine minions to swing with evil glee.

"You're now on the set of The View to a Kill," Wilters sneered.

Hector swore. "With the older bruja, that makes ten of these career devils!"

"That might be enough to last until commercial," Aaron admitted.

"The Feminazi Fembots!" Jesus declared. "I knew you were real!"

"Close but no phallic symbol, you tool of the deposed patriarchy!" screeched the Feminazi who stood appropriately to Wilters' left.

"You tell 'im, sister!" declared her sister Feminazi, who stood even further to the left.

Wilters raised her chin proudly, waving her hair-sprayed mane. "We are not Fembots – we are Femborgs! Part human, part machine, all woman!"

Jesus set his jaw. "That's the last time you'll correct a Christian man."

"We are woman, and hear us roar – your doom!" Wilters declared with glee.

"I guess they were waiting until our backs were turned!" Aaron realized.

"Not that helpful now, man," said Barclay.

A third twisted mockery of womanhood saw the New Disciples. "Matriarch, may we?" she asked Wilters, her voice dripping with eagerness to serve her mistress.

"But of course," said Blabbera. She nodded at her and three of her sisters. "You four take care of those other little men and secure Lily Godwin. The rest of you stay with me." She moved forward with deadly feminist purpose.

"With pleasure!" Four of them split off towards Aaron, Hector and Barclay. "News at 11," said the first one. "You're dead." She brandished her laptop, with protruding spikes on the end of a swinging computer mouse. Three even more vicious-looking Femborgs began whirling laptops behind her.

"I got some truer news for all you," said Jesus. "The only View you're all going to be on is the view of the Devil's hind parts."

"How are you going to do that, shoot us?" Wilters taunted. "Break your word just like a typical man when you're facing a strong woman?"

"I'm a real man, and I'll never break my word. Good thing my word didn't include my men. Blast 'em, boys! Aim for the flesh! Show 'em what God's Second Amendment is all about: lead justice!"

Hector, Aaron and Barclay opened fire, filling the studio with flying lead. The Femborgs took cover. Jesus, trusting in his faith in God more than his team's aim, stepped onto the splintered news desk and leaped over their spray of bullets and high into the air. Like an eagle he saw his prey, and soared downwards fist-first. The Feminazi Femborg second furthest to the left threw up her umbrella, now turned into a speeding and twirling frenzy of knives. His mighty fist went straight through its middle, cracking her across the cheekbones. The plastic right side of her face shattered, revealing a glowing red eye. She screamed and came at him with a roundhouse left. He ducked under it and went straight for her chest. As he'd suspected, that wasn't as well protected. His fist went right into her plastic sternum and tore straight through it. She dropped to the ground, a twitching mass of shattered components, sparking wires and some small remaining flesh.

One down. He looked around. Where had Wilters gone? He couldn't see her, or any of the other so-called Femborgs. That was not good – what if his New Disciples weren't ready to go mano-a-Femi-nazi with this elite liberal force? He needed to draw their attention.

"Which one of you missies should I spank first?" he yelled.

Several of Wilter's Femborgs shrieked in anger, a shrill and fright-ening sound like a PTA meeting from Hell. They rushed out of hiding to grab Jesus. He dropped to a crouch and spin-kicked another Femborg's feet from beneath her. She fell sideways and he stomped her head on his way back up, embedding her metal skull deep into the floor. She jerked and writhed but couldn't break free, her arms flailing against the floor in helpless rage. He stomped again, enough to knock out a bull. She stopped moving. Two down – but another one was hurling some sort of grenade. He grabbed at it, and to his horror discovered it was some kind of exploding feminine product. He dropped it to the ground and kicked it back at her just in time, the explosion shattering her form into bits. The two other Femborgs nearest him were thrown backwards by the blast. He took the time to move backwards as well, trying to find a place where he could get his back against a wall.

Three down. Where could the rest be hiding? His disciples weren't faring as well with their fire as he'd hoped. He heard a sound to his right and whirled just in time to see another three swarm him at once and wrestle him to the floor. He rolled with their momentum and managed to break free. Unfortunately this gave the Femborgs who'd been stunned by the exploding feminine hygiene product enough time to regroup. They came at him again, and he blocked and struck back. The room became a whirlwind of attacks, shattered set equipment and flying Femborg limbs.

Then good American bullets thudded into the Femborgs' plastic, metal and flesh. Jesus' sacrifice play had worked – concentrating the Femborgs on him gave the New Disciples' time to get their aim together. A fourth Femborg went down, and then a fifth. As their plastic coatings became more shredded, ricochets began to fly. Jesus knocked a sixth Femborg's head loose with a flying elbow. There should only be three left! He leapt over another kick and reared back ready to strike – and then stopped with Wilters' Emmy blade right against Jesus' neck.

Like a wily serpent of broadcast sentimentality, she had been waiting for just this moment. "I knew you'd over extend yourself." She raised her voice. "Stop shooting or your Messiah gets it!"

"Don't worry about me!" said Jesus. "Root out her supporters and take 'em out!" To himself, he had to admit he was in quite a pickle.

"What do we do?" Aaron asked Barclay.

"You wanted to be on live television," Wilters taunted. "Now the whole world will get to see your end. Time for your interview, Mr. Supposed Jesus," Wilters said, words dripping with saccharine gloating. "How young were you when you decided this was how you'd like to die?"

"I said shoot!" Jesus repeated.

"We can't, Lord!" said Aaron.

"We follow orders," said Barclay. "Everybody aim for their eyes!"

"Sure you want to do that?" Wilters snarled. She moved the gleaming point of her bladed Emmy to just beneath the perfect bulge in Jesus' jeans.

"We must hold fire!" screamed Hector. "This cannot be!"

"Drop your guns now!" Wilters screamed. "On the floor!"

Feeling no other option, the New Disciples complied, faces contorted in frustration. Smiling in triumph, the three last remaining Femborg assistants emerged from hiding.

"Get behind him and hold him for me, ladies," said Wilters. They did as she asked with smug pleasure. Wilters stepped to the side, keeping her blade less than an inch from the manhood of the man they called their Lord. She noticed Barclay's hand jump. "Ah-ah, sure you want to try for that gun?" Wilters extended her blade even closer to Jesus' most private of parts.

"You cannot sex-change the Son of God!" Hector pleaded. "Madre de Dios, protect your son! Was his circumcision not enough?"

"It's so fun playing with you little boys. But now, the inevitable has come!" She stabbed with all her might. In the last split instant Jesus leapt aside. The Emmy's blade shot past him, into and through the Femborg standing behind him and puncturing some of her last remaining organic tissue.

Wilters pulled her blade back, shocked.

"Matriarch?" the forlorn Feminazi asked, before collapsing to the floor.

"Fix that with your European-style health care," said Jesus with his head held high. The last two Femborg assistants struggled to keep their grip on Jesus' arms with their steel fingernails.

"Alright, you asked for it!" She spun her Emmy up and swung at Jesus' neck. This time he dropped limp in his captor's arms. The blade passed over his head and sliced completely through the Femborg holding Jesus' left arm.

Aaron swallowed his fear and dived for this gun. He grabbed it and fired at the last Femborg still holding Jesus. It glanced off of her weaponized purse. She let go of Jesus and charged at the New Disciples. This one was bullet proof in her massive chest. Barclay and Hector picked up their guns and joined the fusillade. Aaron swallowed and prayed to God to keep their aim straight and sure.

"Looks like it's just you and me now, Wilters." Jesus cracked his knuckles. "Get ready for the Lord's extreme makeover.""

"Bastard!" Wilters screamed. She came at him with a whirlwind of steel aiming again for his holy, handsome head. She altered the arc at the last second and swung for his feet. He leaped over the blade and ducked her next strike, only to be nearly caught by a flashing kick. He dodged to the left, her spike heels shot by so close it sliced off a couple hairs from his manly beard.

"No human man could have dodged that!" she gasped.

"Bad thing for you I'm also the son of God!"

He jumped in the air and kicked. She scrambled out of the way, his boot heel crashing through the cheap plaster wall on the right side of the set. His foot was trapped. He tugged at his leg with both hands to free it. She shrieked in glee and came in with a crushing overhead swing. He pulled his leg out of the fake wall just in time, and rolled backwards, her bladed Emmy striking sparks from the floor where he'd just been.

The three New Disciples fired at the closest remaining Femborg. She advanced with slow and fearful confidence, her barrel-shaped chest shaking off all impact of their bullets. Aaron had a flash of inspiration. "Fire at her hair! Her hair is cut so short it can't be hiding armor! Aim for the top of that feminist hairdo!"

"Bless you, Aaron!" Barclay cried.

Wilters swung her Emmy at Jesus with an overhand chopping motion, missing by millimeters. Her eyes and nostrils widened. "Stand still, you archetype of oppression!" she cried.

"I'm wise to your Feminazi tricks now," Jesus declared. "It's your time of the month to lose, period."

She screamed and came in again - flailing the blades of her Emmy like some sick propeller of the penisless proletariat.

But now he had her timing down. He kicked it from her grasp, and it went flying across the studio to impale the wall mere inches from Lily's unconscious head.

Wilters screamed and swung a karate chop with desperate speed, then turned back to him with a spinning roundhouse kick to the head. "You can't exist! You're a myth!"

He stepped aside to let the strike pass, and kicked her in the vagina. She fell to the floor like a sack of pork and beans.

"I never myth," said Jesus.

He raised his head from the satisfaction of vanquishing his foe. His New Disciples concentrated their fire on the sole remaining Femborg. A stray bullet found what must have been the she-beast's solar power cell, and she exploded. Bits of the Femborg's body rocketed across the studio and her torso flew towards the cameraman. He ducked low as it bounced off of the camera, and readjusted the focus back on Jesus.

Jesus surveyed the rest of room. Among the broken set decorations and sparking electronics lay the bodies of all the other Feminazi Femborgs, some dead and some unconscious.

He turned to the New Disciples. "Look around us, men. Our enemies in shambles, and at our feet their leader." He pumped his fists in triumph. "Damn if it don't feel good to be a Christian."

"Jesus! That was amazing!" Aaron said.

"Yeah it was," said Jesus. He smiled proudly. "Y'all didn't do too bad yourselves."

He whirled around. "Where is that producer?"

There was silence, and then a deeply world-weary sigh. A pile of debris shifted, and the producer crawled forward from beneath an overturned desk.

Jesus knelt down and grabbed him by the shoulders. "Did you cut to commercial yet?"

"Uh....uh...."

"Quickly man!" said Jesus, deeply concerned. "How soon can you go to commercial? Job creators paid for that advertising! It's the only holy thing about your job!"

"About 10 seconds, close enough, I guess?" said the cameraman.

"Cut to commercial," the producer said wearily.

"Don't you have to do make that happen yourself?" said Aaron. "Up in that booth or something?"

"....right," said the producer. He trudged through the wreckage on the floor to the booth, which was now barely standing.

Jesus scanned the studio. "Now where is Lily?"

He heard a muffled coughing sound, and ran over to where Lily lay. She opened her eyes, seeing first him and then the destruction all around them. The studio was littered with the bodies of Feminazi Femborgs strewn about broken sets and equipment in disarray. Near her she could see one Femborg's fake skin falling off to reveal bullet-scored metal showing beneath her chest. Over near the news desk lay

Blabbera Wilters, in a fetal position with her hands on her groin, a double-bladed Emmy lying broken beside her.

"What in God's name just happened?" Lily asked.

"Exactly," he answered.

"What?" Lily blinked, and took in the shell-shocked camera crew and the weary producer, and then back at Jesus. "But - that answer doesn't even make sense."

"Twenty seconds until we're back from commercial," the producer called out from the booth, sounding a bit numb at this point. Jesus pulled Lily to her feet, and nodded to the New Disciples. They stood guard around her, as Jesus darted back before the camera.

The cameraman gave the same hand signals as last time. Three, two...

JESUS FACED THE CAMERA, and through it America. "Well, where were we? I'm'a cut right to it. My name is Jesus H. the Christ, and as you can see, I'm here to kick ass and save souls." He twirled both guns by the trigger guard, and pointed them both at the camera. "And I'm running out of souls. So you better get on the list. Too many of you've just sat back and watched, apathetic or even worse gutless, and let our God-given nation go to rot. Entitlements. Moochers. Taxmen. Unions. The government. Every channel but Fox. Taking away everything that's American about America!"

Jesus shook his head, bemused. "You let 'em do it. You didn't just let the dang media program boys to be gay, by taking away their manly violence and replacing them with Barney and the Teletubbies and cartoons where a villain doesn't even horribly die. You let so-called learning channels teach evolution to boys and girls. You let 'em take away your beautiful God-given gas-guzzling beasts of burden, and replace them with weak and ball-less hybrid cars and public transit – and you even started to believe the lie of Global Warming. You let 'em push that god-awful rappity rap music to the airwaves, and you let their TV shows tempt your daughters and wives into all kinds of sin outside of marriage. You even let the liberals broadcast women kissing women, and worse, men kissing men!" Jesus roared in anger. Aaron, Barclay and Hector wiped away tears. A few members of the studio crew who weren't paralyzed with fear were deeply moved.

Some others were not. "You can't really blame that on the liberals," a college intern interjected. "Sex on TV is driven by advertising, which means the businesses are using it to sell-"

Hector rammed his rifle butt across the intern's mouth. "Silence! Truth is speaking!"

"Yeah, Hector!" said Jesus. "That's the kinda faith I'm talking about! High five." They slapped hands. "Now listen up, America! This is your last chance! Get it together! I'm back, and I'm coming for the Demoncrats, and the coward too many call President, Bomraka the KenyAntichrist – and the dark powers behind 'em. I'm here to clean up the mess they made of this great world - so you can give me a hand, or you can get swept away by the red white and blue tide of God!" Jesus drew his silver-golden revolver with his left hand, and his stepfather's pistol with his right. He spun them both by the trigger, stopping with them pointed directly at the camera.

In Washington, in the Oval Office above Rosio Dawnhell's secret lair, President Bomraka stood in open-mouthed shock. The man who'd taken over the station and rendered some comically bizarre version of Blabbera Wilters helpless with a single kick to a delicate place, had come back from a strangely normal commercial break to call him the KenyAntichrist and a coward, in front of all of America and the world.

All the things he wanted to get accomplished this time around, that he hadn't been able to do in his first two terms. And this quickly, just a few days after he was back in office, it was all going off the rails again with these sideshow distractions.

Back in the station, Jesus came so close to the camera that the cameraman struggled to keep his face in focus. "Have I got your attention, haters of freedom?" He waved a gun at the wreckage of the studio. "I did this with my new disciples. Just three good men and my two God-blessed guns. Imagine what I'll do with all my Christian brothers and sisters behind me. We've only just begun."

Jesus stepped back from the camera a bit. "In the coming days, you'll hear more about us. For now, know this. If you're with us, you'll live with us in the Heaven we build on Earth. If you're against us, you haven't got a prayer. "

He put his stepfather's .45 in the small of his back, and held the gun Hieronymus had made to the camera. "For one among you, you know who you are - I am fulfilling my end of our agreement. I have what you want. So now it's past time for you to do right by me and my Father." He put that gun in his shoulder holster. "All the rest of you, know my sign." He made his sign of the cross, ending with his fist clenched over his heart. "It's called the Crucifist. Those of you who want to be saved, remember."

Jesus signaled to the cameraman. They cut the signal.

IN HER OWN White House office, Rosio sat nearly motionless. Her hand curled around her fine porcelain cup of green tea. Her whole body started shaking with rage. Her hand became a fist, crushing the cup into ceramic splinters. Mingled blood and porcelain dust dripped down onto the carpet.

She brushed the remains of the cup from her palms. "He defeated the entire View staff, in their combat forms – on live television! Before we could cut the signal! And then he laughed." She smashed her fists into her legs. "Laughed!"

"Ma'am," her assistant rang in fearfully. "Ma'am, the President wants to-"

"Not now!" she shrieked. How could this have gone so wrong? How could Wilters have screwed this up this bad?

Her mobile phone rang. It was Michael Max. She snatched the phone off her desk. "What in Hell's name do you want? I'm kind of busy!"

Max was momentarily taken aback. "I guess you've seen the broadcast?"

"Of course I have!" The glass screen of the phone started to bend in her grasp and developed a couple of cracks. She counted to ten, and managed to master her temper. "And next Bomraka will be asking how this happened and why we haven't caught this Jesus yet."

Max cursed. "Does the President know we're involved?"

"I don't know," said Rosio. "I don't even want to see him until I've gotten more of this cleaned up. How am I going to explain this to the media we haven't brainwashed yet?"

Max thought fast. "Tell them it was computer graphics."

"That could work," Rosio said. She calmed down somewhat. "Thank you for actually being useful. I can't believe what a mess Wilters has made of this." She tapped her fingers on the desk. "I think you know what must be done."

"Yes mistress," he said. His tone of servitude was undermined by the sound of a pastry being shoved into this mouth. "Reinstate the media fairness doctrine. With extreme prejudice."

She felt just a bit relieved again. "I knew I could depend on you." Michael Max was a professional documentarian. If anyone could end hope for all Christians it was he.

There was a knock outside her door. She whirled to attack, and managed to restrain herself in the nick of time. It was President Bomraka.

"What the Hell just happened?" he demanded.

"I know it looks bad. But-"

"Bad?" President Bomraka shook his head, as if he could not believe his rather oversized ears. "The whole point of your being my Chief of Staff is to help put out small fires like this. So they don't become four-alarm blazes like this one is now." He folded his arms. "I've had enough of this. I'll handle it myself."

She tried her best to hide the alarm she felt. Since he might not be the Antichrist she'd hoped for, what might happen if he got an inkling of what was really going on? "Are you sure that's a good idea? What if those Ghenbazi investigations begin again? You might not have time to catch him and keep that covered up."

Bomraka rolled his eyes. "You too?"

"What?" she asked.

"There was no Ghenbazi cover up," Bomraka said, exasperated.

"Come on, you can drop that front with me at least. Something must have happened there."

His expression became curious. "What do you mean? Drop what front?"

She scrambled for words. "Just that – well it seemed like there had to be something there for the conservatives to go after you like that."

"Rosio, what is going on with you?" He breathed out. "I'm telling you, there was nothing secret there at all. Some nuts attacked the US embassy before we could get soldiers there to help. That's all there is to it."

"Really?

"Yes, really! Don't you think I'd know? I'm sick of hearing about it." He held up his hands in exasperation. "Almost as sick as I am to hear about yet another stream of failures to catch this terrorist. Schedule a meeting with the NSA and FBI."

"Yes sir," said Rosio. "Will do, sir."

"Good. When you're done, clean out your desk."

It was her turn to not believe her ears. "What?"

"You heard me. If you hadn't been screwing around with off-book agencies that aren't even supposed to exist anymore instead of using actual law enforcement, a lot more people would be alive right now."

"That's not what's important," she said. "What's important is..."

She searched his eyes. Would he get it?

It looked like he wouldn't.

"What?" he said, pursuing her incomplete statement like a prosecutor. "What is more important than using the right law enforcement tools to stop this maniac?"

She was going to say, getting this vexing messiah in a way that would crush the spirit of Christians forever. If the man couldn't be killed in secret, it would have to be in public with a maximum of mockery. He couldn't live on in prison. He had to die in a way that would break their spirits once and for all, so they'd lose their hope for American patriarchal masculinity forever.

It looked like this man she had thought she understood, this man she had served as a fellow tool against the Christian patriarchy for so many years, wouldn't understand that reasoning at all.

Should she kill Bomraka too?

It was still possible he was a deep, deep cover plant. He was doing just too well at his cover. She couldn't take him out until she knew.

"Nothing sir," she said with forlorn voice. "I'm sorry I let you down. I'll - I'll make those appointments and go."

Bomraka's face softened. "You've been with me for a long time, Rosio. I just don't understand what happened to you. You have to understand – I can't keep giving you more chances. It's about my accountability now. I have a country to run, and if someone's not pulling through for our nation, then I owe it to the people to make it right. You understand, don't you?"

Every well-intentioned sentence was further evidence that he was a decent man. Every word of it was like a dagger in her heart. "Stop talking," she said through gritted teeth.

Bomraka eyes opened slightly. "What did you just say?" he demanded. She stared back at him. "I'll let it go," he said at last. "I understand you've had a hard day. This is hard for me too." He left.

On his way back to the Oval Office, Bomraka considered the oddness of their exchange. It saddened him. He'd long observed how often seemingly perceptive people could be so blind to themselves. The way she had carried on, you'd think that *he* had been the one who let *her* down.

32

Jesus faced the camera, and through it America. "Well, where were we? I'm'a cut right to it. My name is Jesus H. the Christ, and as you can see, I'm here to kick ass and save souls." He twirled both guns by the trigger guard, and pointed them both at the camera. "And I'm running out of souls. So you better get on the list. Too many of you've just sat back and watched, apathetic or even worse gutless, and let our God-given nation go to rot. Entitlements. Moochers. Taxmen. Unions. The government. Every channel but Fox. Taking away everything that's American about America!"

Jesus shook his head, bemused. "You let 'em do it. You didn't just let the dang media program boys to be gay, by taking away their manly violence and replacing them with Barney and the Teletubbies and cartoons where a villain doesn't even horribly die. You let so-called learning channels teach evolution to boys and girls. You let 'em take away your beautiful God-given gas-guzzling beasts of burden, and replace them with weak and ball-less hybrid cars and public transit – and you even started to believe the lie of Global Warming. You let 'em push that god-awful rappity rap music to the airwaves, and you let their TV shows tempt your daughters and wives into all kinds of sin outside of marriage. You even let the liberals broadcast women kissing women, and worse, men kissing men!" Jesus roared in anger. Aaron, Barclay and Hector wiped away tears. A few members of the studio crew who weren't paralyzed with fear were deeply moved.

Some others were not. "You can't really blame that on the liberals," a college intern interjected. "Sex on TV is driven by advertising, which means the businesses are using it to sell-"

Hector rammed his rifle butt across the intern's mouth. "Silence! Truth is speaking!"

"Yeah, Hector!" said Jesus. "That's the kinda faith I'm talking about! High five." They slapped hands. "Now listen up, America! This is your last chance! Get it together! I'm back, and I'm coming for the Demoncrats, and the coward too many call President, Bomraka the KenyAntichrist – and the dark powers behind 'em. I'm here to clean up the mess they made of this great world - so you can give me a hand, or you can get swept away by the red white and blue tide of God!" Jesus drew his silver-golden revolver with his left hand, and his stepfather's pistol with his right. He spun them both by the trigger, stopping with them pointed directly at the camera.

In Washington, in the Oval Office above Rosio Dawnhell's secret lair, President Bomraka stood in open-mouthed shock. The man who'd taken over the station and rendered some comically bizarre version of Blabbera Wilters helpless with a single kick to a delicate place, had come back from a strangely normal commercial break to call him the KenyAntichrist and a coward, in front of all of America and the world.

All the things he wanted to get accomplished this time around, that he hadn't been able to do in his first two terms. And this quickly, just a few days after he was back in office, it was all going off the rails again with these sideshow distractions.

Back in the station, Jesus came so close to the camera that the cameraman struggled to keep his face in focus. "Have I got your attention, haters of freedom?" He waved a gun at the wreckage of the studio. "I did this with my new disciples. Just three good men and my two God-blessed guns. Imagine what I'll do with all my Christian brothers and sisters behind me. We've only just begun."

Jesus stepped back from the camera a bit. "In the coming days, you'll hear more about us. For now, know this. If you're with us, you'll live with us in the Heaven we build on Earth. If you're against us, you haven't got a prayer. "

He put his stepfather's .45 in the small of his back, and held the gun Hieronymus had made to the camera. "For one among you, you know who you are - I am fulfilling my end of our agreement. I have what you want. So now it's past time for you to do right by me and my Father." He put that gun in his shoulder holster. "All the rest of you, know my sign." He made his sign of the cross, ending with his fist clenched over his heart. "It's called the Crucifist. Those of you who want to be saved, remember."

Jesus signaled to the cameraman. They cut the signal.

IN HER OWN White House office, Rosio sat nearly motionless. Her hand curled around her fine porcelain cup of green tea. Her whole body started shaking with rage. Her hand became a fist, crushing the cup into ceramic splinters. Mingled blood and porcelain dust dripped down onto the carpet.

She brushed the remains of the cup from her palms. "He defeated the entire View staff, in their combat forms – on live television! Before we could cut the signal! And then he laughed." She smashed her fists into her legs. "Laughed!"

"Ma'am," her assistant rang in fearfully. "Ma'am, the President wants to-"

"Not now!" she shrieked. How could this have gone so wrong? How could Wilters have screwed this up this bad?

Her mobile phone rang. It was Michael Max. She snatched the phone off her desk. "What in Hell's name do you want? I'm kind of busy!"

Max was momentarily taken aback. "I guess you've seen the broadcast?"

"Of course I have!" The glass screen of the phone started to bend in her grasp and developed a couple of cracks. She counted to ten, and managed to master her temper. "And next Bomraka will be asking how this happened and why we haven't caught this Jesus yet."

Max cursed. "Does the President know we're involved?"

"I don't know," said Rosio. "I don't even want to see him until I've gotten more of this cleaned up. How am I going to explain this to the media we haven't brainwashed yet?"

Max thought fast. "Tell them it was computer graphics."

"That could work," Rosio said. She calmed down somewhat. "Thank you for actually being useful. I can't believe what a mess Wilters has made of this." She tapped her fingers on the desk. "I think you know what must be done."

"Yes mistress," he said. His tone of servitude was undermined by the sound of a pastry being shoved into this mouth. "Reinstate the media fairness doctrine. With extreme prejudice."

She felt just a bit relieved again. "I knew I could depend on you." Michael Max was a professional documentarian. If anyone could end hope for all Christians it was he.

There was a knock outside her door. She whirled to attack, and managed to restrain herself in the nick of time. It was President Bomraka.

"What the Hell just happened?" he demanded.

"I know it looks bad. But-"

"Bad?" President Bomraka shook his head, as if he could not believe his rather oversized ears. "The whole point of your being my Chief of Staff is to help put out small fires like this. So they don't become four-alarm blazes like this one is now." He folded his arms. "I've had enough of this. I'll handle it myself."

She tried her best to hide the alarm she felt. Since he might not be the Antichrist she'd hoped for, what might happen if he got an inkling of what was really going on? "Are you sure that's a good idea? What if those Ghenbazi investigations begin again? You might not have time to catch him and keep that covered up."

Bomraka rolled his eyes. "You too?"

"What?" she asked.

"There was no Ghenbazi cover up," Bomraka said, exasperated.

"Come on, you can drop that front with me at least. Something must have happened there."

His expression became curious. "What do you mean? Drop what front?"

She scrambled for words. "Just that – well it seemed like there had to be something there for the conservatives to go after you like that."

"Rosio, what is going on with you?" He breathed out. "I'm telling you, there was nothing secret there at all. Some nuts attacked the US embassy before we could get soldiers there to help. That's all there is to it."

"Really?

"Yes, really! Don't you think I'd know? I'm sick of hearing about it." He held up his hands in exasperation. "Almost as sick as I am to hear about yet another stream of failures to catch this terrorist. Schedule a meeting with the NSA and FBI."

"Yes sir," said Rosio. "Will do, sir."

"Good. When you're done, clean out your desk."

It was her turn to not believe her ears. "What?"

"You heard me. If you hadn't been screwing around with off-book agencies that aren't even supposed to exist anymore instead of using actual law enforcement, a lot more people would be alive right now."

"That's not what's important," she said. "What's important is..."

She searched his eyes. Would he get it?

It looked like he wouldn't.

"What?" he said, pursuing her incomplete statement like a prosecutor. "What is more important than using the right law enforcement tools to stop this maniac?"

She was going to say, getting this vexing messiah in a way that would crush the spirit of Christians forever. If the man couldn't be killed in secret, it would have to be in public with a maximum of mockery. He couldn't live on in prison. He had to die in a way that would break their spirits once and for all, so they'd lose their hope for American patriarchal masculinity forever.

It looked like this man she thought she'd understand, this man she had served as a fellow tool against the Christian patriarchy for so many years, wouldn't understand that reasoning at all.

Should she kill Bomraka too?

It was still possible he was a deep, deep cover plant. He was doing just too well at his cover. She couldn't take him out until she knew.

"Nothing sir," she said with forlorn voice. "I'm sorry I let you down. I'll - I'll make those appointments and go."

Bomraka's face softened. "You've been with me for a long time, Rosio. I just don't understand what happened to you. You have to understand – I can't keep giving you more chances. It's about my accountability now. I have a country to run, and if someone's not pulling through for our nation, then I owe it to the people to make it right. You understand, don't you?"

Every well-intentioned sentence was further evidence that he was a decent man. Every word of it was like a dagger in her heart. "Stop talking," she said through gritted teeth.

Bomraka eyes opened slightly. "What did you just say?" he demanded. She stared back at him. "I'll let it go," he said at last. "I understand you've had a hard day. This is hard for me too." He left.

On his way back to the Oval Office, Bomraka considered the oddness of their exchange. It saddened him. He'd long observed how often seemingly perceptive people could be so blind to themselves. The way she had carried on, you'd think that *he* had been the one to *her* let down.

33

Back in the TV station, the New Disciples bashed the cameras until they would never work again. Those Femborgs that still looked alive had their bionic arms and legs tied down with heavy cables, and were gagged with their own portable latte smoothie bottles that had been found in their abandoned purses.

"Do you think Bomraka knows about this?" asked Aaron. "It's just hard to believe an American President could be this evil."

"Open your eyes, man," said Barclay. "This kinda tech costs a lot of money. It ain't corporations, or we'd've seen it advertised. So that means government." He loaded several more shells into this shotgun. "I think we better get a move on, Lord."

"Right." Jesus addressed the crew members who'd accepted his salvation. "You five are Christians now. Log onto AOL and find the revolution." Three of the crewmembers nodded gratefully and ran.

The makeup girl and hair stylist remained. "Take us with you," the makeup girl begged.

"Why do you want to come along?"

"I was a lesbian," she said. "I never knew a real Christian man 'til I saw you. I can't believe I ever thought literary criticism and jasmine green tea would be enough. I - I need to follow you!"

"Welcome aboard, sister!" Jesus smiled and clapped a hand on her shoulder. "What's your name?"

"Marcia," she said soft and shyly.

"Bring me too, oh Lord!" said the hair stylist.

"And you are?"

"My name is Steve," the hair stylist said, barely daring to meet Jesus' searching eyes. "My dad gave me a strong name and tried to raise me right, but I've always thought I want men. Now I realize that's just not morally right to want them."

"You mean 'wanted' as in past tense, right?" Jesus said. "Because..."

"Well, I do love you," Steve said.

"Um, that's cool ordinarily," Jesus said. "But...uh, love me how?"

"You know, like I look up to, I think you're a great example of a man..."

"Not helping your case, bro," said Jesus.

Steve sighed. "Look, I guess God dealt me an extra tough hand. Or I made a choice I don't remember. But I can see from your example that I can overcome it. I can prove myself to God, and I can procreate as he intended. From being close to your shining, muscular example of a real man."

Jesus stroked his beard and thought a bit. "Think you two can marry each other?"

"For you," they both said. They moved together and held each other's hands as they gazed adoringly at him.

"Good," said Jesus. "Then your name is no longer Marcia. Make it Marci instead. Less lesbian."

"Marci." She tried it out. "I like it."

"Then you're in," said Jesus. "Just don't... just make sure you two stick to each other. Okay?"

"You got it, sir," said Steve. The newly renamed Marci nodded in agreement and shared devotion.

"Then welcome to the New Disciples!" They cheered. Aaron, Barclay and Hector shook their hands. "Okay," said Jesus. "Now let's roll. The Demoncrats at the top aren't slouches. They'll be headed here double time." Jesus looked around at the remaining crew. "Last chance. Anyone else here want to get saved and earn God's mercy?"

No one else spoke for a bit. The intern who'd interrupted the Lord's broadcast gingerly touched the swelling side of his face from where it had met Hector's rifle. He spoke anyway.

"Shouldn't mercy be free, if it's really mercy?"

Jesus laughed. "Ain't your jaw sore enough, boy?" He shook his head. "Only socialists think you should get anything without working for it."

"But mercy isn't a physical thing," the kid argued. "It doesn't even cost anything. It's as cost-free as, I don't know, not being a dick to someone…"

Jesus moved on to the prone form of Blabbera Wilters, still prone on the floor and now bound with cables and a portable latte machine stuffed inside her mouth. "How 'bout you?" He nodded to his vanquished foe. "Even you still get a chance. Nod your head."

She stared back at him, and shook her head now.

"You've made your choice." Surveying the wrecked studio, he found it very satisfying. Yet something was nagging him. What was it? He realized he wasn't seeing Lily. His eyes went straight to the studio's entrance. Sure enough, there she was sneaking towards the door.

Time to see how his newest New Disciples follow orders. "Steve, Marci? You want to bring her back here?"

They scrambled to obey. "Let go of me, you idiots!" she yelled, kicking and pushing as they dragged her back. "What is wrong with you?" Jesus couldn't help but notice what a sight she was, in her torn dress and disheveled hair, more beautiful than ever in her anger.

"This is how it must be," said Steve.

"What are you doing?" Lily demanded.

"We're saving you," said Marci. Jesus saw that Steve barely glanced at Lily's figure, which was encased in a torn blouse and exposed bra. Whereas Marci stared a little longer than Jesus thought she needed to. He sighed. Well, this was what he had to work with.

"I've changed my mind, okay?" said Lily. "I don't know what

happened here or how I got knocked out, but this is a bit crazier than I feel like dealing with."

Jesus shook his head. "You're not safe here anymore. You really have to come with us."

"No way. You go on ahead without me."

He smiled wistfully. "I really wish I had time for this. Fellas, gag her and bring her to the car."

"What the FU-" her unladylike language was cut off by the swift insertion of a cleaning rag into her mouth. Jesus was proud to see how quickly they duck taped her arms, as if they'd been doing this for years. Then Aaron and Barclay picked up the struggling Lily. They entered the hallway.

"There's a stairway that bypasses the security desk downstairs," said Steve.

"There," added Marci, pointing to a nondescript door off to their right.

"Double time!" said Jesus. They ran into the stairwell and took it all the way down. It let them out into the parking lot on the side of the building. No security had arrived yet. "To the car!" ordered Jesus.

They ran for it, Aaron and Barclay struggling with Lily. Hector jumped behind the wheel. Jesus and Aaron helped Steve and Marci wrangle the struggling Lily into the station wagon's third row of seats. At Jesus' direction, Steve and Marci sat on either side of her. Then Aaron and Jesus got into the second row. Barclay jumped in the front passenger seat next to Hector and switched on the police scanner. As the last door closed, they sped off down the street.

Rosio packed her most prized work possessions in a large box, and closed it. She could not risk them being seen by anyone in the Bomraka administration, since she could no longer trust him to be against humanity. This little box of items also meant more to her than she had expected. Here was a piece of the first skull she had used to drink the blood of an enemy; there was a signed invisible ink statement from her fellow feminists showing the secret recipe for soylent green lattes, mixed with the ashes of a flag. The rest of her books, honorary degrees and awards were camouflage and could go into the trash for all she cared.

The box barely fit in her Prius. It was an unwelcome irony that the vehicle created to combat American muscle car patriarchy could barely fit the accumulated artifacts of a lifetime of effort to end America. She opened the back door and tried to wedge the box in. The corner of the box resisted. She gnashed her teeth and shoved, but it still wouldn't quite make it.

She set it on the ground and fought back the need to cry or break a stranger's neck. It hardly seemed fair. There was so much more she could do, and so many more Christians to do it to. This one lone man Jesus had finally appeared out of hiding and it had all gone south so quickly, in a bad way.

Her cellphone rang. She dropped the box in frustration to the ground and snatched her phone from her pocket. Was she going to get any time to figure out what to do with this mess?

She saw the caller ID, and her annoyance changed to anger. She took the call. "Hello?" she said sweetly.

"Mistress!" It was Blabbera Wilters, her voice desperate. "I just managed to break free. We can still capture him! He's taking a captive with him, which just has to mean they'll be slowed down –"

"Never mind," Rosio cooed reassuringly. "No need to worry. It's all going to be resolved. You don't need to concern yourself with Jesus anymore."

"But..." Blabbera didn't quite sound comforted. "Mistress I'm sorry we failed you. We can still get him for you. Just give us a chance!"

"Listen honey, it's okay, I understand. Don't worry, like I said. Just stay right where you are, and we'll figure out the next step."

"Are you sure? "

Rosio's voice hardened. "Damn sure." A thought occurred to her. "I do have a question, though."

"Anything, mistress!"

"What was it like to fight him?"

There was a pause before she answered. Rosio knew that pause –
Blabbera was wondering if she should lie.

Wilters said, "I would like to tell you different. But he was the ultimate patriarchal male, and he was...magnificent."

The speed that Blabbera had blurted out her sentence, led Rosio
to guess that she was telling the truth. Rosio sighed. "Yes, I was afraid
of that. Of course he would be the ultimate in Christian manhood. I
just thought Blabs Strident and I trained you better." She shook her
head sadly. "Together with your government healthcare cyborg
enhancements, that should have been enough to withstand even a
man like him."

"We can still get him, we really can! Please let us!"

"Don't worry," Rosio soothed, like a mother cooing her baby into
sleep. "Just wait right there. I have an operative who's coming
for you."

34

Jesus cautioned his newest two disciples against the sin of using seat belts, and thus agreeing to the Demoncrat game of job creator regulation. The station wagon broke through the closed gate at the end of the parking lot and careened around the corner, throwing the un-seat-belted passengers around the vinyl seats.

Once they had all found their seating again, Jesus pointed out the window at the sky. "And would you look at that glorious sunset!" The skies were yellow, purple and gold, with a red moon hanging low. "The very clouds are on fire with the promise of God's justice. Like God's vengeance, it is beautiful and terrible to behold." He spread his arms and leaned back, causing Aaron to move aside and give him more room. "That's a message. We're on God's track."

Jesus took out a pack, and lit a cigarette. He took a drag and offered the pack to his disciples.

Lily tried to speak. Jesus nodded to Marci, who took her gag off.

Lily then turned to the latest New Disciples. "Marcia, Steven - what the Hell are you doing?"

"Language!" said Steve.

"We're Marci and Steve now," said Marcia. She took Steve's hand. "We're married in Christ."

"And saved forever, by the greatest man who ever lived," said Steve as he stared at Jesus adoringly.

Lily blinked. "Uh-huh," she said. She turned toward Jesus. "Let me go, you son of a bitch."

"Nothing doing," said Jesus. "I took on a job. That includes getting you safely back to your grandfather. But fear not – I will keep my word. I will allow no harm to come to you."

"My grandfather again," she snarled. "What does he have to do with this?"

"He loves you and wants to save your soul. I can relate."

"Alright, that's enough. Let me out or I'll start screaming."

"Go right ahead. Didn't think you liked the gag that much." Lily stamped her foot in anger. "Barclay, any word on us on the police channels?"

"That's the thing," Barclay said. "There's nothing. No chatter at all. Totally quiet. It should be full of what we just did. They should have the po-po looking all over town."

"Who's the po-po?" asked Aaron.

"You know, the 5-oh. The Fuzz. Charlie Bobo. "

"Oh, right," said Aaron, still confused. "Are you messing with me?"

"Little bit," Barclay admitted with a grin.

"The point is, the media blackout is already in place," Jesus mused. "If they've even shut down the police, then..."

"Something pursues us!" Hector called. He barely managed to keep his eyes on the road as all the other passengers looked behind them.

A humming sound approached and gradually grew into a roar. The source of the noise came into view - an approaching squadron of six black helicopters.

The formation swooped, turned and faced the ABC Atlanta building. In unison, as if six of the black helicopters were one strange beast with a single mind, they fired missiles at the building. It exploded in flame and began to collapse. The helicopters continued hovering, sending several more rockets into the growing cloud of debris.

"Keep driving!" Jesus ordered.

"I stop for nothing, mi patron!" Hector gripped the wheel, and slammed the gas pedal all the way down.

"They might think we're still inside," said Jesus. "Make that next corner! Get us out of line of sight!" They turned right with a screech of tires, bracing themselves as best they could without seatbelts.

Lily turned pale. "How – why - "

"Oh my God!" Steve cried. "All those people.... why did they...maybe there are survivors! We have to help!" he started to open the door.

Jesus gripped him by the shoulder. "No, Steve!"

"Lord, I – I don't understand...we worked with them," said Steve. "Those were our friends."

" I know those in the station helped the damned," said Aaron. "But did they all have to die?"

"Yes," said Jesus gently. "Sometimes you have to let those who oppose you die screaming as they beg for mercy. This is what it means to be a Christian."

An amplified cough rang out from above, then the sound of something doughy being swallowed. An oddly familiar voice ricocheted off of all the buildings around them. "Any of you in those cars down there! Do you happen to know anything about Jesus Christ? I just want to interview him for my next movie!"

"Who is that?" asked Aaron. "I've heard him before. So...so smug. So sure."

Barclay took out his binoculars and strained to see the approaching menace. "All of their windows are too dark to see, except the largest one in the center. In that one...." Barclay shook his head. "I wonder if I'm seeing things. I can barely make out a ... fat man in a baseball cap and glasses.

"My God," said Aaron. "I know whose voice that is!"

Jesus nodded grimly. "They're sending Michael Max."

Hector responded with a tire-squealing turn and acceleration which pushed them back into their seats.

Jesus' brow furrowed with thought. "They haven't shot at us yet, they must not know what car we're in. Hector, take the next turn and park anywhere, then kill the engine!"

Hector found a spot and hit the brakes, barely stopping before colliding with the parked car ahead. "Everybody get down and away from the windows! Steve and Marci, hold Lily's mouth shut!"

"You son of ummmmphh!!!"

They all held their breath as the black helicopters flew by.

"Keep your voices low, or their liberal microphones might detect us," said Jesus.

"Shouldn't we fight them?" murmured Aaron. "We've got guns now!"

"Not with the weapons we have right now," Jesus whispered back. "Trust me, those helicopters are a whole 'nother level of deadly. We've got to play it smart. Hector, start the engine and turn around real slow. Take the next right. Then do another half a mile east, and we'll ditch the wagon."

"Our faithful steed?" asked Hector, his low voice now filled with sadness.

"I am truly sorry. It's a beautiful car. And it runs on real gasoline. But we have to do what we have to."

"I understand." Hector started up the station wagon. "This will be our last journey together." They found their way down a series of side streets.

The amplified voice rained down some more, accompanied by the helicopter blades coming back. "We know you're around here somewhere," said Michael Max's voice.

Lily bit down hard on Steve's hand. "OW!" he cried.

"Darn it, Steve!" said Jesus.

"Is that really Michael Max?" Aaron's voice cracked in panic.

"It sure is. And if we let him find us with those helicopters, he's gonna edit us out of the context of America." Jesus gritted his teeth. "All the other cars are stopping. We have to get off the streets before-"

Explosions in the distance shook every building on their block. Debris rained down around the car as they passed. New explosions began as the previous ones faded, coming closer and closer.

"They're expanding the destruction radius!" Jesus knew there were only moments before instant death. "Hector, pull over!" The car screeched to a stop.

"Everyone out! You two, hold Lily and keep her from running!"

"How did they find us?" Aaron asked, stumbling and grabbing for his backpack with shaking hands.

"They're probably just wiping out anything they can find near the station," Jesus said grimly. "We need to get underground, now! We need a manhole."

"What kind of a manhole?" said Steve, a bit too eagerly.

Jesus looked at him a little strangely, but let it go. "There's one, back by the intersection! Hector, get the tire iron from the trunk. The rest of you with me!"

Hector ran back to the car, opened the back door and grabbed a tire iron. Then he went to the driver's side, turned on the car, and put it in gear. It started down the street, away from the manhole.

"Good thinking!" said Jesus. "Gimme that crowbar." He went to work prying the manhole cover with the tire iron. "Rusted shut! Barclay, give me a hand here!"

Barclay and then Hector joined their strength with Jesus, as the driverless car continued its new journey. Lily tried to run. Aaron and Hector saw her and managed to snag her by the tape around her wrists.

Jesus saw that they were occupied. Steve and Marci stood to the side, appearing overwhelmed and frozen in confusion. "Snap out of it!" Jesus bellowed. "Get over here and give us a hand!"

Steve ran over and added his efforts to leverage the manhole cover free. They heard the black helicopters approaching, bringing with them fire and destruction. A rocket came in from around the corner, adjusted course, headed towards the moving station wagon and blew it into bits.

"On three! One, two - for freedom!" said Jesus.

The rust of decades finally gave way before them, and the cover broke free.

"Everybody in!" Jesus pulled out his buck knife and cut the tape holding Lily's hands.

"I don't understand what's happening, but I'm not going in that filthy hole-" Lily began.

"They're blowing up everything!" Jesus yelled. "Do you think they'll stop and ask for your BomrakaCare ID? You get in there before I knock you out and throw you in!"

Angry but aware of his point, Lily stepped into the tunnel and lowered herself down the ladder. The rest of the party followed. Last to leave, Jesus heard the helicopters. He jumped halfway in, grabbed the manhole cover, and pulled it shut behind him - just as a shower of flames sprayed toward them, followed by a massive aftershock.

Jesus muscled the manhole all the way back into place, and descended the rest of the way into the sewer. His boots landed in an inch of dirty water. His eyes adjusted to the darkness, occasionally disrupted by daylight filtering in through gratings.

"Alright," he said. "Now we better get going. They're probably going to keep firing until they've flattened everything they think we could have driven to in the amount of time since the we left the station."

"I'm not going anywhere with you, you maniac," Lily spat.

Any possible response was drowned out by another huge explosion. Gouts of flame shot through holes in the manhole cover above them, followed by a dribble of rubble and ashes.

"I just want an interview," Michael Max's amplified voice came in over the crackling flames and sounds of falling debris. "It'll be a great platform for you to reach people. Just a couple questions. Anybody?"

"Guess what?" said Jesus dryly to Lily. "You're sure not going back up there. Once the black helicopters have saturated the area, they'll send in ground troops. There's no way they'll just accept your word you weren't involved in this. They'll take you away to a FEMA reeducation camp, and you'll never be seen again."

"None of that nonsense really exists," Lily said. "You've ruined my life over a bunch of delusions!"

"If we're so delusional, then why are they attacking?" Jesus pointed out. She had no answer. "I've given you the chance to save your soul. One day you'll see. In the meantime, these are the cards you've been dealt."

"I refuse to accept any of this nonsense."

Jesus scratched his head. "Okay, that's all the time we have. Aaron? Hector? Grab her arms."

Hector nodded, and grabbed Lily. "Get your hands off me!" she exclaimed. Aaron hesitated. "Do it," Jesus repeated. "It's for her own good." Aaron acquiesced and grabbed Lily's other arm.

"Now Barclay, gag her."

"Don't you dare!" said Lily. "You-"

Barclay put a strip of duck tape over her mouth and wrapped it around her head. Aaron and Hector struggled mightily to hold her.

"I guess we gotta tape her arms again too."

"Mmmf!" she protested.

"Look, it's either that or hogtie you," Jesus explained. "It won't be comfortable for anyone, least of all you, and we're going to go where we're going to go anyway."

Lily's eyes flashed rage, but she stopped struggling.

There was a grinding sound. Jesus pressed his finger to his lips and pointed to the manhole cover. They all stayed silent as they looked up. Someone above was trying to see if the manhole cover would open. He motioned them down the tunnel, and they disappeared into the enveloping darkness.

35

***

President Bomraka stared at the desk before him. The time was right, and even necessary, for him to formulate the agenda for the upcoming peace summit. It would set the tone for his entire third administration. Yet try as he did, he couldn't concentrate on it.

He had thought the Thruppence administration had been unexpected, for him as well as many others. As a private citizen again, he'd watched from the sidelines as Thruppence treaded water well over his head. Bomraka did his best to lessen the damage by returning to his roots of community organizing. Then the unexpected happened, and he'd had this third chance come up to move the country forward from the driver's seat.

And then, as soon as he'd started this Christian terrorist group had emerged, and challenged his authority with this situation of total insanity. It really seemed that we would have to wrap this up before he could get his head back into larger things.

His secretary was already busy taking on the workload that was until a couple of hours ago Rosio's, so he chose not to bother her with this additional task. Even if her schedule was less occupied, he wanted to take care of this himself. It took him several rings to get the directors of the FBI and NSA. He put them together on a conference call. Without preamble he launched into his new request - all of the information they could find on this Christian terrorist, on his desk within the hour.

Next, he ordered his new Chief of Staff to schedule a press conference with all the major networks.

Jesus, the New Disciples, and their unwilling captive Lily traveled deeper and deeper into the underground beneath Atlanta. The tunnel inclined downwards, and soon became too dark to see. Aaron reached into his backpack, pulled out three flashlights and gave two to Jesus.

"Good thinking ahead," said Jesus.

Aaron beamed. "Always be prepared, like we were for your second coming."

Jesus kept one and handed the other to Barclay, who he signaled should take the rear.

Soon they were far enough from the surface that Jesus considered it safe to converse in whispers. "Anyone have a compass?"

"Here," Barclay reached into his pack and handed one to Jesus.

"Okay." Jesus shined his flashlight on it. "This way must be towards the river. If we can find tunnels going in that direction, then we should eventually come out there." He examined their faces. All but Lily were with him – and even she did not want to go back the way they came. She might be trouble later on, but for now she would go with them.

"Let's go. I'll take the rear this time."

Jesus let each of them walk past him as he considered them one by one.

Barclay came by him first. He was adjusting his backpack to make sure it wouldn't block his holster. The man was as solid a disciple as one could ask for. Dependable. Reliable. He knew what was right. He was proof blacks could be saved from the evils of government hand-outs and the Demoncratic party.

Next to pass Jesus was Hector. A fine man in his own right, with a good family. With his faith in the Lord and his passion for right-eousness, he had overcome his heritage of immigration and Catholi-cism. A man with fine taste in muscle cars, which was important for any true American.

Aaron came along after Hector, smiling as he passed. Jesus smiled back. Of all his disciples, Jesus related to Aaron the most. The man wasn't the toughest on the outside, but inside he was a true idealist. He knew how things should be, he wanted the world to be that way for the good of everyone - and most importantly, he had the guts not to let the so-called facts change his mind. The man still could be sentimental. It would take time for the holy fires of their job to harden his soft will into steel, so he could clearly see the proper place for compassion – those who followed God's true word before all others.

Steve and Marci walked by him next. They had some distance to go upon their journey. He was sure that with enough faith they could find their way. For now, both looked at him a bit intensely. He gave Steve a bit more room than Marci.

Last to walk by him was Lily. She did not so much as give a frosty glance in his direction. It made him smile. He admired her spirit.

He had accepted the job to save her, and so far that choice seemed to be in accordance with God's plan. Yet he also couldn't deny the attraction and affection he'd felt for her from the moment he'd seen her face. Did his Father mean her to be a path to get great weapons, or as part of Jesus' mission in her own right, or as a simple test of his faith? Was there a chance she'd pull him off his path?

It was difficult enough that she was a woman, let alone so beauti-ful, let alone so much like the woman still in his heart.

As Jesus followed the party, his mind wandered back to his mother telling him about women when he was only 12 years old.

His mother Mary had taken her time in talking with her son about the opposite sex. It was, in fact, the only time she talked at length about the biggest event in her and Joseph's life - her impregnation by the Angel. She told how the agent of God had come to visit her behind the hay at the county fair. There, shielded from others' sight, the Angel informed her that she, of humble birth, had been picked from all the Earth as the most righteous woman of the most righteous nation. If she chose, she could give birth to the savior of all mankind.

She knew this Angel's great beauty meant he must be straight from God. After all, God would surely not allow some demon to appear thus and speak in His name. But Mary had already promised herself in marriage to Joseph, and told the angel so. The angel responded that if Mary loved God before all others, that also meant before her future mortal husband. Would she put her marriage to her love above the will of God?

After a moment of dismay she consented. Twenty minutes or so of naked exertion later, the beautiful angel had placed God's seed within her.

Jesus watched the conflicted emotions on her face as she told the tale, and even at his age he see the heartbreak this had caused her. Gently he asked, "What does that mean for me?"

She took his face in her hands and smiled. "My dear son, what this means is that sometimes you might have to break someone's heart, and I mean *hard*, to do what God asks of you. You might not even know if it's the right thing when you do it. It's just up to you to make your best guess." Mary smiled and sighed, brushing Jesus' tousled hair out of his eyes. "You're too young to pick your wife just yet. You have your whole destiny before you."

"But what if I don't want nobody else?"

"That might not be up to you my son, I'm sorry. You have a destiny." She smiled wistfully. "This girl you like, this Alaine - well, love her or not you're probably gonna have to find your way on past her."

"But surely God wants me to save myself for marriage right? Why have me love other women after if I love her right now?"

"Because even if you weren't the messiah, you're becoming a man. And if men are manly they want to look out a bunch of women and even try out a few before they pick one."

The younger Jesus nodded as he tried to get his head around it. "I don't think I totally get it," he admitted. "Like, if girls aren't supposed to fool around a lot, but guys are supposed to as much as possible and only with girls, then how are there even gonna be enough girls to fool around with? I mean, women are s'posed to want to, you know, do stuff? Right? Or not?"

"I'm guessing you mean make love, sweetheart?" Her eyes twinkled. "Yes, of course. They just aren't supposed to want it as much as men do, or with more than one man in their entire life."

"Okay." It still didn't make sense to him. "Why is that?"

"'Cause they aren't supposed to."

"But what if I love one of 'em?" Like Alaine...

"Never ever love a girl who you wouldn't want to have children with," his mother said. "And you wouldn't want to love a girl who's had a lot of men, would you? That means she isn't choosy."

"Oh." He frowned. "Okay....and I don't have to be choosy?"

"Not as much. That's where God makes it easy. It's the man's job to find the woman, you see. She looks as attractive as she can and waits passively for a man to find her worthy and fulfill her dreams, just as God intended. Says so in the Bible!"

"Where's that?" asked Jesus, surprised. "I haven't seen that."

Mary waved her hands dismissively. "Oh, it's right there in 'Song of Solomon' and 'Leviticus'. You just have to read between the lines."

"What was it like with...pop, once you were with the Angel?" he pressed. For some reason he felt he had to know.

She hid her eyes and lowered her head as she spoke. It was still tough for her to talk about it, after all these years. "Once the angel was...done with me, he reminded me that I was the most important woman in the world. He told me I would need faith to see me through until the Rapture - and I would need it in spades. He was right. But with that faith, all has turned out as it should. I have that future grace, and I also have you to be grateful for." She placed her hands on her son's shoulders. "We real Christians know that God loves the best and strongest above all. When the greater man comes along, all below him must obey him. That man deserves anything he wants, including any woman. It's God's will that the weaker man gives way. Even Joseph had to understand this. And bless his good strong heart and faith, he has."

Jesus had nodded, for once without words.

"We always wanted a boy," Mary continued. "So you are his son, in his heart."

"And you two never wanted another child?"

Mary shrugged. "I guess that just wasn't in the cards. Son, someday the Rapture will come. And on that day your war will begin. Before that, have fun while you can. Go and get that girl while you can. Just don't be so sure she is to be your one and only." She sighed. "On this Earth, no one's in our life forever."

THAT MEMORY WAS one of his clearest of all his childhood, and more than a little bittersweet. It was one of the closest talks he'd ever had with this mother, and one of the last times they'd spoken before the Rapture came and both his mortal parents disappeared. His Alaine had left his life soon after too. For all the women he'd been with after that, both on his mother's advice and on his mission to save as many as he could, he really didn't want anyone else besides Alaine. Other girls looked pretty, hot even. All of that paled next to what he'd had with Alaine - someone he could talk to not as a savior, but as himself. Even though she didn't really believe he was the messiah, she loved him. Even if he was crazy, and even if he might not have been sent to save the world.

As a young man, he had no idea how powerful just being listened to could be. He only found out how much he felt for her when she was gone. He was pretty sure he might never see her again, even in the afterlife. They were headed to different places now....

JESUS WAS BROUGHT BACK to the present by the sound of his disciples and Lily tromping ahead of him in puddles. There was a dark path was ahead, it didn't really serve to be distracted by what was behind him. Still, he was.

36

———

After a few hours, Jesus and his band of New Disciples and one unwilling fellow traveler reached a junction of tunnels. "Here's as good a place as any to take a break for the night," said Jesus. "We need to pace ourselves."

"What do you think it's like up top?" asked Barclay.

"Not good..." said Jesus. "I'll bet Bomraka's men have cordoned off the city, and are searching block by block. Some ruse the EPA will blame on a toxic tanker spill. The only way out is keep going under all their forces." Jesus flicked his spent cigarette onto the tunnel's floor. "We might have to stay underground for a while, like Christians in Roman times."

"I need to get a message to Hannah and my children soon," said Aaron. "They must be so worried about me."

Jesus shook his head. "No can do, Aaron. I feel for you, but we have to stay low. If you've instructed them well enough and they keep their faith, they'll be fine." Aaron was not at all happy with this notion, but nodded his acceptance.

Jesus addressed the group as a whole. "We can follow these to the river, and from there we should be able to find our way free of our oppressors. In the meantime, let's take a break and pray." He smiled at Lily. "I'd take that tape off, but I'm pretty sure I don't want to hear your prayers right now."

Her eyes flashed rage for a second, and then subsided. Then she lunged straight at him with a head-butt.

He dodged and chuckled. "You've got spirit, no denying that. We are about to close our eyes in prayer, so we need to make sure she's tied secure. Hold her, would you, Marci?"

"Sure thing, Lord," Marci chirped. She wrapped her arms around Lily and held her quite close. Jesus made sure Lily's hands were tied a bit more tightly. He then stepped away.

Marci continued to hold Lily. "You can let go of her now," he said, slightly annoyed.

"Oh, right," said Marci. She released Lily from her arms and stepped away.

"Now, let's take some prayer time. After we finish, I'll have a nice little surprise for you all." He folded his hands together and closed his eyes. "I'll start. My Heavenly Father, I pray for victory against your enemies. I pray forgiveness for all my earthly frailties which may make me vulnerable and falter." He opened his eyes and nodded to Barclay.

"I pray to be of help in your mission, and that all our pains and striving are for something that matters. I pray I can lead the Black community away from the Demoncrats and toward true right-eousness," Barclay said.

"I pray to be united with my family as I make a better world for them, and I pray for their safety until I return," said Aaron.

"I pray the same for my family, and also that my grandchildren will be born to live in manly freedom," Hector chimed in.

"I pray for salvation, and God's help with my burdens," said Steve.

"Me too, honey," Marci said. Her smile to Steve held appreciation for the burdens they shared.

"Amen," said Jesus. "Say it with me."

"Amen," they responded.

"And now, let us celebrate our faith, and our togetherness. We will be each other's rocks in these hard times." Jesus reached into his jacket pocket. "And here is our sacrament." He pulled out a bottle of whiskey. "Blood of my blood," said Jesus. He took a swig, and passed the bottle to Aaron.

"I thought wine was supposed to be the sacrament?" asked Aaron.

"They hadn't invented whiskey yet," said Jesus.

Aaron nodded and took a drink. He barely kept from coughing. "Strong!" he said at last.

"You'll get used to it," said Jesus, slapping Aaron on the back with a grin. Aaron sheepishly passed the bottle to Barclay.

"Strong like our purpose," Barclay said, and handled his snort with dignity. He passed to Hector, who drank and then passed it to Steve. Steve looked at the flask, and then Jesus, and knocked it back. He handed it to his new bride Marci, who took a gulp and then exclaimed at the fire in her throat.

Marci passed it back to Jesus. "Thanks Marci, but I got another thought. Now that we're done with communion, why don't you two take the bottle with you and go around the corner? Grab some alone time?"

"Us?" Steve asked, his face scrunching in confusion.

"Ain't no one else married in here."

"Why?" asked Marci.

"Because that's what newly married couples like to do," Jesus said patiently. "Make the beast with two backs." Steve's expression remained confused. "You know, get to it, and get some action," Jesus further explained.

"You mean, with a -" Steve looked at Marci. "Oh yes, yes of course."

Marci's eyes widened in dismay. She tried to find words, but couldn't.

"What is it, my child?" Jesus asked.

"I didn't realize...I guess I was hoping that I could just..."

"Masturbate?" said Jesus.

She blushed.

"Nope," he declared. "It's self-pollution. Only a person of the opposite sex is supposed to have sex with you. Says so right in the

Bible. What God gave you is meant to be a doorway to life, not to pleasure. When a woman plays with herself, her baby door becomes a portal to sin and her clitoris is the Devil's Doorknob."

He saw some motion to his left. Lily was rolling her eyes so hard that for a moment he wondered if she was having some sort of seizure. He swallowed his annoyance. "You two got to be for each other, so you can make babies as God intended. No time like the present to get used to it. Got it?"

Steve and Marci nodded slowly. "We'll be around the corner," Steve said.

"Go to it," said Jesus. "Do God right, make a baby. There must be life in the midst of liberalism. Take your packs with you, they'll make good cushions. Not the best place to get romantic, but you're going to have to make do."

They smiled awkwardly at Jesus and left with their packs.

"As for the rest of us, let's get some shuteye. I've no doubt that whatever tomorrow holds, it's going to be a full day of work fighting for God's American justice. Aaron, you've got first watch. Barclay, you take over in about four hours. Also, can you guys give me a hand here?"

With the help of Aaron, Barclay and Hector, a struggling Lily was tied to a low-hanging steam pipe, and provided with a pack for a pillow. The party settled in. So tired were they all that eventually even Lily closed their eyes to sleep.

Occasional voices drifted over to them from around the corner.

"You want me to do what?" said Marci. "Put it in where?...Well if we do it that way, you won't be able to get me pregnant!"

"Oh right. I haven't done this a lot...I mean, either...way..."

"Well, maybe we can start like this – just go like this..."

There was some quiet for a while. The rest of the party had just about gone under when Steve exclaimed, "Are you crazy? I'm not putting my face in that!"

"Well, I'm certainly not putting my face near your thing either!"

"Ahem!" Jesus' voice rang out. "Less complaining. More doing."

"Sorry, Jesus," Marci and Steve replied together.

"Good. Night." Jesus shut his eyes.

THIS WAS the first press conference of his administration. President Bomraka looked at the door that would open into a large hallway, and from there to the many reporters and all their clicking pens and cameras.

He felt the old electric thrill he always felt before speaking to a crowd. It would have been good to have this be about a planned initiative. But sometimes events set their own agenda.

He opened the door and walked up to the podium. The room silenced, and the camera lights came on.

"Good evening, and welcome. I hope you all had happy holidays, and that you're looking forward as I am to a new year, and a new era of full cooperation.

"I've called this press conference for a specific purpose. As you all are aware, the ABC Atlanta news station WLBS was invaded, and viewers around the world were subjected to a broadcast of bizarre propaganda. Then the entire station and several blocks of downtown Atlanta around it were destroyed. Casualties are still being estimated, but it could have been worse if it weren't for the erroneous reports of helicopters that frightened local citizens into leaving the area.

"Any single life lost is still too much. Among the many dead and missing are the entire staff of the View including the great Blabbera Wilters, beloved newscaster Bret Stormbreaker, and others.

"Let these so-called Christian terrorists be put on notice. You will be brought to justice. I in fact dare you to present yourself in a fair fight. I think you lack the courage to face someone who knows you're coming. If you truly believe in heaven, face your justice here on earth. We will find you in any event, it is up to you whether that reckoning will be with you standing up like men, or hiding from us like cowards." He paused and surveyed the audience. It had been a strong statement, and even something of a risk. If this bible-spouting terrorist leader had any pride at all, he would have to respond directly. If he did not, it would undermine his own authority within his group.

The press corps eagerly awaited the President's next word.

"Now on to foreign affairs. We look forward to our next meeting with the visiting foreign dignitaries of..."

37

The next morning they got started with a breakfast of energy bars.

"Alright, you need to eat too," said Jesus. Jesus took off Lily's gag so she could eat, taking care not to tangle the duck tape on her hair. "We'll just keep it around her neck in case we need it again." He freed her arms and handed her an energy bar. She rewarded him with a stare of blazing hatred, and ate in sullen silence.

Jesus took out his pack of Marlboros, lit a cigarette with his Zippo and passed the pack around. Barclay took one. He didn't even try to offer one to Lily, and passed the pack to Aaron.

Aaron tried a cigarette. When he stopped coughing, he handed the pack to Hector. "Without our watches, we couldn't even tell it's morning. So dark down here."

"How you think the lamestream media is gonna spin all that destruction up top there, Jesus?" asked Barclay.

Jesus shrugged. "Terrorist attack. Lies at eleven. But, did you happen to see the sunset just before we had to go underground? It was amazing. Remember that. That's as close as my Father will get to telling us we have it made."

"Then you don't need me. You shouldn't have me along," said Lily. "What does my grandfather need, money? I can give you money."

"Not even for your weight in God's Good Gold," said Jesus. "Let alone some worthless One World Government Amero. We've got a job to do. To save the greatest country to ever bless the Earth."

"You and your merry band of Christians," said Lily darkly. "Wonderful."

"Not just any Christians. THE Christians. The New Disciples," said Aaron proudly. "We're bringing Godly back," Barclay added.

"Your war on Christmas failed, lady," said Hector.

"You're crazy. You all need help. You'll never get away with this. Just let me go now, and I promise nothing will happen to you."

"Nothing?" asked Jesus. "How do you explain what just happened to the station, and the surrounding city blocks? Your President had to order that."

"There must be some rational explanation. Maybe - maybe you had those helicopters do that!"

"And the Feminazi Femborgs? You saw them with your own eyes, scattered across the floor of the television studio. You saw your own liberal elite media boss there, Blabbera Wilters, face down with her cyborg parts exposed."

"That can't have been real."

Jesus laughed. "Sure is amazing how people can believe what they'd like, rather than even accept a chance they could be wrong."

She screamed with exasperation. "Oh my God!"

"Who?" he said, eyes sparkling.

She closed her eyes and counted to ten. "Look. Whatever's going on, I'm just not of any use to you. I'll just slow you down."

"I knew there was a little more to you than just being liberal." He nodded with satisfaction. "Now you're worried about what happens to us?"

"Get bent!" she responded.

"Language. You know, your grandfather misses you."

"How do you even know him?" she demanded. "What is this really about?"

"About showing you what Christianity is really like. He's just another part of the story. The weapons he's made will help me save America. Yet he defied my will and risked his own soul to save you. That's not wise, but I can't deny that's as strong a love as I've seen in ages." He appraised her critically. "You worth it?"

" He was a sweet old man once...but I never asked him to try and save me. He never did understand why I couldn't stay around in that town waiting for God to come and save us. He knew who he wanted me to be, but he never understood me."

"Uh-huh." Jesus eyes filled with sadness. "I think I understand just fine. You wanted more, and nothing simple and true could satisfy you. So you kept reading, kept going on the Internet, kept listening to strange music that didn't even have guitars. Soon enough that took you out of that small town, and away from people you knew, and into a school of godlessness. You got so lost you couldn't even admit that you were lost. Because the LIEberal media that ensnared you told you that you're a modern woman, and know what you want. You could never admit what you really needed was a man. A real, masculine man who would make you feel not lost, but found. A man you could respect because he's strong enough to tell you what you really need and then give it to you."

Her eyes grew wide with astonishment, then indignation. "You've got to be kidding me. Who's that going to be? You?" She laughed, incredulous. "I don't need to be told what I want by you or any man!"

It was clear to Jesus that no man before him had ever had the guts to tell her how it was. "Ever had the hard love of a good Christian man?"

"Oh my God-"

"Exactly," he smiled.

She rolled her eyes. "Slip of the tongue. How's your kind of Christian man supposed to be different from any other?"

"The fact that you don't know, might be the saddest thing of all." Jesus leaned with his hands behind his head, showing his mighty biceps. She pretended to avoid the sight. A trickster grin came to his face. "If we leave you here, would you rat us out?"

"In a second, you dummy," she said.

"Truthful. Good, you haven't lost that yet. For all your consorting with the Left."

As Jesus and Lily spoke behind them, Hector leaned over to Barclay. "I know that look," Hector murmured.

"What do you mean?" asked Aaron softly, overhearing.

"El Señor, he pretends not to like a fighting woman," said Hector. "But he likes the scent of this tigress."

"He's the Son of God," Barclay agreed, "but he's still also a Son of Man."

38

Steve and Marci rejoined them, a bit more miserable and tired than they'd been the night before. They both perked up at the sight of Jesus. They quietly ate their portion of energy bars.

As they were finishing Jesus stood up, and threw the rest of his cigarette onto the tunnel floor. "We should get going. Lily, we're gonna have to tie your hands, but I'd rather not gag you again. Think you can behave? Screaming won't do you any good anyway, we're so deep down in here."

"I hate you." She said nothing else. Jesus nodded. He could work with that.

They tied her hands, packed up and resumed marching down the tunnels. Soon they found another junction. Jesus consulted the compass. Since they could turn either left or right, he ruled it God's will that they go farther to the right.

Within twenty feet, they ran into a wall.

"That's odd. Don't see no reason for a wall here...why even have a tunnel if it doesn't go through to something?" Jesus kicked away some filth from where the wall met the floor. Aaron kneeled down and joined him, scraping with his hands. They uncovered a manhole.

Barclay scratched his head. "That doesn't make much sense. A manhole cover down here?"

"It must lead further underground," said Aaron.

Jesus decided that, as was almost always the case, this was not a time for thought but for action. "It's still in the direction of the river. Let's take it."

The cover looked quite heavy, but opened surprisingly easily. They were rewarded with a waft of the strongest stench they'd yet been subjected to.

"It stinks like sin," said Jesus. "But we must brave it to defeat it. Forward."

Barclay went down the new ladder first, then Lily and the rest of them. Hector pulled the manhole cover closed behind them.

"Barclay, Hector," Jesus called out. "Get behind us. Marci and Steve, you stay in the middle and keep an eye on Lily. Aaron, you're up front with me." Aaron came up to Jesus who directed his attention to far side of the dark tunnel. "We're heading that way until we find the pipe that hits the river," said Jesus. "Think you can navigate while I keep an eye out?"

"Yes sir," said Aaron. "Is there something wrong?"

"I can't say. Just doesn't feel right." Jesus handed him the compass, as they continued through muck and filth. They passed another junction, and this time continued straight down the same tunnel for a stretch of several hundred feet.

"It's so quiet," said Barclay. "I'm not hearing the same machine noise."

"Yes you're right," said Hector. "Perhaps that was ventilation above? Maybe that is the reason for the smell down here?"

They walked a bit more in silence, punctuated only by the dripping of water and their echoes of their footsteps bouncing through the underground halls. A few more yards and the tunnel went left – to end in a wall as well. This time, they found no further manhole in the floor.

"Dammit." Jesus said.

"You can say that?" said Steve.

" 'Course I can!" Jesus exclaimed. "If I can't damn something, who can?"

"Maybe we should go back a few turns, find another route," said Barclay.

"Looks like we don't have a choice."

They retraced their steps to the section of the tunnel where they'd entered from above.

There was a wall there now.

"Are we lost?" asked Aaron.

Jesus went over to the wall and tapped on it, listening for the sound it produced. He found a section where the sound was hollow. He stepped back and put his hand on his stepfather's .45. "It's not a real wall. Someone's sealed this off."

"Who?" asked Aaron.

"This is really..." Something did not seem right. He stepped forward and tapped again, keeping his other hand on his pistol.

This time, they heard taps back. So faintly they almost couldn't hear it there was a muffled giggle.

"What the Hell..." said Marci.

"Maybe it's someone who's trapped?" said Aaron.

"I vote we not stay and find out," said Steve.

Jesus fixed Steve with a stern expression. "This ain't no democracy. You're my disciples. When I say we gotta do somethin', that's what we gotta do. Got it?"

They nodded. Jesus nodded back. " 'Kay. Now, Steve's actually right. There doesn't seem any percentage in figuring out whatever is going on here. Let's go back to that longer stretch we just passed, and see if we missed a way out back there." Jesus led them back into the main tunnel. As they walked they heard a rumbling ahead of them. Jesus picked up speed and their walk became a run. They turned a corner just in time to see a wall slide into place, sealing off the tunnel a few feet before the end they'd seen the last time.

"Well then," said Jesus. He checked the ammo for his guns. The New Disciples followed suit.

"How did Bomraka's troops find us so quickly?" asked Hector, looking around him with alarm.

"It doesn't make sense!" said Jesus. "We should be completely shielded from satellite view down here. Unless..."

The tunnel wall in front of them started tapping more. Then the wall began to move toward them.

Moments later, a wall slid up to their right. An empty tunnel loomed behind it.

"Should we go in?" asked Aaron.

"Not until we have to," Jesus growled. "I do not like this at all."

"There's something coming at us!" exclaimed Marci. Aaron shone the flashlight down the tunnel. At the bare edge of its range a few hundred feet away, a tiny figure emerged from what should have been a solid tunnel wall. It headed in their direction. As it came closer it became clearer. It was something about the size of a human child, riding what appeared to be....

"Some kind of a giant white lizard?" asked Jesus. "With a.... saddle and a bridle?"

"What the Heaven??" cried Aaron.

"This is...what the..." Jesus essentially agreed.

"There they are!" a tinny voice came from the creature, echoing through the tunnel.

"Huh?" asked Barclay.

"Hand me those binoculars," said Jesus.

It was indeed some form of tiny human, a male one. His proportions and manner didn't quite suit those of a child. He wore a helmet with metallic goggles encrusted with small devices. On his shoulders were what looked like little golden epaulets. His tiny torso displayed a large "1", and a stylized symbol that appeared to be from the zodiac.

More of them followed behind the first. They also had numbers on their torsos, similar signs and numbers on their torsos, and the same strange beasts as their apparent leader. The creatures they rode were as long as a horse and as wide as a bull, but as low to the ground as a dog. The ridden creatures became clearer as they approached, and even stranger. They had no eyes, just bulbs of sealed-over skin where their eyes should be. Jesus' attention was drawn from there to the beasts' teeth - shining like sharp rows of white-grey tombstones as they roared.

As if that weren't strange enough, their tiny riding masters appeared to be wearing velour tracksuits.

The small men's leader signaled to his companions. Jesus saw tiny gold epaulets glitter from his tiny shoulders. His companions all lifted strange little tubes with handles, and pointed them at him and his New Disciples.

Jesus dropped the binoculars and grabbed his .45. "Fire!"

The team pulled out their guns and launched a blizzard of flying lead. The gunshots and their ricochets echoed throughout the confined space. The small men were surprised and took cover, openings quickly appearing near them in the tunnel walls. One pint-sized terror managed to fire his strange weapon. A smoke grenade landed near the team.

"Cover your mouths, and keep firing!" yelled Jesus. In between the blazing bullets of their gunshots in the darkness, Jesus kicked back the grenade.

"I've never shot before!" said Marci.

"Just aim down the tunnel," Jesus ordered between gunshots, "and pull the trigger!"

Then their diminutive enemies were no longer visible, as Aaron dropped his flashlight to grab his gun.

"Put the flashlight back on them!" Jesus ordered. Aaron complied, just in time to see that a half-sized nemesis mounted on an albino alligator was charging. Jesus took careful aim past this reptile-mounted cavalryman, at their leader. The leader saw his intent and ducked low. The pint-sized commander's alligator was shot in the face. It grunted in pain, darted partly up the wall and fled back down the tunnel, with its owner strapped to it trying to regain control. The other mounts became confused and tried to follow it, bunching them together just as the undersized assailants had raised their weapons to send more grenades their way.

Jesus pulled out the special revolver that Hieronymus had made, and held it in both hands. He'd held back from firing it in this confined a space. But the way those tiny sinners were bunched together, if this worked like the last time...

Jesus fired. The shot blew past the half-sized man and his freakish reptilian steed, continuing all the way to the tunnel wall next to the rest of the height-impaired brigade. The masonry disintegrated in a massive explosion. Surrounded in blue flame, the nearby roof and walls creaked and cracked. Then as Jesus had hoped, the tunnel fell in upon their enemies. The cost for this relief was that the way back for Jesus and his team was blocked with damage and debris.

All of the New Disciples stopped firing, stunned. They stood in the silence, Aaron still shining a light forward that now showed smoke, rubble and settling dust.

"That's one Heaven of a pistol," Barclay said.

"You can say that again," said Jesus. He holstered the divine weapon. It probably wasn't safe to fire it again underground.

"Who - what are they?" asked Marci.

"Some strange part of Bomraka's army?" wondered Aaron.

"I really have no idea," admitted Jesus. "I have never even heard of anything like that on AOL before."

"Whatever they are, they could report us to the government," Barclay pointed out.

"If they haven't already," said Jesus grimly. "Gimme that alley sweeper." Aaron looked at him, puzzled. "The machine gun!" said Jesus. Aaron handed him the machine gun.

"Follow me," said Jesus. He ran back to the other end of the tunnel. A door had opened in the side, and was beginning to shut. He jammed his machine gun in and held it open. "Run in!" Jesus ordered.

"Are we sure that's a good idea?" said Steve.

"Do what he says, he's the Messiah!" said Aaron. Marci pushed Lily ahead of them, and shoved her roughly through the doorway. Steve was next, and Hector and Aaron followed.

"Everyone keep running. Barclay!" Jesus yelled. "Help me shut the door behind us!" Barclay put his shoulder to the heavy door, and

Jesus pulled the machine gun free. The door immediately moved by itself. Once it reached the frame around it, large bolts slid out to hold it in place.

Jesus ran to catch up with the rest of the group. Somewhat disconcerted, Barclay followed. Marci and Steve dragged a struggling Lily behind them.

"What are you crazy?" Steve asked. "You want to take your chances with whatever those things are, riding whatever those other things are?"

Jesus caught up with them. He saw no sign of those strange creatures down here. "Report!" Jesus said.

"All here, no wounded," said Barclay.

"Put that gag back on her, in case we need to hide!" Jesus barked.

"No you don't!" said Lily. "You have to mmph! Mmph!"

Jesus stroked his chin in thought. "They're not pursuing us. They didn't even fire at us as we ran. Why-"

Lights flashed on around them. They all instinctively tried to shield their eyes. After a few seconds of blinking, they could see that one entire wall had slid away, to reveal a large chamber with a pool of water about 20 feet below. While they were still half-blinded and off-balance, a flood of sewer water washed them off their feet. Helpless against the deluge they were flung off the edge into the water, then pulled down by currents into a deep abyss...

Where they became entangled in nets. The rush of water pinned them against the ropes, which then lifted them out of the pool. Fighting to breathe, Jesus could just make out movement on a platform above them. As he strained to keep the water from his lungs, he saw what looked like a - yes, another little person, this time pulling a lever down.

The lever clicked into place. There was a massive electric hum. All of their weapons and everything made with metal flew off Jesus and all his fellow captives, straight up to a giant metal plate on the ceiling above.

The nets closed tighter around them and then lifted into the air, separating into two separate nets and shoving those in each net even closer together. Jesus, Marci, Steve and Hector were in the first net. Lily, Aaron and Barclay were in the second. The flood lessened and then disappeared into gratings below.

Jesus twisted to face outside, and grabbed a strand of the net to test its strength. It didn't budge. He looked close and saw plastic green coating on top of steel cable.

Several of the smaller-portioned menaces they had seen just minutes before rode their albino alligators onto the platform above them. They dismounted as one, with eerily similar motions. Together, they reviewed their captured targets. Then as one they jumped up and down, squealing with glee.

"You little jerks!" Aaron sputtered. "You could have drowned us!"

"Wet us out, we'ww dwowning!" mocked the nearest tiny heathen. They all giggled.

Their leader entered, recognizable by his tracksuit's epaulets and the number "1" emblazoned on his front. "Look what we have here," he announced, in his tiny voice. "Excellent catch!" The other creatures giggled. "Yes! Great subjects for our experiments, oh yes." Their leader rubbed his hands together. "Oospek 4. Put a new facade over the entranceway. We won't need more big people for a while."

"Who are you?" demanded Jesus. "Do you have any idea who I am?"

Their half-sized master's only response was a prolonged, high-pitched giggle. It nodded to its compatriots. The strange crew then hopped on their strange alligators, and rode through a door at the end of the tunnel above them. Last to leave, their leader bowed courteously to them before he turned out the light and shut the door.

The room faded into near darkness, save for a soft ambient lighting coming from some phosphorescent fungus along the walls and ceilings.

Hanging in the net next to Jesus, Lily fumed. "Great going, messiah."

"I thought she was gagged," Jesus said moodily.

"Guess what? That gag's working about as well as the rest of your plans, genius," Lily shot back.

"That's Jesus." He shook his head.

Whatever his father was throwing at him, this was a strange test indeed.

Rosio watched the replays of the first press conference she had missed in decades, and then read the analyses on the internet. She was more perplexed than ever.

Bomraka had indeed put this Jesus in quite a box. If the Christian didn't show, it would look as if he was cowed into silence. If he did anything besides attack Bomraka at his strongest, he would look weak.

Yet Bomraka himself still didn't seem to be evil, didn't even seem to be a sleeper agent, and had resisted her most underhanded efforts to help him catch this man.

What was she going to do?

There was going to be an emergency meeting of the Death Panel in a few hours, to deal with the aftermath of her expulsion from the White House. Perhaps with all their heads together they could come up with a way to use this President, towards their own ends.

Jesus knew it was fruitless to strain against the net, but still did from time to time out of sheer frustration. "I can't believe they got my guns. Here we are, disarmed and helpless. Talk about gun control." He pointed to the magnet above them that still held all their weapons, tantalizingly out of reach.

"Let's cut these ropes," said Hector.

"No knives," said Barclay.

Aaron's brow furrowed in thought. "Maybe we can chew through them?"

"Come on, Aaron," said Jesus. "Look through the plastic. That's steel cable."

"I'm just trying to be helpful," said Aaron, hurt.

"I know, I know," said Jesus.

"What do you think they want, Lord?" asked Marci.

"I have no idea," said Jesus. "I don't even know who they are."

"I have heard things," said Hector. "Not much that...I want to share."

"Well, you might as well share it anyway man," said Barclay. "We'll find out if it's true soon enough."

"Does seem like we have a bit of time on our hands," said Aaron.

"Very well. Some who have run into the sewers to hide from the bad President's BomrakaCare, speak in hushed sentences of 'Les enfants de flocon de neige," said Hector. "To translate into American, they are known as 'snowflake children'. They are said to have come from the Petri dishes of abortion labs...and grown in darkness to emerge from the sewers and steal away with lazy children. You know, those so lazy they play rather than having jobs." Hector hesitated. "Those who return never speak of what they have endured but go on to help Planned Parenthood. They can even go far as to vote the straight Democratic ticket the rest of their lives."

"Forever?" asked Aaron, with a hush in his voice.

Hector nodded. "It is terrible."

"Huh." Jesus rubbed his chin, deep in thought.

"What's bothering you, savior?" said Steve. "Maybe I can help. You look tense...do you need a massage?"

"No! No. I'm just thinking." Jesus moved a bit, to make sure he wasn't inconveniently touching any of his disciples. Especially Steve. Jesus definitely wanted to keep Steve's ex-gayness very much 'ex.'

"What were those things they were riding?" asked Aaron.

"Looked like gators," said Barclay. "But really...light-skinned ones."

"Yeah. And they didn't have eyes," said Marci. She shuddered.

"They probably evolved that way, living in the dark," Steve mused. "They don't need light - "

"They didn't evolve," Jesus corrected. "Evolution is a lie. They were bred in some way by evil."

"You're right, sorry."

"That's fine. We've been in a pretty stressful situation for a while.

At least now, like it or not, we can take a breather. We can't get too comfortable, but let's relax as best we can. We just might be here a little while."

"On the upside, they haven't killed us yet!" said Aaron.

"That's a good point, Aaron."

"Or even tortured us or ripped our spleens open!" Aaron added.

"Please don't try and cheer us up any more," said Marci.

"It's weird," said Jesus.

"What is?" asked Marci.

"Just like I have secrets from Bomraka, he can have them from me. This could be one of his secret initiatives like Agenda 21 or Communism Core Math. But it just is not the Demoncrat style." He frowned. "I wonder if he knows about this at all."

Lily snorted. "Gee, you think? Maybe he didn't have a TV station and several city blocks blown up to get you, either."

"You saw it with your own eyes, Lily," Jesus responded, exasperated. "We got a little broadcast time, and dispensed a little justice. And then what happened? Michael freaking Max came in with a crew of black helicopters, and everyone involved was just erased. Put two and two together. It was ordered by your former boss, Mr. President Evil."

"He's not evil. He's just a man. There has to be some other explanation."

"'Course you think there is," said Jesus. "That's what happens when you watch that liberal media filter. Your President looks quite a lot different when you see him through the true lens of the Bible."

"He's your President too."

"I don't recall voting for him. What do you think he's gonna do to you if they catch us? Just set you free?"

"They'll have to turn me loose," said Lily. She held up her bound hands. "I'm obviously here against my will."

Jesus snorted. "If you think telling the truth is enough to save you from Bomraka, then I evolved from a monkey."

"Begging your pardon, Lord and ma'am," said Barclay, "but we have more pressin' concerns right now. Lord, what should we do?"

"I have one idea. It's the one thing we can always do."

"What's that?" Hector asked.

"Pray, of course," said Aaron.

"That's right," Jesus said proudly. "Let us pray. Bow your heads."

"You're going to pray? Right now?" exclaimed Lily. "How about you try to figure out things, make a plan? What use is prayer to-"

"And why don't you put that gag back on little Lily there," said Jesus.

Aaron and Barclay struggled to move around in the net and reach Lily's mouth, all the while roundly cursed with shockingly unladylike language and even a couple of bites. Eventually they managed to slip her gag back on.

"Now, to begin," said Jesus. "Bow your heads. Ready? Dear Heavenly Father, aid us in our time of need. Help us get out, and then get even with whoever put us in here. Then help us continue taking out the enemies of America. Amen." Jesus nodded, satisfied. "You guys can now pray silently to my Father or Me by yourselves."

They bowed their heads except for Lily, who continued to give vent to exasperated huffs. Aaron prayed for his family, and Barclay prayed to be reunited with his daughter who'd strayed from the fold. Hector prayed for his friends, his family, his many cousins and his people. Marci and Steve prayed to stay strong against temptation – for Steve this was symbolized by Jesus, and for Marci this was Lily.

39

———————

Over a thousand miles away, Rosio made it to her apartment. A cute walkup she had purchased as a safe house when she had first begun this journey in Washington D.C., so many years ago. She slumped into her couch. Getting here without murdering every third stupid dupe she came across had felt like walking a thousand miles.

All her doubts and fears were returning with a vengeance. She had just completed moving back into the White House, and here she was not only out, but out permanently and bereft of next steps. If there ever was a time for the Devil to appear and give her guidance, or simply reassure her, it was now. Yet the Devil did not appear.

The coded files of her years of work would show up later, shipped over by movers. Who would rebuild her dreams?

There was a knock at her door.

"This had better be good!" she screamed.

"It's me," said a voice thick with the crumbs of recently deceased donuts.

She got to her feet and nearly ripped the door off its hinges. "Michael Max! Why aren't you out looking for the Christ?"

"I - well, I uh..."

She grabbed him by the collar and dragged him in from the hallway. She slammed the door back into place, and him into the wall. "Don't you dare say you are sparing a single second from looking for them."

He held up his hands in surrender. "I'm looking everywhere I can!"

Rosio Dawnhell held a heavy fist right before his eyes. "Then what are you doing here?"

HER VOICE SHIFTED to a pleasant and perky sweetness. "Please explain, m'kay? Make me understand."

Max tried to shift in her grip. The wall groaned against his weight, but her hand on his collar didn't budge. He swallowed nervously. "They've just gone off the grid, Rosio."

"Nonsense. No one is off grid. As long as they're on Earth, we should be able to find them."

"I know, in theory. I'm telling you they aren't anywhere. Unless they're all six feet under..."

Rosio was about to berate him further, when an idea came to her. She let go of his collar. "They were last seen in Atlanta. Do you recall hearing any information from their Planned Parenthood centers?"

"There's rumors we haven't been able to confirm, about ...lost fetuses."

"You did check if this Jesus and his minions weren't in the sewers?" Rosio said. "Correct? And thoroughly?"

"Yes. All we found were sealed tunnels, an abandoned homeless camp with meal bar wrappers and cigarette butts, and some dead rats." His stomach made a nervous rumble. "Why?"

"The Bush administration left some notes that might refer to this. They aren't very clear, but I recall there being rumors of – some splinter group living in the sewers, known as the Snowflake Children."

"Snowflake – you mean, surviving stem cell fetuses?" His expression became thoughtful. "Do you think they taste as good as human flesh?"

"Food can wait. Focus! Yes, stem cell survivors. We thought it had to be an urban legend. But Planned Parenthood has been consistently low in fetal tissue for our secret human sacrifices. This could explain where that tissue went – and it might explain where this man and his so-called new disciples have gone also."

Max nodded. "I'll get right on it."

"I want surveillance satellites and black helicopters on call, trained on all known exits and outflows from the Atlanta sewer system. I will..." Rosio stroked her fleshy chin. "Yes. I will prepare a note offering amnesty to these so-called Snowflake Children. If they bring me this Jesus and his New Disciples, I will give all of these Snowflake Children positions at the National Institute of Health. Drop this note down each of those tunnels. If they do exist, not only could they liquidate this Jesus, they could even be an asset to our plan."

Max looked at her in awe. "That's genius."

"Yes it is," Dawnhell said, matter-of-factly. "Now, get going back before I get impatient. I will send you the document by courier."

Max shuddered. "Yes, indeed, mistress. Right away." The reverberating fleshquakes from his shuddering continued as he left. Rosio smiled to herself. It felt good to have that power. Maybe she didn't need the White House after all.

After passing through a complicated series of ever-deeper tunnels, the mounted Snowflake Children rode their albino alligator steeds into a large antechamber. Inside were others of their ilk, seated before a row of computer monitors. They left their backless ergonomic chairs and kneeled before their leader and his minuscule raiding party.

The leader jumping off his reptilian mount. "We have trapped so many big people, the nets can hardly even contain them all!" he declared.

"Yay! Success!" the others cheered. "To the decision table!" he squeaked.

The leader and his party led their albino steeds to a recessed pool in the room's center, dismounted and nudged the lizards towards the pool. Once all the scaly creatures were in, rails rose from the floor around the pool to contain them. Bloody food was dropped into the pool, and the albino alligators splashed about in a sudden feeding frenzy.

"Now, to me!" their leader declared. "A quorum!"

"A quorum!" all the others agreed.

"We are the Snowflake Children!" He pounded his fist on the 'I' emblazoned his tiny chest. "I am Oospek 1!"

"Just 12, all stemmed from 1," the rest replied.

"When one falls," he said, and waited.

"Another seed is taken from the Big Person Parent Place upstairs!" the other others finished.

"We are met, and ready," said Oospek 1. "Let us choose what to do with our new subjects! I like the idea of experimenting on them. Other options? Quickly."

Oospek 2 spoke next, to his right. "Clone them and make new snowflakes."

The Oospek to his right was silent. "Eat them," said Oospek 4.

"Sex them, clone them, then eat them," said the one with a large "5" upon his tracksuit, and a leer on his twisted face.

"After the experiments," said Oospek 1. "Other options?"

"Sell them," said an Oospek whose torso displayed a "9".

"Sell? To who?" asked Oospek 1.

"To the big-persons above ground," Oospek 9 responded. "Their President Bomraka people are hunting our prey." He giggled.

"We might have to give our captives back unspoiled," Oospek 5 pointed out. "No experiments or sexing."

"What makes you think the big-person President Bomraka wants them, sexed or not?" asked one of their group with a "6" and the zodiac sign of "Libra" on his chest.

"We have intercepted news reports matching their description," said Oospek 11. "They are Christians who have not stopped fighting the War on Christmas. They apparently blew up a TV station."

"What could the big-person President offer us for his foes?" asked Oospek 2.

Oospek 1 considered this, and laughed. "Hm. Maybe almost anything? Downsides? Quickly."

"We would have to contact the President and reveal ourselves," said Oospek 3.

"The President could destroy us like other fetuses," said Oospek 6.

"Not if we can convince him we are useful," countered Oospek 3.

"That is not all we could do!" said Oospek 4. "I have an idea! We could clone the shiniest of them, the one they call Jesus!"

"Interesting! Why would we do that?"

"We could use him to get followers for us!"

Oospek 1 frowned. "We would have to make it follow my orders of course."

One last remaining member of their group raised his hand to speak. "We could maybe join this big person called Jesus?" Oospek 7 asked haltingly.

"Join?" several others exclaimed at once, incredulous.

"Do you mean by sexing?" asked Oospek 1. "Oospek 5 already said that."

Oospek 7 swallowed in nervousness, then shook his head. "No! I mean by joining the group of big persons we captured. We can join forces to be strong against the evil big person President and the big-person One World Order like it says in the big-person Bible."

"But we Snowflake Children stay hidden!" Oospek 5 smacked his tiny fist to his chest. "Your Libra sign distracts you, this does not need balancing. This Bible is not for us. It is a Big People thing. Also that way we don't sex them."

"Maybe their Bible is for us too," Oospek 7 countered. "I have read their Bible. I like it!"

Oospek 1 examined 7 closely for a moment. "Do a statistical analysis of joining their group."

"Really?" said Oospek 7, hope in his eyes. The leader nodded impatiently. Oospek 7 squealed with joy and ran to the wall of computers. As he began his own set of calculations next to Oospek 3, their leader gave first one and then another of his followers a meaningful stare.

Oospek 7 was ripped away from his calculations by a swarm of tiny hands. He wrestled with all his tiny might, but they were too many for him. "What are you doing?" Oospek 7 cried. "The big person Bible says this big person can save us!"

Oospek 1 shook his head. "You have lost mutuality. You are no longer acting like one of us." He giggled. "But you can join them yourself. Part of the test group now!"

40

———

Jesus and the New Disciples' latest prayers were interrupted when two of their tiny captors returned – dragging a third one of their number by a rope.

The bound figure pleaded for understanding and forgiveness. His former comrades ignored him as they shoved him into a net all his own, and then hauled it up until he hung right next to Jesus' net. They then left their former cohort swaying slightly, giggled, and turned out the lights and left the chamber. The door clanged close behind them, reverberating against the room's stone walls.

In the darkness, they heard the midget sob.

The sobbing went on for a while. Finally, Jesus spoke.

"Stop cryin'," he said.

"What?" their new fellow captive asked. "Why? I feel bad!"

"Man ain't supposed to cry, that's why," said Jesus.

"Are - are you saying I'm a man? Like a big person?"

"Well maybe you could be inside, at least. If you stopped feelin' sorry for yourself."

"But aren't we supposed to let our feelings show?"

"Not if you can help it," said Jesus. "Not men, especially. Don't you want to be a man? Even if you're smaller than one should be, you can still try."

He tried really hard not to cry. "I've always wanted to be a big person man. More than anything."

"Then the time is now for the closest you can get," said Jesus. "You see us trussed up here, we don't even know who the Hell you people are, and we ain't cryin'. We're strong."

Steve wiped his eyes, but otherwise held his peace.

"What's your name?" asked Aaron.

"I'm Oospek 7."

"Oospek? And 7? What kinda name is that?" said Barclay.

"It's how we're called. There are twelve of us, all copied from the First Fetus, the Ooze Speck. We have numbers and signs of the Zodiac, to tell us apart from each other."

"And Hector, you were saying they're called Snowflake Children." Jesus nodded. "I'm starting to get the picture. Why don't you tell us all how you came to be?"

Their new neighbor sniffled a bit further, and then took hold of himself. "Years ago, the first one of us awoke in the sewer, atop a pile of Petri dishes. Somehow, a disposed fetus managed to live, to grow and feed. It found an albino alligator, and raised it as a pet. It learned to speak and read from thrown out televisions, and then computers. It eventually discovered enough of the big-person science that had created it, to create others of its kind."

"My God," said Barclay. "Are you..."

"Yes. I am the seventh clone of the first Oospek. He has given us each a number. Also a different Zodiac sign based on a horoscope found wrapping fish." He pointed to his chest. "I was a Libra, you know, the scales of balance..."

"Astrology," growled Jesus. "Stem cell research and black magic. Do you answer to President Bomraka?"

"Not yet," said Oospek 7. "He knows nothing of us. The other Snowflake Children are discussing whether or not to sell you all to him. We have chosen the shadows up until now. We do not trust the civilization that discarded us."

"Then there's a chance for you yet," said Jesus. "'Cause you know, a true Christian'd have too much compassion to throw you out like that before you were even born, just 'cause you were a twisted mockery of half a normal person." Lily tried very hard to speak, but fortunately her gag was still in place. He continued. "Even though you could never be a full human being, we would still love and treat you like one."

"Really?" said Oospek 7. "You would forgive one like me for existing? You would...you would do that? "

"Yep, you can make up for that. All I need are two things."

"What? What? Anything!"

"You accept me as your savior."

Oospek considered that. "And what's the other one?"

"You decide to kick some ass!" Jesus demanded. "Be a man. Don't go crying when you lose. Get back in there and win!"

"If I did that I could join be one of you Big People?" the half-sized seeker asked, eyes full of wonder. "Like you?"

"Well now, you can't be exactly like me. God created us all in his image, but some people are, you know, more in his image. But you could be a reflection of his image, sure."

"Really?"

"Why not?" said Jesus. "Mirrors come in all sizes. You can be like, you know, the image that gets all bent by a circus mirror. You people must know about circuses."

"That's so wonderful!" The little man began to shake his net in his excitement. "Hey! Maybe that means God can be a midget, and maybe your mirror is just bigger like a circus mirror!"

Jesus' face became stern. "There's no way God is a midget."

"Why not?"

"'Cause I just know. So don't blaspheme."

"But how is it blasphemy?"

Jesus sighed. "Because I said it is. I should know, right? Use your God-given common sense, man."

The tiny seeker bowed his head, chastened. "Yes, sir."

"It's no big deal, little guy," said Jesus. "These are big ideas. It can take a little while for a little guy to get used to 'em." He withdrew his hand. He reached through his own net to pat the little man on the head. "Are you gonna believe with us, or are you against us?"

Oospek 7 took a deep breath. "My people have rejected me for my beliefs. You will accept me because of yours. I choose your side....my savior."

The New Disciples cheered. Jesus caught Lily's eye and smiled. She rolled her eyes. She didn't show it, but Jesus knew she had to have felt moved. Even if it was just a little.

"Welcome aboard!" said Aaron.

"We can't call you Oospek 7, though," Barclay pointed out. "That ain't no kinda name for a real Christian American."

"No, it's not," said Hector. "How you like James?"

"That name's been ruined by too many secular humanists," said Jesus.

"Maybe Gary?" Marci ventured.

"Gary..." the little guy pondered. "Gary. Gar-ee....I like it."

"Then welcome, Gary!" said Jesus. "I'd shake your hand, but we're a little hampered at the moment."

"Thank you, Jesus. I'm so happy I...I feel like crying...but I won't. That way I can be like a real man."

"You catch on quick! So, Gary. Welcome to the New Disciples. Now...how the Heaven do we get out of here?"

"Savior-"

"Call me Jesus."

"Jesus, I wish I had better things to tell you, but we – they – love their traps and make them really good. I don't think we'll get out."

"Time for another lesson, Gary - stop that. That's quitter's talk. We'll find a way. Say a prayer, then wait for an idea. We will too."

There was silence for a bit.

"So, Gary," Aaron asked. "Exactly what are they planning to do to us?"

"I don't know if you want to know," said Gary. "I don't want to think about it."

"Tell us," said Jesus.

"Well..." the small man now known as Gary sighed. "We clone. That's what we do...or what they did. They'll want to...clone of all of you. Especially you Jesus, as you're...clearly superior. Then they'll want to - no! I can't say it!"

Barclay shook his head. "Tell the truth and shame the Devil, now."

"They'll want to - make a midget version of you, Jesus."

No one spoke for a moment. Then Jesus began to guffaw. "Well that ain't gonna work! I ain't the result of no genetics. I'm the son of God!" He snapped his fingers in sudden inspiration. "That could give us just the opening we need! Okay, everyone, listen up. Here's what we gotta do..."

A few hours later, the lights came on with a clang. The captives struggled to wake as several of the Snowflake Children came in with rubber gloves on their tiny hands, holding cattle prods which then shot out electric sparks. Firing the sparks made them giggle, as they walked towards the nets that held their captured prey.

"All right, little fellas!" said Jesus. "Listen up! I know a lot of secrets about Bomraka that I can give you willingly, and you won't have to fear him at all. I'll give myself up right now and spill my guts if you let the rest of my friends go."

"You just might spill your guts, all right! Hee hee!" said one of the half-sized heathens. All three of the tiny nemeses laughed.

"Wait!" the netted Oospek cried. "You can't trust him!"

"Hah! You be quiet," said its jailer.

"We remember how you wanted to join them," said another.

"That was before I knew them!" said the tiny captive. "They are bad big people, very, very bad big people! They were, they were planning!"

"Shut it, you pint-sized Judas!" bellowed Barclay.

"What were they planning, tell us!" said one of the tiny creeps.

"When you open the net and let them down, their Jesus was going to sacrifice himself. He-"

"Damn you!" said Aaron. "Damn you, you oompa-loompa of Satan!"

"He was going to blow himself up so they could be free!" The netted Oospek pointed at Jesus. "He has a grenade on him!"

"Say goodbye to Heaven, you little jerk," said Jesus.

The captive folded his tiny arms. "I don't need Heaven as long as I have my people."

"What does this grenade look like?" asked one Oospek, a skeptical look on his face.

"I think I can find it if you let me out."

"You'll pay for this," said Jesus.

The other Snowflake Children lowered their captive fellow in his net.

As soon as he was free of the net, he ran past their captors and pulled a lever on the wall. The walkway beneath the other Snowflake Children began to fill back up with sewer water.

"What are you doing?" one of their half-pint tormentors demanded. "We're holding electric rods!" His eyes widened in sudden comprehension, too late. A spark jumped from his electric rod jumped to the pool of water at his feet. The midgets jumped up in convulsions, screamed, and then fell and lay motionless except for the occasional muscle spasm.

Gary moved the lever back to its previous position. The water drained off the walkway. "Jesus and everyone, I'm sorry for those mean words!" Gary cried. He manipulated the controls and maneuvered the nets onto the platform. "I'm so sorry!"

Jesus stepped out the net and stretched gratefully. He ran over to Gary and hoisted him in the air. "What are you sorry for?" he laughed. "You did a great job! You sold it so well - my new disciple!"

"Really?" said Gary.

"Yeah!" said Barclay "Greatest little dude ever!"

Jesus set Gary on the ground. "Now, let's get going," said Jesus. "And let's not celebrate just yet. Gary?" He pointed to the magnet overhead, which still held all their weapons. Gary turned off the magnet and the weapons fell. Jesus snatched both of his guns before they hit the ground.

"Make sure your ammo's dry," he said. He holstered his .45, and picked up his buck knife from the ground. "And cut that vile astrology sign outta your shirt," he said, tossing the knife to Gary. "You're with us now."

He went back to looking over his guns. Hieronymus' beautiful revolver didn't have a spec of water inside the barrel or the chamber. He holstered it and picked up his .45, sighted down the barrel from the hammer, dropped out the clip and slipped it back in. "Now let's go kick some half-pint ass!"

"Wait, what?" asked Lily. He saw that she had worked her gag free. "Why don't we just escape?"

"What are you talking about? These pint-sized pagans spurned and taunted me. What kind of an example would I set if I just let that go?"

"I don't know, one of forgiveness maybe?"

Jesus laughed and shook his head. "Retribution has to come before forgiveness...you liberals are so silly sometimes."

"Also, the Demoncrats could get ahold of their technology," said Aaron. "We shouldn't leave this problem for someone else to handle."

"Sure, that too," Jesus said generously.

"Yes!" said Hector. "We are going to take this Planned Parenthood obscenity and defund it – permanently."

"You guys go ahead then," said Lily. "I'll just find my own way out."

They all stopped checking their weapons to look at her, surprised.

"You want to stay here?" asked Marci.

"More than going after a bunch of freaky clones riding albino alligators," Lily retorted.

"Your liberal skills in twisting things won't keep you safe here, " said Jesus. "What if they miss us and come back for you alone?"

She hadn't considered that. "You can leave me with a gun."

"So you can maybe shoot us in the back?" asked Aaron.

"Aaron's got a point, babe," said Jesus. "How are we supposed to trust you?"

"I...." Lily stopped. She had nothing to say. "I could swear to God," she said finally.

"But you don't believe," Jesus pointed out.

"I swear by my love for my Grandfather," she said finally. "You give me a weapon so I can defend myself, and I swear I won't use it to hurt any one of you."

Jesus searched her eyes. "I almost trust you. But you're not quite there yet. You could still change your mind. You're coming with us. No gun, but we'll untie your hands." Hector walked over to her and cut loose her bonds. "Keep her in the middle, fellas. Lily, if you want our trust you're going to have to earn it."

He pointed down the tunnel that the Snowflake children had come through.

"Now let's get to it."

The tunnels were of an ideal size - for Gary. For the rest of them it was claustrophobic and uncomfortable, dark and dirty.

"We have to be careful," said Gary in a low voice. "There are noise sensors nearby."

"What is that weird gunk all over the walls?" asked Marci, pointing to the gray-green patch of soft luminescence that ran along the walls.

"It's a poisonous kind of sewer fungus. Don't eat it," warned Gary.

"Are you sure we shouldn't, Gary?" Steve said drily. "It looks like it might go well with a nice white wine."

"Sh!" said Jesus. Not only did they need to be quiet, but Steve's comment was a little close to irony, a well-known gateway to the gay.

Gary pointed down the tunnel to two tiny metal boxes that stuck out at roughly waist-height, on either side. "I think those are the sensors," he said in a very soft and tiny voice. "If we get too close my – the other – the Snowflake Children will know we've escaped."

"Can we maybe short them out?" Barclay whispered.

Gary shook his head no. "They're waterproof."

Jesus eyed the fungus, and an idea came to Jesus. "But are they fireproof?"

"I don't know," said Gary.

"Everyone get behind me." Jesus took out his buck knife, and scrapped the fungus off the wall for several inches on each of the tunnel's sides. Then he took out his Zippo lighter, and set fire to the fungus patches in front of him.

They all watched as the fire slowly spread over towards the noise sensors Gary had pointed out. Moments later, with a screech and a pop, a concealed panel blew out of the wall. Wires and electronic components on fire burst out, sparked intensely for a few moments, and faded into nothing.

"Super!" said Gary. "The next door is the man...."

A new surge of sparks jumped from the panel, and then a jet of flame shot out.

"After this, the tunnel continues straight through to the main control room," said Gary.

"Okay," said Jesus. He considered a moment. "We better-"

Another pop more flames shot out. Some of the material around the wires started to drip flames along the wall....and the poisonous fungus on the wall began to smoke.

"Uh-oh..." said Gary.

The tunnel wall beneath the electrical panel, then above it, and then on either side began to smolder. Flames emerged and began crawling towards both the ceiling and the floor.

"Move forward!" said Jesus. "Quickly! Past the flames!"

They ran forward through the rapidly increasing smoke and flames, trying to race ahead. The fungus on the walls continued to catch fire behind them.

"Don't stop!" said Jesus. "Our only chance now is to get out of this tunnel!"

Gary stood up to his full height, and stretched his little legs to run full speed. Aaron tried to run crouching and stumbled behind him with Barclay nearly falling on top of him in the growing smoke. Hector helped them back up, holding a kerchief over his mouth. Jesus ran, crouching behind, just in time to catch Lily's arm and keep her from falling to the floor. Her eyes let slip a flash of gratefulness. Then she angrily yanked her arm out of his grip.

Aaron coughed. "I can't see!"

"Just keep moving forward if you want to live!" said Jesus.

The tunnel opened up to a normal person's height. They stood to their full height and ran. The smoke and flame ran just behind them, reaching the tunnel's new height and turning all behind them into an inferno.

They reached junction with several branching tunnels. "Gary, which way-" Jesus began.

"The only way out is there!" Gary pointed to the tunnel on the right.

"Come on!" said Jesus. "It's now or never!"

They launched themselves forward - and ran straight into a door. The group collided into a jumble.

"Can't breathe!" gasped Aaron. They all began coughing. The smoke was making it difficult to see, even through the light from the nearing flames.

"Drop down!" said Jesus. "There's still oxygen near the floor!"

The rest of the New Disciples did as Jesus bade them. For once Lily did also. Jesus looked at the door. "Back up, I need room!"

He threw all his brawn against it, and it barely budged. He took a breath, resisted the need to cough, and searched for God within his soul. He prayed a silent prayer and launched himself against the door again. It still didn't move. He could feel the smoke begin to sap his Holy strength.

Then he remembered the pistol his Father had given him, constructed by Hieronymus. He drew, took aim, and fired.

The gun unleashed a thunderous blast that reverberated throughout the tunnel. The bullet blew the door off its hinges and slammed it ten feet into the chamber beyond. The door caught on it's lower edge and flipped onto its back, its bottom three feet of steel wreathed with dying blue flames, with a dent in the center so deep it might have been punched by God.

Nearly out of air, they scrambled over it - and fell off the other side in what appeared to be a control room.

Eight Oospeks watched with mouths open as the six formerly-captured Big People emerged, from the flaming and smoking tunnel, led by their former fellow Snowflake Child.

41

Oospek 1 and Jesus yelled at the same time "Shoot them!" The half-pint heathens brought their full weapons to bear. Jesus saw his followers were still coughing, and yanked Aaron and Steve back behind the high edge of the still-smoldering fallen door as cover. The rest followed.

Jesus pointed Hieronymus' gift revolver across the room, looked at the domed ceiling overhead and thought better of it. He didn't want a cave-in. He holstered it and pointed his .45 straight at their tiny master, Oospek 1. The wily clone ducked behind the table, just barely in time for the slug to pass over his tiny hard-to-target head.

"Release the albinogators!" cried Oospek 1. Across the room, another hiding Oospek flipped a lever. The cage around the clones' pale and fearsome mounts receded into the floor, and the gators leapt forth.

Jesus concentrated fire on the three gators approaching directly at them. A fourth ran to the side and, with the vicious instinct of a true predator, leapt for the most helpless person in the group - the weaponless Lily. For a split second, Jesus considered firing, but that beast was too close to risk it. He put away his .45 and jumped instead, just barely intercepting its gaping jaws before they closed upon her.

The creature rose to its full height, resisting its unexpected captor, and then the two fell to the floor.

"Shoot the other gators! Shoot them!" cried Aaron.

"I'm trying, they're too close together!" said Barclay.

"Just keep those other ones away!" Jesus yelled. They turned and fired at the other albino gators. "I can help!" yelled Gary. "No! Stop!" Aaron commanded, but Gary was already standing with the stun rod in his hand. A series of bullets from the other Oospeks' weapons flew by him.

Jesus and the creature writhed on the floor, each trying to gain the upper hand. Reaching under its limbs still wet from its brackish home, Jesus managed to get behind it and then get a full Nelson on the creature. Jesus flopped onto its back with the thing on his bellow and struggled to subdue it. From the corner of his eye Jesus saw one of the Oospeks reach for another switch. Jesus gathered his strength, and strained his mighty arms. With a sickening crunch, he broke the albino gator's back. Jesus pushed the dead gator off him and drew his .45, just in time to hit the Oospek in the hand. He heard a squeal of pain as the hand was hastily withdrawn.

"More gators are coming out of the pool!" Aaron yelled.

"Maybe I can hit the lever!" Gary yelled.

"No Gary, you'll be too close to their fire!"

"I have to save my savior!" Gary ran across the room. His former brethren kept firing, the bullets and their ricochets filling the air. Jesus and his disciples spared all the cover fire they could from keeping the remaining alligators at bay.

Gary managed to get the edge of his hand on the lever and pull it down just before the Oospek nearest him shot him twice. Gary fell. The other pint-sized nemesis grabbed the lever and began to reverse it, but Aaron and Barclay's fire drove him back to cover.

The pool's containment wall rose from the floor. Two remaining albinogators who hadn't left it yet tried to climb out but were left inside. With Jesus' help, the remaining creatures outside the pool were quickly dispatched.

Jesus then realized the sinful Oospeks had stopped shooting. "Hold fire!" he ordered his disciples.

The chamber became eerily quiet. The silence was broken only by the still-crackling fungus fire from the tunnel behind them, and the ringing after effects of gunshots in their ears.

"You're not supposed to be here!" Oospek 1 cried. "Why don't you just leave?"

Jesus looked at the rest of the New Disciples. They stared back at him, wordless.

"Well?" asked Lily. "What would the actual Jesus do?"

"My past version would maybe do things a bit different..." he raised his voice. "Listen up, you microscopic villains. That don't work for me. What else you got?"

"Okay," said Oospek 1. "Why don't you put your weapons down, and then we'll put down ours?"

"Not quite sure about that order," Jesus said. "Let's see, how many guys you got left there...looks like eight. There are six of us with guns. We're all in cover, so we don't have clear shots at you and you don't at us." He rubbed his beard. "How about this - two of yours throw down their weapons and come out, hands in the air and no tricks. Then one of ours does. Then when everyone else has gone I'll put down my weapon, and then you can put down yours. And we can work out how to live together in harmony."

"Okay!" said Oospek 1, a little too quickly.

"Jesus, you can't be-" Lily began. "You can't trust them."

"Matters to you?" he said with a smile and a wink. She looked away. He could see that she cared a little bit about him. Any amount would be more than she wanted. "Don't worry your pretty head about it, darlin'." He was surprised to see her expression change to anger – why? Hadn't he said something nice?

He shook his head. He had no time to figure women out right now. "Alright, little feller. If we're gonna do this, then let's get on with it. I got things to do up top, and time ain't infinite here on Earth."

After a pause, Oospek 1's voice rang out, "3 and 8, do as he says."

Two guns were thrown over the far end of the huge stone table and clattered to the floor. Hesitating, first one and then another of the other Oospeks emerged.

Jesus heard a couple of his disciples cock their guns. "Remember, don't shoot now," he said.

"But they could have killed Gary! He could be dead, we don't even know!" said Steve.

"Stay your wrath." said Jesus. "I have spoken."

Steve sighed, put down his gun and stepped away from cover. After waiting a few moments two more Oospeks emerged from hiding, put their guns down and their hands up and walked over to the side.

"Okay, Marci," Jesus said. She threw her weapon out of reach and walked forward. The next couple of Oospeks came forward, and Barclay put down his guns and emerged from behind the damaged door. The process was repeated with another two of the miniature pagans and Hector, and then finally with the last of Oospek 1's remaining minions and Aaron.

The only remaining armed people were Oospek 1 and Jesus.

"Alright big person!" said Oospek 1. "It's your turn."

Jesus pulled out his stepfather's .45, and took careful aim at the ceiling. He fired.

The bullet ricocheted off the ceiling and hit Oospek 1 square in the top of his head. His gun clattered to the ground, followed by his body. He flopped to the side, his head just beyond the stone table, dead.

"No!!!" the other Oospeks cried out as one. Jesus ran straight for the Oospeks' relinquished guns. He got there first, with the New Disciples close behind him. The Oospeks were helpless, and began crying in dismay.

"Quiet!" said Jesus. "Stay still if you know what's good for you."

Lily stood to the side, a bit disturbed. "How could you even do such a thing?"

"I know, right? Wasn't that a Heaven of a shot?" He spun his .45 by the trigger in his one hand his magnificent revolver in the other. "I told you, baby. I'm the Messiah." He put the revolver back in his shoulder holster, and the .45 into his belt.

"That's not what I meant. Wasn't that breaking your word?"

"Do you like being alive?" Jesus retorted. "They were going to kill me and do God knows what else to you and my disciples. I don't have time for your political correctness. Marci, how's Gary?"

Marci and Steve ran over to Gary. "He's still breathing!"

"Thank my Father," breathed Jesus. "Keep pressure on his wounds."

"Can't you just resurrect him?" asked Steve.

Jesus shook his head. "I don't have healing powers this time around."

"What shall we do with 'em, Señor?" asked Hector. He waved his gun at the remaining Oospeks.

"Depends on how these quarter-pint hell raisers want to play it. You!" He pointed to Oospek 3. "Who's the one true God?"

"There - there is no-" the Oospek began. Too fast for the eye to follow, Jesus drew and aimed his .45.

"We came through smoke and flame to get here. Everyone else 's eyes are still red and tearing. How about mine?"

"You're the only one who didn't cry!" said Oospek 8.

"What does that make me?"

His eyes widened. "I don't know."

"Yes you do," said Jesus. "I'm the best man ever made, which proves that I'm the son of God. It's time to pick a side. Do you want the society that aborted you? With nothing but the cold empty and heartless comfort of science?"

Oospek 4 looked down, and dragged his foot along the ground. "Now that you put it that way..."

"That is an awfully big gun you're pointing, so..." Oospek 8 followed.

"Maybe we can reconsider this whole scientific method thing!" Oospek 3 completed.

"You need to do better than reconsider it, son," said Barclay. "Think you better swear allegiance to the Lord Almighty."

"We swear," said the Oospeks, in unison.

"Alright," said Jesus. "Good. Now show us you're ready to help, and get rid of those last couple of sick, twisted alligators you helped the Devil create."

"With our weapons?" Oospek 5 said hopefully.

"Without 'em!" said Jesus. "You gotta fight for what you want in this world! Go get rid of 'em."

"But, uh, your Lordship, they're...they're alligators. And we're...little people."

"Let's not get PC, fellas," said Jesus. "You're half-pints half full of the Devil. And one o'you shot that one good little guy there who joined us of his own free will. So I'm not feeling all that merciful right now. You show me you're ready to go and take care of business on my say-so. Then I'll accept your help in putting the Planned Parenthood that spawned you back to rights."

Seeing no other options in Jesus' steely eyes, the Oospeks wandered over to the alligator pool. Oospek 3 looked back uncertainly, and then climbed over the containment wall. They heard a gator thrashing closer through the water, and Oospek 3 began to scream

"It would be kinder just to shoot them!" Lily said.

"So they all spend eternity in Hell? This way God'll sort 'em out," said Jesus. "Rest of you Oospeks or whatevers, get on in there! Can't just give forgiveness out for free. If people don't work for salvation then they don't respect it, and they'll think you're a pussy."

The other Oospeks climbed over the containment wall. Gary coughed, and a little blood came out of his mouth. Jesus nudged Marci and Steve aside and kneeled next to him. Ferocious roars came from the pool, mingled with tiny screams.

"Hey, Jesus, I'm not sobbing," said Gary.

"I noticed," said Jesus. "You're being a real tough little buckaroo."

Gary began to cough a little more, then subsided. The roars and screams died out.

Barclay leaned over the pool to take a look. "Now don't that beat all I ever saw."

"What is it?" asked Aaron.

"You just gotta see it for yourself."

Aaron saw an albino alligator sticking halfway out of the water, and another floating upside down. Both were dead. The one at the pool's edge had an Oospek stuck in its mouth, choking it. The top part of the Oospek's '5' was barely visible above the alligator's teeth. The stomachs of both the alligators looked very lumpy. Aaron realized the lumps were the outlines of the other Oospeks.

"I did it!" said Oospek 5. "I choked the first one with my body, and then the second! Now, can I be one of you?"

"Yes, you can," said Jesus. "You've proven yourself."

"Yay!" said the Oospek, and died.

A weak smile grew on Gary's face. "That's great...I'll have someone my height to meet, in big-person Heaven..." His eyes began to lose focus.

"Not just yet!" said Jesus. "I order you to stay alive. Let's get you to the table. Who knows any medical stuff?"

"I know he's losing blood!" said Marci. "We need to seal him up!"

"Someone bring me duck tape!" Jesus said. Aaron rummaged through his pack, and brought out a roll. Marci and Steve passed the roll back and forth as they taped Gary's wounds.

"He's looking really pale," said Steve.

"Get him on the table!" said Jesus. "I have a sudden inspiration! They're all into science stuff. And they're all clones. Anybody see any tubes?"

"Along the back wall!" said Barclay.

"And beakers, hoses, stuff like that?" asked Jesus

"Them too!"

"Bring them all over here! With my Holy Father's help, maybe this will work."

Jesus pulled out his buck knife and cut open the vein inside Gary's elbow. He held it shut with his finger until they got one end of a tube into the vein. Then under Jesus' direction, they hung one of the dead Oospeks upside down, and let his blood drip into a funnel above the tube.

After several hours of hard work and prayer, Gary awoke. He saw Jesus, the New Disciples and Lily leaning over him. The fungus flames had faded, and there were no albinogators or other Oospeks to be seen.

"Is this big-person heaven yet?" he asked.

Jesus gave a good-natured chuckle. "Not quite yet. Looks like you're going to pull through." He patted Gary on the head, and stood.

"Now then," said Jesus, "that was quite a day." He brushed the sweat off his forehead. "Steve, you keep an eye on Gary. Marci, you keep an eye on that tunnel. The rest of y'all..." He took out his Marlboros. "How about we all take a break."

42

After a smoke, Jesus led them all in a session of YoGod, the Christian yoga. As he expected, Lily refused to participate. Afterwards, he gathered them around to discuss their next move.

"How can I help?" Gary mumbled.

"Hm," Jesus mused. "You guys got pretty used to sniffing around underground here, didn't you?"

"Best at it ever, my boss!"

"Can you get us information on the KenyAntichrist? His groups, his systems?" asked Aaron.

"Sure," Gary managed to get out.

"How many CD's will that fit on?" asked Jesus.

"We don't even need CDs. We can save that to electronic tablets!" said Gary.

"Wonderful!" said Jesus. "Did you guys have any explosives down here?"

Gary nodded. He pointed to a doorway to their right, then dropped his arm as if it was too heavy to bear.

"If you can save all that information on those fancy tablets,"

Aaron asked, his voice betraying a bit of desperation, "can you also maybe get a message to my family?"

Gary coughed blood and barely moved his head in what seemed like an affirmative gesture.

"Fantastic," said Jesus. "I knew you'd be a great help. Load all that information, and bring it along!" He leapt to his feet, and raised his fists in joyous triumph. "Down here, we could have met our end, and the outside world might have never even known. But God don't work like that. Now, thanks to my Father and a little help from you, our mission is back on track, and we are ready to go all the way to war!"

He indicated the chamber around them. "Someday, we'll be able to sanctify this science and put it to good use. Make sure that properly married heterosexual couples can have all the children they want, so they can be fruitful and multiply all over the face of this Earth. And just delete the Devil's plan for gayness before the kids are even born. My God, it'll be beautiful."

"Amen," said Aaron, Hector and Barclay.

"Amen," Gary whispered, his eyes briefly full of worship before they closed again in rest.

"Amen," said Marci and Steve. They reached for and awkwardly held each other's hands, without quite making eye contact.

"Yep, someday," Jesus nodded. "For now, we're just gonna blow this place up to high Heaven. Let this strange and forbidden science be swallowed up in purifying flames until the overthrow of our enemy. We can resurrect it through Gary's blessed memory, when these scientific tools can only be used by Christian hands."

"You're joking," Lily exclaimed. "Oh my God. You're not. Cloning technology can save so many lives!"

"How many more would it send to Hell?" he pointed out. "Doesn't matter how many cells it is, each fetus is the same as an entire full-grown baby."

Lily grit her teeth in frustration. "Look. If that's the case, why don't you hold funerals for the Petri dishes that fertility clinics discard?"

"'Cause I'm too busy saving America."

She could tell his mind was set. She tried another tactic. "If we blow all this stuff up, won't that give our location away to Bomraka?"

Jesus' face fell. "You're only saying that because you don't want to blow up stuff. But you do bring up a point." He smacked his fist into his palm. "I really want to blow this place up. We need to figure out how."

"How about a timed explosion?" suggested Barclay. "That could even distract Bomraka. Lead him in a different direction once we're gone."

"Perfect! Set it for, say, twelve hours from now. I sure would like to see the explosion in real life, but it'll be enough to know that it was done."

"Maybe you and the explosion can get a room together," Lily muttered acidly.

Jesus shook his head, and didn't even try to figure that one out. Why would he get a room with an explosion? Liberal humor was really too complicated for most real men. "Now let's get to it."

Under Gary's direction, Aaron and Steve found the tablets Gary had mentioned and started downloading maps and information. Aaron was also able to send a coded message to his family in their New America safe house. Lily was kept under Jesus' watchful eye, as the rest of the New Disciples explored the Snowflake Children's lair and brought back as many explosives as they could find.

"Shouldn't we..." Marci paused. "Bury the others? Or something?"

"They're facing their reward," said Jesus. "They can go to ash with the explosion."

"How about that fungus fire?" asked Marci. "It's still smoldering a bit. Should we put it out?"

"Don't backslide and get all environmentally distracted," he warned. "We've got a nation to save and a Bible to avenge. What's the way upstairs, Gary?"

Gary pointed at a door across the room from the still-smoking entrance they'd come in through, and lay back exhausted.

"All right then! Everyone, let's get ready to move out." Jesus directed them to pack, and to assemble a makeshift stretcher for

Gary, from the Oospek's ergonomic chairs. Then he stood over to the side, and took a moment to think wistfully about how cool the explosion would look.

Lily walked over to him. "Jesus..." She shook her head. "I can't believe I just called you that."

"That's my name, you can't wear it out. What's up?"

She glared at him. "I was actually going to thank you for saving me from that - that creature- when you decide to blow up a bunch of technology just to see it blow up. Things that could do more than just help couples conceive - they could make unlimited organ transplants, heal people and save lives. How can destroying that possibly be part of God's plan?"

Jesus shrugged. "It feels right. My Father and I's ways are mysterious. You women ain't so easy to figure out yourselves, you know. Which reminds me. Aaron? You got that duck tape?"

"Sure thing, Lord," said Aaron. He reached in his pack and handed them to Jesus.

He turned to Lily. "Hold out your hands,"

"Make me," she snarled.

"You know I can. How 'bout we just skip that unpleasantness, seeing as how we're starting to get along so well?"

Her response was unladylike enough to make all of them blush.

"Now now," he chided her, smiling. "See? Just 'cause you played so nice, we'll tape your hands in front. That way you can move a lot more easily. You've earned that much trust." Her face held an expression that was beyond skeptical. He switched from her to the adoration of his New Disciples. "Alright people! Let's get going."

In a Washington D.C. Starbucks after midnight, with shades drawn against any public eyes, Rosio held a hastily convened meeting of the Death Panel. Fewer people had shown up than she would have preferred. There was only Strident, George Sauron and Jane Fondue. Others had presented excuses for not being available to meet on such short notice.

This was a bad sign for Rosio's respect and power within the movement. It made her look and feel weak. She decided to keep those who had shown up waiting somewhat impatiently at their simulated wood grain table, as she went behind the counter to complete her own soylent green chai tea. She wanted to establish that even though she had asked them here, she still called all the shots.

When she felt a sufficient amount of time had passed to get her message across, she sprinkled the last bit of cinnamon mixed with human flesh and waddled back towards them. She sat and opened her mouth to speak.

Before she could begin Blabbera Strident banged her own soylent green chai latte on the table like a gavel. "This emergency meeting of the Death Panel is convened," said Strident. "And we have much to talk about."

The rest of the Death Panel nodded in agreement. Rosio grit her teeth but nodded assent. Strident had beaten Rosio to the Starbucks and had thus made her drink first. She was clearly jockeying for position as leader by directing the agenda. Rosio felt confident she could take Strident in a physical confrontation, but to come to blows so quickly could be seen as desperation. Now that Rosio's position of power with respect to Bomraka had become compromised, she had to maintain the appearance of control.

Rosio still had a commanding presence, which she quickly applied. "Yes we do have much to talk about, Blabbera. Let's get to it."

"What first, then?" asked Sauron, addressing Rosio. Good, he was not against her as yet.

"We all know the unfortunate events that have led to this meeting. First and foremost is the question of Bomraka. Is he rogue, is he a sleeper agent, and can he be useful to the cause?"

"Maybe we should wonder about our cause," said Jane Fondue.

Rosio controlled herself from sputtering in surprise. "What do you mean wonder about it?"

Fondue looked very uncomfortable, but swallowed her fear and moved forward. "I don't know....hasn't it seemed a bit weird for a while now? Things keep actually getting better while Bomraka is in charge. How do we even know if we're defeating the patriarchy? Or that the patriarchy even figures into the things we're told to do?"

Rosio stared back at her. "I need you to be very explicit in what you're talking about."

"Well think about it. Bomraka may not know if he's a dupe or not. What if the same is true of us?"

Several other members of the Death Panel stirred as if the very concept was a troubling itch they had been trying to ignore. But once out in the open, it was hard to pretend it wasn't there.

Jane pushed on. "What if we are being duped? What if the same dark power that we seem to get our orders from, that we've never seen directly...what if we're part of some scheme to make this Jesus look good, so he can eventually assume control and do some things that no one wants at all? Not even Christians?"

Sauron put his hand to his forehead, troubled. "I don't like to think of this."

"What about the Rapture?" said Strident. "We know that happened. We helped cover it up!"

"We know small groups of people disappeared...but that's it. What if it's something that has some, I don't know, some other purpose? Like maybe window dressing to fool Christians, and fool us too?"

"Shut it," demanded Rosio. "This kind of talk is unacceptable."

"But I mean, even our names..." Fondue persisted. "What the hell kind of names are these?"

"What do you even mean?" Strident demanded.

"The names themselves seem almost like...caricatures?" Fondue explained hurriedly. "Not that we're wrong, of course we're right. But we're almost also, from a Christian conservative perspective - something you would use to make them feel like they were really right." She paused. "Maybe even convince an unhinged Christian conservative that we're something to fight against."

"Why would our dark masters ever play that deep a game?" Sauron asked with a conviction he did not feel.

"We only hear from them indirectly or in visions or dreams, we've never even met them! We have to take so much that makes no sense, just on faith." Fondue turned to George Sauron. "You. You're supposed to be part reptilian or something, you've got a weird tongue you show every now and then. But why? If Reptilians could run everything, why wouldn't they just do that? Why hide? And if someone asked you if you were a Reptilian, why couldn't you just lie about it?"

"That is quite enough!" Rosio shouted.

Sauron looked uncomfortable. "I'm pretty sure my parents were Reptilians."

"But you don't even know, do you?" Fondue asked.

"No!" said Rosio. "No, no, no!" She smashed her fist into the table. All of their soylent green lattes jumped into the air. As did their owners - looking first at Rosio, and then at the cracking dent she left in the table. She watched with delicious satisfaction as their eyes filled with renewed fear. "We will not consider this," Rosio continued with a voice of iron. "This conversation is over. We can't doubt ourselves, this close to the finish line. Now that all we've dreamed about and hoped for, and literally sacrificed for, is about to come through."

She looked around, daring each of them to say otherwise. Fondue and the rest went silent, still in fear of her power. Even Strident kept her mouth shut.

I have my power back! Rosio thought in triumph. They feared her again, as they should. Their mission could continue, with her at the top. Those other things Fondue had talked about...they could be thought of at another time. If ever.

"Now," Rosio said, leaning back with more assurance of her power. "We need to plan. If this Jesus is killed, then one of our problems goes away. But what shall we do if he is captured?"

43

They went through the door Gary had shown them, finding a tunnel that gradually inclined upwards. Aaron and Steve took the lead, carrying Gary. Lily was again in the middle, angrier than ever and perhaps a little baffled as well. Those were both actually good signs. Jesus decided to let her digest things a little bit.

They eventually came to a junction. Following Gary's quavering directions, they continued moving ever upwards. Barclay and Hector brought up the rear, preparing explosions at key points.

Finally, they reached the last ladder to the upper world.

"Are you ready, Gary?" Jesus asked, smiling.

"Ready, my boss," he whispered.

They came out through a culvert that opened into a clear night sky. It was just about as beautiful a sight as Jesus had ever seen. They fanned out and looked around. They appeared to be in wilderness, with not a human being in sight. They could hear the rushing of a river, and walked toward it.

"What river is that, does the tablet say?" asked Jesus.

"According to the map it's called the Chattahoochee."

"Smell that air," said Hector. "Ahhh."

"Yes my brothers," said Jesus. "Smell the smell of freedom." He looked over at Lily, expecting some sort of barb. Even she had closed her eyes to feel the breeze.

"Where to now, oh Lord?" said Aaron.

"What's nearby?" asked Jesus.

"According to the map, we've got another ten miles to the nearest highway."

Jesus nodded. "This was a good place to come out. God has smiled on us." Jesus took the tablet from Aaron. "Looks like there's a passage over this ravine. East of here? Let's walk along the river until we hit it. Then we won't have to guard our backs as much, and we can take stock of things."

The New Disciples nodded, and began their march. Lily, still bound and still unhappy, was led along between Jesus and Hector, followed by Steve and Marci bearing Gary. Aaron and Barclay found themselves bringing up the rear.

"Been quite a trip so far, hasn't it?" Aaron said.

Barclay laughed. "Got that right. Woo..." He shook his head. "Still woulda joined if I knew what was coming. But I woulda definitely thought about it a bit more."

Lily dropped back a bit, to walk between Barclay and Aaron. "Barclay, why are you here at all?"

"What do you mean?" responded Barclay. "'Cause he's the Lord of course."

"Don't give me that," said Lily, exasperated. "These other simpletons I can almost understand. But you seem to have some sense, some actual real-world experience. Can't you see how he acts. Look at his – his arrogance, his lack of mercy. Even if you believe in the Bible, he's not anything like that guy. Why would you follow him at all?"

Barclay checked the horizon with his binoculars for a second and then lowered them. "You want to talk about real-world experience? Sure, I've had a lot of that. A lot of Black people have. And a lot of it was pretty unfair too." He started ticking points off on his fingers. "We don't have our own businesses. Our schools aren't as good. Our employment levels are always the lowest. Affirmative action hasn't helped the ghetto. Liberals keep saying they'll come through. But they just have not."

"I understand being frustrated," said Lily. "It frustrates me as a progressive. But we've at least tried. And statistics show there's been some good. Social Security, Medicare, Housing and Urban Development – all these things have helped. Conservatives want to get rid of all the things that helped, even if they don't help enough. Why would you throw away what's helped make things less bad? Why get rid of some good because it's not perfect?"

"Because it's been too long. It's time for a change."

"But this guy you're helping blow things up is against government even lifting a finger to help anyone," Lily persisted. "He doesn't want to help the poor or the middle class, as much as he's even thought about it. Let alone black people."

"It's time we gave him a shot," said Barclay. "He's not from the system, and he says the right things. If we believe enough, and we all unite behind the same God, it has to work out. We have to believe more than ever that he can really make things right. Otherwise this whole struggle has really been for nothing." He nodded at Jesus. "This man looks and feels like the son of God. That's all I need to know. An' maybe that little guy can help too."

"You mean Gary?" Aaron smiled and nodded agreement. "Yeah, he is good with the computers, isn't he?"

"Seems so."

"All I need's my family to be safe," said Aaron. "Besides that, all a man can do is hope. That's the whole point, isn't it? For us to keep our faith."

Lily shook her head but said nothing further.

They came to the ravine. The cliff dropped off steeply and a river rushed below them.

"It must have been quite a river once, to cut that deep in only 6000 years," Jesus noted. Lily's snort was a compressed litany of scorn. "Let's take the footbridge over there."

They crossed the bridge into a field with bushes and long grass at the edges, and a tree in the middle. The whole scene was so pretty it could have come straight from a picture book. On the other side of the field lay a forest that went across the nearby hills, and down the other side.

"This is one of the finest days we've seen since the end of Bomraka's second term, when we thought he'd be out of our hair forever." said Jesus.

"At least he can still face justice for Ghenbazi," said Hector.

"Why, what happened there?" asked Steve.

"No one knows for sure," said Jesus. "It must be really awful, because we can't even find the evidence." Jesus walked into the field and went to the tree. He cleared his throat. "Okay everyone, gather around and take a seat on God's lovely green carpet!" The New Disciples did as they were bid, and after some hesitation Lily did too. Aaron sat next to Jesus, and Gary was laid down on his stretcher on Jesus' other side. He coughed a bit but otherwise was quiet.

"Just sitting here and listening is against my better judgment," Lily groused.

"We've gone through more than we expected, and come out a family. For the most part," Jesus added, smiling at Lily's recalcitrance. "Now is a good time to give thanks." He gave Aaron a comradely shoulder punch. "And you man, stop worrying and enjoy yourself a bit. Isn't this so much more interesting than your typical Sunday at church?"

Aaron shuddered. "Feminazi Femborgs and midgets riding eyeless albino alligators are enough new experiences for a lifetime."

"We can't always pick the battlefield," said Jesus. "What matters is the winning."

"Where will we next fight to the Devil?" asked Hector.

Jesus leaned back on his hands. "Well, the job before us is to take Lily back to her grandfather. After that, God only knows where he'll put us."

"I hope Texas," said Barclay. "I want to see the greatest state in America. Also, my daughter lived there for a bit. I might be able to find out where she is now."

"I didn't know you had a daughter," said Aaron.

"She turned lesbian, because her mother was a literary critic," said Barclay. "Last I heard she was in that liberal stain on Texas' honor, Austin."

Jesus nodded. "Texas is a holy place. Where I was born, in fact. Even in Austin, she has a better chance. After all, she's not in California."

"Where in Texas were you born, my lord?" said Hector.

"In a town called Bethlehem. There, the Demoncrats almost prevented my birth with their condoms and Planned Parenthood. But my mother met an angel and then conceived me. Then we moved to Montana, after the Demoncrats increased the tax burden on holy job creators to try and track us down," said Jesus. "So Texas will always be the holy land of my birth and the heart of Real America." He gazed off to the night horizon, wistful. "Someday soon we'll go to Texas and make it right. Maybe after reconnecting with our brethren in New Mexico. Which, if we have our way, soon the world will know as New America." He sat up, a fire in his eyes. "When we-"

Jesus' sentence was cut short by a screaming fiery blast that shattered the tree they sat beneath. The team was showered with flaming fragments of wood.

44

"**S**catter!" Jesus screamed. He pulled out his guns and scanned the skies.

Dark silhouettes moved against the stars over the forest, blocking their light. The silhouettes grew larger, nearer. "Black helicopters," Jesus whispered. The dark beasts reached the edge of the forest and stopped, hovering monsters, trapping Jesus and his crew between the woods and the ravine.

"I know you're here somewhere, you rascal you!" came Michael Max's oily sing-song voice. "Are you ready for your close up?" The helicopters advanced towards them.

Jesus wasted no time. "Steve and Marci, get Gary back across the bridge. The rest of you, lay down some covering fire for 'em! Then let's draw the choppers away to the west!"

Barclay, Aaron and Hector ran apart from each other and started shooting. Hector found cover behind a low hillock, and aimed carefully. He got off a well-aimed shot that ricocheted off the lead helicopter's opaque windshield.

Then an explosion ripped near the ground where he sought cover. Out of the ensuing cloud of dirt, smoke and blood, Hector's lifeless body fell to the ground. Jesus ran towards him, then heard a scream. Lily was running for the ravine in a straight line, panicked. She would be an easy target.

"Keep firing until the others are across!" Jesus yelled to Barclay. "Then join them!" He ran after Lily. She turned back and saw him.

"Run, bless it!" he yelled. He heard one of the black helicopters release a missile. Jesus leaped backwards and to the side - as a blast rocked the ground where he'd just been.

Jesus rolled and aimed his divinely inspired revolver. He sighted directly at the helicopter roaring toward them.

THOUSANDS OF MILES AWAY, safe inside her apartment, Rosio leaned in over her monitor. These live feeds were excellent quality, and she wanted to drink in every detail. This man who called himself Christ and his band of idiots had fallen right into their net. Additional help was on the way, but it looked like Max and his helicopters would be enough for this band of doofuses.

Now their leader was desperate, dumb or enough of both to think he could take down a helicopter with a handgun. That wouldn't even chip the black protective paint on their landing skids. She would get to watch this Jesus' face as he failed, before they all were blown to smithereens.

She would take credit for Max's work, and silence the filmmaker if he dared to disagree. Her status with the Death Panel would be secure, she would find a way to resume her station in the White House, and her promise to her witch mothers would be fulfilled.

She licked her lips. This would be a great video to play over and over again at composting parties.

"I'M READY FOR MY INTERVIEW!" said Jesus, keeping his aim.

"Wait, what?" asked Max's amplified voice. The lead helicopter stopped moving forward, and the other two followed suit. "Did I hear you correctly?"

"Yep," said Jesus. "You can interview me right now."

Barclay and Aaron continued firing. Aaron winged a bullet off of one of the lead helicopter rotors. It shifted to target him.

"Cease fire!" said Jesus. Barclay and Aaron stopped shooting. "Max, this is between you and me! How about you get your fat ass out here and fight me like a man?"

"No need to be sizeist!" Max protested. "Okay guys, let's stand down for a bit. This'll make for some great footage." The black helicopter hovered closer, and explored the ground with a spotlight until it found Jesus and Lily. They stood there transfixed by the light. A smaller second black helicopter came closer, followed by a third.

Jesus looked sideways at Barclay, and inclined his head towards the footbridge in a tiny movement he hoped the man would see.

Barclay got his message, but shook his head in dismay. Jesus stared back sternly. This wasn't a request.

Jesus turned back towards the lead black helicopter. The metal monster turned broadside, and the smooth blackness over the copilot's window slid up. Behind the now-clear window was the pleased and pudgy face of Michael Max.

"Alright," said Max. "We're here with a man who calls himself Jesus Christ. Let's get started. What do you have to say for yourself?"

"I'll just say I hope you're filming." Jesus steadied Hieronymus' pistol with his other hand, sighting down the barrel with all the precision he could muster.

Max laughed. "Of course we are. You know, this is great. It might even go into my next movie. After some tricky editing of course." Jesus could see him rubbing his fat hands. "Okay, next question. Just what do you think you're doing, aiming that pistol? Do you think you could even dent this window I see you through?"

"I don't think it at all," Jesus said truthfully. "I feel it."

"How do you feel about gun control then?"

"Think I'll let this do the talking for me."

"Come on now. You can't be that crazy. I can barely even see that gun from here. Let's talk about the health care system."

"What are you waiting for?" said Lily. "Shoot! Sh-"

Jesus fired. Seven spouts of blue flame exploded from the sides of the barrel. The bullet slammed into the front of the black helicopter and exploded in an expanding firestorm that quickly enveloped the entire vehicle until it burned like a blue sun in the night sky. The flames faded in brilliance but began shooting along sudden cracks in the windshield and the frame. They crawled to the rotors, and engulfed them in a spinning shroud of fire. The engine began to whine as the helicopter shuddered.

An explosion rocked the side of the helicopter, and it shot backwards as if kicked. It turned and struggled to regain its former angle. The front of the cockpit faced Jesus and Lily once more, resembling the head of a half-blind beast.

Jesus fired at the second helicopter behind it. The shot was true and the bullet slammed into the helicopter's nose and blue flames shot out, following along the sides to wrap around the vehicle. The helicopter was knocked backwards by the impact and twisted in the air. Smoke started pouring from beneath its rotors as the flames sought purchase beneath its metal skin. It fired a rocket but couldn't target. The rocket shot plunged into the earth a moment later, without even exploding.

Jesus fired again at the first chopper, which was struggling under the weight of Michael Max. The bullet created another thunderous explosion and storm of flame, but kept flying. Jesus counted bullets in his head. He only had one of Hieronymus' amazing bullets left.

He was just about to fire when the rotors of the second helicopter froze still, and it dropped from the sky. Then the first one listed to the left, the strength of its rotors failing. It crashed next to the first helicopter, with a huge explosion. Flames spread in all directions. The tall grasses around the machines caught fire, spreading to the bridge Jesus, Lily and his New Disciples had come across.

Jesus scanned the horizons. With all the smoke and flame he couldn't see the third helicopter, waiting to strike.

Rosio watched Jesus raise his pistol in glee. She closed her eyes in delicious anticipation.

Then the feed cut. She stopped breathing. She tried reestablishing contact. The video turned to static. She scrabbled for the headset, her frantic motions frustrating her further as she accidentally pushed it away.

She caught the headset with edges of her fingers, and held the mouthpiece close. "Send more helicopters after him! Get him now! Shoot at him from a distance! You have to get him now!"

"We'll need authorization from the whole Panel to do that," said the person answering.

Rosio didn't speak for several seconds, so stunned by what she'd heard.

"It's on my authority. Do you know who you're talking to?"

"Yes ma'am...I understand," the voice responded, fear and tension in it now.

"Then get it done!" Rosio roared. "This has to happen now!"

"Yes ma'am," he said. "Please hold."

Rosio stewed as precious seconds passed, while this man – this *man!* – contacted the other members of the Death Panel. If this specific incident hadn't happened, she might not have even known of this power play for days.

Was someone closing her out of her place at the top of the command chain? Had that not-damned-enough Blabbera Strident undermined her authority? What was going on?

THE THIRD HELICOPTER poked its head from the left side of the previous two helicopters. Jesus aimed Hieronymus' pistol at the third helicopter, rested his finger against the trigger, and held his breath. One shot left. He had to make it count.

The black helicopter rose diagonally to the left, no longer hiding behind the smoke. Then appeared to hesitate in the air.

It turned tail and disappeared over the horizon.

Jesus lowered his smoking revolver and got to his feet. He scanned the landscape around him, and saw Lily was safe. He ran over to Max's black helicopter.

It lay on its side, cracked with its contents spilling out like a black egg. Michael Max had fallen out onto the ground below it, trapped by debris and cushioned by a considerable amount of pastries he must have brought along. Next to him lay the helicopter pilot, motionless behind his black visor.

Max began to stir. Jesus put his magnificent pistol back in its shoulder holster, and drew his stepfather's .45.

Lily caught up to Jesus. "It really is Michael Max? What the Hell?"

"That's not the strangest part," said Jesus. "Check out the pilot. Some kinda half-human half-manatee hybrid. That's why your liberal environmentalists are so concerned about preserving them *and* messing around with stem cells." He shook his head. "Oh, the humanatee."

Lily gaped at him for a second. "You just can't be for real. None of this can be real!"

"Watch and learn." He faced Michael Max, who chose that moment to cough and opened his eyes. They saw Jesus and went wide with fear.

Jesus nodded grimly. "All of this done with your help and your propaganda."

"Well, about that," said Michael Max. "This is kinda awkward, but um, you could, you know, forgive me?"

"What?" said Jesus. "Lily, did he just..." He scratched his head. "What?"

"You know, forgive me. Repentance and stuff," Max said hurriedly, staring down the barrel of Jesus' vintage .45. "I understand that if I ask for forgiveness, I can be, you know, forgiven."

Past the crackling flames of the downed helicopters he saw what could either be a soft and isolated wind, or someone moving in the grass. "Disciples! Report!" said Jesus, as he kept his eyes and gun trained on Max.

"No one else was hurt," Aaron yelled back. "Besides Hector, Hector is..." His voice cracked.

Hector's death was hard enough. The distance that Aaron's

answer came from made Jesus' heart sink. "Lily, where is everyone else?"

"You're asking me?" she said. "They're all on the other side of the ravine."

"Get across that bridge and join them."

"What bridge?"

Jesus' eye followed the trail of flame from the black helicopters' carcasses. The flame had spread to the bridge over the ravine. All of his apostles besides Hector had made it across at least, but the bridge itself lay in ruins.

"About that forgiveness?" asked Max. "I am a Catholic, you know."

The nerve of this man! Jesus longed to just stomp him into a bloody mess in his father's name. But Jesus' commitment to his own principles must stay true. "I can forgive you being Catholic," Jesus admitted. "With my father's infinite mercy, even a Devil's tool as wayward as you can be saved – if you earn it. The last creature that asked me for forgiveness had to fight an alligator. He hadn't even killed one of my disciples! What can you do to prove you really are repentant?"

"Just give me a chance! I can....give up something I really care about. Like...like pastries!"

Jesus snorted. "I thought you wanted a chance. You're even more addicted to carbs than you are to evil."

"Uh, Lord," Aaron called out, his voice stretched taut with worry. "I hate to interrupt, but what are we supposed to do?"

Jesus made the only decision he could. "One moment, Aaron." He locked eyes with Max. "My father's rules say I have to give you a chance. I don't have time to dig you out of that chopper to fight something. Here's what you can do to try and earn salvation. I know what you love even more than donuts - making movies against the Free Market, Guns, and America. If you don't misuse your God-given free speech to ever make another anti-America, anti-business, anti-gun, anti-Godliness film as long as you live, I can forgive you, *I guess.*"

Michael Max's mouth opened and closed. A shocked expression

came over his face. His face twisted as his eyes welled with tears. "It's too much!" he exclaimed. "Please, please I beg of you-"

With a thump, a group of flames spawned at the back of the helicopter. Max saw the orange flicker reflect in Jesus' eyes and began to sweat. He strained against the wreckage pinning him to the ground. It would not budge. "Alright!" Max said at last. "Alright! I promise not to make another liberal movie!"

Jesus nodded. "Okay." He holstered his .45 and turned away.

Max struggled to free himself from the helicopter. "But how – how am I supposed to get free-"

Jesus took a stunned and quiet Lily by the arm, and led her toward the edge of the ravine. Another explosion sounded from the helicopter behind them. Jesus paid it no mind. He reached the edge of the ravine and looked over.

It was deep, and the cliff walls consisted of soft shale that looked prone to easy crumbling under the slightest amount of weight. A risky climb at night even without gear, even if the Demoncrats weren't certain to send reinforcements.

Jesus addressed his remaining flock. "They'll be back soon, in greater numbers! It'll take at least half an hour for us to cross that ravine. There's no way to reunite in time. We have to split up."

"We can't just leave you!" cried Steve.

"You can, you will and you must."

"But - can you trust her alone?" asked Aaron.

"Can he trust *me*?" said Lily, incredulous.

"She's got a large part to play in all of this, and in what I've got to do." Jesus saw Barclay suppress a grin. Did Barclay think he was sweet on Lily too? It dawned on Jesus – was he? He brought himself back to the moment and moved on. "Don't you worry about me. There will be signs in the upcoming days. You will hear of great tribulations as the Enemy's power is challenged like it never has been before. There will be earthquakes and upheavals, and tsunamis and the wrath of unbound nature as good angels struggle to unleash their holy wrath, and fallen angels strive to keep you bound by liberal media deceptions. Watch and prepare, but do not show your growing strength. You will know when the time comes because I will say to you: 'It's time to kick ass!' Can you remember those words?" His new disciples said they would. "Good. Never repeat those again until the time comes!"

"Yes, Lord," said Marci, choking back tears. "Will we see you again?"

"Now, don't cry, child. Have faith. You will."

"Must you go?" asked Aaron, his voice even, but feeling some of the shock and fear they all felt. "It feels like – like everything's breaking apart!'

"This can only be how my Father wants it." Jesus raised his fist in the air. "Be strong! I showed you all the basics. You're gonna have to learn on your own now for a spell. I give you these jobs! Aaron, you must learn how to beat men to death in my name." Across the chasm now between them, Jesus made the sign of the Crucifist. "A good way is to learn yourself some Kung Fu and start getting into bar fights. Get to it." Aaron nodded, wiping at his eyes. "And no more tears!" Jesus added. "Tears ain't for men. Remember that."

"Yes sir," Aaron agreed. Jesus turned to Barclay, and made the Crucifist for him as well. "Barclay, you must learn to use the Free Market to gain God's Good Gold for the cause of Freedom."

"Thank you, Lord," said Barclay. "You know I actually already know quite a bit about the stock market. I've been investing in-"

Jesus moved on. "Marci, you must learn how to make any man desire you, and any woman want to not be gay by seeing how much men want you. Not while cheating on Steve, mind you. Just by how you look, and smile, and say things that are pleasant to right-thinking people."

"Thank you, Jesus!" Marci said. She paused. "Umm.... how?"

"You gotta learn how, that's woman stuff. That's what you're gonna have to figure out. I dunno, maybe grow your hair longer and lose a couple pounds. Go to a tanning salon and get your nails done. Maybe a lotta YoGod, a crash diet and some liposuction. Try wearing a lot more makeup too. Maybe some implants."

Marci hesitated. "Wouldn't that...make me like a Femborg?"

Jesus laughed. "Ah, you adorable thing... no, don't worry about that. If helps make you pleasing to a good Christian man, then it will always have my and my Father's blessing." He addressed his next New Disciple. "Steve!"

"Yes, Lord?" asked Steve, most humble.

"Steve, you have to learn how to help any man not be gay, and any Christian woman want to give fruitful Christian birth from Christian seed."

"Thank you!" Steve breathed. "Seed!"

Jesus frowned a little. "Make sure you stay focused," he admonished his disciple, and turned to Gary, still on his stretcher. "Last and least, Gary, you must learn to always use your science skills to advance the will of God – and never to disprove true Christians."

"I will sir!" Gary said. He struggled his hardest to salute, and barely lifted his tiny hand to his forehead.

Jesus chuckled at the huge spirit in that little frame. "Now you all act wisely and righteously! God is watching, and the Devil is scouting for any chance he can to trip us up and strike us down."

"Wait - what about Hector?" asked Aaron. "We can't just leave him here."

"We must. We've left him where he fell - a warrior's end. His family will know he rests in heaven for helping Real America rise again." Jesus held his arms high in pride. "I know I've got some solid fighters in you, ready to do God's work. Learn what I've told you. Keep the Enemy guessing. Find my people in New America, train with them and lead them, and tell them the time of God is not past, it's come at last."

"Yes, my Lord," they said as one.

"Rise, and be glad!" Jesus pumped his fist in the air. "This is a glorious day! We are one! With this group, I will save the Heaven and Earth and all inside it so help me Me! Amen! Now - get!"

Jesus waved farewell to his followers, and headed for the woods with a wide-eyed Lily in tow.

Rosio slumped to the floor, and laid there, stunned from the shock of her total defeat.

Michael Max was not enough. No lesser servant of their dark cause could be enough. The Death Panel could not be depended on to help her either. In the end it might only be her, maybe it was only her from the very beginning.

She could only keep to her faith and soldier on. She had contacts deep within the government that Bomraka would never know about. They could be turned against him and the rebel Death Panel members soon enough. For now there was one thing in front of her vengeance on the man who'd failed her – disposing of the Christ who still stood in the way of all that was unholy.

She began to lay the groundwork for the less favorable scenario, of President Bomraka and his all-too-human forces finding Jesus first.

45

The road stretched out before Jesus and Lily, as they walked beside the highway. The night grew cold as cars flashed by.

"Here," he said. He took off his denim jacket. and tried to drape it over Lily's shoulders.

She shrugged it off. "I'm not cold! Don't try to help me when you've kidnapped me under false pretenses - and keep almost getting me killed!"

"Actually, the jacket's to hide the fact your hands are tied. So some driver doesn't call the police."

She gaped at him. "Why wouldn't I want that?"

"Come on! You want to give your Demoncratic party another chance to kill you? You just saw the truth of Michael Max. How much more of your supposed scientific evidence do you need?"

For once she had no response. Jesus succeeded in draping his jacket over her shoulders. She walked next to him in baleful silence for another 15 minutes.

"You never did say what danger my grandfather was in," Lily said finally. "Or how I could help save him."

"Oh, that," he sighed. This probably wouldn't go over too well. "The danger is, he'll go to Hell if he doesn't give me what I want. He said if I brought him back to you, he'd help me. Unless you go back there and talk with him, he's destined to go to Hell."

She grit her teeth. "You're an absolute liar."

"No, not one thing I told you was a lie. You just didn't need to know the full picture right off."

"The full picture!" she sputtered. "That's what makes everything make sense. What the Hell is wrong with you?"

"It's more like what the Heaven is right with me. Why should anything be wrong? Isn't all this beautiful?" He held his arms open to the night sky. "Look at those stars! Smell that night air."

"One of your followers was just killed!"

"Can't heal or resurrect people this time around. Hector'll be fine in Heaven. Why cry about a man going to his glorious reward?"

"Did you give them the full picture, or are you hiding things from them as well?"

"Who?"

"I'm talking about that bunch of dipshits you sent to revolt against the President."

"You worried about them?" he asked, one eyebrow rising. "You care about what happens to us? Maybe me?"

"I don't have to care to feel sorry for those brainwashed idiots. Don't change the subject. They haven't got a chance in the world."

"Remember that. Remember what you just said. 'Cause you know what? You're right. Just not the way you think. They don't have a chance in the world – it's going to take Heaven to make it happen. The sky will have to open and rain down miracles. Why, an amount of miracles that's miraculous all by itself!"

"That's as crazy as you are."

"Why don't you have the Mark of the Beast implanted yet?"

"The what?"

"You heard me."

"Yes, and I have no idea what you're talking about."

"That implanted chip that helps the government track you, without which you aren't allowed to do business with the Beast."

She shook her head impatiently. "There is no such thing. That's just crazy. Why would the government even need to do that? They can track us all with cell phones."

"This is a whole different level. Among other things, it means they can blow your head up any time they want. Which means forcing people to fit into the secular humanist system. I bet not having that chip made it a bit hard to find a man. I bet it caused some trouble with that career of yours. But not having it yet also means that maybe they weren't quite ready to trust you. It's why I still have hope you can be saved. It's why I'm going to do this."

Jesus took out his buck knife, opened it and cut through the duck tape on Lily's wrists. Surprised, she took off the rest of the tape and rubbed her hands.

"Good," she said. She took off his jacket and threw it back at him. He caught it, momentarily taken aback. She started walking in the opposite direction. Jesus looked after her a bit, shook his head, and continued on his way.

She glanced backward after a few steps, and saw his back receding.

"You're going to just let me go, after all that?" she said incredulously.

"Well, you want to go, don't you?" said Jesus. "I ain't gonna keep you. I showed you all I can. You saw what I can do. You saw the facade of the Devil's plans crack open in Atlanta. How's six black helicopters supposed to just show up and wipe out a city block? How's a half-human half-manatee supposed to pilot one?"

"What are you talking about? There wasn't any evidence that pilot was – was anything but human, let alone half-manatee!"

Jesus threw up his hands. "See? I can't make you believe. You don't want to go back and see your grandfather? You want to take your chances with Bomraka and the One World Order? I'll be sad to see what happens to you. But I've done all I can do."

Jesus resumed walking. After a few moments, he heard her walking back towards him.

"I suppose after all this I should see my grandfather," she said.

"I suppose you should," said Jesus with a smile. She wanted to pretend she didn't like him. Who was she really fooling? She was beginning to like him, in spite of herself. Just like Alaine.

Love moves in mysterious ways. Because God is love, he realized. And righteously ass-kicking was God too, of course. Just another form of love.

"What are you smiling for? You ruined my life!" said Lily. "You – you got my entire TV station blown up, you got people I worked with killed! You turned Blabbera Wilters into some sort of – of cyborg!"

"Now, don't put that on me. That was probably Blabbera Strident did that."

She lapsed into an angry silence. He glanced over at her from time to time. She avoided his eyes. So willful! So beautiful. Smart as a whip too. And strong. Like it or not, she had guts. Too much guts for other men, perhaps. Just right for him. Her beliefs were just so wrong-headed. Just the worst combination of liberal thinking – all about excuses for the weak, and nothing about kicking the ass of evil. All about the facts, not at all about the truth. If he could only get her to let go of all that liberal nonsense and just believe.

They walked for miles in relative silence. Eventually they could hear something coming down the road. It sounded big. Jesus coughed. "We better get off the road and see who it is."

"Don't you trust in God?" Lily taunted.

"All the time," said Jesus. "All others pay cash."

"Some Messiah!"

Jesus grinned. Then he paused. "Get down!"

"Oh, right. What is it this time, a submarine-"

"DOWN!" he shoved her, and lay down too. He put his finger to his lips. She withheld her angry rejoinder.

Anxious seconds went by. Jesus abruptly leapt to his feet. "This is it! Can you hear that? It's a sign!"

"What?" Lily strained her ears. "That just sounds like a truck, you lunatic."

"You're blessed right it does," said Jesus joyfully. "A truck the likes of which I ain't heard in years."

The truck came around the bend in the road. Just as Jesus said, it was a truck – but not just any truck. A true gas-guzzling tractor complete with a sleeper cab, meant to haul an entire 18-wheeler. It had no cargo behind it, but drove by itself in these times of vile computer-aided hybrid drone delivery. It was a lonely and majestic beast, in its own way like the blessed dinosaurs of 6,000 years ago.

Jesus got onto the shoulder and waved his arms. The tractor slowly pulled over to the side of the road, a few feet ahead of them.

Jesus headed toward the truck, a joyful skip in his step. Unsure of what to do, Lily stood up and brushed off the dirt. After a bit, she followed.

The driver climbed down from the 18-wheeler's cab, and went over to the shoulder to meet them. He had medium build, blue-collar clothes, a red baseball cap and a broad smile. "How's things, people?" he asked.

"You tell me!" said Jesus with a broad smile. "What in Heaven's an honest-to-God diesel tractor trailer truck doing on these highways? I thought all that was left were hybrids and public trains!"

"Ah, friend, please don't twist the knife," said the trucker. "This here's this lovely lady's final run. Ain't even haulin' no cargo. I'm taking her straight to the recyclin' camp."

"My God, brother," said Jesus. He put his hand on the man's shoulder to comfort him. "Was she yours?"

"Yep, and my father's before me. She hauled goods all around America, no matter day or night. But now we got to move things with more fuel efficiency." He spat the last word out like a curse. "So generations of our way of life must bite the dust."

"It won't be this way for much longer, my friend. Things will turn."

The man snorted bitterly. "How you figure? Who's gonna stand against the President? Who's brave enough to fight against fuel efficiency standards, black helicopters, gays marrying, and men who take our guns? Who's gonna help us fight the blue helmets when the UN sends 'em in?"

"You're lookin' at 'im." He stuck out his hand. "The name's Jesus."

The man left Jesus' hand in the air, unclasped. "That's ain't no kinda joke, mister," he said, anger rising in his voice. "Was a time that name meant something."

"Still does. Glad to hear it means something to you. What's your name, brother?"

"Gus." He looked Jesus up and down. "Damn if you don't look like the pictures I used to see on Sunday mornings before they took our church shows off the Devil's cable."

"Except this time, I ain't here to make no peace. I'm here to take care of business."

Gus started to say something else, and then thought better of it.

"Come on," said Jesus. "Out with it, whatever it is."

"If you're the messiah, then why aren't you fighting the Bomraka?"

"Doing what I can," Jesus said patiently. "I got a plan, he's on my list."

"But he called you out."

"What?" said Jesus.

"You telling me you didn't see the news?"

Jesus waved his hands dismissively. "You should know better to believe the media."

"I do know better - but I saw the President himself stand there and call you out. Said you were a coward for not fighting him."

Jesus paled. "What did you say?"

"I didn't say it," Gus said hastily. "He did. He just up and dared you to respond. To take him on directly."

"I see," said Jesus slowly. "Well."

"What are you going to do about that?" asked Lily. "Doesn't your macho code require you go risk yourself?"

"That it does," said Jesus. He considered it. "If my disciples were around, I might not have a choice. I can't look weak in front of my troops. But they're on their own right now. The President's just going to have to wait until I get this job done. Once I get you back to your grandfather's, I'm gonna show the President and his media a fight like they ain't never seen before.

"Gus faced Lily, as if noticing her for the first time. "What you think of him?" he asked her.

"He's a lunatic who ruined my life," said Lily flatly. "If it weren't for him, I'd still be sitting pretty in a penthouse in Atlanta."

"Atlanta?" Recognition dawned on Gus' face. "You're that news reporter! I read about you on AOL." His eyes widened "You're both supposed to be dead." His eyes fixed again on Jesus. "You took over that station, defeated Blabbera Wilters and The View and then blew the whole thing up!"

"I didn't blow that place up. But the rest is right."

Gus jerked a thumb toward Lily. "What's her story?"

"I'm right here!"

Jesus smiled by way of apology. "She's a mite testy. I guess I earned it, seeing as how I saved her liberal butt multiple times from the devil's dark creatures and all."

"You-!"

Jesus chuckled. "Let's not argue just now. Gus, that's a fine hat you got there."

"This? Just my high school baseball team." Gus took his hat off and showed it to Jesus. As he did, Jesus surreptitiously checked the man's hairline and his temples. He appeared to have no Mark inserted.

The hat's label said "Vernon Valley Kings". Jesus grinned and handed it back to Gus. "Local baseball team?"

"The best kind. American."

"Where you headed?"

"West."

"Ha! What a coincidence. Why, that's exactly the direction we're headed. On the last real 18-wheeler in America." He winked at Lily. "Almost like a miracle."

"Or a lot of chance!" said Lily.

"Where's your stop?" Gus asked.

"Little town by name of Egypt."

"Sure, I know it." Gus considered them both. "Well, I got to get going to reach the recycling plant before nightfall. I do think it just might suit me to have along two more hitchhikers, for this ol' girl's final run." The last trucker reached out his hand, and Jesus shook it. Gus reached out to Lily, who folded her arms crossly.

Gus shrugged. "Well, if you want to come aboard too, ma'am, you're welcome. But do please make it snappy." Gus went back to the driver's side and climbed in. He opened the passenger door. Jesus went up the steps.

After a few more seconds, Lily climbed in the cab. She started out the window, trying to hide that she was feeling more than a bit unnerved.

Jesus leaned back and enjoyed the sight of nighttime melting into dawn. Why say anything more? They were sitting in a miracle. The point was being made all by itself.

The first couple of hours were blessedly uneventful. Gus felt no need for extra chit-chat. Jesus spent most of the time gazing at the road and letting his thoughts wander.

"What happened to you?" Lily broke in.

"What do you mean?" said Jesus.

"What made you this way? What made you so sure you're the Son of God?"

"I was raised like it seemed I could be, and then a vision came that made it clear."

"Doesn't it seem a bit contradictory to you that the other Jesus said 'Do unto others', but you go around ready to punch and shoot and kill?"

"Nope. The last time I was a lamb. This time I'm a lion."

"That's just what I'm talking about," asked Lily. "How did you decide to be so aggressive? How did that begin?"

Jesus smiled at her, and then at Gus driving. Gus said nothing, but seemed interested as well.

"Alright, I'll tell you," said Jesus.

46

As Jesus had approached maturity, it became clear that his physique was not only intended to be a paragon of manly male beauty. He had also been gifted with the build and talents of a fighter. Like any man born of woman, he had to learn to use those tools. He started learning at age thirteen.

He was already a good strong boy, able to work harder and longer than grown men twice his age and starting to turn the heads of girls with his clean good looks. The only thing that put people off was his long hair. Since his parents were so godly otherwise, it was a cause of some confusion.

At his parents' request, Jesus had kept his divine origin a secret. Thus, inevitable questions arose from his appearance. The townsfolk gossiped - were his parents just turning a blind eye to his behaviors? Was their son, who they actually dared to call Jesus, which was funny enough - was he maybe going a little "that way"? Pink, pinko, or both?

One time Jesus came back from a hard day at work in the fields to find his beloved mother and stepfather at the kitchen table. Mary was holding ice to Joe's hands. Once he saw Jesus was home, he tried to hide his bloody knuckles.

"What happened?" Jesus asked.

"Nothin'," said his stepfather. "No big deal."

"Tell me," said Jesus. "Don't I have to know, if I'm gonna grow up to be the messiah?"

Joe sighed. "I went to the store to get some feed, and stopped by the bar to play pool. Some fella had a bit too much and gave me some crap about your hair." Joe held up his left hand. "That was that one." He smiled. "Then his friend came up. That was the two knuckles on the other hand, before he got me in the ribs with his thick skull." His smile disappeared. "Then we split before the cops come. 'Cause the government don't want men to fight like men no more."

"This has been going on for a while?" asked Jesus. Joe hesitated, then nodded. "Why didn't you want to tell me about this?"

"You're here to save us America and mankind from Hell, not to deal with idiots' distractions."

Jesus thought about it. "It's a problem, though."

"Yes it is," Joe said.

"So this must be part of what I have to fix too."

Mary stood up from the table, alarmed. "Now son, it's bad enough when your stepfather fights. If you fight too, you're both going to get hurt, and maybe hurt someone else too much!"

"That whole nonviolence thing didn't work too well for the last me," Jesus pointed out.

"I'm glad to hear you say that, son," said Joe. "'Cause I've been thinking about that too. I think it's just like Kenny Rogers says. 'Sometimes you have to fight when you're a man.'"

Mary sighed. "They got that Kung Fu place in town. Maybe he can learn some of that at least. That looks less hurtful than just swingin' at things."

Joe laughed. "That stuff? That's for the movies. There's only one place you can learn to fight like a man. And that's a bar."

Jesus rubbed his chin, which was just starting to grow a fuzz. "Maybe I should learn both."

"I don't know if I like you fighting," said Mary. Jesus was about to say something, but Joe said, "Mary, can you get some more ice?" Mary sighed and went back to the fridge. He leaned in to his stepson Jesus and whispered, "Don't bother her with the details. Do what you gotta do."

Jesus sweated and practiced every evening for the rest of the summer. He sparred and struck against other fighters and fixed and swinging targets, and learned all the Kung Fu master could teach while also trying to reform the teacher's pagan ways. Jesus also learned to hunt and catch animals, to always hold his hand over his heart when an anthem was played, to despise the French, and all the other things a real American man should know. Finally the end of the summer came, and a long harvest began. They rented equipment, and did their best. When all their crops were gathered and shipped to market, they went to the bar for a good, cold beer.

Jesus was too young to be in there, according to the law. Anywhere else that might have been a problem. In this small and righteous Montana town, people didn't care much about the law when it got in the way of what was right.

Jesus and Joe had just gotten their cool cans of Budweiser and sat down at a pine wood bench, when Jesus saw two men looking at them across the room. They were sitting at a table next to a couple of other fools who looked even ornerier.

Joe had noticed too. He took a sip, saying nothing.

"That's them isn't it?" said Jesus. "The two you fought back at the start of the summer."

"Yep," said Joe.

Jesus looked at them, and him. "What do you want to do?"

"You're asking me?" said Joe with a twinkle in his eye. He put the can down. "I thought you were the Messiah and all."

"I want to know what you think," said Jesus.

"I think you gotta decide if you want trouble or not," said Joe. "And if it's trouble, when you can you head straight for it like a freight train."

Jesus nodded and stood up. Joe stood up too. Together, they

walked over to the table in question. There sat two man, one tall and thin and the other short, thick and mean.

"Well, if it ain't Joe and his daughter," the tall man said.

"Aw, don't give him a hard time," said the short one. "His pa got so worked up the last time before he got his ass beat. Got to be embarrassing. Maybe he's a pacifist-"

Jesus caught him right across the jaw. The man fell off his seat while his friend stood up in surprise. The fellows at the next table followed.

"I'm more of a double fist," said Jesus.

"You son of a bitch!" the tall man said, and dove at Jesus. Joe caught him mid-lunge with a boot to the gut. The man hit the floor and doubled over, gasping for air.

"That's my boy AND my wife you're talking about this time!" said Joe. "You want to stay down if you know what's good for-"

The table cleared, as they launched themselves at Joseph and his stepson. As Jesus would remember it later, a glorious whoop filled the air as the bar was filled with their flying fists. This was man time. The harvest was done, and the women weren't around. It was time to fight with the free abandon that was all men's birthright.

Later, in the wee morning hours, Jesus and Joe came back to their home. Jesus was half-carrying Joe who was equal parts concussed and drunk. "That wash beautiful, son," said Joe.

Mary waited for them in the doorway, clearly angry. Joe put his finger to his lips, in the universal signal of "Don't tell it to the wife."

She held the door and they stumbled in. Knowing what he was in for, Joe got his pillows and set up for the couch. She turned and left the room.

"Why you sleeping on the couch this time, pop?" said Jesus. "We didn't do nothing wrong." He had seen his mom get cross if she caught Joseph staring at another woman too long. Then Jesus' stepfather might bring up the angel, and things might go south from there. But they hadn't even been to a strip club this time.

"Shometimes you got to pick your battlesh, shon," said Joe. He belched mightily. The bedroom door slammed behind Mary upstairs.

"You did good," said Joe. "Real good. Looksh like there'sh not even a mark on ya."

"I let myself get hit just to feel it," said Jesus. "It hurt." He laughed.

"Good boy," said Joe. "You got to know you can feel pain shometimesh. Jush to know you're shtrong enough to take it." He patted Jesus on the head. "Night now. Pleashe don't wake me up early."

Joe drifted off to sleep. Jesus sat there a little while, and then went up to his room. He thought about asking Mom why she was mad. She seemed a bit too upset to talk to. Maybe he'd ask later.

Jesus looked down at his knuckles, and smiled. There was a lot to like about being a man.

"And that's how it is," said Jesus. "All men have to fight sometimes. When you believe in what's right, you have to fight for God. When you're the Son of God and man, you have to fight all the enemies of America."

Lily started to respond, when Jesus pointed to a police car's flashing red-and-blue lights emerging over a hill. As they drove closer, they saw a car pulled over and a policeman getting out with a somewhat bored manner. The policeman paused to admire the truck, and waved as they went by. It was a hard vehicle for men not to like.

They rolled on down the express lane, past the poor, deluded masses in their meaningless, environmentally emasculated so-called vehicles that almost apologized for being on the road. Most of those cars' drivers stared in wonder at the mighty beast of a truck on its bittersweet last trek.

The cars and the police car's flashing headlights faded into the rear-view mirror.

"A good man doing a tough job," said Jesus.

Lily stared at him. "You mean that policeman? He isn't a government thug to you?"

"Nah, not that guy. He's keeping the peace. Probably just making sure that driver isn't some Muslim terrorist. We just need to be sure that real Americans have enough guns that the police leave us alone."

She shook her head. "See, your background doesn't explain that kind of.... whatever that is. Something else happened to you."

"The only other thing that happened was..." he stopped.

"What?"

He closed his eyes. It was a part of his life that hurt to relive. But tell the truth and shame the Devil. "There was a girl I loved."

47

"Loved?" Lily asked softly. "As in, past tense?"

"That's right." Jesus looked away for a moment. "She died in that thing you liberals don't like to call the Rapture."

"That unexplained disappearance of a few thousand people?"

He snorted in derision. "That's the one."

"Tell me about her," she said.

He faced the horizon ahead, and his mind went flashing back.

JESUS HAD BEEN SO eager to tell Alaine of his adventures, he could hardly wait. He was sure they would impress her. What girl wouldn't like a good strong fighting man?

However, that wasn't how Alaine responded. When he told her of his and Joe's victorious bar fight, at first she didn't believe him. When he showed his bloody knuckles as proof, what flashed into her eyes was not approval. Instead her face went white and she looked away.

"What?" he asked, bewildered. "You should see the other guy's face."

"I don't want to see the other guy." She bit her lip. "I'm kind of wondering if I want to see you."

"I'm here to make things right! I can't just take people's crap. They'll think I'm weak."

"Who cares what they think? Why do you?"

"I have to care. I'm gonna be representing God. I'm gonna be the messiah!"

She took his hand, and saw again his scarred and bloody knuckles. She let go of his hand, becoming more upset. "You're hurting people and you don't have to." She shook her head. "I just don't see why a loving God would want that."

"You don't understand," he said.

"You're right, I don't. And I don't want to." She touched his chest. "There's someone beautiful in there, who is even prettier than you are on the outside," she said. "I'm going to keep on your butt to bring him out."

He grinned in spite of himself. "Sounds like something I should say to you." She wasn't a believer. No matter how good she was to him, she was still going straight to Hell. He had to save her. Like he'd have to save all mankind, once he was fully grown. That was the job his heavenly Father had set before him. "I worry about you, you know."

She laughed. She came in close, just a few inches from his own face, and stopped. "Not all sinners need saving."

He looked into her eyes. How different they were. The left one blue, and the right one green. He'd never stared this deeply into them before. He moved his gaze from one eye to the other. Blue was often thought the clear grace of an angel, and green the unknown temptations of a witch's mystery. What lay behind those eyes? Was there one side more of her that held more sway than the other – and if so, was it the angel or the witch?

He decided that he just didn't know enough yet to make that call. He put aside knowing that answer for that moment, and instead went in for a kiss.

He never talked with her about his fighting again. His dad was right about that. Women didn't need to know about every little thing.

Back in the cab of Gus' truck, it had felt easier to tell this to Lily without looking at her. He kept his eyes straight ahead. "I was in love with her from the moment I first saw her. She was beautiful, like you. Sweet, and free, and smart, and all these wonderful things. My parents always made me feel like I had to be the Messiah. With her, I could just be myself." He smiled at the memory. "Just a randy teenage boy with a whole fun life ahead."

When Lily said nothing else, he continued. "Her father was a liberal. A defense lawyer, even. He would come home and just hang out. He should have hated me, but he didn't seem to mind me. I think it was because of how much Alaine liked me. Even though we were nothing alike at all."

"That sounds like they completely accepted you," said Lily softly. "Why do you sound so sad?"

"'Cause then it came. The Rapture. Chaos. In these liberal modern times, few true Christians remained for God to summon to heaven. My parents were among them, as were several others in our unusually faithful town. Alaine and her father..." He stopped, holding back tears that as a man he could not show. He realized he never healed from this, even after all these years.

"They disappeared too?"

"No! They didn't!" Jesus' eyes closed, and a clenched fist went to his brow at the painful recollection. "They died in an accident instead! And they went straight to Hell because I hadn't done my job to save them. They stayed secular liberals. There they were, sittin' in their car, seatbelts on, waiting patiently at an intersection. A car came that had been driven by a true Christian just moments before. In the blink of an eye it had no driver, so it blasted through the red light and ploughed straight into them. The girl I loved, the one person I knew who was good to me because of me, and not because of anything I was supposed to become – is now being tortured in Hell. Forever. Because I let her down."

He dared to look at her eyes, half expecting to see more biting sarcasm. Instead, if he didn't know better, he saw something that looked like sympathy.

"That can't be your fault," she said gently. "Even if you believe that, it would have to be God's will, wouldn't it?"

Jesus laughed bitterly. "I'd blame it on anyone else if I could, even my Holy Father. But I have no excuse. I understand my burden all too well. It was just that some part of me still wanted to stay a boy. To not take on so early the mantle of the man I'd have to be." He sat up straight. "If I falter in my job, then people will die before they know the true Word of God. Good people or not, good works or not...people I love, or not, they will go to Hell and be tortured for all eternity." His eyes lost focus for a bit, haunted by the memory.

"What was her name? Was it Alaine?"

He looked a little startled. "Yes. How did you know that?"

"That's what you called me before, well, you blackmailed me and then kidnapped me."

Jesus sighed inwardly. They were back to that again. Well, it had been nice. "You look enough like her almost to be her twin."

"You do know I'm not her, right?"

"Oh, I'm very aware of that," he said drily. "You're also so much like her that you could be her twin, and not just in looks. She was very like you. A well-meaning liberal, ultimately doomed to Hell unless you stop taking facts and so-called science over the truth. You looking so like her might mean God is giving me a second chance."

Jesus caught her looking at him with something like compassion. Gus continued driving, saying nothing. They must be more interesting than any hitchhikers in years.

"So that's me," Jesus concluded. "We've got some time ahead of us. How is it that you came to this pass yourself? You have a brave heart, came from a good Christian family. You have a grandfather who's willing to risk the pits of Hell itself to save you."

Her eyes sparked with anger. She moved away from him and faced forward, folding her arms. "And thanks to you, I have no other place to go."

"Here we are. How about you tell us what led you to work for the Demoncrats at ABC?"

"Demoncrats," she said in amazement. "You really want to know?"

"Said so, didn't I?"

"Well, I went to college and -"

"Ah." He nodded.

"Do you want to let me even finish before you show how ignorant you are?"

Jesus smiled indulgently. "By all means, go ahead."

"I went to college, and I met people from other backgrounds and other religions - who were happy. It was such a contrast to how unhappy my grandfather's beliefs made him. When I was very young he was kind and happy, but then he started thinking he had this destiny. Instead of bringing him peace, all it seemed to do was make him angry and bitter. Sure, he had a story now that made him feel important, even central to all mankind. It gave him a lot of pride. The price he paid was spending most of his waking life on whatever he thought was his secret mission. It helped him feel justified no matter what he did, so he never had to think anything through. It gradually cut him off more and more from others who had the slightest disagreement. It was like he – he built a fortress, a lonely castle where he could feel like a king – and to protect that feeling, no one who thought different was allowed into his heart. I thought, if God only wanted one view of things then why would he give us so many different views? How could he condemn so many to Hell for thinking differently, about a narrow set of doctrines that he himself was supposed to have made?" She sighed. "It was easier for me to think that fallible men made their own ways and called them God's. I chose my own way. I know it broke his heart. I tried to be diplomatic, but after a certain point, I just couldn't see the use in living like he was. I couldn't stand to live a lie of pretending to believe."

Jesus smiled at her. So much potential in her, such a big heart just waiting to be filled with faith. "It's true, sometimes God's gifts are also tests. He gave you wit and spirit and intelligence, to see if you would let them overpower what your heart knows is true. You let them lead you astray. Let me lead you back."

She stared at him, and then at Gus. The truck driver was looking at her also with a deep sympathy that could even be pity. She slapped her own forehead in frustration. "It's amazing! How did you both do that? It's like you didn't hear a single thing I said."

"It's alright, don't worry about it. We've got a few more hours on the road, and then you can talk to your grandfather. If you aren't convinced at the end of that, you'll still have a great story you can sell to your liberal media you love so much." He chuckled, and blew her a kiss. It was so out of nowhere that she couldn't help but smile before she turned her face away.

"You're not supposed to like me, are you?" said Jesus.

"I don't!" said Lily.

"Uh-huh." He leaned back into the seat. "Baby, you ain't even fooling yourself."

"You're such an egotist," she rolled her eyes.

"Maybe I am. Does that make me wrong?"

"You're just unbelievable!"

"What's unbelievable is how hard you want to smile right now," he teased. "Shouldn't you be too angry to do anything but scowl?"

"Humph!" She closed her eyes and appeared to count to ten, before placing her hands flatly on her legs.

"That all you got to say?" said Jesus.

His sentence hung in the air for the next few miles, until Jesus started to wonder if that really was all she would say. He was thankful that Gus did not have a need to fill silence with conversation.

"No," she said at last. "You did save my life more than once down in those tunnels, quite bravely. I wouldn't have even been in that situation if it weren't for you... but still, that was brave and I thank you." She paused, and grit her teeth. "And I must admit - I don't understand what was going on with those black helicopters and Michael Max."

Jesus stroked his chin in mock surprise. "That mean I'm getting closer to receiving your secular liberal forgiveness?"

"I wouldn't go that far..., but," she said with a rueful smile, "I always did like bad boys."

Jesus sat frozen for a second. "Bad boy?" The son of God, a bad boy? He shook his head. Women. "We got to you in the nick of time, you know. The next step in your climb up the ladder is the Mark."

This was her cue to roll her eyes. "And there we go. Back to insanity."

"What's the Mark?" Gus broke in. Their heads both swiveled at the sudden sound. They had gotten so deep in conversation with each other, they had momentarily forgotten he was even there.

"It's a computer chip. Like Bill Clinton's V-chip, but for people instead of computers. It gets inserted when people are high up enough the ladder to be introduced to President Bomraka's true mission. Usually under cover of vaccination. After that, all their words are monitored and their positions are tracked, and anything that veers from the Devil's plan means their heads can be exploded just like that." Jesus snapped his fingers.

"In other words it's totally insane," said Lily.

"That's exactly what a liberal would say," said Jesus. "But something like that has to be going on. You see it all the time. It's how a band is great until they make it big. How a star does right until he gets too famous, and gets that chip put in so he won't step too far out of the liberal line."

Gus looked thoughtful. "I always wondered about what keeps real conservatives out of Hollywood."

"That's why it all makes sense. There's a few who are smart enough to slip out of Hollywood's grasp and not get a Mark, like Stephen Baldwin or that kid from Growing Pains. For the rest of 'em, that chip is calling the shots on behalf of the KenyAntichrist."

Gus nodded. "Like they must have gotten to President Thruppence, seeing how he never built that wall."

"Is that why my Grandfather sent you to get me, and ruin my life in the process?" asked Lily. "To save me from these things that don't even exist?"

"That wasn't the main reason. The worst was that you might die before you had been saved, and thus go straight to damnation."

"And that's how it came to be that you're taking me back to my grandfather - to save my soul."

"That's the job I took on."

"Got any other reasons, besides that supposed main one?" she persisted.

"You sure are a reporter, huh?" he chuckled. "You dig right to it. It is a fair question though." He reached into his shoulder holster, and pulled out the pistol Hieronymus had made. "I get more things like this."

Gus gave out a low whistle. He put his eyes back on the road with some difficulty. "That's – man, that is beautiful."

"Yeah it is," said Jesus. He holstered the revolver and patted it. "Making something like this takes more than just skill. It's divine inspiration, the kind that can only come from powers beyond man. With a supply of weapons this powerful, I can fix this nation and save mankind from Bomraka, the Devil, their Demoncrat party and all their secular humanist tricks."

Lily looked out the window. "If you need to fight to prove your point, you've already lost it."

Jesus lifted an eyebrow. "Is that why you're fighting to pretend that you don't want me?"

Lily's face burned with embarrassment. "Why is it that you're so determined to think I want you? What is it about me, some godless secular liberal, that makes me so interesting to you?"

Jesus breathed out. Tell the truth and shame the devil. For some reason he didn't understand, these next words felt very hard to say. "You just...matter to me. Ever since your grandfather showed me your picture."

The moment hung in the air around them, quiet and electric. There was only the noise of the truck's engine, revving and releasing as they drove over low hills.

Jesus took out his pack of cigarettes.

Gus' eyes widened at the faded Marlboro label. "Are those really pure tobacco?"

"Yep. Getting' pretty hard to find, what with all this modern obsession with health. Want a smoke?"

"Sure! Seems fitting too, on this ol' diesel lady's last run."

"How 'bout you, Lily?"

"Absolutely not!" she said, exasperated. "Bad enough you kidnapped me and ruined my life, you want to fill this tiny cab up with the smell of burning leaves?"

Jesus shared a grin with Gus, and put the cigarettes away. The first rays of sunlight were starting to appear around them. Gus put in a Gordon Lightfoot CD. Jesus settled in to enjoy it. Even Lily seemed to relax a bit to the classic traveling music.

Jesus wondered to himself if this was kind of like the sunset he'd seen from Hector's station wagon. A pretty moment before unexpected threats, bringing risk, death and near-disaster. He didn't even have disciples to lead right now. He'd gotten to like having some backup. If anything went south now, as in to Hell, it was back to how things had been since the Rapture - pretty much up to him.

48

The express lane ended, and they merged back into ordinary lanes of traffic. "Look at 'em scatter out of our way," Gus said. Ahead of them, electric motorbikes and Segways were pulling over to the side of the road to let the truck roll past, like so many frightened deer.

"They chose the path of less resistance. The way of so-called sustainability," said Jesus. "Sad, really. They made their bed, and they'll lie in it until God's judgment."

"God's Judgment," said Lily. "For driving a low-pollution car."

"Of course," said Jesus. "That's just not having faith that God made us a good strong planet."

Lily held her hand to her head as if in pain. "According to the Bible, didn't God say that we're supposed to be good stewards of the Earth?"

"Oh-ho! We're quoting the Bible now?" He stretched. Might be a good time to get out and stretch their legs. "Yep, that's right. Stewards. In power over it. Not servants to it." He nodded at the vehicles they passed. "Every one of these poor bastards has given up their God-given birthright of mastery, for the Devil's environmental lies."

She shook her head. "We belong to the Earth."

"Wrong again, babe. The Earth doesn't belong to 'us' - the Earth belongs to man," said Jesus. Gus shared another grin with him. Lily threw up her hands.

Jesus slipped his arm around her. "Come on, girl," he said. "I saved you from a pretty bad fate back there, being middle-management for the media wing of Satan's little helpers."

"You must really be nuts," said Lily. She tried to shrug off his arm.

"You're a babe," said Jesus. "A babe who needs a good strong man. Don't hold out too long, 'cause you know you won't find no better."

Lily continued shrugging off his arm. Smiling indulgently, he pulled his arm away. He left his shoulder brushing against her. She didn't have much room to move, but Jesus also had the feeling she didn't completely mind. How could she, how could any real woman? He was God's perfect man.

"So hey, Gus," he said, to change the subject. "How'd you keep this truck going against the EPA's plots, for all these years?"

"We had to compromise a bit," said Gus as he adjusted the heat controls. "They made us put in an electric battery system." Gus nodded, acknowledging the truth. "We kept the whole old engine separate, though. We couldn't let them take something that beautiful."

"That must have been a bit of a mechanical job," said Jesus.

"Yes indeed," said Gus. "There could have been many ways to do it, but we started with the flywheel..."

Gus told the long tale of working on this mobile treasure. Jesus nodded politely at first. He soon found himself lulled by the rhythm of the speech and the roll of the road. He let Gus' voice drone on, as he drifted into sleep.

It was nearly sunset when the truck pulled up to a fenced industrial area at the edge of Egypt. Jesus woke, and looked over at Lily who was stirring as well. They must have both needed the rest.

"You all should probably get out here," said Gus. "The EPA's been surprise inspecting a lot of vehicles towards St. Louis. Last time I was here, bringing up the last of our family's gas cars, they started to give me crap for having holes in my muffler."

Jesus and Lily climbed out. Gus turned off the engine, pocketed the keys and followed.

Jesus slapped the side of the truck with some affection. "This proud steed, of a once proud and prosperous country....full of mighty jobs and job creators, taking what they wanted from the environment as God intended." He leaned on one hand against it. "Today, this heads to a recycling shelter. A place of huge magnets attached to cranes, drifting overhead like buzzards. Waiting to swoop in and prey on what was left of man's proud, magnificent metal beasts. Machines turned against machines – to recycle them! Can't you feel the shame?"

"Do you have some sort of head injury?" Lily asked.

He chuckled and took out his pack of Marlboro's, offering a cigarette to Gus.

"Seems like now's the time," Gus said as he took it.

"Here, let me get that for you." Jesus pulled out his Zippo, lit Gus' cigarette and then his own.

He then looked deep into Gus' eyes until Gus began to feel a bit uncomfortable. "You and your Pa might've been big in the EPA's sights, having such a beautiful truck."

"Yeah, I don't mind admitting it was tough. We just kept reading between their lies and dodging the regulations as best we could."

"What if I asked you to give this truck to me? Give it a good life for what life it has left?"

The proud truck driver averted his gaze. "I would if I could. I can tell you'd do right by the old girl. I just can't. I need the money they'll give me. Even if it's in Ameros. If I can't feed my kids...what good's a memory?"

"Well, to tell you straight, you know you gotta be tough in this here life," said Jesus. "You gotta have faith in what the Lord will provide."

"I've had faith, for many years. Every year I've seen the little life I have be whittled away. What the Hell good is faith now?" Gus appraised him. "If you really are the son of God come to save us, why'd you take so long to get here?"

Jesus nodded, sad. "I wish I could have gone public sooner, and made it easier for you and yours, and everyone who lives in Christ. But timing? That's up to my Father upstairs." Jesus blew out the rest of his cigarette, dropped it, and crushed it beneath his boot. Gus looked away from the sudden intensity of Jesus' gaze.

"Coulda woulda shoulda," said Jesus. "Don't matter. Now is now, brother. Hard times are comin' like you ain't never seen before. So you listen good. As sure as you believe in me, my Father, and the Constitution written by his prophets, you go home and build a boat. 'Cause my vengeance is comin'. And when you see it come to fruition, you won't have a lot of time. When that time comes, you grab your kids and folks and get in that boat. And wait out the storm."

Gus scratched his head. "Wasn't the next time supposed to be fire instead of water?"

Jesus scowled for a moment at being questioned. "Gonna be fire too. You'll see."

Gus voice broke. "How'n Hell am I supposed to afford to build a boat big enough to save my family?"

"With this," said Jesus. He reached into his jacket's lining, and there was a sound of stitching being ripped. His hand came back out with several coins of gold in his palm.

"Are those...real?" the man gasped.

"Of course they are," said Jesus. "You don't even know me, so I'll let that go. This is God's Good Gold. They'll be worth a fortune when the banks fail, the government's computers crash, and Ameros ain't worth the paper they're printed on. You feed your family, you build that boat, and you be ready to mop up the rest of the Devil's helpers when I command you."

The man looked from the gold to Jesus' eyes, and back to the gold. "You're serious aren't you?"

"He's certifiable, is what he is!" Lily interjected. "You're walking around with freakin' gold coins sewn into your jacket?"

"Like there isn't already a price on my head?" said Jesus.

Gus shook his head. "I can't just take that gold."

"'Course you can't. This ain't charity. It's a trade. Give me that truck."

Gus grinned from ear to ear. "You don't have to tell me twice!" He pulled the keys from his pocket and handed them to Jesus, taking in return the handful of gold coins. Gus looked at them briefly, his eyes basking in their warm glow. He took off his baseball cap and dropped them inside, before folding the hat closed.

"You believe a little stronger now?" ask Jesus, sure that he knew the answer.

"I'm a little closer to believing in miracles," Gus admitted.

"Good. When you get back to your house, pack up your family, and follow these instructions." Jesus handed him a pamphlet. "You'll find more people like you there, and the space to build that boat. Now get going. I got a job to do."

"Yes sir," he said, and shook Jesus' hand once more. "Ma'am," he said to Lily, waving goodbye. Without further ceremony, he walked off into the coming night.

"Let's get a move on," said Jesus. "Your grandfather's bound to be anxious, even with his faith."

Jesus climbed into the cab, followed by Lily. It had been a long time since he'd been behind the wheel of a tractor this size. With a little rustiness at first and then increasing familiarity, Jesus wove the truck through the town's small streets.

Some of the townsfolk gazed in wonder as they passed by. A few tried to remember when last they'd seen its like.

"You sure know how to keep a low profile," said Lily. "How are you still alive?"

"I don't know," said Jesus. "Why, it must be another miracle."

"Fat chance," said Lily.

"You're admitting there's a chance now."

Lily snorted. "More like people just don't expect you to be so dumb and brazen."

"See that place?" Jesus pointed at a nearby building that was once a gas station. "It's supposed to be America. They only take Ameros, and they only give hybrids a recharge. It's probably owned by a man who's Marked. If I really wanted to brazen, I would go in there right now and give them a choice: return to God's Good Gas or I'll blow the place up. But I don't need to be brazen because I'm right."

Lily asked, incredulous. "You would consider blowing up that station just to make them use gas instead?"

Jesus nodded. "It'd be a mercy. I'm forcing them to pick a side, before it's too late. You've still got a chance to pick yours."

"I already have."

Jesus' face hardened. "I didn't hear that." She could not go to Hell after all this. He pulled the truck over to the side of the road, and engaged the parking brake.

"Because you've got a thing for me?" she pressed.

"I do," said Jesus. "I freely admit it."

"You flatter yourself if you think I'd ever return that feeling, you two-bit Christian thug."

"I can't help what I feel," said Jesus. "I also know that, deep inside, you know I'm the man for you."

"Because you're physically attractive and a macho patriarchal mess, I can't resist you?" She looked away. "Let's just finish getting me to my grandfather. I can salvage something out of this whole disaster, if I can at least help that misguided old man come back to reality."

"We'll see about all that. But first, this." In the cab of the last 18-wheeler left on earth Jesus leaned over, took her in his arms and kissed her.

Moments passed like minutes - or was it the other way around? Then they both opened their eyes and, he thought for a second, looked into each other's souls. Her eyes became teary, and she pulled away.

"Jerk!" she cried. She slapped him once, and then a second time.

The third time he grabbed her arm. "Now that's all of my cheeks I'm gonna turn. The next one might be yours when I spank you."

"Try it, you son of a bitch!" she slapped at him with her free hand. He grabbed that too.

"That's my mother you're talking about," he said. "She gave me some advice about girls once that I'll never forget. Truly wise, like only a good Christian mother can be. And like any wisdom, it ain't always quite easy for me to follow."

Jesus lowered both of her hands, without letting go. "She said, never love a girl you wouldn't want to be the mother of your children." He sighed and leaned back. "But I am as God has made me, so I must be born to love you. It wasn't right of me to force that kiss upon you, and I apologize. I just had to do that before we're done. Anyway I guess it's only right that you should have a taste of what awaits you if you chose to side with me."

She spun around in her seat, opened the door and jumped down out of the cab. "I'm going to see my grandfather," she declared. "If you care for me at all like you say, you'll leave me right now and never look back."

"Nothing doing," said Jesus. "I gave your grandfather my word that I'd see this job through. I'm taking you straight to his door." She slammed the door shut. Jesus turned the engine off, and climbed out.

It was colder outside than she expected, now that the sun had gone. She rubbed her arms to warm them.

"You want my jacket?" Jesus offered. He started to take it off.

"I'd rather be cold."

"Suit yourself."

"We're on the whole other side of the town from my grandfather's house, you know," said Lily.

"I know it," said Jesus. He went over to a nearby Prius, unfolded his buck knife and stabbed into a panel on the vehicle's side. He probed this wound with the knife, then pried the panel open. From his pocket, he took his whiskey flask, his lighter and a bandana. Lily's eyes widened as he soaked the bandana in whiskey, lit one end of the rag, and stuffed the other in the tank.

"What are you up to?" she asked.

"I figure you grandfather's house is about half an hour's walk. We might want to get moving."

They walked to the next corner, where Jesus took a right. Just as they turned, the hybrid exploded in flame.

"Why did you do that?" Lily shook her head. "Just to hurt the environment?"

"I was thinking of blowing up the truck. Beautiful old beast like that deserves a Viking funeral. That's one thing those old pagans got right. They were wrong, but at least they were manly." He took a swig from his whiskey bottle and put it away. "Much better to blow up that so-called hybrid that doesn't deserve to be called a car. That battery should glow real hot. If the fire spreads it could burn up some other hybrids too. Keep anyone looking for me clear on the other side of town."

They made their way through the town by back alleys, steering clear of well-lit streets lit by solar-powered long-life bulbs. First things first, thought Jesus. Their time would come as well.

Soon they heard the town's police and firemen's sirens heading back toward where the Prius' existence had been cleansed by fire.

WHEN THEY WERE three houses away from her grandfather's house, she spoke. "In spite of everything, I know that you...are trying to do what you think is good. You actually do believe in these things. You somehow keep thinking you're doing good for people, and you'll risk anything to do that. You're just so wrong. You're just wrong and you're just destructive. You won't stop, and you should be stopped." She breathed out. "So somehow after all this, I still don't hate you."

He couldn't believe his ears. In all his years since the Rapture he'd never really believed this could be possible - a love like he'd once had with Alaine.

She next did something that shocked Jesus even deeper – to his core. He could swear that, for a second, before she thought better of it - Lily reached out to touch his hand.

She let go and headed up the steps. Jesus followed and waited as she knocked politely.

There was a pause, a rustle from behind the door, and grumbles that gradually increased in volume as an old man approached. The old man jerked the door open, his mumbled oaths mixing with the sound of cracking varnish and rusted hinges.

"Do you know how late it -" Hieronymus began, and saw Lily. His face froze. He closed his eyes for a long second, and then opened them again.

"There you are," he said, his eyes becoming watery. "I'm not only dreaming." He noticed Jesus behind her. "You did it. You brought her back to me. It is a miracle. Oh, Lily...." He opened the door all the way, and went out onto the porch.

"Grandpa, I-"

"Shhh," he said, and held his arms open. She hugged him. Jesus couldn't see her face, but he expected she was crying as well. "Look at you," Hieronymus said, over and over. "Look at you."

They stood there for a few moments longer. He disengaged, and held her by the arms.

"Come on in."

49

They walked into Hieronymus' living room, to find a complicated jumble of decades-old furniture piled high with books, tools and equipment, strewn haphazardly atop scripture magazines and technical blueprints.

Hieronymus went over to a couch-shaped pile and shoved all of its contents to the floor to reveal ancient cushions. "Take a seat, my Lord. You've done well."

"You don't really believe he's the Son of God!" Lily exclaimed. Jesus started to speak, but Hieronymus caught his eye and gave the barest shake of his head.

The old man shut the front door. "We can talk about these things later." Jesus decided to go along with him. For once, maybe it was not the best time for an argument.

Perhaps unsurprisingly, Lily wouldn't let it go. "You really do think this lunatic is the messiah?"

The old man nodded. "We'll do something about that."

"About what?" she demanded.

"Your unbelief. I've lived too long and worked too hard for you to go that easily to Hell."

"You can't, so don't even bother." Lily responded. Jesus smiled at the fight in her. Damn if he didn't love her spirit.

The old man pointed at a chair next to the revealed sofa, piled high with books. He shoved them roughly the floor as well. "Don't worry about it. Sit tight, right here. Nice and comfy. I'll go get us some beer."

"You know I don't like beer," said Lily.

"You'll like some today, come Hell or high water." A glint of anger showed in Hieronymus' eyes. "It's been too long since I've seen you, and it's taken a lot of work to get you here. I've risked Hell itself. You can blessed well sit down and have a beer with me, and the man who brought you back to me." Hieronymus tottered out to the kitchen.

Jesus looked over at her, and could see conflicting emotions on her face. "What troubles you?"

"What do you think? Take a look at this place. He's just been living here, alone...all these years, and nothing but these plans."

Jesus nodded. The plans for weapons to help him win back America.

The old man returned with a couple of opened beers. He pressed one into her hands, and gave the other to Jesus.

"Do you honestly think a beer makes up for this? Letting your delusions control you to the point that you get this guy to wreck my life, and drag me half across the country?" asked Lily.

"However you came here, you're here now. Let's break bread together first," he said. "We'll have a good meal. Then we can talk."

"I'm more'n hungry enough," said Jesus. "It's been quite a journey."

Hieronymus went into the kitchen and opened cupboards, taking out pots and pans. After a few moments of awkward restlessness, Lily got up to join him. Jesus stayed in the living room with his beer, and listened to them talk. The conversation was halting at first, like an old engine warming up. As it ran longer it ran smoother, until the old grooves were found again.

Jesus leaned back against the wall and stretched. It felt really good to not have anything that needed doing right this moment. He hadn't had a real chance take a break since back in the Motel, before his great vision had started him along this path.

He pulled out the magnificent gun that Hieronymus had built for him, and laid it on the couch to his right. Next to it he put his stepfather Joseph's .45. Both were fine weapons. He had a real attachment to the history of that good ol' World War II .45. America's last great war against the godless Nazis had an honor that could never fade. But the beautiful artifact just couldn't bring down a black helicopter.

Jesus picked up the revolver Hieronymus had made. He felt its heft and the way the pistol grip fit his hand. Only one of its bullets were left. He could get more now. This was also only a small and portable token of Hieronymus' gifts for making weapons. What other larger, more powerful, even more miraculous tools of salvation could the old man have?

"Come to the table, Lord," the old man called out. "We've set a place for you, and this time you're even here."

Jesus entered, and beheld a lovely feast. There on the table were barbecued ribs, chicken-fried steak, baked beans and hot dogs. Corn bread, stuffing, mashed potatoes, and biscuits. And neither a vegetable nor a salad, not so much as a sprig of parsley.

They sat, with Lily between them. "Would you like to say grace, ironically enough?" she said.

Jesus could feel the spite in her jab, but was also heartened to see her being just a bit playful. "I think your grandfather's earned that right," he said. "This looks like quite a meal."

"Oh yes, indeed," Hieronymus said. The men both bowed their heads. After a bit of reluctance that Jesus couldn't help but notice, Lily did too. "Heavenly Father," Hieronymus intoned, "we thank thee for those gathered here at our table. I thank you for the miracle of my beloved granddaughter returned. Now I have the chance to truly save her." Lily was predictably irked, but for once she held her tongue. "May all be as it should be. Amen."

Hieronymus set the baked beans in front of Lily, who spooned some on her plate.

She tried some. "Ok, those are really good." She passed the serving dish to Jesus, but Hieronymus intercepted and grabbed the dish. She almost spoke, but let it go.

Hieronymus passed plates of ribs and other delicacies to Jesus and Lily, and they all began to eat. After a while, Lily cleared her throat. "This is a lovely meal, and it's wonderful to sit down with you. But there's something more going on here. What's this all about?"

"All I know is, he's supposed to give me what I have coming," Jesus said.

"You better hope it's less than that," she said.

"Ha! What happened to miss lovey-dovey?"

"Maybe I had to be reminded what it was like to live with patriarchal assholes," she muttered under her breath.

"Not anymore," the old man said. He got up from the table.

"What do you mean?" said Lily.

"I mean you won't have to wonder any more. At least, not soon."

Something about that tone struck Jesus. He fixed his gaze on Hieronymus' eyes. "What exactly do you mean? Exactly."

"My dear, you know you mean so much to me," Hieronymus spoke to Lily as if Jesus had not said a word.

"I know," said Lily. "And I've tried so hard not to upset you. We just see the world so diff... different..." she blinked rapidly.

The old man nodded. "And that's the whole problem in a nutshell."

"Why do I feel...." Her eyes closed, and she slumped in her chair. Jesus leapt to his feet, knocking his chair back. What was happening to her? My God, was she dying before she'd been saved again?

Jesus rushed to her side. As he did, Hieronymus touched a knot in the kitchen's wood paneling. A section slid aside, to reveal a row of switches. Hieronymus flipped one.

Clamps erupted from the chair beneath her, locking onto her arms and legs to hold her firmly in place.

"What the Heaven!" cried Jesus. His hands became fists.

The old man held up a hand. "This is how it has to be," the old man said.

"Grandpa," Lily said weakly. "What are you...stop..."

"I'm fixing you. Gonna rip that liberal demon that's wrapped around your soul right out."

50

Hieronymus began flipping other switches. Jesus watched in confusion as a cone-shaped device, apparently built around a colander, extended from the fluorescent lighting of the kitchen ceiling and approached Lily's head. She struggled with fading energy against her bonds.

Jesus grabbed the old man by the collar, snatched him away from the switches and slammed him against the wall. "Get her out of that chair right now, you old nut!"

The old man didn't bat an eye. "I'll do no such thing. You and I both know where she's headed. If she doesn't change her mind soon, she's going straight to Hell for all eternity."

"She's starting to warm up to me," Jesus protested. Her eyes pleaded with Jesus one last time, before they closed completely. Her eyelids tensed but could not open. They fluttered with an increasing slowness, like a dying hummingbird's wings.

"Nuh-uh," Hieronymus said. "Right now, you're her captor. Maybe she has a bit of Stockholm syndrome. Maybe she really does love you. But will it stick?"

"It could!" said Jesus.

"I think not. The modern world with its so-called nuance has ruined her. She thinks too critically. Given even half a chance, liberalism could suck her right back in. I can't take that risk."

"You're gonna change that by tying her to a chair and putting some stupid cone on her head?" Jesus took tighter fistfuls of the old man's shirt, pulling him close enough to head butt. "You need to do better than that."

The old man unperturbed by the closeness of Jesus' wrath. "I surely will. I'm going to change her mind for her! I'll change those wrong things she believes into the right ones."

"The Hell you are! You are going to unplug her from that - that lounge chair of the Devil right now! Or I swear by my Father I'll-"

"You'll what?" Hieronymus laughed. "Hurt me? Go ahead, do your worst. I'll suicide right out of it. She'll never get out of that chair." He smiled knowingly. "Is that something you're willing to risk?"

Jesus sought for words. For once he had none. He let go of the old man and paced around the room.

"I knew it," the old man said with triumph in his voice. "You've loved her ever since you saw her picture, haven't you? That's how the powers in Heaven would have it - bind my beloved granddaughter to you, and you to her, as I provide you with the tools you need! Well, it would have been nice for God to ask, but it's still an honor to have my granddaughter marry the Messiah. It just ain't gonna happen until I know she's safe from Hell."

"Not like this, you son of a bitch. It's not her choice!"

"Would you rather she be tortured in Hell for all eternity?"

Jesus' mouth worked. "This can't be right. Of course she can be convinced. Why, right out there in your front yard she reached out for my hand-"

"Was that because you're a man, or because you're the Son of God? Is she convinced of the one true path?"

"Maybe not all the way. But someday she could be!"

"Your Holy Father tests all of us," the old man said, softer now. "Now I think he's testing you. I can give you the weapons you need for what is supposed to be your mission - what are you willing to do to bring Heaven to Earth?"

Jesus glared at him. The answer tasted foul even as it sat in his mouth. "Anything," he said, spitting the words as if they burned his mouth.

"Are you willing to give up this notion that she must choose Heaven on her own?" the old man pressed. "Are you so sure that she will?"

Jesus had no answer. Hieronymus' point made holy sense. He just wanted to snatch the words from the air, tear them into bits, and jam them down the old bastard's scrawny throat.

"Once I install in her the proper will to live for God," Hieronymus said, "The real God we know from Scripture, she will be saved. In all her waking moments and all her dreams, she will have a filter in her mind. It will keep liberal lies from her beautiful mind, those wrong motivations from her actions. She will at long last be saved. She will no longer be of this fallen World, but of God."

"How long will it take?" Jesus asked, his mouth twisting.

"A few hours," the Old Man said. "It is a complicated process. I suggest you get some rest." He smiled. "Take heart. When this last part of the job is done, I will give you all the weapons you were destined to receive. You can take back the world and make it right again, for my granddaughter and all mankind."

The room began to swim. Everything Hieronymus had said fit with the one true Christian faith of which Jesus had to be the best example. Unlike Alaine, Lily would go to Heaven. And at long last, Jesus would be less alone. He would have a true-believing woman as his wife to walk with him every mile.

Wordless, Jesus left the room. The old man pulled more panels loose from the wall. Rows of instruments emerged, sticking out the mechanical arms of dentists' drills. Surveying his handiwork with an expert craftsman's eye, he was pleased and satisfied. The old man went to work.

In the living room, Jesus paced.

Why did it feel so wrong? It was supposed to be right. His faith told him it was right. The visions of his childhood, his upbringing and the Bible itself all told him that Hieronymus was right.

Saving Lily had to be his redemption for Alaine. Lily's similarities and the way she had opened his heart again had to be a message from his otherwise absent Holy Father. Once God had sent him the sign, this must be the first test in his path. Everything about his faith told him how the test must be passed.

Then why did he feel more powerless than when he was just an ordinary child?

He kicked an end table to pieces in his growing anger. There was nothing else he could do. Everything he knew told him he had to let this happen.

And then, in one instant of clarity, he realized: faith be damned, he loved her. In the same way he now realized he'd loved Alaine – as her own person. Not the someone, the something she would be with her mind altered against her will.

He didn't care for all the Heavens or the Earth more than he cared for her.

HE RAN BACK into the kitchen, seeing various instruments bathing Lily in strange lights. The cone extending from the cylinder was glowing rapidly as well. Her eyes were still closed, and her jaw was clenched so tight he could see every muscle in her throat. "Stop!" Jesus cried.

"What?" said Hieronymus, startled. "Why?"

"It ain't right. She has to find her way to me on her own!"

"To God, you mean."

"Same thing." Jesus knocked aside the glowing cone over Lily's head. She relaxed only slightly. He began tugging at the clamps around her wrists.

"She won't, don't you see?" Hieronymus cried. "Her mind's too much her own! I tried for years to convince her. This is the only way to save her from Hell."

"I don't care," said Jesus. "You ain't doing it."

"Watch me," said Hieronymus.

Jesus drew the revolver Hieronymus had made for him. "One last bullet left in here," he said. "One last warning."

At that exact moment, all the lights in the house went out. Lily slumped in her chair, then began to stir.

"What trick are you trying to pull now, you old hyena?" said Jesus.

"It isn't me. I don't understand - "

"I swear, if you are Judasing me again, I will send you straight to St. Peter so you can take it up with him."

Blue and orange lights flashed outside. Then more. A large vehicle screeched to a halt, and doors slammed open. There was the unmistakable sound of multiple boots hitting the pavement.

"Jesus!" a man's voice announced through a bullhorn. "We know you're in there!"

Hieronymus froze. "I've barely had time to start!"

"We don't want any trouble, Jesus," the policeman's voice continued. "Come out with your hands up!"

51

———————

"Get down!" Jesus hissed. He crouched and made his way over to the kitchen window. He leaned against the wall below the window and pulled off his buckle, revealing a mirror. He stuck the mirror above the windowsill, so he could catch a glimpse without exposing his head to a kill shot.

Several military vehicles had converged upon the house. Behind a soldier with a bullhorn stood several more soldiers, guns trained.

"You have to stall!" the old man whispered. "Maybe I can get her out of here-"

"You aren't taking her anywhere, you bastard." This couldn't be happening. Not now! It would be hard enough to escape by himself – how could he make it with Lily?

"We've got you surrounded, Jesus!" the same bullhorn voice declared.

"Deal with me later," Hieronymus hissed. "If you really care for her, let's at least work together to get her out of here!"

Jesus gritted his teeth. There was nothing else for it. This time the old son of a bitch was right.

He took the magnificent pistol Hieronymus had made, and stuck it in the back of his pants. He scanned the living room floor until he found a loose floorboard, ripped it loose, and stuffed his jacket and remaining gold into the space inside. He replaced the board and pulled the rug back over it again. Hopefully that would keep the government from taking the gold as his death tax.

Then he pulled out his Zippo and his last remaining pamphlet, with secret directions to New America. He burned it into ash and scattered its remains with his boot.

"Hieronymus! I'll take their attention," said Jesus. "When I shoot, you make a break for it. If you start brainwashing her again, I'll make you wish you were in Hell."

He stayed crouched until they had entered the living room, then stood. It was his job to draw attention now.

He pushed the front door aside and emerged onto the stoop. There were several soldiers arranged in a basic semi-circle. They wore standard issue Army fatigues and had their rifles trained in his direction. Back by the police car stood a local police officer with the bullhorn, and an Army officer who Jesus guessed was a major. Behind them were several scattered Humvees and an unmarked hybrid van with tinted black windows.

Jesus chuckled. "Local police and soldiers? What, you couldn't get UN Blue Helmets here on such short notice?

The policemen with the bullhorn looked at the major. "What's he talking about?" the policeman asked.

"Like I know?" the major responded.

"Keep playing your roles, that's fine," said Jesus. "Who wants the taste of the Devil's privates slapped outta their mouth first?" He strolled towards the soldiers.

Four of the soldiers kneeled and cocked their rifles. "On your knees!" the man with the bullhorn yelled.

"Devil take you, and he will," said Jesus. "I ain't doin' any such thing. If you know what's good for you, get on your knees and beg my forgiveness." None of the soldiers followed his advice. "Go get your master, dog. I know he's here for this."

The soldiers looked at each other, now uncomfortable.

"He dared to call me out," Jesus persisted. "I'm here. Is he now too scared to face me?"

The back doors of the unmarked hybrid van snapped open. A man emerged. His famous grin split his face.

"I must say, I'm impressed that you knew I was here," President Bomraka said. "It's interesting to finally meet you in person."

Jesus nodded. "I knew Michael Max's footage wouldn't be enough. You had to see for yourself." Two of the soldiers split off and took positions behind Jesus, their rifles pointed at him. He let them be – this way there were fewer bodies between him and Bomraka.

"Hm?" Bomraka frowned. "What do movies have to do with anything?"

One of the soldiers behind him exclaimed "He's got a gun!"

"Damn right, I do. You touch me, and you can get a good look at the barrel before you go to Hell express."

Bomraka smiled indulgently. "We can wait a second, soldier. He's not going anywhere, and this moment is definitely worth savoring."

One bullet left, Jesus thought. "Why'd you bring so few people for me?" he asked. "The way your black helicopters have been failing, I'd've thought you'd bring the cannons and the cavalry."

Bomraka shook his head. "After the mess you've made, it was important to track you down with simple law enforcement. Making a big deal of a two-bit terrorist like you only serves your kind of cause."

Jesus laughed out loud. Inside, he planned the shot. "Nothing two-bit about me. I'm a solid gold double Eagle for the Lord." He willed his arm to relax. If he dropped down to the ground and fired as he shot, and he got the angle just right, the soldiers behind him might overshoot and miss just long enough for his bullet to hit his target.

He would have failed in his job for his Father, but at least Lily would be her own. His holy mission failed, he could hope to at least remove this Satan's pawn from America before he answered to his Father in the afterlife.

Then Jesus saw a smile of satisfaction spread across the President's face, and a moment later heard a whimper behind him. When he whirled around, he put his plan on hold. Other soldiers emerged from the house, holding a vainly struggling Hieronymus and a half-conscious Lily.

"There she is," said Bomraka, grinning from ear to outsized ear. "The woman who led us straight to you."

Jesus' face went white. It just couldn't be.

"You lie!" Jesus declared.

"Touchy subject for you there?" said Bomraka. "How do you think we found you so quickly?"

"My grandfather goes free!" Lily cried. "That was the deal!"

The President nodded. "If he cooperates and testifies. That part is up to him."

Hieronymus said nothing, tears in his eyes.

"You really did betray me?" Jesus asked her. She looked away. It felt like his heart was being torn to shreds. "When did you even have the chance?"

"When we first met, and I picked up my smart phone. I thought that if my grandfather was involved with terrorists, I could free him by getting you captured. That's what I mumbled into my phone and emailed to the police, before I put the phone away."

"If my assistant Rosio had been checking her email, she would have seen the Atlanta police department's follow up. This would all have been resolved so much sooner." Bomraka frowned. "I'm honestly a bit perplexed at how she missed it. It took just a few minutes of my own search. But those are just a few of the frustrations that have made this moment oh-so-sweet."

Hieronymus glared at Bomraka and then Jesus, still saying not a word.

"You don't have to say it, old man," said Jesus. "I know you're sorry, for all the good that does. If only you had given me what I needed without question, long before this all began."

"Which was what?" asked Bomraka, with surprised curiosity.

"His granddaughter, of course," said Jesus.

"Oh, right," said the President, smiling. "Nothing else? A Christian wouldn't lie, would he?"

"I owe no truth to the enemy of God, in time of war." Jesus stroked his chin. "You know what though? If you wanna get rid of all of Satan's little helpers here, why, I can promise you a very honest and direct discussion." Jesus cracked his knuckles. "If you're not too much of a pussy."

"My, oh, my, aren't we something fierce and bold when we're forced out of hiding," Bomraka laughed. "Well, whatever you wanted this man to do for you-"

"You'll never find out," Jesus finished. Hieronymus face washed over with anger and grief, and then resolve. He spat, at Jesus, Bomraka or both. Then he bit on his cyanide tooth, and collapsed.

Lily screamed. She slipped her guards' grip and ran towards her grandfather. The soldiers converged almost immediately.

Quick as a viper, Jesus pulled Hieronymus' pistol. He shot right for Bomraka's torso.

With lightning speed, Bomraka threw himself to the ground.

The bullet passed above the President with barely an inch to spare, and slammed into the military personnel carrier behind him. The entire vehicle was shot backwards into the air, flying into the house behind it.

The President rushed back to his feet. Jesus aimed at Bomraka's head and pulled the trigger again, in the vain hope that Hieronymus had left some kind of final surprise. The hammer thudded onto an empty chamber. Stunned, he let his hand drop to his side.

In desperation, Jesus threw the empty gun at Bomraka with all his might. The President batted it away. Jesus charged the President. A stream of machine gun fire split the dirt between them.

Jesus paused. He was utterly surrounded, with a group of trained soldiers holding guns at him at point-blank range. Was this how it was to be? He was to die in a hail of machine gun fire for God?

Bomraka got to his feet, brushed off his suit. "Ah-ah-ah!" he admonished with a wag of his finger. "You'd best relax there, Mr. Christ." An expression flashed across Bomraka's face that Jesus didn't understand. If Jesus didn't know better, he could have sworn it was sadness. "I expect you won't believe me, but it gives me no pleasure to say this. This just seems the only way to conclude this with no more deaths." He indicated Lily. "Take one more step I don't like, and one of my soldiers will shoot her in the head. If I understand your own beliefs correctly, she would then go straight to Hell unsaved."

Jesus thought furiously. Try as he might, he could see no way out of this. And even worse, Bomraka saw it in his eyes.

"Checkmate," said Bomraka.

"It isn't fair!" Lily protested. "He was my only family!" She struggled with the soldiers holding her, trying to turn away.

Bomraka shook his head, in a way that left Jesus further mystified. The Demoncrat KenyAntichrist seemed sad and even sympathetic as he spoke. "Fair or not, it's what happened. He made his choice."

Lily's knees gave way, and she collapsed in sobs. Only the soldiers' grip kept her from falling to the ground. Bomraka gestured towards one of the vans. They half-carried, half-dragged her to it. She put up no struggle.

"You picked the wrong side, babe," Jesus said to her. "It's all been for nothing, unless you let yourself have faith." He fixed her in his steely gaze. "It won't be for nothing if you believe. You can turn this into a win, you can defeat the President and all his Demoncrats and all the harm they've brought you, if only you believe."

"Really?" she said, dazed. "If I truly believe you're the Messiah, then it won't have been for nothing?'

"Yes, baby, yes!" Was he at long last getting through?

Her eyes lost their focus. "Then I believe! I have faith like he wanted...wanted me too..." She went limp again with sobs.

Jesus' heart leaped. "Yes! At long last you have opened your heart to God's messages of truth!"

Bomraka shook his head as the soldiers picked her up bodily and placed her in the back of a waiting van. As they closed the doors she began to struggle. "I believe now, you bastards! I believe!" When the doors were completely shut, her screams went silent.

"That was interesting," Bomraka said.

"She has faith in me now!" Jesus declared. "She can resist all your FEMA programming, and your Delphi 21 and Common Core math as well!"

Bomraka gave his soldiers inquiring looks. "Are you guys sure you didn't hit him in the head while I was in the van?"

"Nope, that's how he came out," said a soldier.

"Not even a flash-bang grenade? Nothing?"

The soldiers all said no.

The President faced Jesus. "What are you even talking about?"

"Why are you even bothering to pretend anymore," Jesus snarled. "You know! Delphi 21! The UN Agenda! Part of the Feminazi Femborg coalition!"

Bomraka stared at him for a second. "You mean like with that bunch of special effects at the TV station before you blew it up? You actually believe all that nonsense?"

Jesus blinked. This wasn't the reaction Jesus expected at all. "Are you trying to say you don't know?"

"Know what?" Bomraka gave an abrupt bark of laughter. "That you're a lunatic?"

Jesus repressed his confusion and rallied his faith. "You'll be hurting in Hell, no matter how much you keep pretending you don't know the path you're on! I'm wise to your games!"

Bomraka shook his head. "You might be a whole bunch of things. But I don't think wise is one of them."

"Sir?" said a soldier emerging from Hieronymus' house. "The old man had some interesting technology in his kitchen. It seems to be some kind of - cerebral manipulation?"

Bomraka raised an eyebrow. "It sounds disturbing, but maybe it can be of some scientific benefit. Pack that up as well."

"Your days are numbered, Bomraka," Jesus stated. "And the count ain't all that high."

"That sounds like a lovely dream you're having there," Bomraka said. "Here's what's going to happen in reality. You are going to be paraded before the press. Then you will go on trial for murder, and will be judged by a jury of your peers."

"Ha!" said Jesus. "How can I have peers? I'm the Son of God!"

"When you are likely sentenced, you will not be executed and become a martyr. You will serve time like any other common criminal. America and the world will know once and for all that it is time to move forward." Bomraka smiled.

The man's smile was like a knife twisting in Jesus' gut. "Go for it," said Jesus.

Bomraka nodded. "Indeed we will."

Jesus wondered, were the soldiers trying to fry him with some sort of mind ray? Because for the second time in a minute, Jesus saw the President's face flash an expression which made no sense. This time, it was weariness and sadness. "You three, put him in the other van."

Three jackbooted government thugs approached Jesus in their tactical gear. Jesus stopped the closest one with a stare. "I will not suffer one of you dogs to touch me. You will go to your judgment now, not later."

The soldiers looked at each other, and then President Bomraka. "Get on with it!" he ordered. They surrounded Jesus as he stood motionless. A soldier behind Jesus placed a hand on his arm. With the speed of a striking eagle, Jesus spun and caught him with a boot in the gut and then roundhouse kicked his head. He fell unconscious.

The other soldiers raised their rifles. "Don't shoot him!" said Bomraka. "We need him alive for the trial. Just cuff him and put him in the van."

"But sir," said a soldier. "I mean, Jesus Christ!"

"Even your minions can't help but say my name," Jesus taunted. "Gonna kill him for me now?"

"Kill him?" Bomraka asked, bewildered. "For saying 'Jesus Christ'? What is wrong with you?"

Jesus searched the Demoncrat's eyes. Just what was his game? "How about you come and cuff me yourself, President Evil?"

"I just had this suit dry-cleaned," said Bomraka. "I'd rather not have your blood stain it." He spread his hands. "And I don't think you want to risk that girl going to Hell, as you believe she will."

Jesus knew the bastard had him. Lily's faith was new, but not yet strong. For all Jesus knew she had begun to doubt again already. He couldn't bear to risk her going to Hell. His love for her had finally given his enemies a hold on him.

"You can't hide behind her forever," Jesus managed to respond.

Bomraka shrugged. "Here we stand right now. What is your reply?"

52

———

Once again, President Bomraka was at his desk deep into the morning hours. What a strange set of evenings it had been.

He had tracked down the Christian terrorist himself. Which logically shouldn't have been possible. The best resources in the world for tracking down terrorists, criminals and fugitives had been put to this task. Yet none of them had turned up the needed lead for Jesus Christ.

Strange groups and organizations had been involved in the hunt that had no business being near it. Almost laughably so. The EPA. PBS and NPR. Teachers unions. If one report was to believed, ACORN - which not only wasn't a government agency, it was supposed to have been disbanded years ago. Even stranger, these groups were using immense resources from unidentified origins.

The capper was that they had all failed, when all he had needed to do was follow up on a single email that should have triggered alarms all the way to the FBI.

After all the trouble this man who called himself Jesus Christ had caused, all the attention he'd received, displaying him as a successfully captured terrorist would be a successful and useful resolution. With this accomplished, they could at last return to incrementally moving the country forward to a better future.

53

Jesus sat in the back of the hybrid government vehicle, heading to the Devil knew where. His hands rested in his lap, cuffed. He had demanded to keep his own vow that no officer would touch him, and put them on himself. Bomraka had not objected in the slightest. And indeed, why would the President object? Jesus had lived his whole life free of big government until today. Now he had voluntarily surrendered himself to the government's blood-red red-tape grip.

"Tex" Adamapoulos had faced this same defeat. That was not long ago, Jesus realized. It felt like ages.

What were his new disciples up to? He could only hope they were still free. Surely if they had been caught the Demoncrats would throw that in his face as well. He prayed that they would stay alive to continue the fight, now that he had failed them.

The walls around him did not yield to his mood. He lay down and tried to rest. There was not much else for him to do.

The last time he had felt this lost was when Alaine died.

He had been practicing in the barn's makeshift dojo and listening to the Patriots game, as he liked to do most every Sunday after church. The call of yet another ingenious play was interrupted by a mighty car crash. It sounded like it was just down the street - at the neighboring farmhouse where Alaine lived with her father.

Jesus ran, hoping against hope that she was not involved.

When he got there, his hope failed.

Alain's father's car had made it almost into their driveway. It lay half in and out of the ditch next to the entrance, wrapped around the front of the unmanned truck.

THEIR BODIES LAY MANGLED and dead inside the car, looking absurdly like bloody rag dolls.

He fell to his knees next to the them. When the police arrived, they found him still kneeling in shock. Once they got him to speak, he told them the accident was caused by the Rapture. Of course they didn't believe him, just nodded politely and closed their notepads.

"Got somewhere you should be, son?" one of the policemen asked.

At that instant Jesus realized his parents must have been Raptured as well. He leapt up and ran back to his house. All he found were a pair of holes in the ceiling, and empty clothes lying on the living room floor.

His parents had been taken together, without even leaving bodies to be buried. He paced the room, wondering and worrying over many things before he rallied and pulled it back together.

All he had left now was the job that his visions had set before him.

Before he could start in earnest, the government had to get as little property from their anti-Christian Death Tax as possible.

Jesus' job became clear. It was time to jam his feelings deep inside and do his duty like any Christian man – in this case, hide anything of value from the Feds. In the bottom of the master bedroom closet, he found a shoebox with a note saying "To Jesus".

He placed the box on his parent's empty bed, and opened the note.

If you're reading this then your mother and I have gone to our reward.

In this box you'll find a sack of gold coins I've been saving for you ever since our country's honor was stained by the Amero.

You'll also find a Zippo lighter and an old .45. My father's father wielded them with honor on the fields of Normandy. I pass them on to you. Use them against all of God's foes, be they foreign or domestic.

Last, take with you our hope and faith. Know that the hope of all America – and with her, all of mankind - rests within your hands. So always do your best and fight your hardest. With God above to guide you, that will be enough.

For even though you are the Son of God, we have been proud to know you as our son for many years.

Your loving stepfather and mother,
  ~ Joseph and Mary

Jesus had closed his eyes and prayed Joseph would hear his own response in Heaven: that he would always think of Joseph as his second dad. Not in a false and sinful way, like gay marriage, but for real.

Jesus returned to the present. This was in its own way much like that time right after the Rapture – the space of a few hours that had changed everything forever. Since the Rapture he had been doing his best to shove those feelings into the center of his heart, and use their banked fires as fuel for his faith. Today he took a rare full look at all those questions instead.

Saving Lily seemed to have doomed his mission. Had he chosen wrong?

His heart said no. Keeping her from being brainwashed felt righter than anything he'd done since the Rapture. He resolved that if he had chosen wrong, so be it. He would face his reward.

With this resolution, he found himself at ease. He stretched out, and realized now that he was caught he could relax. The worst had already happened. The background noise of travel soothed him into sleep, his easiest transition to the land of dreams in years.

At least at first. After several gradually worsening dreams, he saw a whirlpool of lava. Was this the Lake of Fire? In the center was a hole that drained into nothingness. He floated on a giant cross made of guns tied together with strips of flesh. Clinging to the sides with their feet dangling above the fiery surface were the disciples - and Lily.

The giant cross circled the whirlpool ever faster towards the drain. Made crazy by the pace, Lily let go and fell towards the lava. From above, Jesus grasped her wrist. She struggled, and Jesus slipped and fell off the cross as well.

Right before they hit the lava's surface it became a meadow. He lay on his back on the grass, and Lily leaned over him to block the sun. Behind her head, in the sky itself, angry clouds formed throwing thunderbolts. She smiled. She could hear them too. She lay down atop him and put her lips against his.

JESUS WOKE to the van stopping. He felt like he'd been asleep for about five hours. If they had driven relatively straight and respected their own meddling big-government speed limits, that might mean they'd made it to Chicago.

The van's back doors opened. A soldier poked his head in. Behind him Jesus glimpsed a parking garage. The soldier opened his mouth to speak.

Jesus cut him off. "Before you do a thing, you should know that the first one of you gutless worms to touch me gets it."

The man closed his mouth and swallowed. He moved back out of the way.

Jesus emerged from the van, to find two corrections' officers waiting with hands on their guns. They kept their distance from him.

"Which way?" asked Jesus. They led him into an elevator. The soldiers fell in behind Jesus, and crowded into the elevator.

The muzak inside was sub-par even for muzak, but there was no point in making a fuss.

They went up several floors, and led him through a series of increasingly heavy doors until they eventually reached Jesus' new quarters – a cell. One of the soldiers reached toward Jesus' arm to guide him in, and received a warning look. The soldier swallowed and carefully dropped the key into Jesus' hands.

Jesus unlocked his cuffs, dropped them into one of the corrections officers hands, and took stock of the cell. He found an orange jumpsuit laid out for him, and next to it a beard trimmer and a comb for his flowing hair. "I need to look good for the audience, is that it?" said Jesus. "Your boss should be careful what he wishes for."

No one responded. Jesus laughed. "See you all soon." He sat on his bed and faced them. "Unless you die, in which case, I expect we're going to quite different destinations."

54

———

Rosio Dawnhell struggled to clear her mind for hours, in the approved Satanic yoga meditation her matriarchs had taught her. It was deep into the night, and she had yet to receive a single vision. She knew being tense could not help, so she tried her hardest to relax. Being tense wouldn't make receiving any easier.

3:30 came and went. She tried thinking of the few human pleasures she enjoyed. When the clock edged close to 4:00, she could take no more. She leapt up from her seated pose and punched a bookcase into splinters, then began smashing the sculpted busts of various patriarchal historical figures. She kept them for just this soothing purpose, and they usually were enough - but not this time. She brushed the stone dust from her hands, remaining tense as ever. Still not a single sign.

She should be happy, she thought. At long last Jesus had been captured. It wasn't ideal that Bomraka had done it in public, but at least this obstacle to the coming matriarchy had been removed.

Obstacle? Who was she kidding. The man had become a wrecking ball. The question was, had the threat been stopped with his capture?

They would have to call soon. They had never contacted her before in her entire life, but if the faith she was raised in meant anything at all then the dark powers would have to call her now. Even if it was to judge her as a failure and send Rosio to her doom. Even that would be better than this silence.

55

The media trumpeted Jesus capture and upcoming trial for a solid week. All of America and a large portion of the world prepared to tune in to MSNBC (known to Christ's followers as the One World Channel) for opening arguments. Jesus had no doubt this would solidify Bomraka's grip on the United Nations. The world would be united at last - through doubt and dishonor. Maybe after his fourth term Bomraka would run for President of the UN, if there was still time left for more charades before the sky started raining blood.

On the day of the big event, two corrections officers led Jesus from his cell and through the prison halls. As before, he insisted on cuffing his own hands in front. He was otherwise compliant. He had even accepted the wearing of an orange prisoner's jumpsuit. It felt something like a badge of honor.

His fellow inmates went silent as he passed. He nodded to some and ignored others, raising his bound hands to clasp with those prisoners who had the courage to reach through the bars.

Far faster than he had expected, he entered the van that would take him to his trial. The doors were closed behind him. This van had windows at least. He watched as the city and its people passed by.

After a few minutes they pulled up to the curb next to a court-house. It must have been a lovely building once. The skeleton of its former marble glory was still barely visible beneath the gathered crowds – as well as the modern shame of handicapped-access ramps. Such seeming conveniences were particularly dastardly liberal Demoncratic Trojan horses – they robbed those who had been blessed with the challenge of a handicap from working a little bit harder as God intended.

Jesus also noticed an empty hole on the lawn to the right of the main steps. He tapped his cuffed hands on the panel that separated him from the front seat. The panel slid aside, and Jesus saw two soldiers. Both were dressed as if they were corrections officers, but carried themselves like Demoncrats.

He addressed the corrections officer behind the wheel. "Say, hell-bound. What used to be on the right of the steps there?" He pointed to the lawn.

"The Ten Commandments," the man said.

The other officer drew his gun. "Before we got rid of them in the same court where we'll be getting rid of you." He cocked the gun. "Just like we won the war on Christmas."

Jesus smiled without animosity. "You've got guts. I respect that. Shame you chose the wrong side. Maybe when the time comes, I'll give you another chance."

"You'll give me a chance?" The Demoncrat laughed. "Well thanks so much!"

Jesus nodded. "You're welcome." He leaned back, and his eyes became thoughtful. "I am now in the hands of my enemy, while my disciples are stranded in the wilderness. They aren't the lost babes they were when we first met, but it will take a miracle for them to toughen up enough to stay free." He looked off into space past his chaperones' heads. "Still, I was caught because I wanted to save a woman I loved. I can't shake this feeling that all is as it should be."

The Demoncrat thug's brow furrowed in confusion. Maybe he wasn't expecting this kind of – what was the word?

Introspection, Jesus thought. That's what this was called. Jesus could understand the guard not expecting it. It was a pretty unfamiliar experience for Jesus as well.

The corrections officer leaned in closer, so that Jesus could almost feel the man's breath coming through the mesh that separated them. "What makes you so sure you'll get into Heaven yourself?"

"Ha!" said Jesus. "'Cause I'm the messiah. How do you guys come up with this stuff?"

The van pulled to a stop, and its back doors opened. A cleared walkway led up the courthouse steps, through lines of police restraining crowds. Some of the crowd were apparently reporters, while others of the teeming civilians were bold enough to carry signs in support of Jesus. Most were apparently not there to support him.

A second van pulled up, and more government thugs emerged. These wore police uniforms, but Jesus' keen eye noticed one had a pen from the PTA. The crowd spotted the van. A great number of civilians began to scream for Jesus blood, and the sides of the van rang with thrown debris.

Two Demoncrats dressed as corrections officers led the way before Jesus, and four followed behind. As they walked up the steps, the thugs attempted to duck the flying rocks and rotten vegetables. Jesus ascended the steps with head held high, as if the attack of curses, insults and garbage wasn't happening at all.

The crowd became confused at Jesus' lack of reaction. Their volley of projectiles and curses slowed, and faded into silence. Jesus and the guards had made it all the way up the steps into the building when a young man called out, "Why is he just letting us do this?"

"'Cause he's a big wussy chicken," said another voice. Jesus turned to see these wayward souls. They both wore T-shirts and jeans, like any normal Americans. The first speaker was tall and lean, and the man who'd responded to him was short and rather fat. They even looked strikingly like those two barstool warmers who'd challenged Jesus and his stepfather Joe in that Montana tavern so many years before.

Jesus shook his head sadly and went to face whatever his fate would be.

"Go ahead and run away, you girly man!" the fat one cried as he lobbed a rotting apple at Jesus' head with all his might.

Almost inside the doors, Jesus turned and caught the apple in his handcuffed palms right before it hit his head. The thrower jeered Jesus in defiance.

Before the guards could stop him, Jesus whipped the apple back. It sailed through the air to strike the man with such speed and force he was knocked off his feet, and did not rise.

The crowd fell into stunned silence.

"I was trying to let this happen all dramatic-like, where I'd enter serene and sullen and dignified," Jesus' exasperated voice ringing out along the steps. "But no, you just had to run your mouth."

He entered the courthouse, shook his head and sighed. What else could he do? He had done his best to prove his divinity, and save as many as possible.

This had been such a long road to this place. Jesus found it was a bit of a relief to know it was likely coming to an end, one way or another.

The crowd was still debating his behavior as the doors closed behind him.

Jesus was led through a series of metal and bomb detectors, up several flights of stairs, and from there into a darkened room. The Demoncrat thugs exited, and the door was closed behind him. Puzzled, Jesus examined the room. After a few seconds he heard a sound behind him. The wall at his back slid aside, to reveal a video screen showing a darkened room.

The lights in the room came on, and he could not help but laugh.

On the other side of the glass, arranged around a boardroom table, sat a veritable rogues' gallery of self-admitted liberals. George Sauron, leader of the One World Media. The Feminazi Dominatrix pair of Blabbera Strident and Jane Fondue. To their left was the elderly celebrity succubus Madonna, representing the Pope in Rome. She leered in her black leather emblazoned with Papist crosses. Jesus mused that her leather gear might as well have been made from the skins of so many girls she led astray from proper married submission into wanton slutdom, and thus to Hell. Next to her sat the saboteur of America's righteousness with so-called facts, the diabolical academic mastermind Noam Chimpsky. Trying vainly to hide behind him from Jesus' searching eyes was the pathetic George W. Botch, his chair chained to post that showed the carved face and figure of the infamous secret master of community organizing, Saul Stalinsky.

Last and perhaps least of all except for his sheer size, sat Michael Max. The fat documentarian bore bandages from his most recent encounter with Jesus. Of all the liberal enemies of Christ he was having the hardest time meeting Jesus' gaze. He was finding comfort in hiding behind a large submarine sandwich.

"Welcome to the Death Panel," said Chimpsky.

"Get this glass out of the way and I'll deconstruct you limb from limb," said Jesus. Chimpsky laughed the dry academic squeak of the tenured liberal hellbound.

Jesus addressed G. W. Botch. "And you. I always knew you hadn't choked on that second pretzel. Good - I don't think you've paid enough for your betrayal. You let the so-called economic stimulus happen, rather than let the whole economy collapse as God intended."

"Enough!" declared George Sauron. "We are doing the judging here!"

"I thought that was going to happen in a courtroom with the cameras. Ain't that gonna be a better circus?" Jesus sneered at Michael Max. "But I expect you will be in charge of that, won't you?"

"You're - you're darn right!" said Max.

"I knew you'd return to evil. Already planning your next documentary, aren't you?" Michael Max took solace in his submarine sandwich rather than face Jesus' steely gaze. Jesus nodded. "Thought so. You've had your chance. Now you're Bowling for the Devil."

"Well Jesus, if you're bowling for God looks like you got a big ol' gutter ball," said a woman's voice.

"Yeah?" said Jesus. "You got the guts to say that to my face?"

"That and more, you two-bit chauvinist." Rosio Dawnhell emerging from the shadows, furthest to the left.

"Chauvinist is just feminist for 'winner'," he snarled.

"Then what are you doing here?" She beamed like a pig enjoying a bath of filth. "But ya still have a chance, ya know. Ya still could score some kind of a win."

"Oh yeah? How's that?"

She folded her bulky arms. "Let us know where your followers are, and you can save 'em from destruction."

Jesus' mouth gaped open. "You're supposed to be smart enough to lead this gang of evildoers, and you'd think something as dumb as that? You think I'll give up a single man, woman, or child who believes in me? Do I seem to you like a man who's afraid to die?"

"It's just a matter of time before we have them all anyway, you fool. Mr. Sauron just bought AOL. We own all your communications now."

"We already have your other follower," said Strident. "That newscaster you took from the station before Max blew it up. All we have to do is get her out of FBI custody first-" Rosio silenced her with a glance.

"What are you talking about?" said Jesus. "Are you trying to trick me? You already have her."

"Yes we do," Rosio said quickly. "I should have remembered you're no fool."

"Blessed straight," said Jesus.

"Then listen. We can leave all your current followers and their families alone, isolated but alive, if you'll admit to the world you're a fraud."

"A fraud!" repeated Bush.

"Yeah!" said Michael Max.

"You son of a bitch," Jesus snarled. Even through the telescreen, Max squirmed under Jesus' stare like an ant under a magnifying glass. "God's got you on a short list for Hell. He's just waiting for the right cheeseburger." His eyes roamed the rest of the room. "Ain't nothin' any of you can say that'll make me do a single thing for you.

Even if you track down my followers, what use is the little torture you can mete out now compared to the perfect and all-powerful Godly torture they would meet for all eternity?"

"Told you he wouldn't go for it," said Strident.

Dawnhell nodded agreement. "It seemed worth a shot. I guess we still can't pussify all men."

"We've got a script all set up, you penis-having dupe," Fondue said. "You haven't got a chance. You'll be found guilty, and we'll kill you."

"So be it," Jesus said.

"You aren't going to even fight?" Strident said. "You're just going to give up, that's it?"

Rosio cut her off. "Enough. We gave the easy way a shot. We'll see you in the trial, Mr. Christy-wisty."

The lights dimmed, and the wall slid back into place. Before it closed completely, Jesus said so softly that only Dawnhell heard it:

"Be careful what you wish for."

56

Jesus was left alone in the darkened and quiet room. After some restless pacing, he spent his unexpected free time on prayers, then YoGod, and then shadowboxing at his doubts and fears. This last was an interesting challenge with his hands bound. Jesus was at it for a good couple of hours before he heard voices in the hallway.

"You sure want to do this, kid?" asked one of the Demoncrat thugs outside.

"He's entitled to a legal defense," a younger male voice responded.

"You really should have someone in there with you," said the other government thug Jesus had spoken with, the one who'd tried to taunt Jesus with his gun.

"I'll talk with my potential client in private, thank you," the younger voice asserted.

"You know how many men he's killed?"

"Allegedly? Yes, I've read the charges."

Jesus could almost hear the second guard shrug. "It's your funeral. If he starts to kill you, try to scream."

The door opened. A young man walked in, carrying a briefcase and a manila folder. The door shut behind him.

Jesus waited for him to speak. After a moment the man said, "Hello. I'm Josiah Greenwood, and I'm your court-appointed attorney."

Jesus raised an eyebrow, and gestured at the room they stood in. "That so? I'd offer you a seat if there was one."

"I'm alright standing, thank you."

"Me too. All my life. That way other people can see what it's like, and stand up too."

"I'm not here to express an opinion on that," the kid said quickly.

"Well if you got one anyway, you might as well say it. I promise you'll get a warning before you piss me off enough to kill you." The young man's eyes widened. "Oh yeah, I heard what the guards outside were saying. I respect how you came in anyway. That shows guts, and earns you a listen. Go ahead and speak your piece."

"Alright then," said Josiah. He sighed. "Mister...."

"Christ," he said. "Jesus H."

Josiah set his briefcase on the floor and poked around inside his folder. "I didn't see that here. What's the H for?"

"Heaven."

"Okay, mister...Christ. It's not my job to have any opinion on your religious beliefs. It is my job to defend you. You are facing charges for fifty-seven counts of murder, one hundred and ninety-two counts of assault, and other counts too numerous to mention including but not limited to trespassing, breaking and entering, theft, resisting arrest, unlawful disobedience of safety regulations, violation of the EPA, arson, terrorism, treason, wanton disregard of correct political language, interference with public broadcasting, and the impersonation of a Mexican civilian."

Jesus considered the charges. "They forgot kidnapping."

"You really shouldn't-"

"Tell the truth? Shame the devil?" said Jesus with a taunting tone.

"Look. The authorities could be listening to us. It won't be admissible in court, but if you give them ideas they'll find other evidence."

"You know I'm guilty, right?"

"Guilty or not, I'm here to defend you."

"What's your name again?"

"Josiah Greenwood."

"Josiah," mused Jesus. "You're Jewish."

"On my Dad's side. So?"

"Josiah's kinda close to 'Jesus', isn't it? That's how it works right?"

"You'd have to ask my parents."

"Sounds like they ain't around no more."

"They were...part of that unexplained worldwide mass vanishing."

Jesus snorted. "It is explained. It was the Rapture."

"My parents didn't practice any religion at all."

"Nah, they musta been secret Christians without telling you. I understand why, considering modern times."

"That doesn't make any sense."

"Not if you're liberal." Jesus cocked his head sideways. "You probably believe global warming too, don't you?"

"Of course I – look, this is getting us off track. We need to prepare for your defense."

Jesus' eyes narrowed as he stroked his beard. "How much money you getting to defend me?"

"I'm a public defender. You're one of a hundred people I'll represent this month. If you must know, I barely make my rent."

"But a big case like this could make your liberal defense lawyer career win or lose, huh? And let me clue you in, you'll lose. Even if the fix wasn't already in, I don't intend to counter a single charge against me. As a matter of fact, make sure you put kidnapping down like I said. Lily Godwin is probably in a FEMAnazi reeducation camp right now, after the KenyAntichrist took her away. "

"Do you mean President Bomraka? Please don't call him that."

"How 'bout 'President Evil'?" Jesus raised an eyebrow.

Josiah shrugged. "There's one possible benefit to you talking like that. It does mean that we can use-"

"Don't even say it, boy."

"I have to. It's my job. Anyway, how do you know for sure what I'm going to say?"

"Alright, that's fair. You might as well get the words out before I reject 'em."

"We can try for an insanity defense."

Jesus grinned. He had known that was coming. "Absolutely not. That's just what Bomraka and his LIEberal Demoncrats want everyone to think. I'll plead guilty - but I am not going to claim insanity. There's a good Christian reason for everything I do."

Josiah blinked. "Let me be straight with you. You're already guaranteed to do life in prison. The only choice you have left is how bad the rest of your life is. They could put you into solitary confinement. The insanity defense might be the only chance you have of ever seeing a human being again."

"Let's get back to you. You're Jewish."

Josiah threw up his hands. "I'm not religious. What's that got to do with anything?"

"Here you are, defending me. Sounds a bit different than the last time, huh? When Jews had me killed. What do you think of that?"

"Honestly?" said Josiah.

"Of course I want your honest answer," said Jesus. "You don't know me, so I'll forgive you for thinking otherwise."

"Alright, I don't really want to be here. You're almost certainly guilty of terrible crimes, you talk like a stupid bigot, and now you're wasting my time. Time that I could be spending on other people who want a good defense."

"You think I'm guilty. Why defend me?"

"Because the justice system is the bedrock of our society."

Jesus chuckled fondly. "By my Father, they sure sold you a bill of goods." He began to walk around Josiah in a circle, examining him from different angles. "The bedrock of our nation is the Bible, boy. Our founding fathers were Christians, every last one of them, and any other so-called history is a damn lie of the Devil." Jesus' face twisted in a sad half smile, and he shook his head again. "As for your ol' justice system, the Bible shows that treating the guilty as same as you treat the innocent is as much a sin as treating the weak the same as the strong. God's the only Supreme Court there is. And he don't much listen to legal arguments."

Josiah shifted uncomfortably under Jesus' inspection. "Do you want me as your lawyer, or not?"

"You sure are persistent, I'll give you that." He considered it. "Okay, be my lawyer then. Just keep those big innocent eyes o'yours wide open."

"For what?" Josiah asked. "A trial? I've seen plenty of them. Ten this week."

"Not like this one. I guarantee you'll see things you never seen before. If you're lucky it might even lead you to the truth."

"Okay, whatever," said Josiah. "We don't have a lot of time left today. Now that you'll accept me as your lawyer, let's talk about your defense. If you won't plead insanity, your best chance is to-"

"I'll make things really short and sweet. Here's how it's gonna go." Jesus counted off points on his handcuffed fingers. "You plead me guilty to every single charge. You add that kidnapping charge. Also you add how I've traded in gold, owned guns without a license, and disavowed the lies of global warming, stem cells, liberal economics and evolution. You put all of that in there, every word. Then you go to court with me, and watch how it goes down. Got it?"

Josiah raised his hands helplessly. "Sure, I guess. I can only advise you, you don't have to take it."

"When's the trial start?"

"In a few hours. There's a press conference beforehand that I can't seem to get you out of."

"Good. I think I got a last meal comin'."

"That's supposed to happen right before the execution. You haven't even had your trial yet."

"I'd rather have it now. See what you can do. I want a Chic Fil-A sandwich, and a slice each of Godfather's pizza and Papa John's with all the meat it'll hold."

"Those last two haven't been in business for fifteen years," said Josiah. "The Empty Caloric Consumption Act."

"That's my request. And one more thing," said Jesus. "Shake my hand like an American."

Josiah held out his hand. Pleased, Jesus shook it to seal the deal.

His new lawyer picked up his briefcase and knocked on the door. It opened, and Jesus briefly saw the same guard who'd taunted him earlier. He looked at Jesus and then Josiah. "You aren't even hurt?" he asked, sounding just a bit disappointed.

57

Two hours later, Jesus received his requested meal. Whoever the chef was, he did a fine imitation of good ol' Chic Fil-A. The pizza was a passable meat-lover's style as well. The Devil's plan to replace the divine magnificence of meat with the soulless emptiness of tofu hadn't even worked with all of the Devil's own servants. Jesus chuckled briefly. There was even a brand of tofu named 'seitan' - how could anyone miss such a message in plain sight? Anyway, whoever the cook was he knew how to make manfood. There might be a chance for him to get to heaven yet.

Just as he was finishing up, the door opened. The same two Demoncrats dressed as correction officers threw a package in. Jesus opened it, and found his jeans, shirt and boots. The clothes were cleaned, and the boots were even polished.

"Well, well, well," said Jesus. "At least I'll get to face whatever happens dressed right."

He put on his familiar clothes, and then the Demoncrats led him out. Jesus felt no need to ask where he was going, he would find out soon enough. After several flights of stairs, he caught a brief glimpse of the outdoors. The sun shone gloriously. They came to a stop outside a courtroom's double doors. Josiah came around the corner, briefcase in hand.

Jesus smiled at the sunlight. "Nice day for a trial, huh?"

"Sure, sunny days are great for mobs howling for blood." Josiah scowled as he pressed a pair of sunglasses into Jesus' hands. "There'll be a lot of flash photography too."

Jesus slid on the sunglasses. "Think I'll have some things to say then."

Josiah looked pained. "I really don't think that's a good idea. For some reason they're having the conference in front of the jury pool. I tried to get them excluded and got nowhere – it's really weird. Anyway you don't want to prejudice the jury by-"

Jesus was already stepping around him and through the courtroom doors. He entered and the liberal media pounced. They were 10 people deep and maybe 20 wide, producing an onslaught of shouted questions and camera flashes. Josiah followed him as he made his way through their ranks. The clicking cameras sounding to Jesus like a descending swarm of hungry locusts.

After the massed reporters were several liberal network broadcasting cameras. They were on raised platforms apparently built for the occasion. One camera was manned, of course, by none other than Michael Max. Once again he hid his eyes from Jesus' gaze.

As they walked on, Jesus turned his attention to the courtroom itself. The room itself was rather grand, with high vaulted ceiling, fine marble walls and stately wood décor. It must have been built in Chicago's better days. Rows of carved wooden pews were packed with spectators, some against and some clearly for. Jesus winked at a little old lady holding her Bible. She blushed.

They reached the end of the spectator section, and passed through a hinged half-door to arrive at two tables before the judge's bench. Josiah and Jesus were apparently to sit on the right - the left table was already occupied by a suited man in his early 50s, with his arm in a shoulder sling. Jesus surmised he must be the prosecutor.

Jesus then realized he'd seen the man before, quite recently.

"Bret Stormbreaker?" Josiah blurted out. "You can't be prosecuting this! You're – you're one of the – alleged victims." He looked around the room, and back to Stormbreaker. "You don't even have a law degree!"

Stormbreaker just gave an amused smile. "I guess we'll have to see how it goes."

Jesus regretted that he'd only shot the man in the shoulder. He noted what must be a Mark near his man's temple. It must have been newly implanted, the skin around it appeared slightly raw and red. Stormbreaker himself looked serene and confident, notwithstanding his wounded shoulder.

"We'll straighten this out right away," said Josiah. "Just as soon as the judge gets here."

Jesus glanced to the right of the judge's bench and saw the juror's box, currently empty. Jesus wondered which Americans would decide his fate. The saved ones, or the damned?

Josiah and Jesus took their seats at the table. Josiah placed his briefcase on the table, took out a pad and pen and handed them to Jesus. "If you need to tell me something," Josiah whispered, "write it on there."

A bailiff went to the front of the courtroom and turned. Jesus noted that she was unusually pretty for a bailiff. He sensed a bit of feminism hiding beneath the surface.

"All rise," said the bailiff. Jesus stayed seated. "That means you too, buddy." Jesus didn't move. She pointed to a bailiff who stood to the table's left. "Jones! Get over there and pull him to his feet."

"Try it," said Jesus.

"The trial hasn't started yet," Josiah said hurriedly. "This isn't yet a court in session."

The bailiff sneered. "You might be right legally, but the judge ain't gonna like it."

"I'm representing my client's wishes," said Josiah.

"On your own head be it, punk," the pretty bailiff sneered. "All the rest of you, rise."

Josiah started to rise. Jesus grabbed his arm and dragged him back into his seat. Josiah was startled, but stayed seated.

"Hope for you yet," said Jesus.

A door opened behind the Judge's bench, and a woman came out in black robes. As she walked the steps up to the bench, the audience recognized her and gave a collective gasp. This had been rumored, but no one had thought it would actually happen. She was returning to television, after several years as a behind-the-scenes White House staffer.

The pre-trial press conference would be conducted by none other than Rosio Dawnhell.

58

"Hey everyone!" the beloved female idol of millions announced. The crowd warmed to her smile. "Why am I in judge robes? 'Cause today we're having a surprise special edition of The View! We're going to look over the crimes and follies of this - Mr. Christ, can you believe it?"

"You better believe it, swamp witch," said Jesus.

"I'm sorry, did someone ask you? I tell ya, these Christians, am I right?" She stuck her tongue out at him. The crowd responded with laughter and scattered applause.

"I'm not just A Christian," said Jesus. "I'm THE Christian."

"Fine, whatever. Counsel, can ya shut him up? We're getting' ready to judge here." She sat down. "Alright everyone, be seated. What shall we do first? Go through the charges?"

Josiah jumped up from his seat. "What's going on here? I had thought this was a press conference before the trial. We can't actually be going into the trial itself."

Rosio snorted impatiently. "The judge has authorized me to take over in his place. You don't like it, take it up with him."

"This is highly irregular-"

"You're highly irregular," Rosio zinged back. The crowd laughed. "Now where were we?"

"The jury selection hasn't begun yet," said the Prosecutor.

"Alrighty then!" She banged the gavel. "Jury selection! Let's get to it."

"What are you talking about?" Josiah sputtered. "The – both the Federal and the Illinois criminal codes clearly state-"

Rosio rolled her eyes. "Listen you little mansplainer, the judge is letting me go ahead and set things up for him. It's gonna be constructive and educational for everyone watching at home." She leaned back and sneered. "You can either represent your client or leave him here alone. Up to you."

Jesus pulled Josiah down and whispered, "Are those going to be the jurors?" He jerked his head towards a group of people sequestered from the rest of the audience, near the jury box.

"I guess so," said Josiah.

"Then go along with her."

Josiah saw his client's mind was set. By now he knew better than to argue. He faced Dawnhell. "I withdraw my objection." He sat down.

"Who does the prosecution want?" Rosio asked. Stormbreaker named four people.

Rosio nodded. "Great! You got 'em. Now how about you, for the Christian terrorist?"

"I think you mean 'alleged'", Josiah corrected. "And this isn't how jury proceedings are supposed to go at all!"

Her eyes flashed fire. "Whatever."

Jesus took another sidelong glance at the jury pool, and hid his grin. He whispered to Josiah the five specific people he wanted to make sure got to the jury. The public defender didn't bother arguing. He stood up and named four jurors - not one of whom Jesus had requested. Jesus frowned. Josiah covered his face with his legal pad and mouthed "Trust me."

Jesus chose to wait and see.

"I don't think they'll be properly unbiased," said the prosecutor.

"Agreed," said Rosio. "Defense, pick another four."

On Stormbreaker's next round of jury selection, one of Jesus' picks made it through. Jesus was careful to conceal his elation from his enemies. Josiah's turn came and named three jurors, and then pretended to forget the fourth name as if it didn't even matter. The first three were denied, while the fourth was allowed in. The fourth was another of Jesus' picks.

Jesus relaxed. His lawyer could be trusted to follow his will. Whatever would happen, he now had the best shot he could. He stopped following the play by play, and spent the rest of the selection process doodling angels battling with swords, guns and rocket planes on the pad Josiah had given him, mumbling phrases like "Eat it, Satan!" and "Pew pew pew."

When the prosecutor and Rosio were satisfied, the jury selection was abruptly concluded. The twelve jurors and six alternates took their place in the jury box to the right of the judge's bench.

"How you all doin' out there?" Rosio asked the crowd. "You wanna take a break, or you want to jump right ahead?"

The courtroom cheered, eager to move ahead. From behind the cameras in the back of the room, Michael Max gave her a thumbs up. "Alrighty!" Rosio declared. "Just call me Judge Dawnhell!"

The trial began. Brett Stormbreaker presented the charges. His presentation amounted to little more than listing each crime Jesus was accused of. It took quite some time.

At long last, in the fading hours of the day, Dawnhell declared it was Josiah's turn to state Jesus' plea. He leaned in close to Jesus, his face pained. "Are you sure that you don't want to change your mind?" Josiah cautioned him in whispers. "This so-called trial is a joke, there's no way it can stand on appeal. But your statements could still be introduced as evidence against you."

"I appreciate that you think you're looking out for me," Jesus responded, his voice as low as Josiah's. "No change. Say it all just like I asked."

Josiah sighed, and rose. "May it please this bizarre media event that is pretending to be a court-"

Rosio banged her gavel. "Smart mouths get contempt. "

Josiah continued as if she hadn't spoke, "My client plans to plead guilty. He also pleads guilty to kidnapping, and ..." Josiah pressed his hand to his forehead, recalling the additional charges his client had requested. "Trading in gold, owning guns without a license, and... defying the lies of global warming, stem cells, feminism, vegetarianism, liberal economics and evolution."

Brett Stormbreaker and Judge Dawnhell laughed incredulously.

"Okay then!" Dawnhell said perkily. "I'm happy to accept. How 'bout you, Mr. Prosecutor?"

"Sounds great to me," the prosecutor affirmed.

"Does the government wanna call anyone to the stand?" Dawnhell asked the Prosecutor.

Stormbreaker shrugged his healthy shoulder. "What for? The defendant admits all the charges."

"Very well." She raised the gavel in her fat fist. "Looks like we can get outta here in time for supper! The jurors will now go and - "

"Wait! Objection!" yelled Josiah.

"What?" said Dawnhell, her eyes flashing at his impudence.

"Don't I get to call anyone in my client's defense?"

"Don't make me laugh. He's confessed to everything."

"My client has the right to testify as to the reasons-"

Dawnhell's slammed the gavel into the wood with surprising force, sending a splinter flying. She grit her teeth. "You are getting on my nerves. Shut it. Your client is guilty. One more word out of you and you're guilty too. We don't have time for this. I'm getting hungry." She addressed the crowd. "Hey everyone, maybe once we're done here the whole courtroom can go out for tofu steaks, on me. Who wants some?"

The courtroom full of spectators responded with very sparse, half-hearted clapping and an isolated cheer.

"Do you want to see a miracle, Josiah?" Jesus said. "Remember this." He stood up, straight and proud. "All you fools who clapped for tofu - you better get right, before your time runs out!"

Rosio began to smash the gavel into the bench. "The defendant hasn't been told to rise yet!" she protested.

"Only God tells me to rise! I was going to go along, all the way to the gallows if need be. Instead my father intervened. Here in this courtroom, with the very jurors you would presume could judge me!" He made the sign of the Crucifist, ending with his fist on chest. "Those of you who have walked this journey with me, I give to you the five words I gave you in secret. Step forward now and let the American people behold that, at long last: IT'S TIME TO KICK ASS."

"And we're just the New Disciples to do it!" a voice rang out from the jury box. Josiah turned towards the jury box, to see a slightly chunky man with short sandy hair brandishing a shotgun. Josiah wondered why he looked familiar, then it clicked into place - that man was Aaron, one of Jesus' accomplices. How had Josiah not noticed him? How had no one else?

Next to Aaron a strong Black Christian pulled off his sunglasses and stood revealed as Barclay. A man, a woman and a little person next to them also removed their disguises. Together they were the five jurors Jesus had requested.

"We are the New Disciples," said Barclay, "And you get your dirty fingers off our Lord!"

Jesus saw with pride that they were acting as a unit. Aaron and Barclay had leveled weapons at Rosio Dawnhell, while Marci, Steven and good little Gary were aiming at the bailiffs and Michael Max's camera crew.

"Yes!" Jesus raised his fists in triumph. "Now it's time for all to see! All who love me will now join us, to rise and put an end to you. We're here to beat the truth, the whole truth, and nothing but the Holy Truth straight into you - so help me, me!"

"You will all sit down!" yelled Rosio. "We know those guns can't be real!"

Barclay fired his shotgun into the ceiling, spraying chunks of plaster and concrete across the courtroom. The rest of the jury fled, screaming - to run into the audience and the media as they also scrambled for the door. The mass exodus created a jam at the exit doors, and the nearby bailiffs had to flee to the other side of the room or be trampled.

"What are you all standing around for?" Rosio demanded. "Shoot them!"

"The cameras are still broadcasting, mistress!" the head bailiff exclaimed, panic in her voice.

"Blast! Make sure you don't hit Jesus yet!" Rosio turned a furious face towards the back of the room. "Max! Turn off all of those cameras immediately!"

Jesus jabbed his finger at Dawnhell. "Last time I said 'Judge not lest ye shall be judged'. Now I'm here to do the judging!" He punched his fist into his palm, and strode toward Rosio with deadly purpose.

"You will not touch the matriarch!" The head bailiff cried. She drew and fired at Jesus. He ducked just in time.

"I said don't shoot him yet!" Rosio bellowed.

The New Disciples ducked down behind the edge of the jury box and fired back. The rest of the bailiffs took cover and answered fire, filling the courtroom with flying lead.

Josiah ducked beneath the table.

"Stormbreaker!" Rosio roared at the would-be prosecutor, now crouching beneath his own table. "Grab him!'

"Can't we just wait for backup?" he asked.

Rosio brandished her gavel at him like a club. "Do you really want to make me angry!"

The man paled and rushed at Jesus, swinging his briefcase with his one good arm.

Jesus spun, jumped and kicked Stormbreaker in the head so hard it flew clean off his shoulders. Stormbreaker's head bounced off the courtroom railing, as his body slumped to the floor and spilled blood across the marble floor. Some of the arterial spray landed on Josiah, still beneath the table.

"You've just been cross-examined," Jesus declared.

Rosio saw to her shock that Michael Max's cameras still flashed red "recording" lights. "Max! Stop the broadcasting, you idiot!"

"The cameras aren't shutting off!" Max punched at buttons, on the control board in front of him. "They've been taken over! It's some kind of virus!"

"Not just any virus!" yelled Gary, his head barely poking above the railing in the jury box. "It's a Holy One!" He waved his tiny arms in excitement. "Your Devil-based Apple operating systems don't stand a chance! Just like the Apple your Devil gave to Eve!"

"Good one, Gary!" thundered Jesus.

Rosio stood now, swinging her gavel left and right. "All of you bailiffs - stop firing at the idiots in the jury box! Shoot Jesus instead!"

"No, look at me!" Marci demanded, and opened her shirt.

"Why is she showing us her tits?" asked the head bailiff, bewildered.

"Focus!" yelled Rosio Dawnhell. "Shoot Jesus, you idiots!"

"But those are really nice tits," said another bailiff. Barclay took him out with a well-placed shot.

The bailiffs responded by concentrating fire on Barclay. Seeing they were no longer so distracted by her now, Marci ducked down and buttoned up her shirt.

Rosio gripped her hair in frustration. "Max, this can't be broadcasting live! If you can't turn off the cameras, smash them!"

"Aaron!" Jesus ordered. "America needs to see this! Take care of Michael Max!"

"Yes my Lord!" Aaron vaulted out of the jury box and ran to the back of the room.

Max snarled and stepped off the platform to meet Aaron, making the room shake slightly. Aaron raised his gun to shoot. Max produced a donut from his pocket and threw it, knocking Aaron's gun from his hand. Aaron ran at him - and bounced off. Max sneered and grabbed a microphone from the platform, and swung it by its cord. It whirled faster and faster until it resembled a spinning morningstar.

"Time for your interview," said Max.

In the front of the courtroom, the head bailiff ran out of bullets.

"You, she-bitch," said Jesus. "Do you dare to face me in your real form?"

"With pleasure, you man!" The head bailiff tore off her uniform, revealing her cyborg chassis for all the world to see.

"Viewers at home, take a good look!" Jesus preached. "See the fruits of liberalism – a Feminazi Femborg! A twisted mockery of God's plan for women - not only was this woman paid what a man would earn, she was given free access to bionics to challenge man's strength! A witch born of science used for evil - not the technology that comes from holy job creators, but academic socialists instead - all to end God's plan for manly domination"

"That's enough, you man! This is for Blabbera Wilters!" The head bailiff snarled and leapt for Jesus' throat, her Femborg bionic legs turning into rockets and launching her all the way across the room at Jesus. He ducked out of the way and kicked her as she passed. She wobbled in the air and rose to the ceiling, turning around for another pass. Barclay took her out with a blast of his shotgun. She crashed at Jesus' feet, next to the headless Prosecutor.

Jesus saluted Barclay a graceful sign of the Crucifist, and pointed to Rosio. "Now it's your turn."

"Jesus, have you lost your mind?" Dawnhell dropped the gavel and balled her fists. "Don't you know what will happen to your little girlfriend?"

"It's too late for that, demon!" said Jesus. "My disciples are here. God's playing this hand now."

"What are you all doing?" Josiah asked, bewildered. "What's going on? This is supposed to just be a press conference!"

Jesus looked under the table and caught Josiah's eye. "I told you to look, Josiah. Don't come this far and close your eyes! This is the time to see what stands before you."

59

———

Jesus walked with slow confidence towards the judge's bench and Rosio Dawnhell. Bullets flew past him as if he wasn't there.

"Very well then!" said Rosio. She took off her judge's robes, to reveal a standard smart business suit and skirt tailored to her stout figure. "What do you think you see, doomed Son of Man?"

"I see you, bitch!" Jesus spat. "You stand between me and humanity's salvation, and I will END YOU!"

Jesus ran the last few steps and vaulted onto the judge's bench, swinging for Dawnhell's throat. Dawnhell dodged with unnatural speed, and made it out to the side.

He stalked towards her like a cat. Rather than be frightened, a vicious leer came across her face. Then a curious transformation began. Rosio's already extra extra large business suit stretched, and stretched again. Then 9 tentacles burst forth from her torso and shot at Jesus. He leaped to the side in the nick of time, the ends of the tentacles smashing the judge's box to splinters.

Rosio laughed maniacally as the tentacles returned to her form. They were each the size of a thick tractor trailer's exhaust pipe, and beneath an odd green slime they shined like steel. On closer examination, Jesus saw that they were built from interlocking cylinders, which could mostly likely spring forth again or shrink at her command. At the end of each vile tendril was a famous face of the evil feminocracy. All told they were Ellen DeGeneres, Eleanor Roosevelt, Billie Jean King, Melissa Etheridge, Rachel Maddow, Roseanne Barr, and the Indigo Girls.

"It all makes sense now," said Jesus.

"Huh?" said Josiah. "How the Hell do you figure that?"

Rosio's tentacle heads joined in her laughter. The tentacles writhed and twisted, then struck out for Jesus again.

The New Disciples stood, aghast. "Keep the bailiffs pinned down!" Barclay ordered. They resumed firing at the bailiffs. Barclay ran forward into the fray and attempted to aid their savior. He fired at the tentacles, but his shotgun blasts had no noticeable effect on their steel skins and the heads ducked and weaved to dodge his aim. Some were distracted away by the gunshots and began to wend their way across the courtroom, telescoping as they twisted and turned. The rest of the tentacles continued straight towards Jesus.

Aaron swung at Michael Max with all his strength. No matter how he tried, he couldn't hit anything solid in Max's body. His fists kept bouncing off Max's fat-swaddled softness. Max used his gut to push Aaron sideways, and then pin him against the marble wall.

"Got you now!" said Max. "Time for your close up!" He pushed into Aaron, crushing him against the wall. Aaron gasped and struggled. Beyond Max's head Aaron was stunned to see the former talk show host now sprouting eight tentacles with a total of nine heads. Jesus ducked and dove, struck and twisted as he fought two of them with his bare hands.

"And now, I will deliver my sentence upon you!" all of the Dawnhell-creature's mouths intoned as one.

"All with eyes to see, look at what the Bible prophesied!" said Jesus, as he dodged her fighting limbs. "Behold in all her wickedness – as foretold by the Book of Revelations – the ultimate Feminazi Femborg – the *Whore of Babblin'!*"

All nine heads laughed with Rosio as the Dawnhell's body gloried in her transformation into an even more horrific beast than her human form.

Aaron struggled desperately against Max's bulk, but could find no purchase. He felt his consciousness slipping. "Someone stop her!" Aaron cried with fading breath. "She is the dark queen of the liberal media, the great beast's lieutenant!"

"She who turns the Devil's Doorknob to open the portal of your doom!" Rosio laughed. "Ah, to be revealed at last! To use my power to crush you with my bare steel tentacles!"

"Die bitch die!" yelled Barclay as he pumped shell after shell into the Dawnhell-monster's torso. The shots bounced off her layers of tough-skinned blubber.

"Have I just lost my mind," Josiah wondered aloud. "Maybe I can leave the dream?" He stood up from beneath the table, and began to walk towards the back door. A bailiff noticed him unprotected, and pivoted to take aim.

"Get back under the table!" bellowed Jesus. He ran back to Josiah and shoved him down, just as a bullet rang overhead and a tentacle whizzed past where Josiah stood. "You might not be saved yet!" said Jesus. "You can't take those kinds of risks, you still could go to Hell!"

"Cover me!" Barclay yelled. "That lawyer's with Jesus, I'm going in to get him!" Steve pulled his gun and took aim. "You too Gary - stop fooling with the laptop, and pick up your gun that's an order!"

"I'm getting so much information from their systems!" Gary protested. "Just a few more seconds!"

"Now, son!" Jesus commanded. "We need you to join the fight!"

Gary put down his laptop and pulled out his gun. Together, Gary Steve and Marcy returned fire at the bailiffs. Barclay jumped out of the jury box and ran to Josiah.

"I'm dreaming," said Josiah. "That's it. I fell asleep before I went to talk to that Christian terrorist."

The Dawnhell reached out two tentacles in a pincer for Josiah. Barclay shoved him out of the way, just in time. The tentacles smashed the table next to them to bits.

Steve and Gary switched their fire to the Dawnhell-creature.

Their guns did no better against her hide than Barclay's shotgun blasts. In retaliation her nine steel arms smashed and slammed against the pews, long tables and chairs all across the courtroom.

The tentacle bearing the head of Billie Jean King shot forward to Barclay and Josiah. It pursued them as they crawled backwards, darting left and right to catch them as they dodged with mere inches to spare.

"I was a tennis pro," the head of Billie Jean King taunted. "And I was as good as any man - OR BETTER!" It lunged forth with gnashing teeth to take a bite from Barclay's groin.

"Devil bitch!" yelled Barclay as he dodged and fired straight between her eyes. Her head bobbed around his shot and back again with an eerie precision, as if the bullet were moving slower than a tennis ball.

It lunged again, but stopped hard and recoiled - it had reached the maximum length of its tentacle. Outraged, Billie Jean King snarled and snapped her teeth together.

"I don't think I'd dream that, though," said Josiah.

"This is happening, son," said Barclay. He looked around. The thing had them pinned against the wall. "It's been happening all your life." He handed Josiah a .45. Josiah looked at it like something that had appeared from another world.

Aaron's vision began to go black. He swung in wild desperation and caught the extended brim of Max's baseball cap. Max yelped in sudden pain and the pressure on Aaron eased off. Not understanding the reaction but sensing some kind of an opening, Aaron aimed a punch straight at the hat. It flew all the way off – taking part of Max's head with it. Max fell back from Aaron and stumbled, then fell twitching to the ground. Aaron leaned in to press his advantage and saw to his horror that Max's head was not entirely his own. Another tiny human head jutted from Max's crown that looked strangely familiar, like an old and painful memory.

Aaron held his stomach quiet through sheer force of will.

"Why in God's name do you look like that...that liberal talk show host from the 70s?" Aaron asked, his voice soft in horror. "My father used to hate him. Dick Cavil? Dick Cravitz?"

"My name is Dick Cavity, actually," it bubbled smoothly. "Isn't this something we should perhaps introspect about? There's many ways to talk about it. Why, I think I would like to have you on my show-"

Aaron steeled his nerves and kicked the vile mockery of an entertaining intellectual into the afterlife. Max's body collapsed, lifeless.

"Aaron!" said Barclay. "Barricade the doors, they'll be sending reinforcements!"

Aaron snapped out of his daze and began moving debris in front of the court doors. He stopped paying attention to the whirling limbs of the Donnel-thing. This was nearly his undoing, as a tentacle shot out and whipped at his head. He dove and rolled as it smashed a nearby row of spectator's seats to kindling. Roseanne Barr's head shot forward, at the end of grotesque appendage attached to the Dawn-hell-creature's vile bulk.

"You want to see a heartwarming comedy about a hard-working liberal family?" she asked.

"You never fooled us, you whore!" screamed Aaron.

The head gave a dead-eyed laugh. Its tentacle then whipped the head straight at him, with biting teeth. He ducked out of the way with an inch to spare, and was barely missed again as the tentacle lashed back like a stinging whip.

The head of Ellen DeGeneres chased Steve back and forth inside the jury box. "One of us, I know you are!" the face said. "Come back and join the gay agenda!"

"I'm with a stronger power than you!" Steve ventured, his voice cracking.

"With this face, perhaps! But how about this one?"

The face at the end of the tentacle transformed into the head of George Clooney. It fixed him with a charming smile that matched a knowing glint in its eye. Steve bit his thumb, and thought of Jesus. He fired at the Clooney-head. It snarled and thrust in for the kill. Steve scrambled to the side as it smashed into the juror's seat behind him.

At the other end of the jury box, the head of Eleanor Roosevelt had trapped Gary in the corner. "You sad little cripple!" said the evil Mrs. Roosevelt. "Just like my husband! Let me weaken you with handicapped help, like I did him! I made him betray his fellow job creators to feed the poor! Join us, so you can do the same!"

"Don't let their words fool you – remember your training!" Jesus encouraged his disciples, as he fought the tentacles aimed at him. "Stay real Americans!"

Gary heeded his savior's words. "I don't have to listen to you! You disagree with me!"

From the corner of his eye, Jesus saw the tentacles headed for Marci. "Steve, instruct your wife! Make sure she doesn't listen to them!"

"Resist them!" cried Steve. "If I must resist George Clooney then you must resist them!"

The heads of the Indigo Girls smelled weakness in Marci, and slinked towards her. "You want me, don't you... Marci?" the conjoined heads asked as one. "Admit it, sweet Marci. You like our music, don't you?"

"No!" said Marci. "Jesus will save me, you evil wenches!"

"That's not how you felt in college," said the Indigo Girls their voices linked in harmony. "That's where you fell in love with us. You came to our concerts, signed our mailing lists, and your name was recorded for all eternity on our list of slaves."

"Jesus saved me!" Marci cried.

"No one can save you from our sweet...tongues," the Indigo Girls intoned. "Your Jesus can't save you. All your other friends are fighting on their own, and sure to lose. Join us...it's almost as good as a man, you'll never miss it...Come back! Stop fighting us..."

The head of Melissa Etheridge saw the Indigo Girls were making headway. Her tentacle shifted to bring her over too. Together all three cooed to Marci in a hypnotic lesbianic three-way harmony.

Across the courtroom, the head of Roseanne Barr joined them in song. The cacophony brought Aaron to drop to his knees. The tentacle slammed into him and threw him against the wall. He struggled to resist, but was so dazed he could hardly see.

Only Jesus was left free. All of the New Disciples and Josiah were captured by Rosio's steely tentacles. She bellowed laughter as her remaining appendages dove for Jesus.

Jesus saw an opening in the tentacles swinging at him. He leapt towards where the last two bailiffs hid. He caught them by surprise, kicking the gun from one man's hand and punching the other bailiff in the throat. The first bailiff ran, scrambling to find his lost gun in the empty courtroom seats.

Jesus grabbed the dazed second bailiff's head by the hair, and gave a piercing whistle that cut across the room.

"Alright, you Femborg she-bitch from the fires of Hell!"

Silence struck the courtroom. All nine of Rosio Donnel's heads focused on him.

Jesus slammed the bailiff's head into the prosecution's table. "It's time someone gave you a real mansplanation."

Rosio's screamed with all ten of her mouths. Her nine tentacles dropped their other prey to focus on Jesus. As the New Disciples struggled to recover and find their guns, Jesus dodged and threaded through Donnel's telescoping tentacles like the magnificent warrior he was born to be. Frustrated with rage, the Dawnhell-thing brought her own torso forward from behind the judge's bench, attempting to crush him with her bulk. Ruined wood, flying tables and broken chairs filled the air, but she was unable to catch him with any solid blow.

As she emerged from cover, the New Disciples fired at her torso. She flinched but kept heading towards Jesus. "We still can't get through her skin, dammit!" said Barclay.

"At least they seem to hurt her!" said Aaron. "Keep firing!"

The Rosio-beast's tentacles encircled Jesus and took turns thrusting at him, like individual wolves in a pack harrying their prey. His punches and kicks would momentarily make a head retreat, to then come back in for more.

Soon her bulk was close enough to charge in. "Look out Jesus!" Aaron cried.

Just in time, Jesus noticed her. Rather than avoid her attack, he leapt for her throat. The tentacles worked against her for once, getting in their own way as they flailed to stop him. Her body's head and human limbs fought against him with all the strength and speed they had. He attacked like a man possessed, and got behind her in a sleeper hold. He wrapped his hands around Rosio's fat-protected throat.

The last remaining bailiff emerged from hiding behind a smashed table, at point-blank range behind Jesus. Just as Jesus began choking out the Dawnhell thing's last breath, the bailiff took aim at his head.

Aaron pulled his trigger, but the gun's hammer clicked on an empty chamber. "Get that bailiff!" Aaron ordered as he hastily reloaded. "Behind Jesus, at that table! Barclay, Steve, anyone!"

Jesus couldn't get a grip around her huge neck. He let go, and surprised her with an uppercut. Then he jumped back, crouched, and sprang forward, spinning backwards in midair for a final two-booted drop-kick to her exposed neck

Steve aimed at the bailiff as Barclay ran forward to stop him.

Jesus' boots struck Rosio's throat with all his weight and might. The sheer force of the blow pushed her back five feet. The Dawnhell thing tottered, stunned. All of the tentacles went to her main throat as she tried to gasp. Her knees buckled and she dropped to the floor, a perplexed expression emerging on her face.

Jesus whooped and raised his fists. "Looks like I've had my day in your liberal court - case closed!"

The last remaining bailiff took aim at Jesus' head.

"No!" cried Barclay. Steve and Barclay fired at the bailiff, just as he pulled the trigger.

Jesus' head snapped back.

The New Disciples had been just a split-second too late. Their messiah fell backwards and crumpled to the ground.

The bailiff fell next, already dead from Steve and Barclay's bullets. Aaron and Josiah ran to Jesus. They turned him over. His forehead bled from a bullet hole. All life faded from Jesus' eyes.

Josiah sat down hard. "My God."

”Marci!” screamed Steve. “I thought you were making all men in the room love you?”

“I tried to use my God-given femininity to distract them,” said Marci. “Maybe the bailiffs hated God too much!”

Rosio Donnel's main head tried to speak, but remained choked. “Ha Haaaaah, hahhh,” its other heads whispered, using the last of its remaining breath in their separate tentacle-throats. “Your savior dies! We've won!” She smiled as she closed her eyes. “My faith is proven true at last...”

Her last breath left her, and her tentacles retreated back to her bulk, to disappear inside one single seemingly human corpse.

60

———————

"Open up!" a voice demanded. The barricaded doors shook from battering rams, the resulting booms thundering across the courtroom. "Somebody open these doors!" The doors shook again. Gun blasts fired, taking chunks out of the barricaded doors, sending shards paneled wood flying into the air.

"Gary, we need a way out of here," said Aaron, his voice halfway between an order and a plea.

"Maybe over there?" said Gary. He pointed to a ventilation grill in the lower part of the wall, next to the remains of the judge's bench. "That could lead to a shaft that'll go below the building?"

"No way Jesus would ever retreat!" said Barclay. "We'll go to heaven with him!"

"We can't save America if we're dead," said Aaron. "We have to retreat. I'm in charge, so listen! Barclay, shoot back at that door. Slow them up." He saw Josiah, sitting and still holding the gun Barclay had given him. "You – lawyer. Help me with our Lord's..." He didn't want to say body. "Help me with our Lord."

Josiah stared at him. "She – he fought her with – Rosio Dawnhell had nine tentacles?"

"Hey!" Aaron slapped him. "Snap out of it! Stay or go, but if you're coming along, give us a hand."

Josiah's mouth worked for a second. His eyes snapped into focus. Moving as if he was sleepwalking, he stuck the gun Barclay had thrown him into one of his suit pockets, and grabbed Jesus by his cowboy boots.

Aaron reached under Jesus' mighty shoulders. Together they dragged his body over to where Gary was frantically removing the ventilator grill.

"Does it go anywhere?" asked Josiah.

"Somewhere away from here," said Aaron.

Aaron entered first, then reached out and took Jesus' body by the hands. Josiah lifted as Aaron pulled, and together they moved Jesus' lifeless body into the ventilator shaft.

Josiah and Gary followed. Steven and Marci went next. Barclay took up the rear.

The courtroom doors burst open and Elite troops stormed in, bearing the symbol of ACORN. They took up positions and started shooting. Barclay kept up returning fire as long as he could, and then dove into the shaft.

"Clear!" said the squad leader. Fondue, Sauron, Strident, and the remaining members of the Death Panel entered.

"Where are they?" demanded Sauron.

"Down that shaft sir," said the Acorn leader.

Strident saw the cameras, and cursed. "We're still broadcasting, you idiots! Wreck them!" The soldiers destroyed the cameras with several short quick blasts. "Now where did the Christians go? Quickly!"

All their eyes scanned the room. Sauron's eyes lit upon the vent. "They must have gone in there. Follow them!"

The squad entered into the ventilator with guns drawn, one by one.

Almost immediately after the last man had entered, an explosion blew fire from the vent and rocked the courtroom. Dust and debris shot across the courtroom in a cloud.

Strident clenched her fists. "They left a bomb!"

"What do we do now?" asked Fondue.

"We can't be seen here," Strident said. "The media will be back in here soon. Without Rosio to run interference, the public might get wind of our presence."

Sauron frowned. "We have to get ahead of this. We have to explain away what they all saw."

"The country saw us win," Fondue cooed. "The Christians failed and their leader died."

"That's true," said Strident. "But we still need to keep the Christians from being believed, if we're going to really defeat God."

Fondue sighed. "I mourn the glory of Dawnhell's true form. Not even a bra!"

"We can celebrate her later," Strident scolded. "Fondue, take a squad of your best Feminazis and look for other ways into those tunnels. Sauron, you must immediately connect me with the lead show producer from ABC."

Before they left the courtroom, Strident took one last look at her former colleague, Rosio Dawnhell.

This was more than just inconvenient. Their overlords would be enraged. On the other hand, it was not a total loss. If they spun it correctly, they could use this as leverage to push their agenda in other ways.

No matter what they chose to do about Bomraka.

With digital copies of official blueprints and his own experience underneath the streets of Atlanta, Gary was able to bring them deep into the tunnels beneath Chicago. The New Disciples crawled through hundreds of feet of ventilator shafts. Eventually they reached a main room that linked up with a sewer line. After several more hours, they tapped and found a hollow space behind a sealed wall. They pried the bricks loose, and entered into a deep underground lair that hadn't known a human breath for at least fifty years.

"We should be safe here for now," said Gary. "I've changed their blueprints in their main system. I couldn't reach the backups, but they shouldn't be able to find this place for at least a few days."

"Good work, Gary," said Aaron. "And good to hear you talking like a man." Gary blinked back tears of gratitude.

"Hell, what's it matter?" said Barclay, despairing. "The Man is dead."

"He'll rise," said Aaron "Just like the last time."

"How do we know?" said Steve.

"Faith!" barked Aaron, his voice cracking.

"If only we had acted sooner," said Gary.

"If only I had been able to hold all those bailiffs' attention!" said Marci, her voice breaking. "That horrible, horrible Rosio...and that unChristian folk music..."

"Did you really expect they'd stay distracted by your tits, while they're also being fired at?" asked Josiah.

"It's a long story," said Aaron. "We'll tell you later. For now, do you believe?"

Josiah stared down at Jesus' corpse. "I always felt something wasn't quite right with the world, but there was always a plausible explanation. Now I have seen things I can't explain. So either I am mad – or this man is Jesus Christ." He closed his eyes. "I'll believe."

"Glad you're on board. Know how to use that?" Aaron gestured at the gun Barclay had thrown Josiah, now sticking out of Josiah's waistband.

"Not really," Josiah admitted.

"You're going to have to learn."

"Why bother?" said Steve, tears streaming down his face.

"No! We have to believe! He would want us to believe!" Aaron laid a hand on Jesus' shoulder. "We must care for his body and carry on. As best we can."

"Should we, I don't know, anoint him or something?" asked Marci.

"That's what they always did in the Bible," said Steve. "They were always anointing people."

"What we got?" asked Barclay.

Aaron reached into his backpack. He pulled out Jesus' redone

American flag with only forty-nine states. "I've held onto this ever since Jesus first showed it, back in Hector's living room so long ago. I thought it could help us celebrate our victory before the cameras." Aaron swallowed. "Perhaps we will still. But for now..." He choked up. "Now we use it for our savior."

Barclay took the flag from Aaron. "What else do we have?" he asked the rest.

"I've got some tobacco," said Josiah.

"I've got some of his whiskey," said Marci.

"I've got some gold coins from our stay in New America," said Steve.

They wrapped Jesus in his holy flag, and anointed his forehead with tobacco, gold and whiskey. They arranged his hands so that they crossed his chest, and in each of his hand they put one of their .45s.

Then they waited.

One day passed. There was no light to tell by, but their watches confirmed the passage of time. They began to run out of water. They made a sad little meal of the couple of exercise bars they'd managed to bring with them.

"We haven't been found yet, at least," said Aaron, trying to stay upbeat.

Josiah looked up at the ceiling, imagining the world above them. "I wonder what my parents are thinking?"

"They might not understand until they've seen it for themselves, son," said Barclay. He shook his head. "It's still hard even for me."

Two days passed. Gary wandered some distance and broke a pipe to find some water. The water was cloudy and smelled badly. Barclay put together a water filter through combination of shirts and a lighter, but even after going through it the water still tasted a bit too sickening to drink.

Their fallen savior's body began to smell. Marci found herself gagging, and the rest of the New Disciples weren't far behind. By the evening, a few rats encroached. The New Disciples kept shooing them away. The rats' numbers increased, waiting at the edges of the shadows.

"If only we had some way to - to embalm him..." Marci said.

"We've given all we have," said Steve. He embraced her. No one had anything to say. They all stood in silence.

"We can't stay here much longer," said Barclay finally. "We're out of food and water. If we keep staying here we'll get weak, then sick, then die."

"We have to stay another day," said Aaron. "I know it's a risk. But he's got to come back to us."

The third day came.

And passed.

Then came the morning of the fourth day.

"Maybe we can find some food," said Aaron. "Maybe we can cook the rats. Maybe-"

"We're gonna get food poisoning and die if we try to eat any of those creatures," Barclay asserted. "An' if we don't die o' that, the government thugs could find us. They could be searching in infrared even now. They'll pick up anything that gives off heat." Barclay looked away from Aaron's pleading eyes.

"He's just not coming back to us right now, Aaron," said Steve. He held back from sobbing only by the utmost exertion of his Jesus-given heterosexuality.

"I don't understand," said Marci.

"None of us do," said Gary.

"We have to keep believing," said Aaron. "It's all got to be part of God's plan."

"Well, if we stay here, we are gonna get got!" said Barclay. "That can't be part of God's plan."

"How are we going to bring him with us?" said Marci.

No one spoke for a while. Finally Aaron broke the silence. "We won't be able to bring him with us. And you're right, Barclay. We can't stay here. We'll have to leave him." Aaron wiped at his eyes and stood. "At least no matter what happens to us, they won't be able to show him like some trophy. Bomraka, that devil, he won't be able to desecrate our - our fallen savior-" Aaron began to cry again, and turned his face to hide his tears.

"Can I go with you?" Josiah asked.

"Of course, man," said Barclay. "You're one of us now."

"Where are we going?" Josiah asked. No one had an answer.

Gradually, Aaron realized they were all looking at him. He cleared his throat. "Out into the wilderness. Somewhere they won't find us. Let them think that we're dead, while we spread the story of Jesus' last fight across the world. So we can unite all Jesus' children together and bring the enemy to flame, ruin and destruction." His voice cracked. "Just like He would have wanted."

Aaron reached beneath Jesus' crossed arms into his jacket and removed the blessed silver flask of whiskey. They drank a final glass, and Aaron returned the flask to its jacket pocket. They gathered together their gear and left the room, sealing it as best they could. After another day of weary march by flashlight, they emerged just outside of Chicago near the Joliet River – headed for, as Aaron put it, God knows where.

EPILOGUE 1

"Mr. President, Mr. President!" the reporters called out. When Air Force One had landed at Jerusalem International airport a few minutes ago, there had only been about thirty of them. Yet in the few minutes it had taken to extend steps from the plane and set up a podium, the group had grown to a hundred. Bomraka sighed. They were already shouting questions before he reached the microphone.

"Mr. President! Have they found the terrorist's body yet?"

"Do we know for sure the man who called himself Jesus is dead?"

"Do you have a comment on the strange video appearance of Rosio Dawnhell at the pre-trial press conference?"

Even after so many years in office, he was disgusted. Several people had died. Here were these reporters circling like vultures over a corpse, and upset he had one less body to provide them.

Bomraka ran through his statement again in his mind, and then spoke. His amplified voice rang across the tarmac.

"I am on my way to a peace summit, which is the main focus of my statements today. So I will be brief. We are examining the evidence that remained in the courtroom, and we are reviewing the bizarre computer-generated footage that was broadcast by the terrorist group that calls themselves the New Disciples. From the information we have so far, it appears that this group killed Rosio Dawnhell, several officers of the court and their own leader and then attempted to frame the Federal government for their crimes."

He watched the reporters' faces as they took in his words. That was of course his own experts' best guess at what happened. They still had no real idea exactly how or why this series of events had occurred. It was all quite strange. All he knew was that he had a country to run, and a world to keep incrementally moving forward. This surreal distraction had to be put out of the public's minds as quickly as possible.

"Rosio Dawnhell was more than just a beloved entertainer and my Chief of Staff, she was a personal friend of many years. This desecration of her memory with insane computer footage is an insult on top of a great injury. We will find those responsible, and they will be brought to justice."

At which point, he hoped he would at last have some relief from these explosive disasters. This third term was turning out to be even more difficult than he had expected. "That is all I have to say on that. And now, onto the Middle East peace summit. We have gathered many great nations here, for the purpose of securing a lasting world peace."

EPILOGUE 2

J esus woke and leapt to his feet, fists out, ready and eager to fight some more against the Whore of Babblin', or any other foul servant of the Demoncrats and President Bomraka.

But she was not there, nor was there any other enemy. Nor were his loyal New Disciples. In fact he wasn't even in the courtroom.

He was wrapped in an American flag, which held the fading American incense of whiskey and tobacco. That was easier to accept than the growing strangeness of his surroundings.

For it was dark, but he was not in total darkness. He was outside, and yet there was no sky. Everything was in shadow, with just enough light to show surroundings of surpassing ugliness that was so complete it was a kind of anti-perfection. The light appeared to come solely from towers of flames and lava that surrounded him, coloring all he could see a crimson red.

As he surveyed the landscape, he saw no sign of any life. At the edge of the horizon were jagged and foreboding peaks, closer up were dark pits, and in between them were broken earth and desert sand. The land beneath his feet was cracked and broken as burned skin.

There was only one place he could be. He tried to understand what twist of fate, what turn of God's plan could have led him here.

"By my Father," he said.

Jesus was in Hell.

NOTES ON THE MANUSCRIPT

I was unemployed and just back from a week of camping in an attempt to clear my head, when what should I find on my front stoop but a brown-wrapped package from someone named "Theodorus Hardwicke, D.D."

The package was stained with whiskey, chewing tobacco and what I hoped was ketchup and not blood. Inside were seven numbered cassettes. Intrigued, I tracked down a cassette player from a nearby thrift store and began going through the tapes. The first started with an old man's voice, scratchy from years of smoking and twisted with passion like a gnarled old tree. He promised to follow up with me via AOL, and then launched into a dictation that eventually became this novel. The entire 90-minute tape was narrated in one feverish sitting.

I checked my email's spam folder and found his message. He promised "gold and salvation" if I would transcribe his prophecy, which he would then spread across America to save mankind.

Having only so many remaining "Rockford Files" episodes to catch up on, I dove in. After months of hammering the crazed narrative into something approaching intelligibility, I emailed him to collect my first installment of gold. He said I'd have to come to Maryland and pick it up in person – he refused to use the government-tainted US Postal Service, or any other institution that required paper currency. When I pointed out that getting to his location would cost more money than he owed me, he never responded. I was left with this manuscript.

So I've chosen to publish it instead.

Prophecy, insanity, or both?

You be the judge.

~ JAMES M. BEACH, Esq.

WHAT'S NEXT?

What happens next?
What's Bomraka's master plan?

**Find out in Book 2 of the
Two-Fisted Jesus Tales Trinity:**

Doublecrossed

ACKNOWLEDGMENTS

First, I must thank Lise Miller for encouraging me to run with an idea so crazy that I couldn't stop laughing just thinking about it; and David Neil Black, for his constant encouragement throughout this entire process. Without his constant camaraderie and persistent, nearly relentless positivity, this book would not have been as fun to write and might not exist at all. The credit is theirs, the blame is mine.

I also owe thanks and favors to those who have seen this manuscript during its dare I say evolution – or if you prefer, across its many iterations of striving for somewhat intelligent design. This includes and is definitely not limited to: Sean Gannon, Robert Baker, and Ryan Bradley; the Sideways Invisible; Joshua Franklin Sigal; Kelly Gerstbacher; the Castaways, including Layla Skramstad, Chanterelle Grover, Vrie Shmidt, Kayla Foley, Daniel Lenders, Adam Taubenheim, Martin Lucas and many more; the East Bay critique group including Beth Haskell and Rebecca Gomez; the Post Genre Group of Eduardo, Miguel, and Jessica; Jude and Jared of Borderlands Books; the Gerstle Park Literary Salon of Pat Morin, Susannah Solomon, John King, Robert Evans and Christie Nelson; and the many others too numerous to list under whose noses I thrust this tale.

I was also quite fortunate to engage the help of Laurie Kingsley, as an editor with near psychic abilities; Jason Heuser, an amazing artist whose cover painting raised the bar for me; and Kerry Hynds as a cover designer and fellow heathen who got it so quickly it was further inspiring.

For their constant generation of a truly stunning amount of inspiring nonsense, I would also be remiss if I did not thank the entire Republican party.

Lastly, I dedicate this novel to the memory of my beloved grandfather, the Reverend Hugh John McNelly. A true Christian in every good sense of the word that matters to me: a man who cared about love, mercy, charity, honesty, integrity, bravery, and who also had a full and joyful appreciation of the great importance of a good sense of humor.

ABOUT THE AUTHOR

James Beach is a writer, photographer and recovering musician. He was born and raised in New Jersey, and was once told he was a bad Photoshop superimposition on the East Coast. He successfully escaped and now lives in San Francisco, a perfect locale for exploring his emerging super powers.

For more declassified information, visit
jimbeach.net/

www.ingramcontent.com/pod-product-compliance
Lightning Source LLC
Chambersburg PA
CBHW050613170726
48283CB00001B/227